"Do you have a wife, Bairn?"

"No, Lord," Bjorn replied. In truth, he would not have wed for yet another thousand years. It was amazing how much the truth was a matter of perspective.

"Well, then," Rylur said, "it certainly seems as though you are well suited for apprenticing. You suffer from no . . . distractions. You may join the others now."

"Yes, Lord," Bjorn said. A woman rose and drew the curtain aside, revealing a door between the compartments. She opened it and held it for Bjorn as he passed. His eyes met hers briefly before she submissively averted her gaze. But not before he could see the fear hidden in her eyes. If that fear in every person who looked at you was the price of being a MageLord, Bjorn wanted no part of it. Unfortunately, he had little choice. . .

Ace Books by Thomas K. Martin

A TWO-EDGED SWORD
A MATTER OF HONOR
A CALL TO ARMS
MAGELORD: THE AWAKENING
MAGELORD: THE TIME OF MADNESS
MAGELORD: THE HOUSE OF BAIRN

Magelord

The House of Bairn

Thomas K. Martin

ACE BOOKS, NEW YORK

This book is an Ace original edition,
and has never been previously published.

MAGELORD: THE HOUSE OF BAIRN

An Ace Book / published by arrangement with
the author

PRINTING HISTORY
Ace edition / May 1999

The Penguin Putnam Inc. World Wide Web site address is
http://www.penguinputnam.com

Check out the ACE Science Fiction & Fantasy newsletter
and much more on the internet at Club PPI!

ISBN: 0-441-00623-X

ACE®
Ace Books are published
by The Berkley Publishing Group,
a division of Penguin Putnam Inc.,
375 Hudson Street, New York, New York 10014.
ACE and the "A" design are trademarks
belonging to Penguin Putnam Inc.

PRINTED IN THE UNITED STATES OF AMERICA

10 9 8 7 6 5 4 3 2 1

This book is dedicated to my loving family.

Be sure to visit my official web page at:
http://ourworld.compuserve.com/homepages/tkmartin

Magelord
The House of Bairn

Prologue

Chapter One

Abdul ben Yosif rode through the darkened streets. The Call tugged at his mind with the desperation of a lost soul wailing for help. But who was sending it? This touch did not feel like that of anyone he knew. Ben Yosif had never felt such a strong summons. It was as if Bairn himself sent the Call.

He had found the High Magus awakened by the Call as well. It had likely woken every mage in the entire city. As Guardian, it was his duty to find out from whom this strangely powerful Call originated.

He followed the Call out the east gate of the city. The black woolen scarf over his face hid his identity along with the black robe and sash.

The horse pranced nervously beneath him. Abdul did not doubt that it too could feel this summoning, so strong was it. He turned the horse to the northeast and rode away from the city.

The Call led him to a low hill several miles northeast of the city, beyond the vegetation that grew around the oasis. Abdul slowed the horse to a walk and rounded the hill to meet the man who Called them with such strength.

Gods above! Abdul thought when he saw the man. The man's aura shimmered around him like the full desert moon. He was an old man. His hair was white as cream, and his skin was almost as pale. Abdul had never seen such a man. Could he be a MageLord?

Cautiously Abdul dismounted and approached this frightening figure.

Theodr sat just outside the planted fields that surrounded the strange city, sending out the Call. He was far, far from home. Far from Bjornshall and from the warm bed he shared with Freida.

He had travelled for three moons to reach this place. Over

mountains and across vast snowy plains of grass with no sign of man to a burning land devoid of both snow and grass where only sand and strange, tough-skinned plants had prevailed.

Eventually he had left even the strange plants behind and had ventured into a realm where only the sands ruled. Until he had found the city.

Here, like a green island in a vast ocean of sand, the city and its surrounding fields rose from the barren sands. Here he had come to kill a friend.

Theodr continued to send out the Call, hoping against hope that the magi existed in this foreign land as they did in his own and that they shared the laws of Bairn. The laws that required any Circle to render aid to one hunting a renegade who sought the forbidden Power of the MageLords.

As he poured forth the Call, he wondered for the thousandth time how it had come to this. How he had come to leave the lands he knew far behind to kill Bjorn. What could he have done to change things?

He should never have gone with Ian to help him build his lodge. The Guardian's place was with his Circle, with his Magus, to protect them from events like this. But Bjorn had commanded him, and Theodr had gone. As a result, he now sat here calling for help to kill his Magus.

There was no way I could have known, Theodr thought. No way he could have realized that Bjorn would continue to study the ancient book in violation of his promise to wait. No way to know that the book would tell Bjorn of an entire vault of the forbidden knowledge and no way to know that Bjorn, of all people, would succumb to such temptation.

But fate had conspired against them. Bjorn had convinced himself that he sought the knowledge to save his people from the Hunt when Gavin came with his armies in the spring. Had convinced himself that this was the only way to protect them. But if Bjorn gained this Power, who would protect them from him?

Even so, fate or not, Theodr should have seen the signs. The ardor with which Bjorn had pursued his study of the ancient tome should have warned Theodr of the danger. He was Guardian—it was his *duty* to see such things. But he had been unwilling to believe that his friend was capable of such a failing—until it was too late. And so he had disserved them both.

The sound of a horse and the touch of another mind on his own startled Theodr from his reverie. His Call had been answered. Now he would see what manner of men lived in this strange land.

Theodr watched as the strange man dismounted from his night-black horse. The horse looked as lean as the man beneath his black robe. The eyes that looked wide-eyed at Theodr were like two black coals surrounded by white in a face dark as walnut. A strange cloth covered his head and fell across his shoulders. A black cloth drawn over the man's mouth and nose hid the remaining features from Theodr.

The man approached timidly. For a moment, Theodr wondered why the man was so frightened. Then he realized.

'Tis your aura, you old fool! he thought. Even though he had discarded the Power of the Cords, Theodr's aura was at least twice as powerful as any mage this man had probably ever seen. The stranger was probably wondering if he faced a MageLord. Theodr held his hand up in the Sign, hoping to reassure him.

The mage returned his Sign, seeming to calm a little as he seated himself across from Theodr.

"Hello," Theodr said, nodding pleasantly and smiling.

"*Solam, sahib,*" the man said. Theodr blinked in surprise.

"Can . . . you understand me?" he asked. The man said something else as unintelligible as his first remark. Theodr had never encountered a completely foreign tongue before. He and this man shared no common language. Or did they?

"You . . . understand . . . this?" he asked haltingly, in the ancient tongue of the MageLords.

"I . . . understand," the man replied. "Are you . . . Lord?"

"No!" Theodr assured him. "I Guardian. I Theodr."

"I, too, Guardian," the man replied. "I Abdul."

"Ahb-dool?" Theodr asked. The man nodded.

"I seek . . . man . . . try be Lord," Theodr explained. "Need help. Need . . . guide."

"He here?" Abdul asked.

"Yes," Theodr said. "He seek for . . . old place. Seek for . . . bad knowledge. He has . . . book . . . guide."

"Come," Abdul said, standing. "We help."

The city was unlike anything Theodr had ever seen before. Towers rose from behind the wall, topped with strange, onion-shaped domes. Abdul led them through the unguarded gates into the dry, deserted streets.

This entire land was bizarre. By day the sun had burned down on him even though it was the dead of winter. By night, the chill was enough to freeze a man's bones. Just when Theodr had despaired of finding food or water to continue his hunt, Bjorn's trail had led him to this city. Certainly there had to be water here. Otherwise, how did people survive?

Abdul stopped at a door in an alleyway, and Theodr realized he had been following the foreign Guardian blindly, lost in his reverie. Abdul knocked, and a small window opened in the door. A pair of eyes peered out briefly, and the window slid shut. Theodr heard a latch being removed, and the door opened.

Abdul ushered him into a small room—a foyer, apparently. Their host stared at Theodr with much the same expression of awe that Abdul had first displayed. Abdul spoke to him rapidly in their strange tongue, drawing the man's attention from Theodr.

Eventually the man turned back to face him.

"You . . . Guardian?" he asked in the Lord's tongue.

"Yes," Theodr replied.

"You . . . seek . . . man try be Lord?"

"Yes," Theodr replied again.

"You speak . . . mind to mind?"

"Yes!" Theodr said. Communion would help overcome some of the difficulties they were having with speech. He hoped these people would be able to help him.

"Come," his host said, beckoning for Theodr to follow as he left the room.

Some time later, Theodr climbed into bed gratefully. He was fed, bathed and in clean clothing. His host, Harif, was a generous man.

Even better, his new friends apparently knew where Bjorn was headed. There were some ruins less than a sevennight east and south of here that were believed to have been the palace of a MageLord.

Tomorrow night, he and Abdul were going to leave for this place. In the meantime, Theodr was enjoying the first bed he'd seen in far too long.

Perversely, sleep eluded him. He could think of little else

besides the fact that Bjorn was probably already there. Had he already opened the vault? Had he found the forbidden knowledge he sought? Would Theodr be *able* to kill him once they found him, or would Bjorn have become too powerful?

Theodr closed his eyes and gathered the Power. He focused it inward into a single commanding thought.

Sleep!

Theodr tightened the woolen scarf across his face as the wind tried to force the ever present sand into his lungs. This was a strange land, and that was reflected in the local clothing. Loose, white, woolen robes and baggy trousers that kept the wearer cool by day and warm by night. Scarves to protect the face from both the sun and the constantly blowing sands.

His hosts of last night had been more than helpful. They had given him the use of a fine horse and supplies, including some of the local clothing. Abdul rode along with him, on the same night-black stallion that he had ridden last night.

Abdul led yet another animal carrying their supplies—an ill-tempered beast called a camel that was as likely to bite you or spit at you as it was to obey. Theodr had vowed to never call a mule stubborn again after dealing briefly with the beast.

"When we be there?" Theodr asked. As they rode, he and Abdul had been working to improve their understanding of each other. Between the three languages, they were managing.

"Four, five days," Abdul said. "We ride hard. Make good time."

Not as good as Bjorn, Theodr thought. He had probably already found the vault.

Bjorn looked at the ruins that thrust up through the barren sand in the light of the quarter moon. The last traces of life had long ago disappeared from this permanently blighted land, leaving nothing but the sand and the wind. And the ruins of the House of Soren.

There wasn't much left. Just a few feet of wall sticking up through the sand here and there. The remains of one tower actually rose taller than Bjorn's head.

For this, he had left everything? For a few bits of stone in a ruined land? He had pinned his hopes of saving his wife and his newborn son and all of his people on this?

The ruins seemed to go on forever. Bits of stone thrust up here and there through the sand. Magic suffused the entire ruin. Swirls and loops of permanent magics floated on the sand.

However, none of the patterns that he could see matched the pattern that Bjorn was searching for—the pattern described in the ancient book. Perhaps one of these would reveal the other. It was a risk, but there was no telling how close Theodr was behind him. He did not have time for caution.

Bjorn examined one of the patterns carefully, searching for traps. Only one lead sat free from the pattern. No other lead was hidden in the pattern—there was only one attachment point. The spell should be safe. Should be.

Bjorn's mind took hold of the pattern, and he directed Power into it. As the Power flowed through the lines and figures of the spell, nothing untoward happened. No trap killed him.

The last figure was filled with the Power. And then the earth began to shake. Bjorn's eyes snapped open as the ground shook beneath his feet. It was a trap, after all!

Stone rose up through the sand like a tree growing toward the sun. Sand flowed away as stone rose around him and over him. The ground continued to shake even after the stone had closed over him.

Finally, it stopped. Bjorn looked around. He was in a circular, stone room. Stairs climbed up the wall to the roof high overhead. Before him stood a door.

Slowly, Bjorn walked over and opened the door. The sand of the plain stretched out before him. Bjorn stepped out and looked behind him. A tall tower stood behind him, rising over forty feet to the battlements above.

Gods above! Bjorn thought. He had just raised a portion of the ancient House of Soren—just like Valerian had done outside Star Hall. And it had been *easy*!

Bjorn stepped back into the tower. For a time he just stared at the walls, at the stairs and at the roof high overhead. Then he climbed onto the roof and looked out over the sandy plain. He had done *this*?

He had been right about one thing, though. On the tower's rooftop, new patterns of spells waited for someone to activate them. These patterns were trapped, however. Half a dozen leads hung free from each pattern. Only one would be the correct attachment point. The others would probably kill him.

Bjorn walked back down the stairs and out into the desert. Since raising the tower had revealed new patterns, it was possible that the pattern he was searching for was in another part of the palace.

Bjorn picked another pattern floating on the sand. It, too, was untrapped. Bjorn pushed his Power into the pattern. A section of curtain wall grew from the desert sand and attached itself to the tower Bjorn had just built.

This looked like a section of outer wall—not part of the palace itself. Presumably, the palace itself would be on the side of the wall where the tower door opened. Bjorn rose to his feet and walked around the short section of wall.

Once again Bjorn selected a pattern from those among the sand and fed Power into it. This one was different. When the Power reached one of the figures of the spell, his progress stopped. Bjorn poured more and more Power into the spell. He was just beginning to consider abandoning the effort when the Power flowed past the figure into the remainder of the pattern.

The sand flowed away, revealing a broad section of plaza. A large, ornate marble structure began to grow in the center of this section. As it grew, Bjorn recognized it as some sort of fountain. Then, without warning, water burst from the top of the fountain to run streaming down the layered bowls until it reached the main basin of the fountain.

For a moment, Bjorn just stared at the water cascading down the fountain. He reached out and placed his hand into the falling sheet, feeling the cool water splash over it. He brought his cupped hand to his mouth. The water was sweet and pure. The basin filled and water began running along a small channel in the plaza that Bjorn had not noticed before. The water ran into a small opening in the curtain wall and out into the sand.

Although this had not been what he was searching for, he now had a source of water. There were no new patterns revealed on the plaza itself.

How convenient, Bjorn thought. He ought to go get the horse and tether it to the fountain while he searched. The fountain was certainly large enough for Bjorn to bathe in. *That* would be nice, once the sun rose.

Bjorn went to get the horse, examining the layout of the visible portions of the palace. The door of the tower faced directly toward the fountain. That probably meant that the palace itself lay further along that same line.

He relocated his camp by the splashing fountain and then walked off the plaza into the sand beyond. A pattern floated on the sand in front of him. Bjorn took a deep breath and gathered the Power. It was beginning to look as if this could take a while.

Ian waited outside the lodge, watching for Arik's return. In the deep winter, the days were as short as the nights had once been. This was a strange land which they had made their home.

It had been one of the happiest days of his life when his father and Arik had arrived at the lodge last autumn. Ian had thought he would never see his father alive again, but Baron William had arranged Ivanel's escape from Gavin's dungeons. Someday, if he ever had the opportunity, he would have to thank William for that unexpected act of kindness.

Surprisingly enough, his father had not taken Ian's place as chieftain of this lodge. Instead, he had insisted that Ian stay on as chieftain and had taken a place on Ian's council.

Ian felt Arik approaching from the west. He waited anxiously for the scout to appear from the forest. Would the people at Herroldshall accept his proposal? If so, it could possibly save them all.

Herroldshall. Until this winter it had been Bjornshall. But Bjorn had gone renegade—fled south in pursuit of forbidden knowledge three moons ago. Since then, Herrold had been named chieftain of the neighboring lodge.

Arik's sled emerged from the forest, laden with furs. The trapping had been good. Of course, it usually was in the forest. Ian waved to the scout and then rapped on the heavy door behind him. It opened.

"My lord?" Wiegel said.

"Get some men out here to unload Arik's sled," Ian said.

"Yes, my lord," Wiegel said.

Arik drove the sled to the barn, and Ian followed. Even through the layers of fur that he wore, the cold bit at him. He wondered how Arik could stand to spend days at a time out with his traps.

"Greetings, my lord," Arik said. Ian was finally starting to grow accustomed to the title. He almost didn't notice it anymore.

"Greetings, Arik," Ian said. "What news?"

"They think it a sound proposal," Arik said. "They believe it will work."

" 'Tis our best chance," Ian agreed. He and his father had arrived at the answer to their dilemma over the long winter. Come spring, Bjorn's family and Herrold would travel to Ianshall. When Gavin arrived, those of Herroldshall would claim that Bjorn had merely been a guest in their lodge and that he had travelled southward with Ian back to Nalur's Ridge. Once Gavin had withdrawn, Herrold would return to his lodge, but Bjorn's family, including Freida and Theodr, if he ever returned, would stay on at Ianshall.

Ian, Ivanel, Arik and Finn would have travelled ahead to Nalur's Ridge, where they would attempt to finish what Ian had begun last summer. Mathen had to die. This would also lend credence to the story of those at Herroldshall. Hopefully, they would be able to escape after assassinating the First Knight.

Hopefully.

"Father is waiting for us," Ian said. "Let us go and tell him. Wiegel is getting someone to unload your sled for you."

"Yes, my lord," Arik replied.

"We are close to the ruins," Abdul assured Theodr. In the last four days, their command of each other's language had improved markedly. Communion had helped considerably.

"Just over these dunes," Abdul added.

"Thank the gods," Theodr replied. He rode alongside Abdul as they climbed the steep sandy hill.

"In Bairn's name!" Abdul said when they came within sight of the ruins.

Ruins hardly seemed to be the appropriate word. Although large portions of the structure before them were definitely in ruins, much of the palace looked as if it had been built yesterday. In the noon sunlight, Theodr could even see water cascading down a fountain in a section of plaza surrounding the palace. Delicate towers reached scores of feet toward the sky. Ornate buttresses supported the walls of the palace, and beautifully colored glass adorned the windows that were visible.

However, entire sections of the palace were missing. Not destroyed—simply missing, as sharply as if they had been sliced away with a knife.

Long ago, Bjorn had told him of the tower that Valerian had raised against Gavin's army—how it had looked as if it had been cut away from a larger structure and placed on the hilltop. This was the same thing. Bjorn had raised most of the House of Soren by his own Power.

"We are too late," Theodr said.

"We must try," Abdul said. "Now, while he still does not know we are here. We will find him and take him from behind."

As he spoke, Abdul dismounted and drew a long, curved dagger from his belt.

"Bjorn will think I am alone," Theodr said, also dismounting. "We can tether our horses behind the last dune. I will lead the search. You remain hidden behind me. While I speak to him, you approach him from behind and kill him."

"A good plan," Abdul agreed. Theodr did not think so—conspiring to assassinate a friend.

Gods forgive me, he thought. They led the animals out of sight behind the tall sand dunes and approached the palace.

"What are those tracks from?" Theodr wondered. A trail circled around the palace in the sand just beyond the structure.

"I do not . . ." Abdul began. Then the answer to their question rounded the corner of the wall. An armored figure, a full head taller than Theodr, walked in its own trail through the sand toward them. It looked their way and continued walking.

Cautiously, Abdul and Theodr backed away from the palace. The thing walked past them and continued its patrol around the palace.

"Not very bright for a guard," Theodr observed.

"It has no mind," Abdul said. "It is a *golem.*"

"A what?"

"A living statue," Abdul explained. "With no soul or spirit. A creature of the Power which exists only to serve its master. We have legends of such things. Supposedly, they cannot be harmed."

Theodr watched as the metal monster walked around the side of the palace. Was this thing under Bjorn's Power? Or had it slain him and resumed its ancient post?

If it was under Bjorn's command, which seemed more likely, this was proof of Bjorn's true motives. If he truly only desired something that could aid them against Gavin, it was walking around the palace. Yet he was still here, still searching for the forbidden knowledge.

They waited until the golem had passed back out of sight around the palace. Then the two of them ran across the sand to the palace, eager to be out of sight when the thing returned.

Bjorn's horse was tethered to the sparkling fountain. The horse seemed well. At least Bjorn was still taking care of it. Then they were in, through a short section of wall missing from the palace. The room was empty. They slipped through a door into another room to hide.

A small window faced outside from their hiding place. Theodr and Abdul watched to see what the golem would do when it came upon their trail.

Soon the iron monster came back around the small bit of outer wall that was standing. It stopped when it reached their trail. Then it turned and followed the trail toward the palace, stopping at the plaza and casting about for them.

"It's following us!" Theodr whispered. "Come on!"

They fled deeper into the palace. In a large hall, water splashed in another fountain similar to the one outside. Marble columns reached more than a score of feet to the ceiling overhead.

"Even the *kaftan* does not live in such splendor," Abdul whispered.

"We can gawk later!" Theodr admonished. "We have to find Bjorn before that thing finds us!"

The golem appeared to know the palace better than they. It systematically searched through the rooms looking for them. Theodr and Abdul watched it briefly from beneath a door. The monster disappeared through a doorway.

"Now!" Theodr said, slipping out of the door and crossing back the way the golem had already come. Perhaps it would not search where it had already been.

They never found out. Apparently the thing could hear quite well. They had barely made it through the door when it came back into the fountain chamber at a run. Theodr slammed the door behind them and they both took off running.

The door opened behind them with a crash. Theodr slowed to open another door and heard Abdul cry out behind him. Theodr ran through the door without turning to look behind. There was nothing he could do for the other Guardian.

An iron hand closed around his right arm and pulled him back from the doorway. Theodr's struggles were as ineffective as Abdul's who was tucked up under the creature's left arm like an angry child.

The thing walked out of the palace, carrying the struggling Abdul and dragging Theodr backwards by the arm. Soon they were back outside, and the golem dumped them unceremoniously on the sand. Then it just stood there, waiting.

"Well," Theodr said, shaking from the experience, "that was certainly . . . humiliating." He backed away from the golem, moving crablike on his back. Still, it just stood there, watching them.

"It did not harm us," Abdul said. He sounded surprised.

"Perhaps it has been ordered not to," Theodr said. Bjorn would not want him dead. Only out of his way.

"It dropped us just outside its path," Theodr added, noticing that the golem now stood in its original track. "Bjorn must have ordered it to keep trespassers out, but not harm them."

"I am glad this man you seek is not vicious," Abdul said.

So am I, Theodr thought.

Chapter
------- Two -----------

The areas beneath the House of Soren were almost as extensive as the palace itself. Bjorn had activated over a dozen nascent spells. He had found dungeons, torture chambers, storerooms—everything but the vault.

Now, however, he had found something different. A large, circular room laid out with patterns of inlaid gold in the floor. A five-pointed star inside a circle that lay within yet another circle. Between the two circles, figures had been scribed, also in gold. Bjorn recognized some of these figures from the spells he had seen around the palace.

Bjorn carefully approached the center of the star and gasped, almost sobbed, in relief. There, in the center of the star, lay the pattern he had been seeking.

It was, of course, trapped. Heavily trapped. But, with the knowledge he had gleaned from the Silver Book, Bjorn knew the traps of this pattern. Finally!

Bjorn carefully reached out and took hold of what the book had claimed was the attachment point of the true spell. Soon, very soon, he would know if this was indeed what he sought. He would know if he could find something here with which to save his people.

Bjorn summoned the Power.

Half of the afternoon had passed since Abdul and Theodr had attempted to gain entry to the palace. They had used the time to make camp. Neither of them could think of a way to get past the iron sentry and find Bjorn. The golem marched in relentless patrol through the sand.

"Theodr?" Abdul said, breaking the silence. His voice sounded odd, frightened, and he was looking behind them. Theodr looked back, following Abdul's gaze away from the palace.

Two men and a woman faced them. All were clad in black

robes. Strange belts fashioned of gold mesh circled their waists, and another mesh strap ran from the waist up over the right shoulder. The auras of all three were clearly visible and easily as powerful as Bjorn's had become. All carried swords at their waists.

Gods help us, Theodr thought. *Who* are *these people?*

"Do not be alarmed," the darker man said, raising his hand in the Sign. The other two moved to surround them. Theodr noticed, to his surprise, that the mark of Bairn was blazoned on their left breast.

"Who *are* you?" Theodr asked.

"I am Guardian," the man replied. "For your own safety we must insist that you leave here."

"We pursue one who . . ." Theodr began, knowing that his statement was about to fall on deaf ears.

"We know why you are here," the Guardian interrupted. "If you remain here you will die."

"Is that a threat?" Theodr asked.

"A warning," the Guardian assured him. "A battle is about to occur here. One you cannot survive. Begone."

"Theodr?" Abdul asked. The other two had completed the triangle. The point lay toward the palace, and the open side lay away from it. The meaning was clear.

"I think we do as they say," Theodr said. "Let's break camp."

"Leave it," the Guardian said. "Take your horses and your supplies and go quickly. Your lives depend upon your haste."

"As you wish," Theodr replied. "Come, Abdul."

"Yes, *sahib,*" Abdul said.

This spell craved more of the Power than any pattern Bjorn had yet charged. Several of the symbols within the pattern had already consumed huge amounts of the Power before allowing the flow to proceed on through the rest of the pattern.

Sweat dripped from Bjorn's brow as the Power flowed through him. Never had he wielded the Power of the Cords for this long before. Time ceased to have any meaning, and it seemed as though he had sat here all of his life, feeding Power into this pattern.

Bjorn trembled from the exertion of maintaining the flow. It was becoming a race. Would he finish the activation before his own body betrayed him?

Finally, after an eternity, the Power traced along the pattern toward the last figure in the spell. Bjorn had long before collapsed to his knees. Now he fought to maintain his control over the Power long enough to finish.

The Power touched the last figure of the spell, and the world dissolved into a roaring maelstrom beneath him. Bjorn cried out as he was sucked into the gray whirlpool, and then the world went black around him.

He awoke in a place that was . . . no place. Around him was nothing but featureless blackness stretching away into infinity. And he was not alone.

Another stood before him. His aura shone more brightly than Valerian's ever had. Bjorn met his eyes and saw nothing but disdain, contempt and amusement.

The man's flesh was darker than leather, and his eyes were black as jet. A thin moustache and strangely pointed beard surrounded his mouth, but his cheeks were bare. He was dressed strangely in loose-fitting, robelike garments, and his head was wrapped in a cloth.

"Who . . . who are you?" Bjorn whispered, although he feared that he already knew the answer.

"I am Lord Soren," the MageLord replied.

"Why . . . ?"

"Be silent," Soren commanded, and Bjorn found that he could no longer speak. The MageLord raised the Power, and the maelstrom once again swallowed Bjorn.

Theodr, Helga—forgive me! he thought before he again lost consciousness.

When the maelstrom had vanished from the Circle chamber, a lone figure stood within. Soren looked around the room and smiled. That pathetic fool! He should have known that no Lord would leave his library for the common worms to find!

Soren had known that the time of the Lords was coming to an end. So he had prepared to do the one thing that could save him—to flee through Time. But one could not travel blindly into the future. There were many possible futures, but only one true future. Travel down the wrong path, and one could arrive into nothingness to be forever trapped.

No, it had been necessary to have someone from the true future reach back and pull him forward, and so he had set the spell on the Circle chamber and scattered dozens of copies of his book throughout the world. It had taken well over a thousand years, but one had finally brought him forward and taken his place in the doomed past.

Now, he could pluck this world like a ripe melon, unopposed and undefeatable. What he had learned from Bjorn's mind told him that there were none alive who could oppose him. The House of Soren would rule again—this time forever.

Soren walked over and opened the door that led from the Circle chamber. Someone stood on the other side. As Soren stepped back in surprise, the other entered the room.

"Greetings, Lord Soren," he said.

"No!" Soren cried. "You *cannot* still live!"

Theodr felt the distant rumble before he heard it. They had travelled perhaps a mile from the palace since the MageLords, if such they were, had warned them away. Now Theodr turned to look back.

Balls of fire rained from the sky while a pillar of smoke as black as night climbed into the sky. Even at this distance, the earth bucked and heaved beneath them like a thing alive, panicking the horses. Theodr fought to control his mount, both with reins and with Power.

There was no doubt now. Bjorn could not possibly have survived the battle that now raged behind them. Theodr's head dropped in grief. Whether it was for his friend or for his world he was not certain.

"The Lords battle," Abdul whispered.

"Gods help us," Theodr said.

•

One

CHAPTER THREE

AGAIN, [illegible] woke from unconsciousness [illegible] lay in the center of the circular room in which he had [illegible] the spell that had released [illegible] [illegible]

[illegible]

[illegible]

[illegible]

Chapter
------ Three ----------

Again, Bjorn woke from unconsciousness. He lay in the center of the circular room in which he had activated the spell that had released a true MageLord upon the world. This was no mere apprentice as Valerian had been, but a Lord in the full of his Power.

Bairn forgive me! he thought. He had been such a fool! He had to warn the others—warn Theodr. Bjorn raised himself onto his elbows to look around the room and stopped.

A circle of people stood around him. Each bore an aura easily as powerful as Soren's had been. Bjorn felt himself seized by the Power and lifted to his feet. One of the Lords stepped forward and examined the gold amulet around his neck.

"This says his name is Bairn," the Lord announced to the others present. He dropped the medallion. Bjorn's senses reeled. Soren had sent him back to the Time of Madness!

"So, Bairn," the MageLord asked, "where is Lord Soren?"

Bjorn stood by the window in the lesser apprentices' quarters. The barren, desolate landscape he remembered was no longer there. Or, more accurately, it was not there yet.

Outside, a fountain, exactly like the one Bjorn had raised a thousand years from now, splashed in the sunlight. Beyond the wall, lush vegetation reached toward the sky. Strange trees with bare trunks and all of their leaves at the top grew in the forest beyond. Bjorn had seen their like before outside the city in the sand.

The Time of Madness. Actually, the years *before* the Time of Madness. The MageLords held absolute power in this time. There was no escape.

Yet their very arrogance had saved him—thus far. They were so unlike Valerian. Valerian had been confident in nothing, had assumed nothing. These Lords were so powerful that it never even occurred to them that Bjorn might lie to them. After all, they were the Lords and *he* was the apprentice.

So they believed him when he told them he did not know where Soren was. When he told them that his "Lord" had performed a ritual in the Circle chamber and then simply vanished. From that point, the MageLords had fashioned their own explanation.

Apparently, Soren's attempts to pierce the future had been known. Bjorn had listened as the assembled Lords had decided that Soren was now lost, trapped in a future that had never come to be. His House would now fall to a new Lord.

Bjorn heard someone walk up behind him. He turned to face one of the apprentices. The man was dark of skin and beardless. His aura was more powerful than Bjorn's, currently, since he had released the Cords to avoid notice. Thank Bairn his Power had been exhausted when he had arrived here!

"Who are you?" the apprentice asked.

"I am . . . Bairn," Bjorn replied.

Am I? he wondered.

"I can see *that*!" the apprentice snapped. "Who *are* you?"

"An apprentice," Bjorn lied.

"Not of *this* House!"

"At least not that *you* knew of," Bjorn replied. That answer seemed to take the other off guard for a moment, giving Bjorn a little more time to think.

"I had just been taken," Bjorn added. "This morning, from my home to the north."

Bjorn prayed that the legends of the MageLords taking their apprentices from among the magi were correct. If not, he had just shown himself a liar.

The apprentice's eyes narrowed as he studied Bjorn carefully. Bjorn did his best to meet that gaze squarely.

"You're a little too cocky for a new apprentice," the apprentice finally said. "Learn a little humility before it gets you killed."

"I . . . am sorry," Bjorn replied, averting his gaze in what he hoped was an expression of submission.

"Welcome to the House of Nobody, Bairn," the apprentice said with a sardonic smile. "I am Haresh, Chief First Apprentice. You may address me as 'First.' Come with me."

"Yes, First," Bjorn replied.

"This will be your bunk," Haresh told him, indicating the bunk furthest from the door.

"Not that I think you will be here long enough to use it," Haresh added. "We will have to get your bedding, some clothes and a first's tunic. Then you can burn these . . . rags."

"Why do you say that I will not be here long?" Bjorn asked.

"None of us will, after today," Haresh said. "I suspect we will be parceled out among the other Lords, leaving the new Lord of this House to gather his own apprentices. Some of us may even be . . . discarded."

He looked pointedly at Bjorn as he said the last. Clearly, Haresh expected him to be among the latter group.

"I . . . hope not," Bjorn said.

"Naturally," Haresh agreed. "To be accepted into a great House and then lose it in the same day would be unfortunate."

Bjorn supposed that was one word for it. "Fatal" might be another word. According to the legends, anyone with the Power who was not apprenticed to a MageLord was killed.

Haresh turned out to be wrong about how soon the apprentices would be parceled out. Choosing a new Lord for the House of Soren was taking longer than Haresh had thought.

During this time, Bjorn moved through the palace in blessed anonymity when he was not at his lessons. Haresh had scheduled Bjorn's time as if the House were conducting business as normal.

The interesting thing was that *none* of his lessons had anything to do with the Art. He was tutored in the Lord's tongue to "get rid of his peasant accent," as Haresh put it. Other lessons dealt with etiquette, mathematics, cosmology and herbalism.

The lessons in etiquette turned out to be the most helpful. As a new apprentice taken from the populace, Bjorn was assumed to be just a notch above an ox as far as his knowledge of "polite" society was concerned.

He now knew that his off-white tunic marked him as an apprentice of the First Rank. A "first" for short. There were three ranks of apprentice before one became a journeyman—white, silver and gold. The journeymen wore black tunics and trousers. They alone among the apprentices bore arms.

There were three orders within each rank, including the journeymen. Again, they were denoted by white, silver or gold sashes tied around the waist of the tunic.

Bjorn was, of course, First Rank, First Order. These were, by far, the most numerous of the apprentices, about a hundred in all. They were taught nothing of the Art and were responsible for most of the menial work inside the palace.

Another thing that surprised Bjorn was that none of the apprentices were women. It was not that they were not capable. Bjorn knew that all too well. Many times when he was a boy, Aunt Freida had shown him exactly how powerful her Art was during his training.

Come to think of it, none of the Lords Bjorn had seen had been women, either. Apparently women were allowed only one role in MageLord society.

And they consider me *a barbarian!* he thought.

It took three days for the Lords to select a new master for the House of Soren. In the end, they selected the highest-ranking third-order journeyman among Soren's apprentices solely because he had no allegiances to any of the *other* Lords in the Alliance.

This news pleased Haresh immensely, as it meant that any apprentices not claimed by the senior Lords would still have a place here—even Bjorn. That was good news, indeed. Now he just had to make it past the selection interviews with the other Lords.

Bjorn waited outside the council chamber with the other first-rank apprentices. Over the last few days he had refined the story he had given Haresh. As long as the Lords did not question him under truthspell, Bjorn's story should hold up.

And, according to his etiquette classes, apprentices were only questioned under truthspell when there was active suspicion of betrayal. This courtesy was only extended to apprentices, however. The other subjects of the MageLords were afforded no such courtesy.

Courtesy. Hardly! To Bjorn it was obvious that the custom was in place simply to protect the MageLords' secrets. Magical interrogation of another Lord's apprentices could give an adversary vital information about the master's defenses.

"Bairn!" the guard called. Bjorn looked up in surprise, as did Haresh. They had just gotten down to the first-order firsts, and now they called him before all the others? Why?

Bjorn walked into the council chamber and knelt before the assembled MageLords. His heart pounded in his chest, but a lifetime of hiding from the Hunt allowed him no outward sign of nervousness. His breath was calm and his voice even as he spoke.

"You summoned me, Lords?" he asked.

"Yes, Bairn," one Lord said. "You may rise."

Bjorn rose to his feet, but kept his gaze averted.

"Bairn," the same voice asked, "where are you from?"

"Hunter's Glen, Lord," Bjorn replied. Bjorn had decided earlier that answers with as much truth in them as possible were the safest course of action. Hunter's Glen might not exist, but he doubted that the Lords knew the local names of every village in their lands. They just weren't that interested in their subjects.

"Is that near here?"

"No, Lord," Bjorn said. "It is far north of here."

"I thought so!" he heard another Lord whisper to the others. The one who spoke was blond-haired with a full but close-trimmed beard. He could have been from any of the clans north of Reykvid—in Bjorn's day.

"How long have you been apprenticed to Lord Soren?" the first Lord asked.

"Only since the day he disappeared, Lord," Bjorn replied.

"Three days ago?"

"Yes, Lord," Bjorn said.

"Who is the Lord of your homeland?" the blond Lord asked.

Bjorn's heart beat even harder. This was one area in which he was almost completely ignorant. What *were* the names of the reigning Lords? Valerian may have given him one answer, long ago.

"Lord Rylur, Lord," Bjorn replied, giving the only name he knew other than Soren. If Rylur had indeed been Valerian's Lord, that was also much nearer to Bjorn's home. The ruins of his castle had been near Star Lake.

Gods, let Rylur be alive! Bjorn thought.

"Damn him!" the blond Lord said. Bjorn was startled by the outburst.

"Soren has taken this apprentice from *my* lands!" the Lord continued. "No doubt to use as a spy against me!"

"Calm yourself, Rylur," the first Lord replied. "Soren is

gone and this one has only been in his service for three days. Three days that he was not here, at that. No one here will challenge your claim to him.''

''Good,'' Lord Rylur said. ''However, he is completely untrained. As he is of my lands, he should not count toward my allotment of Soren's apprentices.''

The Lord who had spoken conferred quietly with the other Lords at the table.

''Agreed,'' he finally said. Rylur smiled with satisfaction.

''Welcome to the House of Rylur, Bairn,'' he said.

''Thank you, Lord,'' Bjorn said. ''I am honored.''

''Have you any family?'' Rylur asked.

''No, Lord,'' Bjorn replied. ''My mother died in childbirth and my father died two winters back from an illness. I had no brothers or sisters.''

''We will speak more later,'' Rylur assured him. ''Lower your wards.''

''Wards, Lord?'' Bjorn asked, feigning ignorance. He had discarded those long ago. A first-order first should not have any. Bjorn felt Rylur's mind touch his, and his heart pounded. If Rylur read his memories, Bjorn would soon be dead.

But Rylur was not reading—he was placing.

''You are now bound to me,'' Rylur said. ''When I Call, you will hear.''

''Yes, Lord.''

''You may go, Bairn.''

''Thank you, Lord.'' Bjorn bowed, then turned and left the council chamber. Haresh was waiting for him when Bjorn returned to the hallway.

''Well?'' Haresh asked.

''I have been claimed by the House of Rylur, First,'' Bjorn replied.

''A noble House,'' Haresh told him. ''Congratulations, Bairn.''

''Thank you, First.'' Bjorn bowed and then quickly left the corridor. He wanted to find someplace where he could tremble in private.

Chapter
------ Four ----------

"First Apprentice Bairn!" a journeyman shouted at the entrance to the barracks.

"Yes, Master?" Bjorn replied.

"You are to come with me to Lord Rylur's coach," the journeyman told him. He already had a great deal of the arrogance of the Lords—at least when dealing with a lowly apprentice.

"Yes, Master," Bjorn agreed.

"Where are your things?" the journeyman asked. Bjorn spread his arms.

"This is all I have, Master," Bjorn replied.

"Very well," the journeyman said. "Come along."

Bjorn followed him from the apprentices' barracks into the palace and then out into the palace courtyard. A coach ride almost all the way back to Reykvid was going to take a *long* time. How would Bjorn keep his secrets safe while in such close contact with the MageLord for so long?

A strange . . . thing waited for them outside the palace gates. It vaguely resembled a sled, in that it rested on twin runners. However, these runners were of some highly polished, grayish metal, and the resemblance to a sled ended at the runners.

The body of the coach, if such it was, was fully twenty feet long and just taller than a man. It was all fashioned of some beautifully polished wood. Perhaps cherry. Glass windows, with drawn curtains, adorned the coach.

The body was strangely shaped—rounded in the front, with the . . . nose about one third of the way up the coach. The back was flat. Two doors opened in the back to allow entry. All of the corners of the body were gently rounded. There were no horses, nor any place to attach them that Bjorn could see.

Bjorn started for the back doors, but the journeyman caught him by the arm.

"Lord Rylur wishes you to sit up front with him," the journeyman said.

"Yes, journeyman," Bjorn replied. Bjorn could see other apprentices sitting on cushioned benches in the back. They looked out of the glass windows at him as the journeyman led him to the front of the strange coach.

The journeyman opened a door near the front, and Bjorn stepped into the front compartment. The coach was divided into two sections. The back section, where the apprentices sat, had been fitted with a three-sided bench along the walls of the compartment.

This section was much more ornately furnished. A sofa, two comfortable chairs, and a small table between the three filled the compartment. To one side was a small, ornate wooden cabinet. Fine crystal glasses sat neatly on its top. A large glass window dominated the front of the coach. Smaller windows were set in the sides. A curtain covered what was probably another window, this one looking into the rear compartment.

Bjorn bowed his head to the man lounging comfortably on the sofa. A beautiful woman, sparsely clad in almost transparent silks, sat on a cushion on the floor at his feet. Her hair was deep red, and her eyes were greener than the sea. The woman's skin was pale as ivory. An exquisite beauty with an empty smile.

"You wished me to ride with you, Lord?" Bjorn asked.

"Yes, Bairn," Rylur replied. His blue eyes belied his pleasant smile. Their suspicious gaze missed nothing. The MageLord took a sip from the crystal goblet in his hand and then handed his wine to the woman, who then set it on the small table. Bjorn ignored her.

"As you are the only one of my new apprentices from my own lands, I wanted to get to know you a little better," Rylur said.

"Yes, Lord," Bjorn replied.

"Sit down," Rylur said, gesturing expansively to one of the chairs. "We will depart soon."

"How, Lord?" Bjorn asked, forgetting to stifle his curiosity for a moment. Rylur looked at him curiously.

Oh, gods, Bjorn thought. He had slipped up already.

"You've never been in a coach before?" Rylur asked.

"N-no, Lord," Bjorn replied.

"Then how did Soren bring you hence?" Rylur asked. *Good question. Stick with the truth—to a point.* Rylur could very well be employing a truthspell on his new apprentice.

"I was just suddenly . . . here," Bjorn replied.

"A *translocation*?" Rylur asked. He sounded incredulous.

"I . . . do not know, Lord," Bjorn replied.

"Of course you don't," Rylur said. "A translocation! Of two people. How could he have done it without me sensing the Power?"

"I do not . . ." Bjorn began.

"I wasn't asking you!" Rylur snapped. Bjorn fell silent. Rylur's attention was diverted from him by a knock on the back wall. Rylur reached behind him and opened the curtain a crack. In the back, the journeyman bowed his head to his Lord.

"Excellent," Rylur said. He dropped the curtain, looked back to Bjorn and smiled. With a gesture, the floor beneath their feet became glass.

"Be silent for a moment," Rylur said. "Enjoy your first coach ride."

"Yes, Lord," Bjorn replied.

Bjorn watched as Rylur sat up and placed his hand on the wooden ball at the end of the sofa arm. Bjorn saw the flow of Power from Rylur's hand. He was activating a spell. Of course, Bjorn was not supposed to know that. In fact, he probably wasn't supposed to be able to sense the use of the Power yet.

Bjorn looked down through the clear glass beneath his feet. They rose to about a foot above the ground and then began to move forward. Soon they were moving about as fast as a horse at full gallop.

Magic, Bjorn thought. He should have known—these people could do *anything*, after all. At this rate, it would only take a fortnight or so to return to the House of Rylur.

Once they had passed through the garden, the coach took them into a city surrounding the palace. Bjorn watched out the window with interest. It was not as destitute as Bjorn had expected. Buildings and shops in good order lined the streets. It was not an unpleasant-looking place.

However, people watched the coach pass with concealed fear in their eyes. These people looked well off. What did they fear?

It was not long before they passed the outer wall of the city and were travelling along well-tended fields and meadows. Again, things looked pleasant. Perhaps the Time of Madness had not been quite so mad as the legends had painted it to be.

The coach began to rise further into the air. Once it was twice the height of the tallest trees, its speed began to pick up as well. Soon the tops of the trees were flashing past beneath. Bjorn's breath caught at the sight. They were travelling even faster than when he had ridden Arcalion! *Much* faster!

Still the coach climbed until the trees were far below them. At this height, their speed did not seem so great, but Bjorn knew that it had not lessened. Lord Rylur would be home by morning.

"You said that your family was dead, did you not?" Rylur said.

"Yes, Lord," Bjorn replied, tearing his gaze from the window beneath his feet. Rylur gestured, and the floor became opaque once again.

"No brothers or sisters?"

"No, Lord."

"Why did you wish to be apprenticed to Soren, Bairn?" Rylur asked.

"I was not given much choice in the matter, Lord," Bjorn replied.

"Oh?" Rylur said. "Do you not *want* to be apprenticed?"

"Oh no!" Bjorn said. "It is not that, Lord. I simply . . . that is, it *never* occurred to me that I could be apprenticed to the House of Rylur, or to any great House."

That was certainly true enough. The Houses of the Mage-Lords had been ruins for a thousand years before Bjorn's birth. It never would have occurred to him that he would live among them someday. Rylur smiled.

"I understand," he said.

I'm sure you think you do, Bjorn thought.

"What did you do before?" Rylur asked.

"I was a trapper and furrier, Lord," Bjorn replied.

"Not much of a life," Rylur observed.

"It was not . . . unpleasant, Lord," Bjorn said.

"I suppose not," Rylur conceded. "Still, did you never yearn for anything more?"

"Constantly, Lord," Bjorn replied. He had. He had yearned for a time when his people did not need to hide from the Hunt or when they could practice their Art for the benefit of their neighbors without fear of the fire. But Rylur would not understand such yearnings. He would simply assume that the person he knew as Bairn had yearned for power.

"Well, I suppose that the last few days have been very fortunate for you, then," Rylur said.

"It is hard to believe, Lord," Bjorn replied, carefully avoiding giving a direct answer to that question. He did not consider these events fortunate at all. So, instead, he answered with a diversionary truth.

"I'm sure it is," Rylur noted. "Do you have a wife, Bairn?"

"No, Lord," Bjorn replied. In truth, he would not have wed for yet another thousand years. It was amazing how much the truth was a matter of perspective.

"You seem to be extremely . . . unattached," Rylur noted.

"I have been alone for some time, now, Lord," Bjorn explained.

More alone than you could imagine, Bjorn thought.

"How unfortunate," Rylur noted, caressing the hair of the woman at his feet. She looked up at her master and smiled that empty smile.

"Well, then," Rylur said, "it certainly seems as though you are well suited for apprenticing. You suffer from no . . . distractions."

"No, Lord," Bjorn agreed.

"Very well," Rylur said. "That is all I wanted to know. You may join the others in the back now."

"Yes, Lord," Bjorn said, rising and bowing his head.

The woman rose and drew the curtain aside, revealing a door between the compartments. She opened it and held it for Bjorn as he passed. His eyes met hers briefly before she submissively averted her gaze. But not before Bjorn could see the fear hidden in her eyes.

If that fear in the gaze of every person who looked at you was the price of being a MageLord, Bjorn wanted no part of it. Unfortunately, he had little choice.

The bench along the back wall of the rear compartment was split to make room for the doorway. Bjorn walked into the rear compartment and took his seat among the other apprentices. He looked out the window at the trees rolling past below. However, all he could see were green eyes filled with hidden fear.

Rylur did not know quite what to make of this new apprentice. According to the truthspell, Bairn had answered all of his questions with complete honesty. All of them.

Still, there was something about him that simply did not seem . . . right. There was something . . . missing from Bairn's demeanor. Something that set Bairn apart from all of the apprentices Rylur had trained before.

And then Rylur realized what it was. Ambition. Bairn appeared to have *no* personal ambitions.

Rylur smiled. An apprentice without ambitions could be a great asset. Rylur would have to watch Bairn and see if that persisted as Bairn rose in ability. If so, he could become *very* valuable to Rylur, indeed.

The woman returned to her cushion after closing the door and offered him his goblet. Rylur waved it away with a smile.

"Not now, Rowena," he said. "But there is something else you can do for me."

"Yes, Lord," Rowena said softly as she rose to join him on the sofa. She smiled at him. Unlike Bjorn, Rylur did not notice the emptiness of her smile.

They arrived at the House of Rylur with the sunrise. As the coach settled into the main courtyard of the palace, Bjorn's gaze took in the whole of the great House. The House of Rylur was even more grand than the House of Soren. The palace itself was approximately the same size, but the grounds were much more extensive.

The palace was surrounded by a closely trimmed bailey, green and lush. That was surrounded by the inner wall. An outer wall sat at least another thousand feet out from that. The area between them was nothing less than . . . magical.

Sparkling crystal streams flowed into sculpted ponds before eventually joining and flowing out under the wall into a larger stream. Meadows, glens and forests were all recreated in miniature in Rylur's gardens. Bjorn caught glimpses of small herds of deer and other animals roaming the garden between the walls.

Bjorn blinked and then looked more closely at something. A small herd of horses grazed in a small meadow in the garden. However, they weren't horses—they were *unicorns*!

Before Bjorn could see more, the coach dropped behind the inner wall and landed on a stone patio attached to the palace. Once they were down, the journeyman rose and threw open the doors to the back of the coach.

"You will all be given one day of rest," the journeyman told them. "Tomorrow you will be given assignments appropriate to your rank. Welcome to the House of Rylur."

It was clearly a dismissal. The journeyman stepped down from the coach and departed. The apprentices disembarked by rank. Bjorn and one other first-order first were the last to leave the coach.

A man in a white tunic with a gold belt waited outside the coach.

"I am Chief First Jorgen," he told them. "Come with me."

Bairn's first fortnight, or first two "quarters," as they were called by the MageLords, in the House of Rylur was little different from his experience in the House of Soren. Chief First Jorgen ordered that he receive the same instruction he had begun under Haresh.

Bjorn still did not know what he thought of being given the name "Bairn." Was it possible that he and that legendary figure were one and the same?

That thought made him uncomfortable. It was far more likely that there was another Bairn somewhere in another House. Or maybe among the magi. The legends had said nothing of Bairn being a MageLord.

Whatever the truth, Bjorn was beginning to think of himself as "Bairn" now. That was how he was addressed. That was the only name he heard now. If someone walked up to him and called him Bjorn, he probably would not react to it at first.

As he stared at the ceiling above his bed in the barracks, Bairn found himself wondering about those who had known him as Bjorn. Sometime around a thousand years from now, would Helga wonder what had become of him? Would Theodr continue to search for him forever?

No. Bairn had loosed Soren, a MageLord in the full of his Power, onto his world. The lives of his loved ones would never be the same after that. With luck, Soren's attention would not make it as far as Bjornshall within his son's lifetime. With luck.

Theodr would not be so fortunate. Close on Bjorn's trail, he would run headlong into the MageLord. Hopefully, the Guardian would kill himself before Soren could learn his secrets.

And Bjorn—Bjorn would never see his wife or his son again. His friends would be lost to him, and he would never know what fate had befallen them at the hands of the terror he, himself, had unleashed upon the world.

Silently, in the darkened barracks, he wept.

Bairn's mornings before dawn were consumed with his chores. In the mornings, the duties of readying the House for the day occupied all of the firsts. Breakfast had to be prepared, drapes had to be drawn and shutters opened. Floors had to be swept and polished. During breakfast, beds had to be changed and linens washed before the firsts had their own breakfast.

After breakfast were the lessons. Mathematics was grueling. Bjorn had thought he already knew all there was to know about *that* subject. Now he was rapidly beginning to understand that he had only studied one tree out of a forest, so to speak.

Cosmology was not difficult, but it was fascinating. The MageLords taught that the sun did not circle the world. Rather, the world was a small ball of rock and water and air circling the sun along with other planets, inhospitable to life and devoid of Power.

Oddly enough, the most important thing that Bairn learned in cosmology was what time of year it was. He had been brought into this time from the dead of winter in his own time. Apparently, he had been transferred into the middle of spring in this time. He had already seen that it was not winter during his flight from Soren, but now he knew exactly when he had arrived in the year. In another two moons the summer solstice would arrive.

Fascinating as they were, Bairn was careful not to excel at his studies. The watchwords of the magi were "avoid notice." In his studies, that was exactly what Bairn did. He paced himself to match the progress of his fellow apprentices. Fortunately, this was not difficult. Bairn seemed to grasp the new concepts more quickly than the others, which made it easy for him to lag behind at their level.

After his studies, the afternoon chores waited to be done. Dinner had to be prepared, and the uncountable glass windows in the palace had to be washed. Floors and latrines had to be cleaned. It seemed endless.

However, there was a short time, between their dinner and sunset, that the apprentices held to themselves. Bairn had little to occupy himself during these times. He did not associate much with the other apprentices. Their talk and dreams of power did not interest him.

During these times, Bairn would find a quiet corner of the palace and look up at the stars. What was he doing here? Here—learning the Forbidden Arts of the MageLords to an extent he had never desired.

Surviving, he thought. But for what? What end did his survival accomplish?

None, he thought. But, for now, death would not accomplish anything, either. So, he who was once Bjorn would continue to survive until he had a reason not to do so. Or, until he had *found* a reason to do so.

At the end of Bairn's third quarter-moon in Rylur's service, the apprentices were given a holiday. Jorgen handed Bairn a small purse, after informing him that this was his monthly stipend as a first-order apprentice of the first rank.

Ten silver coins jingled in the pouch. All of them bore the stylized mark of the House of Rylur.

The coin of the realm, Bairn thought with a smirk.

The apprentices were free until the next morning. A day and a night to spend as they pleased. The next morning, however, they had all best be back at the gate. They could return early, or not leave, if they wished.

Curiosity led Bairn out of the palace and into the city that surrounded it. Like the city outside the House of Soren, it surprised him.

The city seemed much like any city that Bairn had ever seen. Houses and shops of stone and wood lined rough, cobbled streets. People bought and sold, haggled and shouted, laughed and cried. All appeared normal.

Appeared. When the apprentices began to go about their holiday, Bairn saw the difference. No request of an apprentice was denied, no matter how outrageous. No one haggled with the apprentices. They took whatever offer was made, if any.

So, what was the point of the stipend? Bairn tried an experiment. As he walked past a vendor selling spring apples, Bairn openly reached out and plucked an apple from the cart without bothering to pay. The man said nothing. When Bairn met his gaze, the vendor simply smiled and nodded to him. But Bairn saw the fear in his eyes that kept him silent. He also noticed that the man had a faint aura. Very faint.

Bairn fished one of the silver coins from his purse and handed it to the man.

"Thank you, Lord," the man said. So, even the apprentices were "Lord" as far as the townsmen were concerned. When it came to women, Bairn realized that he had seen nothing but old women. That was odd.

Bairn turned his palm up, and the man counted nine copper coins and a single bronze coin back to him.

"Is there a place in town where I can take a room?" Bairn asked, dropping the pennies and half penny into his purse.

"First holiday, Lord?" the man asked.

"Yes," Bairn replied.

"Most of the young Lords prefer the Golden Hare," the apple vendor said. Bairn already knew that from overhearing many of the apprentices making their plans for today. It was apparently a brothel.

"I just want a room," Bairn said. "Is there a place in town the young Lords *don't* like to go?"

"Not . . . that I know of, Lord," the man said. The fear had returned to his eyes. That was interesting. Bairn laid another penny in the man's hand.

"Thank you for your time," he said, turning away.

"Lord?" the man said.

"Yes?" Bairn replied, turning back.

"There are some . . . less expensive inns on the north side of town," the vendor told him. "You might try there."

"Thank you," Bairn said, smiling. He turned northward. As soon as he was out of sight of the vendor, he circled back toward the south.

What's on the south side that he doesn't *want me to see?* Bairn wondered.

Bairn wandered through the south side of Rylur's city. It had no name, other than the House of Rylur. This city, so close to the MageLord's Power, was simply considered an extension of his House.

However, Rylur's control did not extend into every portion of this city. Bairn had found a tailor's shop shortly after leaving the apple vendor. He was now wearing clothing that was much less obvious than his apprentice's tunic.

He had also banished almost all of the Power, muting his aura to an almost unnoticeable level. He only retained enough of the Power to keep his magesight—to let him see the auras of those around him. He felt more like the Bjorn of old here than he had since he had arrived at the House of Soren.

I could simply not return, he thought. *I could take back my name and disappear.*

But he knew that would not work. Rylur had marked him. If Rylur called, his apprentice, Bairn, would return. Rylur was powerful enough to make certain of that.

This part of the city was much less pleasant than further north, near the palace. The cobblestone streets had been replaced with packed earth, and open sewers ran alongside the streets. The smell was . . . potent. Bairn doubted that the apprentices ever came near this place. For that matter, Rylur himself probably avoided it.

It also looked rough. Now that he had shed his tunic, Bjorn no longer enjoyed the protection of the House of Rylur. To make matters worse, he was starting to look out of place. A little too clean, and much too well fed.

Still, if he were to find the magi, this was the most likely place. A place where they could be reasonably safe from discovery. Bjorn wasn't even certain why he was looking for them. Perhaps just to find a link, however tenuous, back to home.

But it appeared that he would not find them today. The sun was sinking toward the rooftops, and the shadows would soon start filling the streets. Bjorn did not want to be out in a strange part of town after dark. It would be best to return here on his next outing.

For now, he would return north and find a room between here and the palace that he could rent on a permanent basis. He would need a place to keep his clothes and from where he could come and go as either Bairn *or* Bjorn.

Chapter
------- Five -----------

It was another moon before the apprentices were given their next holiday. During that time, Bairn's studies proceeded at a steady, unremarkable pace. Part of him yearned to speed ahead, but it was best not to draw attention to himself.

Jorgen handed Bairn his monthly stipend of ten silver coins and instructed him to return to the palace by sunrise. Bjorn fastened the purse to his belt. Apparently Lord Rylur had an endless supply of leather purses.

Probably plucks them from thin air, Bairn thought. *Along with the silver.*

He passed the same apple vendor he had met on his first trip into the city. Bairn plucked an apple from the cart and tossed the man a half penny, left over from his last holiday. The merchant deftly caught it.

"Good day, Lord," the man said.

"Good day," Bairn replied. He wandered off, seemingly aimlessly toward the west. He stopped and looked over the wares of a few merchants briefly and then continued on his way.

As soon as he was out of sight of both the vendor and the other apprentices, most of whom were heading straight to the Golden Hare, Bairn turned to the southwest. On his last holiday, Bairn had secured a room in a part of town that was not too unpleasant. It had cost him his eight remaining silvers to secure it against his return in a moon.

All conversation in the inn stopped at his entrance. Bairn walked up to the counter, and the nearest people made room for him as he approached.

"Good day, Lord Bairn!" the innkeeper said cheerfully. His pleasant demeanor did not hide the trace of fear in his eyes, however.

"My room?"

"Hasn't been touched, Lord," the innkeeper quickly assured him.

Bairn smiled. He was sure it had not been.

"I meant, how much do I owe you for the next moon?" he explained.

"The same, Lord," the innkeeper told him. "Eight silvers."

Bairn counted the coins onto the counter. That left him only two silvers and a few pennies for the day. Fortunately, his expenses were small.

"Send dinner up tonight," Bairn instructed the innkeeper. "I will need no other meals."

"Yes, Lord," the innkeeper said.

The ward shimmered behind the door when Bairn opened it. As the innkeeper had said, no one had disturbed his room. The lattice, while weak from his absence of a moon, was undisturbed.

Bairn took hold of the lattice and passed through. There was not much to the room—a bed and a cabinet for the chamber pot, which was still outside the door. He picked up the chamber pot and closed the door.

The room had accumulated quite a bit of dust over the last four weeks. Bairn had not needed the lattice to warn him if anyone had entered his room. He would have seen their tracks on the floor.

With the addition of a locked trunk, he could leave the room unwarded and allow the innkeeper to clean the room during his absence. Bairn placed the chamber pot inside the cabinet.

So, his first order of business was to buy a trunk. That would take up precious time, but it was a necessity. Bairn dusted off the foot of the bed and sat cross-legged on it. He closed his eyes and reached out to the lattice.

It took much less time to dispel the ward than it had taken to raise it. Before, he had been very careful not to empower it too quickly. He had not forgotten Rylur's comment regarding Soren's supposed use of Power in his own lands. Apparently the MageLords could sense the use of the Power within their realms.

Now, dissipating the almost wasted ward was near effortless. Bairn opened his eyes. No trace of Power lingered in the room. Excellent. Bairn took the clothes he had purchased on his last holiday and folded them to look like a package.

Again, room was made for him at the counter.

"Yes, Lord?" the innkeeper asked.

"My room needs to be cleaned," Bairn told him. "Could you see to it while I am gone?"

"Of course, Lord," the innkeeper replied.

"Thank you," Bairn said. "Do you know where I might purchase a trunk?"

"Sven, the barrel maker, would know," the innkeeper suggested. "His shop is on the second street south, to the right."

"Thank you," Bairn said.

"My pleasure, Lord," the innkeeper replied.

It was early afternoon by the time Bjorn left for the south side of the city. It felt good to be out of his apprentice's uniform—to have people look at him without the immediate presence of fear in their eyes. To leave Bairn behind and to just be Bjorn again.

Again, he had shed most of his Power with his clothes. People jostled around him on the street, paying him no mind. It was wonderful.

Bjorn wandered aimlessly about the city, heading southward. Slowly the condition of his surroundings worsened. The cobblestone streets were replaced with gravel and, eventually, with earth. The smell of rotting sewage and garbage lingered constantly in the background.

This was a part of town into which the apprentices never ventured—except Bjorn. Not from fear or danger, but from distaste. As such, it should be the safest part of town for the magi.

If they existed. Bjorn could have been imagining things when he thought the apple vendor was attempting to throw him off the scent of something. The man could have simply been trying to be helpful. So far, he had found no sign of their presence.

A woman across the street caught Bjorn's eye. She was middle-aged and portly. That in itself was enough to catch his attention. She seemed more well fed than anyone on the street except Bjorn. She had just emerged from a shop, and her basket weighed heavily on her arm. And she had an aura.

It was not strong, even by his preapprentice standards, but it *was* there. Bjorn forced himself to remain calm. Not everyone with an aura was of the Circle.

Once she had gone a little way down the street, Bjorn began to follow her. He kept over a score of paces distance between them. Mage or not, she was the best lead he had come across yet.

The sun kissed the rooftops as Bjorn followed her. He really ought to head back to the inn, but he wanted to see where the woman was heading. If she were Circle, watching her home might lead him to others of the Circle on his next outing.

She climbed a flight of stairs on the outside of a small two-story building. The bottom floor was a shop, closed for the night. Its sign identified it as an apothecary. Bjorn smiled.

Some things never change, he thought. Many among the magi had posed as apothecaries and healers in his own time and, apparently, for centuries.

Of course, he still was not certain the woman was Circle. However, it certainly seemed likely. Especially given her choice of profession.

The shadows were beginning to fill the streets. Now that he knew where to find his quarry, Bjorn began to hurry back to the inn. Somehow, he didn't think it would be too healthy to be out in these streets after dark.

Bjorn was only halfway back to the inn by the time the sun had fully set. The streets were deserted except for a few rats and the occasional stray dog or cat.

Closer in to the palace, Bjorn knew that a near carnival atmosphere would prevail until dawn. But here, in the back streets and alleys, no one was about. Doors and shutters were tightly closed against the night. No one ventured onto the streets.

"You!" A shout came from behind him. Bjorn whirled to see three men in armor with weapons. They wore the livery of the House of Rylur.

Almost no one was about, Bjorn thought.

"Hold!" they commanded as they broke into a run. Bjorn turned and ran. He couldn't afford to be caught by the guard! He would *never* be able to explain it—Rylur would learn the truth and have him killed!

Unencumbered by armor, Bjorn quickly gained the lead. However, he heard the high shriek of metal whistles behind him and soon, another group of guardsmen burst onto the road ahead of him.

"Damn!" Bjorn cursed as he turned down an alley. If only he knew this part of town better, he could elude them. He heard the jangle of armor behind him in the alley.

Thank the gods they're not carrying crossbows, he thought.

The alley ended in a blank wall. Actually, a fence. Bjorn jumped onto a crate in a pile of garbage and leaped for the top of the fence.

He caught the lip of the fence and strained to pull himself over. The muscles in his arms strained, and his chest burned for lack of air as his heart pounded in his chest. Gods, he was getting soft!

The sound of running feet gave him renewed strength, and he hauled himself over the fence to fall to the ground on the other side.

He was on another street. Bjorn staggered to his feet and ran off down the street. Behind him he could hear the curses of the guardsmen.

He made it back to the inn without further incident, although he was forced to hide several times to avoid patrols of guardsmen.

Whom were they looking for? Him? If so, why? Had Rylur somehow stumbled onto his secret?

If that were the case, Bjorn was certain he would already be dead. Rylur had only to Call and Bairn would have no choice but to obey.

Bjorn slipped into the inn, which was still crowded. No one, not even the innkeeper, noticed his entrance. Bjorn smiled. It was completely unthinkable to them that a young Lord would divest himself of his robes of station.

Bjorn climbed the stairs up to his room. It had been a *long* night.

When the Call woke him before dawn, Bairn groaned at the stiff and sore legs that wobbled beneath him. His adventures of the night before had taken their toll. It was amazing how much damage only two moons of easy living had done to him.

He was going to have to do something about that. Last night's encounter had been too close for his taste. He dressed quickly as the Call tugged at him and headed downstairs. The innkeeper was waiting for him.

"Good morrow, Lord," he said.

"Good morrow," Bairn replied. "You may now clean the room during my absence. Be careful not to disturb my trunk."

"Yes, Lord," the innkeeper said. "I will see to it."

"Thank you," Bairn replied. "I shall see you next moon."
"Yes, Lord."

"As many of you know," Chief First Jorgen was saying, "tomorrow is the summer solstice. You may take the first half of the day for rest. After that, we have much to do to prepare."

That was fine with Bairn. The day of rest following a holiday was always more than a little boring for him. For the other apprentices, who had been up all night at the Golden Hare, the news was dreadful.

"Chief First," Bairn said.

"Yes, Bairn?"

"I got enough rest last night," Bairn said. "If there is anything that needs to be done now, I can help."

"Thank you, Bairn," Jorgen said. "I am certain we can find things for you to help with."

"I have had sufficient rest as well, First," another apprentice said. Bairn glanced over to the apprentice who had spoken. His dark skin and lean features identified him as one of the apprentices from Soren. His white tunic and sash placed him at the same rank as Bairn.

"Very well, Raoul," Jorgen said. "If anyone else wants to start work immediately, I'll be in my chambers."

Atop the central tower of the palace was a double circle of stone obelisks. The inner circle was raised a full manheight above the outer circle. Bairn knew, from his lessons on etiquette, that this double ring of stone was where the apprentices would gather at dawn tomorrow for the solstice.

Rylur, the journeymen and the third-rank apprentices would occupy the raised circle. The second- and first-rank apprentices would occupy the inner circle. Together they would all participate in some great work of Power. The lessons had not been explained beyond that point.

There was some work preparing the circle, but most of the work took place in the great hall preparing for the feast that would follow. Summer garlands of roses and other flowers were woven and draped over the chandeliers. Similar centerpieces were fashioned for the tables.

The work brought back memories of preparing Lars's hall for similar events. The women weaving the garlands and the men slaughtering the cows for the feast. Bjorn and Helga sitting together at the high table with Lars and Bris or, later, just with Bris. Pleasant memories—filled with pain.

The apprentices gathered atop the palace in the cool, predawn air. Once all had gathered, Rylur and the higher-ranking apprentices raised the Circle.

It was not a Circle as Bairn remembered them, however. Rylur was its center. The apprentices remained apart from it, feeding their Power into it from without. They did not join with each other through the Circle as the magi would have done.

Of course not, Bairn thought. The Lords, and the apprentices, did not want the others to know their thoughts. They did not trust one another enough for that. This was a Circle of strangers—a Circle of enemies. It was not a Circle of brothers and sisters such as those Bjorn had known before.

As the Circle expanded, the second-rank apprentices added their Power to it. The expanding ring swept toward the first-rank apprentices. Those of the first rank did nothing. As yet, they had been taught nothing of the Art.

And then, the sun rose over the horizon. As it did, the stone circle isolated a single beam of sunlight to strike the central dais where Rylur stood. The light brightened beyond the point of mere sunlight into a blinding sphere of radiance.

The sphere grew, expanding outward through the Circle. As it did, the Power of the Circle soared and expanded.

As the Circle, now made visible, swept over the roof, the palace was transformed. Cracked stones and cornices fused together. Weathered stone was polished to the point of brilliance. A season's wear was undone in a heartbeat.

The lowest-rank apprentices gasped in awe, save for Bairn who simply observed. As the Power swept through the courtyard toward the inner wall, fountains burst into sparkling water, flagstones shone like polished gems.

The line of transformation climbed up the inner wall. Even the guardsmen were affected, their uniforms, armor and weapons mended and polished to perfection. And then the Power hit the gardens.

Flowers bloomed behind the wave of renewal. Trees blossomed and then hung heavy with fruit in the space of a heartbeat. It was amazing—and frightening. It had taken Bjorn days to raise a portion of the House of Soren even with his exaggerated Power. Here, an area a hundred times greater was transformed in seconds.

It was a sobering sight.

The great hall was a sight to behold. When the wave of Power had passed through the great hall, the garlands and centerpieces had taken life and grown throughout the chandeliers and over the tables. As a result, the smell of roses and wildflowers filled the hall.

As all the apprentices filed into the great hall, Bairn wondered who would be serving dinner. That chore usually fell to the lowest-order, first-rank apprentices. Today, they were all sitting in the hall as equals.

The feast was already upon the table. Another aspect of the Power that had swept through the hall, Bairn supposed. Or perhaps others had been hired to prepare the feast so that the first-rank apprentices could join in.

Scarcely clad wine girls moved throughout the hall, tending to the goblets of the apprentices. From their number, Bairn supposed that they would tend to other needs as well later on as the level of intoxication rose.

In other circumstances, Bairn might not have minded such a feast. In fact, he had participated in a few similar rites as Bjorn before his own marriage. However, these women were slaves—forced to serve, not partaking as equals. There was no sanctity here, only debauchery.

He would stay just long enough to eat and then, when things had progressed to where no one would notice, he would quietly slip out. Bairn chose a seat near the door.

The festivities began with the meal. The wine girls filled all the goblets, forced into close quarters to pour the wine. The apprentices took full advantage of such close quarters. Bairn successfully ignored the women until a cascade of red hair brushed across his face.

He glanced up into the same green eyes he had seen in Rylur's flying coach. These were not just women brought in from the city—at least some of these were Rylur's own women! How large was his harem?

"I am sorry, my lord," she said, smiling and leaning against him as she filled his goblet. Bairn flushed at the feel of her warm flesh against his arm.

"That's . . . all right," he stammered. "Thank you."

"I live to serve, my lord," she said. As she left, she ran her arm across his shoulders.

I'm sure you do, he thought. *That's the problem.*

"Lords, Bairn!" a voice said to his right. Bairn turned to see Sven, another of the first-rank apprentices, sitting two seats away. "She practically threw herself at you!"

"I . . . didn't notice," Bairn said.

"Perhaps he hasn't figured out what they're for yet?" an apprentice Bairn did not know suggested.

"Aye," Sven agreed. "I did not see him at the Golden Hare this holiday. Is that it, Bairn? Are you an innocent?"

The entire table found this immensely funny, and Bairn returned his attention to his meal.

Promising young MageLords, every one of them, he thought.

Rowena watched the apprentice at the far table carefully. She had heard the others call him Bairn as they taunted him. Bairn. That was also the name by which Rylur had called him in the coach, she remembered.

He ate quietly, paying no attention to the festivities around him. She had been forced to hit him in the face with her hair simply to get him to notice her. He was different from the others. She had known that when their eyes had met in the coach.

She made her way back over to his table, filling goblets as she went, ignoring the groping hands that roughly caressed her exposed flesh. Somehow she knew that his hands would not be rough.

Finally, she was at his chair. She placed her left hand on his left shoulder as she leaned over his right shoulder to fill his goblet. She felt the muscles of his back tense as she pressed against him, even though he gave no outward sign of any unease.

He looked up at her and she smiled at him. There was a touch of surprise in his eyes. Beneath that she could see his desire. It had been there in the coach as well. Still, he would not touch her.

She turned away to fill other goblets.

• • •

"I tell you, Bairn," Sven said, "that woman is practically begging you!"

"You're imagining things," Bairn replied, although secretly he was beginning to agree with Sven. There had been no fear in the woman's eyes that Bairn could see, and her smile had been nowhere near as empty as it had been in Rylur's coach.

Bairn had to get out of here as quickly as possible.

"Where are you going?" Sven asked.

"To the privy," Bairn replied.

"I'll bet!" Sven chuckled.

Bairn slipped out the doors of the great hall. No one would notice when he didn't return. The apprentices were starting to get drunk. Bairn doubted it would be much longer before the real festivities began. He doubted that he would be missed.

Rowena saw Bairn leave the hall. Fortunately, she was still near the doors. She set the ewer on a nearby table and glanced toward the high table. Rylur was engrossed in his conversation with the journeymen. She turned and walked out of the smaller side door to the kitchen.

She would have to hurry to catch him.

"Bairn?" a soft voice said behind him. He stopped. Before he turned, he knew what he was going to see. Red hair, green eyes and alabaster skin covered with entirely too little clothing.

She knows my name, he thought. That was not a good sign.

"Can I . . . help you?" he asked.

"I think we can help each other," she replied, walking toward him. "Are you coming back?"

"No," Bairn said.

"Is it me?" she asked. "Do you . . . dislike me?"

"I don't even know you," he said, taking a step back. She continued to advance. "How could I dislike you?"

"Then why?"

"I don't want to be here when . . . it begins," he said. He took another step back, but she was already within arm's reach.

"Why?"

"I . . . cannot," he said.

"Are you unable?" she asked. "I can help."

I'll bet you could, he thought. This woman could stir passion in a stone.

"No," he said. "That's not it. I . . . had a wife—a son. I . . . lost them less than a year ago."

"I am sorry," she said. Then she was in his arms.

"I knew you were different," she said. "You know love. The others are animals. Let me help. Let me ease your pain."

"What . . ." Bairn began. He cleared his throat—this woman was making his head swim.

"What is your name?" he asked.

"Rowena," she said.

"Rowena," Bairn said, "please, don't think that I don't find you . . . desirable. You are probably the most insanely beautiful woman I have ever seen. I just cannot. Forgive me."

Bairn broke from her embrace and walked quickly down the hall. If he didn't get away from that woman now, he never would.

Rowena watched him walk away, realizing she loved him. She had to get back to the feast before she was missed.

She turned around to come face to face with Lord Rylur. She gasped in surprise.

"My Lord!" she said, kneeling before him.

"You know you are not supposed to leave the hall, Rowena," Rylur said.

"Forgive me, Lord," she said. "One of the apprentices left quickly. I . . . feared he was . . . unwell."

"I see," Rylur said. "Come back to the hall, Rowena. We have much to do."

Chapter

------- Six -----------

"Let me see if I understand this," Jorgen said. "You *want* me to give you harder work?" The Chief First still seemed a little bleary-eyed from the previous night. Most of the apprentices had slept, or rather passed out, in the great hall.

"I need something that will give me back my wind," Bairn added.

"Very well," Jorgen said. "You may work in the gardens from now on."

"The gardens?" Bairn asked. He had never been in the gardens before.

"It is usually reserved for punishment," Jorgen said, guessing Bairn's thoughts. "You've never had to be punished, Bairn."

"Is it . . . safe?" Bairn asked.

"As long as you wear that and stay clear of the ponds," Erik replied, indicating Bairn's medallion. "But it will be difficult work. You will have to trim and prune the trees, remove dead stumps—and animals, chop wood and so on. It's probably the most tiring work in the palace."

"Thank you," Bairn said. He had been wanting to see the gardens ever since he arrived. Now, it seemed, he would get his chance.

"Don't thank me yet," Jorgen said, smiling.

As Jorgen had warned him, the afternoon work in the gardens was exhausting. But it was also rewarding. The gardens were beautiful, and it pleased Bairn to have a hand in their beauty.

Apparently, there were no apprentices in need of punishment today, for Bairn was alone in the garden. That suited him just fine.

He was eating the evening meal he had brought with him atop a hill overlooking the largest of the ponds in the garden. Occasionally the tail of some large fish would splash out of the water and slap the surface of the pond. Bairn wondered what they were. Whatever they were, they were *big*. No wonder Jorgen had told him to stay away from the ponds.

As Bairn took another bite of the chicken leg and idly watched the rippling pond, one of the creatures leaped from the water. He dropped his food in surprise.

She had flowing, golden hair, and water streamed from her bare, ample bosom and from her outstretched arms as she soared out of the pond. At the waist, her smooth skin blended into a fish's tail, also seemingly smooth—not scaled like the tail of a normal fish.

Bairn rose to his feet, his meal forgotten, as she arced over the pond to dive back beneath the waters. The heads and shoulders of other women rose briefly above the water where she had entered. There was the sound of women's laughter.

Mermaids! As if in a trance he wandered toward the pond, stepping on the forgotten remains of his meal.

Mermaids! Where had Rylur found them? Bairn had always believed them to be nothing but sailors' fancies after too long at sea without female companionship. These were real creatures!

As he neared the pond, a flash of red hair emerging from the water caught his eye. She turned toward him as he approached, and Bairn's breath caught as he looked into her bright green eyes. Green eyes that had looked away from his in fear in Rylur's coach, that had held his eyes spellbound at the feast, that had looked up at him while he held her in his arms.

"Rowena?" Bairn said, hardly believing his own eyes. "Oh, gods. Rowena!"

There was his answer. Rylur had *not* found them—he had made them. These were his women—or his former women. Bairn felt his stomach revolt against the food he had eaten.

"Damn you, Rylur," he said. "*Damn* you! Oh, gods, Rowena—forgive me."

The redheaded mermaid swam toward him, then rose a little from the water and held out her arms to him. There was nothing in her eyes but animal passion—no trace of intelligence or reason.

Bairn turned and ran.

Bairn avoided the ponds by a great distance after that. He asked Jorgen about the mermaids that night. Apparently, if one of Rylur's women displeased him greatly enough, that was her fate.

They were condemned to an existence of consuming passion. If they tried to take a male, they almost invariably drowned him in the attempt. So their desires could never be sated. The crime that usually sent them to the ponds was infidelity. Bairn had a fairly good idea who her paramour had been—himself.

The trees around the pond were typically those unfortunate lovers. Always near, but never together. Rylur found the punishment appropriate. Bairn found it monstrous.

He had been close, *so* close to joining those silent, wooden ranks. If he had succumbed to her potent charms, he would now be forever rooted in the banks of her pond.

All of the mythical creatures in the garden were fashioned by Rylur's magic. The unicorns were simply smallish horses with horns. They were also more aggressive than regular horses. Without his medallion, Bairn would likely be dead by now.

There were other, normal creatures in the garden as well. Deer, rabbits, mice, wolves—all lived within the confines of the walls. Hawks and owls came to feed on the smaller game.

On some days, Bairn worked in the garden alone. On other days, other apprentices worked in the garden as well. On those days, regardless of their rank, Bairn was put in charge of them because of his knowledge of the gardens. Bairn much preferred the days he worked alone.

Over time, the timid animals came to know him. Before a moon had passed, even the wolves and unicorns would let Bairn approach them. When he ran through the trees, the wolves would follow around him, as if he were one of their pack.

Today Bairn was going to attempt to groom the unicorns. He had noticed that, although bright, their coats were matted and dirty, so he had borrowed some grooming equipment from the stable hands.

He combed out the mane of the lead stallion as the herd grazed in one of the meadows. The mane was matted and tangled from almost a moon of neglect. After about an hour, Bairn was able to get it combed out. Then he set to brushing the animal. At this rate, he would only be able to groom one animal a day if he wanted to get his other work done.

The brushing went much quicker, and Bairn turned his attention to the hooves. *This* was the risky part. It would probably be best to start with the forelegs. Less chance of upsetting the animal that way.

Bairn lifted the animal's foreleg and inspected the hoof. The unicorn snorted, but tolerated his actions. Bairn dug a small stone out of the frog of the hoof and then took the rasp to a few rough places on the hoof itself. It was in surprisingly good condition, considering how little attention these animals received.

That was true of all of the hooves. Bairn patted the stallion on the flank and gathered up his tools. It had been beautiful before, but now the animal shone. Bairn smiled.

"That was amazing," a voice behind him said. Bairn turned to see Lord Rylur standing behind him. He dropped to one knee and bowed his head.

"Lord!" Bairn said.

"Rise, Bairn," Rylur said. "I am amazed that they allow you to approach them, let alone groom them."

Bairn rose from his knees.

"They know me, Lord," he said.

"Apparently so," Rylur noted. "Walk with me, Bairn."

"Yes, Lord." Bairn fell into place behind Rylur and to his right—the correct place for an apprentice.

"Do you like my gardens, Bairn?" Rylur asked.

"Yes, Lord," Bairn replied.

But not enough to become a part of them, he thought. Was he about to join the silent grove by the mermaids' pond?

"When I first noticed you working out here, I thought you were being punished for some infraction," Rylur said. "Then I noticed that you were out here several days together. So I went to Jorgen and he told me that you had requested this work."

"Yes, Lord," Bairn said.

"My next thought was that you had found a unique method for slacking off," Rylur said. "After watching you for a few days, however, I determined that that was not the case."

"No, Lord," Bairn said.

"How are your studies progressing?"

"Well, Lord," Bairn replied.

"That is not what I hear from Jorgen," Rylur said. "He says that you are only an average pupil. I had hoped for better from you."

"I . . . am sorry, Lord," Bairn replied. Apparently he had lagged a little *too* much.

"Jorgen also tells me that you never spend any time in the library after hours," Rylur noted.

"No, Lord," Bairn replied. Since he was deliberately lagging to keep pace with the other apprentices, he had not required extra study time. In his most difficult subject, mathematics, he was still keeping pace with the average apprentice. Even so, Bairn should have *pretended* to take extra study.

"Why are you out here, Bairn?" Rylur asked.

"I wish to stay fit, Lord," Bairn replied.

"I think that is not the only reason."

"Lord?"

"You don't get on well with the other apprentices, do you?" Rylur asked.

"No . . . Lord," Bairn replied. There was little point in lying—Rylur obviously knew the answer.

"I thought not," Rylur said. "Much as I hate to do it, you will only be allowed to work in the gardens in the afternoons. I want you to have more contact with the other apprentices."

"Yes, Lord," Bairn replied.

"And I want to see more progress in your studies."

"Yes, Lord."

"Oh, and Bairn?"

"Yes, Lord?"

"My gardens have never looked better," Rylur said, smiling. "You do good work—when you want to."

Bairn forced himself to smile back.

"Thank you, Lord," he said.

The library was located between the barracks of the first-order firsts and the higher-order firsts. Small alcoves off the library were used for study. Each alcove held two desks with hard-backed chairs. As it was everywhere in the palace, light filled the room from no discernible source.

Bairn was familiar with that, however. He had empowered several of the light spells in the resurrected House of Soren himself. Bairn could see the spell that lit this room plainly on the wall. He doubted that any of the other first-rank apprentices could, however.

Bairn found the last empty alcove and claimed a desk. He opened the math text and began reading. He didn't really need to study anything else. If Lord Rylur wanted him to progress in his studies faster, he ought to tackle the one that was giving him the most difficulty.

Of course, he had also selected works appropriate to his other studies. He wasn't going to make *that* mistake again. It would not do for him to suddenly improve in all of his other subjects without ever raising a tome about them.

"Excuse . . . me," a voice said timidly. Bairn looked up from his work to see another apprentice standing just outside the alcove. He, too, was first rank, first order.

"Yes?" Bairn asked. The young man was dark-skinned and black of hair—like the apprentices at the House of Soren had been. Bairn recognized him as the other apprentice who had volunteered to help with the solstice preparations. He was obviously one of Rylur's new acquisitions—like Bairn.

"May I . . . take the other desk?" the apprentice asked.

"No one is using it," Bairn replied, returning to his book.

"Thank you," the apprentice said. Bairn glanced up in surprise. He didn't think he had heard those two words directed at him inside the palace since he had arrived.

"You're welcome," he replied and turned back to his book. The apprentice sat and began quietly working at the desk next to Bairn.

"Raoul!" someone said. "You finally found someone to study with!" Bairn looked up. It was Sven—red-haired, large and loud. First rank, second order. He had worked under Bairn twice in the garden.

Bairn glanced over to Raoul. The apprentice looked back and then away, back to his books, but not before Bairn could see a trace of fear in his eyes. Bairn looked back to Sven.

"It figures you'd take up with the gardener," Sven added.

"Sven," Bairn said, "is there some reason you are interrupting me? I have work to do."

"Oh, pardon me, Lord Bairn," Sven said, bowing to Bairn. "But in case you haven't noticed, we're not in the garden tonight."

"Not tonight," Bairn agreed. "But I *will* be there the next time you are. Perhaps I'll have you clean the banks around the mermaids' pond. Can you swim?"

"N-no," Sven said.

"Then you'll have to be careful not to . . . fall in," Bairn said. "Now, if you'll excuse us?"

"Watch him, Raoul," Sven warned. "The unicorns let him groom them. You know what *that* means!" He turned and walked away.

"What does that mean?" Bairn asked, turning back to Raoul.

"I . . . do not know," Raoul said. "I am sorry. I will go."

"I wouldn't," Bairn said. "If you go somewhere else, he'll corner you again. He's gone for now. Let's get back to our studies."

"You . . . do not mind?"

"Not as long as you're quiet," Bairn replied. He heard nothing else from Raoul for the rest of his time in the library.

Bjorn left the inn and walked toward the south side of the city. As before, he had discarded all but the barest amount of Power. Today he would find a place to watch the apothecary and see if any others among the magi sought the woman out.

His work in the garden had taken some of the plumpness out of his face, making him seem less out of place in this part of town. An hour's walk brought him to the apothecary. Bjorn looked about the street.

Almost directly across from the woman's shop was a tavern. Bjorn smiled. He still had over a score of pennies left from his month's stipend. Apparently, he had found where he was going to spend them.

The tavern was almost empty. Only a few old men sat around a single table, playing some type of game with colored chips of wood on a grid pattern in the tabletop. They glanced at him as he entered and then looked back to their game.

Bjorn claimed a table by an open window, from where he could watch the shop with ease.

"G'day, sir," the tavern owner said. "What'll ye have?"

"Ale," Bjorn replied.

"Tha' 'ill be a penny, m'lord," the man said. Bjorn took one of the copper coins from his purse and handed it to the man. He had traded his two remaining silver coins for copper back at his inn. Bjorn had had a feeling it would not do for him to pay for anything with silver in this part of town.

"Right back, m'lord," the taverner said. Bjorn watched the street, sparing only a glance and a brief smile at the taverner when he returned with Bjorn's ale.

As usual, there was a noticeable lack of women on the street.

Only older matrons, such as the herb woman whose shop Bjorn was watching, were in evidence. Many of them, Bjorn noticed, had old scars on both cheeks.

A middle-aged man came down the stairs from above the shop and unlocked the doors. Like the woman, he had a visible, if weak, aura. He went into the shop and opened the shutters, announcing to the neighborhood that he was now open for business.

As Bjorn watched, a few patrons entered the shop. After a time, the woman, presumably the apothecary's wife, came down and went into the shop with an empty basket. She left shortly afterwards with the basket an obvious weight on her arm.

House calls, Bjorn thought. That left Bjorn in a bit of a predicament. Should he follow the woman to see if the people she called on were magi, or should he stay and watch the shop?

He decided to watch the shop. It was the safer course, and he was as likely to find what he was searching for here as elsewhere.

Near noon, the tavern began to fill with patrons for the noon meal. Bjorn ordered lunch and another ale, for which he was charged three pennies. More customers visited the apothecary as well. Several of these bore noticeable auras. If other customers were in the shop, those with auras emerged last.

Gotcha! Bjorn thought. This shop was the center of *some* type of gathering of the magi. A person could wait all day in a city and only see one, or maybe two, people with a noticeable aura. Here, a total of nine had just passed through.

Now all that remained was to decide on the best means of contacting them. If the magi in his own time were wary, these people should be downright terrified of new faces. Bjorn smiled.

So he should let them contact *him*. That would be the best approach.

Several hours past noon, the traffic into both the tavern and the inn had slowed considerably. Bjorn drained the last swallow from his goblet of ale and left the tavern.

For a moment, he simply stood on the sidewalk, watching the street. He saw no one about with an aura. Good.

Bjorn took a deep breath and gathered the Power. In his own time, Bjorn had been more powerful than any of the magi he had seen thus far. It was to that level that he now raised his

Power. Then he walked across the street to the apothecary.

The old man's blue eyes widened in surprise as Bjorn walked into the shop. It was just a flicker of surprise before the old man's composure returned, but it told Bjorn what he wanted to know. The apothecary could see his aura quite clearly.

"I need a straining bag of comfrey, coltsfoot and mullein," Bjorn told him.

"Chest problems, m'lord?" the old man asked, as he gathered the ingredients from the shelves behind him.

"Just a little wheeze," Bjorn assured him. "But if I don't head it off now, it'll get worse."

"Aye," the old man said as he dropped the herbs into a mortar.

"Haven't seen ye around before," the old man noted as he ground the herbs.

"I'm just passing through on my way north," Bjorn lied. "My father's brother has a farm north of here. I'm going to help him with it while he's ill."

"Will that be all, m'lord?" the apothecary asked.

"Yes," Bjorn replied.

"Three pennies, then," he said. Bjorn fished the coins from his purse.

"Is there a place nearby where I can get a room for the night?" Bjorn asked. "I don't have a lot of money."

"Aye," the apothecary said. "The tavern across the road has a few rooms. I don't think Jergen has any guests right now."

"How convenient," Bjorn said. "Thank you."

"Ye're welcome. G'day, m'lord."

"Good day," Bjorn replied. He smiled as he left the shop. Now they not only knew he was here—they knew where to find him as well.

Hervis hurried to the apothecary. It wasn't like old Olaf to summon him so urgently. Something had to be wrong.

There were no customers when Hervis arrived behind the shop. Olaf let him in to the back storeroom. It smelled pleasantly of herbs and roots. Olaf looked down the narrow alley behind his shop before closing the door.

"What is wrong, Olaf?" Hervis asked.

"We have a problem," Olaf replied.

• • •

Bjorn lay on his side on the uncomfortable straw mat that passed for a bed in this room. What was worse was that this room had cost him five pennies for the night—almost four times as much as his much better room north of here cost.

Of course, that might be due to the fact that he rented *that* room openly as an apprentice. It would not surprise Bjorn to learn that the innkeeper was charging him less to avoid the wrath of the House of Rylur.

The night was warm—much warmer than it would have been in the palace. Still, this was more like the summer night Bjorn would have anticipated for this time of year. Even so, he missed the evening coolness of the apprentice's barracks.

He heard someone try the door behind him. Bjorn had considered leaving it unlocked, but that might have aroused the suspicions of his quarry. He assumed that they had ways around locks.

He was not disappointed. He heard the click of the bolt as the lock was released and then the soft creak of the slowly opening door. Then he heard the door close.

Bjorn rolled off the mat to a sitting position against the wall. As he did so, he reached out with his mind and ignited the wick of the oil lamp on the wall above him. Light filled the room.

The two men froze in surprise. They carried drawn knives, and their faces were covered. Bjorn was not surprised to recognize the aura of one of them from his vigil today. He had just met the local Circle.

"Good evening," he said to them. "I have been expecting you. Please, sit."

"And why shouldn't we just kill you?" the one Bjorn had recognized asked.

"Well, for one thing, I've given you no reason to," Bjorn replied. "For another, if you do, you will die. The apothecary and his wife probably will as well. Mind you, that won't do me much good, and I would rather avoid it altogether."

"Who are you?"

"I am Bairn," Bjorn replied. "Apprenticed to the House of Rylur against my will. And I would like to be your friend." He drew the full of his Power, without the Cords, to himself and watched as the eyes of the men before him widened in fear.

"Why . . . should an apprentice want to be our friend?" the second man asked.

"If you will sit for a while, I shall try to explain that," Bjorn replied. Reluctantly, the two of them lowered themselves to sit on the floor across from him.

"This is a long story," Bjorn explained, "and it begins long, long from now . . ."

Bjorn walked the darkened midnight streets of the town back to his room further north. He proved much more able at evading the guard than during his previous holiday, now that he knew to do so.

He had learned a lot tonight. The cheeks of the women were scarred because they mutilated themselves while still young. It was believed to be a better fate than being taken as a Lord's concubine. Bjorn remembered the pond full of mermaids and found that he had to agree with them.

Most women stayed completely out of sight in their homes. Weddings were arranged by parents, with the new bride being shuffled from her parents' home to her new husband's home in the dark of night.

It was a horrible existence. Bjorn had thought that the towns looked too normal from the stories he had heard told of these times. It was not normal at all. It simply appeared that way.

And the magi! Bjorn had arrived well before the time of Bairn, apparently. The magi did not know the most basic secret of hiding—how to rid one's self of the aura. He was going to have to teach them that before he had too much more contact with them. Teach them the law against workings of Power in one's own home, lest it betray you to the Lords. The magi had much to learn.

Bjorn stopped in the alley as an unexpected thought struck him. If he taught the magi the teachings of Bairn in this time, then . . . then he *was* Bairn. Not just *a* person named Bairn, but *the* Bairn of legend.

After a moment he resumed the walk back to his inn. He felt a sudden need for the illusory safety of walls around him.

Olaf, Hervis and Ingrid sat up in the old couple's home above the shop long after the stranger had left.

"Do you believe him?" Hervis asked.

"We have little choice," Olaf replied. Even so, Bairn's story of being pulled from far in the future by an escaping Lord sounded preposterous.

"I think he is mad," Hervis said, echoing Olaf's own thoughts. "We should kill him and be done with this."

"If we kill him, then Rylur will purge the city. Scores will die, including ourselves."

"So, we are simply going to take him at his word?" Hervis asked.

"Not quite," Olaf said. "For now, at least, only the three of us will meet with him. We will expose no others among the magi. If this is a trap, then only we three will be snared by it. And we have a moon to prepare. Warn the others, Hervis. Tell them what has happened."

"I will," Hervis assured him.

"Gods help us," Ingrid said.

CHAPTER

------ SEVEN ----------

"MAY I JOIN you?" Raoul asked. Bairn looked up from his books at the younger apprentice. Raoul was late for study tonight.

"I've been saving your table," Bairn replied. In the quarter-moon since the holiday, Bairn had found the quiet apprentice to be pleasant company.

"You have?" Raoul asked. He sounded surprised as he set his books on the study alcove's other table.

"Yes," Bairn said. "I like you, Raoul—you're quiet."

"Thank you," Raoul replied.

"M-hm," Bairn replied, already absorbed in his latest text on mathematics. His other lessons came almost naturally to him, but the math of the MageLords was still his weakest area.

Bairn was quickly, but not too quickly, advancing toward the lead in his classes. This was true even of mathematics, but only through great effort. By the end of the moon, if he paced himself correctly, he should hold the lead in most of his lessons.

Hopefully, that would be enough to satisfy Lord Rylur. Bairn wanted to avoid as many audiences with the Lord of the House as possible.

Bairn's standing in his classes was not the only thing that changed that moon. Chief First Jorgen was advanced to second rank, first order. The new Chief First was to be introduced to the apprentices after Jorgen's ceremony.

The ceremony was held in Rylur's throne room and consisted, quite simply, of the removal of Jorgen's gold sash and white tunic, to be replaced with the silver tunic and white sash of his new rank.

Once attired in his new uniform, Jorgen knelt before Rylur to receive some sort of blessing. Then Rylur dismissed his new second-rank apprentice, and Jorgen departed from the throne room.

The other second-rank apprentices followed him, leaving only the first-rank apprentices.

"And now it falls on me to select a new Chief First," Rylur announced, turning toward the assembly. "The choice is simple. He is a man who comes to us just today from the stronghold of Journeyman Sigmund where he has made astounding progress through the ranks. It is with great pleasure that I name Valerian to the post of Chief First."

Valerian! It was all Bairn could do to keep from rising to his feet in surprise and rage. He coughed to cover the involuntary gasp of surprise that escaped his lips. Bairn should have expected this meeting. After all, he had known that Valerian was one of Rylur's apprentices. Since he had not seen the apprentice around the palace, however, Bairn had completely forgotten about him.

Bairn watched as a younger version of the man he already knew rose to his feet in front of him. He fought not to glare at Valerian's back. Dark of hair, clean-shaven, and slender against the tendency of the lower-rank apprentices, he looked every bit the viper that Bairn remembered him to be.

You bastard! he thought. This man was, or would be, responsible for the death of Bjorn's father, Rolf, as well as countless other people in his mad war of conquest. It was his fault that Bjorn and his father had been driven from their home into the northlands, where Rolf had caught the cough that had eventually taken his life.

Unless Bairn killed him now—in the past, before he could do all of these things.

But, if he murdered Valerian, he would be killed. There would be no Bairn to teach the magi. No Bairn to prepare humanity for the Time of Madness. No Bairn to start the war that ended the tyranny of the MageLords.

And if Valerian did not survive into the future, Bjorn would never learn what he needed to know to return here and *become* Bairn. Not only could he not kill Valerian, but he had to ensure that Valerian found the magical sleeping chamber in which he had been discovered.

Curse you! Bairn thought. *Even now I cannot defy you!*

Bairn remained silent for the remainder of the ceremony.

• • •

Bairn threw himself into his studies for the next few days. If he was Bairn, then, by the gods, he was going to *be* Bairn. He was going to learn everything the MageLords knew and use that knowledge to destroy them.

By day, he worked himself to exhaustion. By night, he dreamed of Valerian's face, gloating over him, and of his dying father coughing by the fire. And he dreamed of rats.

Finally, one afternoon, the moment Bairn had dreaded arrived.

"Bairn?" Raoul said.

"Yes, Raoul?" Bairn asked, looking up from the books on mathematics he had taken from the shelves.

"The Chief First wishes to see you in his chambers," Raoul replied. For a moment, Bairn simply stared at him. Raoul looked away uncomfortably.

"Thank you," Bairn finally said.

Bairn rose from behind his study table and walked from the library to the chambers that had formerly belonged to Jorgen.

Calm yourself, he thought. He traced the patterns of calm in his mind that he had learned from the Silver Book. That, in conjunction with a lifetime of training, served to cement his composure by the time he reached Valerian's chambers.

Bairn knocked at the door to Valerian's chambers.

"Enter," the all too well remembered voice called through the door. Bairn opened the door and stepped into Valerian's presence.

"You wanted to see me, Chief First?" Bairn asked.

"Yes, Bairn," Valerian replied. "Please, sit down."

"Thank you," Bairn replied, taking a seat.

"There are two things I wish to discuss with you," Valerian began. "First, I would like to compliment you on the progress you are making in your lessons."

"Thank you, First," Bairn replied.

"That is *Chief* First," Valerian said. His dark eyes narrowed in precisely the way that Bairn recalled. Bairn swallowed the lump that began to form in his throat. At this point, Bairn knew more of magic than Valerian. He had nothing to fear.

"Forgive me, Chief First," Bairn said.

"No need," Valerian replied, his tone turning pleasant again. "Jorgen got you in the habit of only using half his title. I anticipate a few slips."

"Yes, Chief First," Bairn said. There would be no more slips from *him*.

"The second matter I want to talk to you about is your assignment to the gardens," Valerian continued.

"The gardens, Chief First?" Bairn asked.

"Yes," Valerian said. "I understand you have been doing some good work out there, but I need you in the palace. The gardens will tend to themselves."

Bairn swallowed. He did *not* want to lose his time in the gardens. These last few days, that had been all that had kept him sane.

"That might not be a good idea, Chief First," Bairn said.

"What do you mean?" Valerian asked. Again, his eyes narrowed dangerously.

"Lord Rylur has expressed a great deal of satisfaction at my work in the gardens," Bairn explained. "If I am removed from that, he might be . . . displeased."

"Are you threatening me, apprentice?" Valerian asked.

"No, Chief First!" Bairn replied. "It is just that . . . neither of us would benefit from upsetting Lord Rylur. I will do whatever work you assign me. But it might be wise to check with Lord Rylur before you reassign me."

"It might be, at that," Valerian said. "Very well, I shall leave you assigned to the gardens until I have the opportunity to check with Lord Rylur."

"Thank you, Chief First," Bairn said.

"You may go, Bairn."

"Yes, Chief First," Bairn replied.

"Oh, and Bairn?"

"Yes, Chief First?"

"I appreciate your . . . candor," Valerian said. Something in his voice told Bairn that he did not truly mean that.

"Thank you, Chief First," Bairn replied.

And may you burn in Hell, he thought. Valerian returned to the papers before him, and Bairn turned and left the room.

The next holiday came none too soon. To Bjorn it almost felt like an escape to a more normal life. That illusion would prove all too fleeting today, however.

He quickly made his way to his room, where he changed into

his commoner's guise. He slipped unnoticed out of the inn and made his way south to the apothecary.

The town was in the height of summer, and the day was hot. Bjorn had lost touch with the seasons while in the palace. The palace and its grounds, including the garden, were locked in an eternal spring.

Bjorn almost sighed with relief when Olaf answered the back door. He had been half afraid that the magi would flee since they had been discovered.

"Inside, quickly," Olaf said. Bjorn slipped into the back of the shop. It smelled wonderfully of herbs and roots, reminding him of Aunt Freida's kitchen.

"Is Hervis here?" Bjorn asked.

"He is," Olaf replied.

"Good," Bjorn said. "We have much work to do before I leave."

"The cellar is this way," Olaf said. As he led Bjorn down the stairs, the lingering trace of Power was obvious. This was not good.

"This will give you away," Bjorn said.

"What?" Olaf asked, stopping on the stairs and turning to face him.

"You have performed workings of Power here," Bjorn explained. "I can sense the Power here yet. No work of Power should ever take place in your home. It will lead those with the sight straight to you. At the very least you should cleanse it."

"Cleanse it?" Olaf asked. They did not know how. If possible, Bjorn would have to teach them this today, as well as how to ground out their auras.

"Watch," he said. He closed his eyes and reached out to the remnants of Power drifting around him. Bjorn took them into himself, draining the Power from his surroundings. Then he directed the gathered Power downward into the ground. When he opened his eyes, there was almost no trace of the Power that had been used here.

"How?" Olaf asked. "How did you do that?"

"That is what I am here to teach you," Bjorn replied. "Among other things. Come—let's get started."

Over the next quarter, Bairn had no direct contact with Valerian except for one written message left on his bunk informing him that he would remain on duty in the gardens in the afternoons.

After that, he had noticed something akin to anger in Valerian's gaze. Valerian apparently felt that he had been slighted by a mere first-order apprentice under his command. Bairn would have to be careful in his conduct from now on—he had made an enemy.

Even so, it was worth it to keep his afternoons in the gardens. They gave him release from the pressures of the palace. The gardens also gave him a private place to think.

As he fought to clear the gardens, he also struggled with thoughts of his own destiny. It was becoming increasingly apparent that he *was* the Bairn of legend. If that were true, there were things that he had to accomplish.

Teaching the magi the laws of Bairn would be the easiest of those chores. Preparing the deep refuges that Bairn had provided to shelter humanity from the war and its aftermath would be much more difficult.

However, even that would be child's play compared to Bairn's most important achievement. Somehow, Bairn had set off the war that had brought an end to the MageLords themselves. How?

Bairn had about as much chance of triggering a war between the Northern and Southern Alliances as he had of stopping the sun in its path across the sky. His position was too low, too unimportant to trigger an event of that magnitude.

Which meant that he needed to gain a higher position. There was currently only one way Bairn knew of to do that. He was going to have to make even greater progress in his lessons. He would have to rise to at least the rank of journeyman.

As he had planned, Bairn had advanced to the lead in all of his lessons—except one. If he were going to start advancing in ranks, he was going to have to work even harder on his mathematics.

Bairn slammed the book shut with a whispered curse. A few startled apprentices glanced his way and then returned their attention to the shelves in front of them.

Bairn was almost ready to believe that the MageLords had devised this entire system of mathematics solely for the purpose of tormenting their apprentices. There was no other explanation for it.

"What is wrong, my friend?" Raoul asked.

"Hm?" Bairn said. "Oh, nothing. This math is about to drive me nuts."

"What are you studying?"

"Mutual equations," Bairn replied, opening the book back to where he had been studying. Each equation, by itself, was impossible to solve. However, when the two were taken together, one was supposed to be able to solve both equations. So far, the technique was eluding him.

"Oh, that's simple," Raoul said.

"Excuse me?" Bairn said.

"Forgive me," Raoul said. "I did not mean to imply that you . . ."

"You understand this stuff?" Bairn asked.

"Yes," Raoul said. "Would you like me to . . . help you?"

"Yes," Bairn said. "If you don't mind."

Raoul moved his chair next to Bairn's at the table and began showing Bairn how the equations worked together toward a solution. Raoul proved to be a very able instructor. He was patient and did not mind explaining the same thing several times—trying to find a different means of explaining it each time.

Over the next few hours, Bairn came to understand the techniques involved. By the end of the study period, he could solve most of the equations himself with only a little prompting from Raoul. Neither realized how much time had passed until the gong heralding the end of the evening sounded.

"I'm sorry," Bairn said. "We've used up your entire study period."

"That is all right," Raoul said.

"Is there anything you are having difficulty with?" Bairn asked.

"Much," Raoul said.

"Tomorrow we will see if there is anything I can help you with."

"That would be most appreciated," Raoul replied, smiling. Bairn thought it was the first time he had seen Raoul smile. Of course, come to think of it, he didn't smile much himself anymore, either.

"If you don't mind my asking?" Bairn began as they replaced their books on the library shelves.

"Yes?"

"Exactly where *are* you in mathematics?"

Raoul glanced away as if embarrassed by what he was about to say.

"I . . . believe I hold the lead," he replied.

"Really?" Bairn asked.

"Yes," Raoul said.

"That's great," Bairn said. "Thank you for helping me."

The two of them walked back to the barracks chatting about their various lessons.

In the days remaining in that moon, Bairn and Raoul took the lead in all of their lessons. Bairn never came close to taking the lead from Raoul in mathematics—the young apprentice had a gift for it. However, no one else was close to taking Bairn's second-place standing, either.

With Bairn's help, Raoul actually wrested the lead from him in first-rank physics, although Bairn enjoyed a comfortable lead in all of the less concrete subjects. Herbalism, etiquette and history were all securely his.

The two of them took turns at holding the lead in cosmology. Raoul dealt best with the concrete aspects of that subject—the nature and motions of the planets and stars. Bairn dealt better with their nonphysical aspects—how those motions affected the world around them.

Throughout all of this, Raoul and Bairn developed a strong friendship. Bairn found that Raoul was not at all like the other apprentices. He was not ambitious or full of himself. He was not out to rule his own House and force his will on all around him. He simply was. Much like Bairn had been before he realized that he *was* Bairn.

What Raoul *did* have was a thirst for knowledge. He desperately wanted to understand, and that made him an ideal student. That Bairn could understand—but his own thirst was now augmented by an equal, if not greater, measure of purpose.

He had a world to destroy.

Bairn joined the line of first rank apprentices preparing to go out on holiday. One by one the apprentices were handed the purses containing their monthly stipend. Bairn walked up, and Valerian met his gaze with a glare as he handed Bairn his purse.

Go ahead and glare, Bairn thought. *A thousand years from now, I'll kill you.*

"Thank you, Chief First," he said. Valerian said nothing.

His purse felt . . . different somehow. Bairn waited until he was through the gardens and out of the palace to examine it. He counted out thirteen silver coins. That explained the difference. He had three more coins than normal. Why?

"Bairn!" Raoul called from behind him.

"Hello, Raoul," Bairn replied, distractedly.

"Is something wrong?"

"I don't know," Bairn said. "I have three more coins this time. I was just wondering why."

"You hold the lead in three lessons, do you not?" Raoul asked.

"Is that it?"

"Yes," Raoul said. "You are given another silver for each lesson in which you hold the lead. I imagine some of the other apprentices are not pleased with us today."

The extra money would come in handy. Bairn would be able to buy himself another set of clothing as well as some paper and writing tools. It was time he began codifying the Laws.

"May I accompany you on holiday?" Raoul asked.

"What?" Bairn asked, shaken from his thoughts. "No, Raoul. I'm not going to the Golden Hare."

"Neither am I," Raoul said.

"You don't go?"

"I went once," Raoul said. "I . . . did not like it."

Well, there's another good point for Raoul's character, Bairn thought.

"Where do you stay at night?" Bairn asked.

"I normally return to the palace at sunset," Raoul replied.

"Raoul, please don't think I don't want you with me, but I have things to do today," Bairn explained. "Things I have to do alone."

"I understand," Raoul said, obviously disappointed.

"But we can spend our rest day in the palace together tomorrow," Bairn offered.

"Very well," Raoul said, cheering a bit.

"Have a good holiday, Raoul," Bairn said.

"You too, my friend," Raoul added as Bairn left. As he

walked away, Bairn did not see the expression of curiosity on Raoul's face.

Bjorn arrived at his inn roughly an hour after he had left the palace. Summer was beginning to wane, and the day was not as hot as it had been on his last holiday. Bairn had taken advantage of the pleasant weather to stop and purchase a sheaf of parchment and some quills and ink.

Bjorn barely had enough left to pay for his room. That was fine, though. He did not need to spend any more of his money today. He would spend the rest of the day in Olaf's shop teaching his three pupils.

The paper and writing supplies went into his trunk with his apprentice's uniform. He would work on writing the first of Bairn's epistles to the magi tonight. Bjorn smiled—it was a good thing he had it memorized.

Raoul could scarcely believe his eyes when Bairn walked out of the inn garbed in the dress of a commoner. It had not been easy to follow him unnoticed to this place in his apprentice's uniform. However, Raoul had spent too long living in the streets of Soren to allow something like that to stop him.

But now it would be almost impossible to follow Bairn unnoticed. Bairn would blend into the crowd on the street, which would continue to react to Raoul in his apprentice's uniform.

He would have to give up at this point. However, he should be able to do the same thing Bairn had done. He could buy some commoner's clothing. After all, he had been saving most of his stipend for the last three moons now.

Even so, clothes would not serve to hide Raoul's other distinguishing features. Even garbed as a commoner, he would look out of place with his dark skin and lean features. Still, it might be enough for him to follow Bairn unnoticed next moon.

Raoul wondered whether he should be spying on his friend like this. It should be all right, though. It wasn't like he was trying to get Bairn in trouble, after all. He just wanted to know what his friend was doing.

Once Bairn was safely out of sight, Raoul began to walk back toward the palace, looking for a tailor.

• • •

Bjorn exhaled in relief when Olaf opened the back door to the apothecary. He kept expecting to find the building abandoned.

"Greetings, Lord," he said. "Come in, quickly."

Bjorn followed Olaf into the back room, breathing in the smell of dried herbs.

"I am not your Lord," he said, once Olaf had closed the door. "Nor do I wish to be."

"Then . . . how shall we call you?" Olaf asked.

"I am Bairn," Bjorn replied. "If you must have a title for me, then I am your High Magus and you may refer to me as 'Magus' when we are alone."

"High Magus?"

Bjorn smiled. Apparently today's lesson was going to be on the structure of the Circle. It was as good a lesson as any, he supposed.

"I will explain when we are downstairs," Bjorn replied.

Bjorn sat at a table in the common room of the inn, writing Bairn's first missive to the magi. He did not like writing this out in the open, but it had proven impossible in his room. His first three attempts were now burning in the inn's fireplace.

Fortunately, at this hour, the inn was deserted. In the future, he would have to get some sort of writing desk for his room. That would be expensive.

Still, he could commission the desk to be made on his next holiday and pay all but his room rent then. Then, on the holiday after that, he could pay against the balance when he picked it up. And probably for the next two or three moons afterward.

Bairn folded the parchment carefully into thirds and then sealed it with a drop of wax from the candle he was using. Tomorrow he would meet Hervis on his way back to the palace and pass this off to him. If Hervis showed up.

Hervis returned to the apothecary with the letter that Bairn had given him. He handed it to Olaf and left.

He had not been pleased with this apprentice when they had first met. However, as time went on, Hervis was beginning to trust him. They were learning valuable things under his guidance. Things that would help them survive under the very noses of the Lords.

Hervis still did not believe his story of coming from a time far in the future. A time when there were no Lords, but the commoners hunted the magi even more fervently than did the Lords.

However, in exchange for what they were being taught, he would claim to believe anything.

Olaf closed the shutters to his shop. His neighbors had initially expressed concern over his monthly closings, inquiring about his health. Olaf had simply told them that he was feeling the need to take a day to rest occasionally. Age had some advantages after all, it seemed.

He broke the blank wax seal on the letter and opened the sheets of parchment. Fortunately, he could read. Many of the magi could not. That was going to have to change. So many things were changing so quickly with the coming of this person Bairn.

Olaf read.

These are the first of the Laws of the Circle, Bairn's letter said. *These Laws are not intended to give me mastery over you. They carry no penalty save that which will be enacted by the people who discover you if you fail to obey them. Learn them well. Keep them well. Teach them well.*

Let no work of Power occur within your homes, nor your shops, nor upon your lands, lest it guide your enemies unto you . . .

CHAPTER EIGHT

PREPARATIONS FOR THE autumn equinox began nine days after the holiday. Bairn now had another painful memory to join with those that had occupied his mind during the solstice. Rowena. Her fate had been the result of her own actions, but Bairn could not help but feel responsible, somehow. If he had remained at the last feast until everyone else was occupied, Rowena might not now be trapped as a mindless half-woman in Rylur's gardens.

However, there was no changing the past. Bairn had acted on his conscience at the last feast. Had he done otherwise, he would have lost something of himself.

After the equinox, the remainder of the moon passed quickly. Soon, another holiday was upon him. This time Bairn was not surprised by the extra coins in his purse. He had five coins above what his room would cost him to put toward a writing desk.

Raoul did not attempt to join him today, thank the gods. Bairn would be free to conduct his business. He looped the thongs of the leather purse over his belt and set off in search of a craftsman.

Raoul followed his friend at a safe distance. With his apprentice's uniform wrapped up and tucked under his arm, he looked like just another commoner—almost.

Bairn was behaving most oddly. He went into several shops and simply spoke with the shopkeepers briefly before returning to the street. From the gestures of one shopkeeper, it was obvious that Bairn was being directed somewhere.

Eventually Raoul followed Bairn to what looked like a furniture maker. Raoul could not approach the shop too closely. Even without his uniform, he looked little like the other townspeople.

Bairn spent a fair amount of time in this shop. From across the street, Raoul saw Bairn count out several coins from his purse. Why would he buy furniture? He had no use for it.

Raoul smiled. Unless it was a gift. Perhaps for a woman? That could explain Bairn's odd habit of sneaking into town dressed as a commoner. Perhaps he did not want this supposed woman friend of his to know he was apprenticed to Lord Rylur.

That had to be it. It would certainly explain why he would not want Raoul to go with him. If Raoul had a lover, he certainly wouldn't want Bairn around while *he* was visiting her!

Bairn emerged from the shop after apparently concluding his business there. Raoul waited until his friend was a safe distance down the street before following.

Now that he had figured it out, Raoul considered leaving his friend to enjoy his holiday. Of course, this was a lot more interesting than spending the day in an almost empty tavern watching the street traffic. And it wasn't like he was doing any harm.

Besides, he might be wrong.

Bairn smiled as he walked to the inn, enjoying the cool autumn morning. In the eternal spring of the palace and its gardens, he was like a hermit living in a cave. On occasion he was able to poke his head out and see what the seasons were *really* doing.

He climbed the few steps to the front door and walked in.

"G'day, Lord Bairn," the innkeeper said, meeting Bairn at the door as he walked in.

"Good day," Bairn replied, cautiously, his previous mood shattered. This was unusual, and the unusual typically meant trouble.

"I was wond'rin' if I might have a word wi' ye', m'lord?" the man asked.

"Very well," Bairn said. He sat down at a corner table with the innkeeper.

"M'lord," the innkeeper began, " 'tis about the room ye keep wi' me."

Bairn said nothing, just waited for the innkeeper to go on. The man was obviously nervous. After a moment he continued.

"Right," he said. "No offense, m'lord, but 'tis cuttin' into my business."

"How so?" Bairn asked.

"I normally charge five pens a night for the rooms, m'lord," the man explained. "For a moon that comes out to, eh . . ." He began counting on his fingers.

"Fourteen silver," Bairn calculated for him.

"Tha's right, m'lord," the man agreed automatically. "Fourteen sils. Ye see my problem?"

Bairn did. The man was losing almost half his income on that room. Bairn had suspected that he was being undercharged. Undoubtedly the man had also lost a few customers due to Bairn's presence.

"I sympathize with your problem," Bairn said, "but I'm afraid that I cannot afford to pay you more at this time."

Bairn leaned forward, toward the innkeeper. He hated to do this, but he had little choice. This room was too important to his plans.

"I trust that you will continue to honor our previous arrangement," he added coolly. The innkeeper paled.

"O' course, m'lord!" the innkeeper said. "I ne'er meant to imply that I wouldn't! The room is yours as long as ye need it."

Bairn sat back in his chair. Several of the customers in the tavern were now watching them covertly. A few, near the door, slipped out quietly. Probably to avoid having an angry mage bring the place down on their heads.

"I'm glad to hear that," Bairn said, smiling and speaking loudly enough for those nearby to hear. "Now that you have made me aware of your predicament, I shall see what I can do to increase your payment. It will take me some time, however."

"Oh, bless ye, m'lord," the innkeeper said, relaxing. "Tha's all I was askin'."

"Good," Bairn said. He counted out his remaining eight silver and set it on the table.

"Now, if you'll excuse me," Bairn said, rising.

"Aye, m'lord," the innkeeper replied. "Thank ye, m'lord."

Bairn walked up the stairs to his room. That had been distasteful. A man could grow accustomed to that sort of power. Bairn prayed that he never did.

It seemed like ages before Bairn emerged from the inn. Raoul watched as his friend quickly blended into the traffic on the street. He would have to follow dangerously close to avoid losing track of Bairn.

Raoul followed cautiously, careful to remain where he could duck out of sight around a building, or behind a cart or simply behind the crowd if Bairn turned unexpectedly.

As they travelled southward, the condition of the city worsened. Raoul had never seen this part of Rylur before. It reminded him very much of the poor quarter of Soren where he had grown up. Where he wished, many times, that he still was.

Not that his life in Rylur wasn't comfortable. It was vastly more comfortable than anything Raoul had known before. But it was lonely. Living on the streets in Soren, he had had friends—true friends, not two-faced ones who would stab you in the back as soon as it benefited them.

Bairn wasn't like that, though. He had befriended Raoul without benefit to himself. Indeed, at the expense of the respect of the other apprentices. Of course, Bairn did not give camel spit about the respect of the other apprentices. He was his own man. Raoul admired that.

Bairn led him into the poorest quarter of the city. He turned off the main street into a narrow back alley with no traffic. Raoul crept up to the edge of the alley before cautiously looking down it. Bairn walked quickly down the alley before stopping at the back door of a building. Raoul ducked back out of sight as Bairn glanced back behind him.

Raoul cautiously peered around the corner. Bairn was nowhere to be seen. He had obviously been let in. Well, now Raoul knew where he was going—but he still didn't know why. He started down the alley toward the building Bairn had stopped at.

Before he was halfway there, Raoul heard a foot scuff behind him.

Fool! he thought. He had forgotten how dangerous this part of any city could be. Before he could turn around, something hard struck the back of his head, robbing him of consciousness.

"What are you going to teach us today, Magus?" Hervis asked.

That was a good question. Bairn had not quite decided how to proceed from this point. He supposed that the next step would be to teach them how to raise the Circle before they met.

No, the first step would be to find out if they were capable of Communion. That was a necessary prerequisite to forming the Circle.

"We are going to . . ." Bairn began. Before he could finish, an obviously coded knock came from the back door upstairs.

"Who is that?" Bairn asked.

" 'Tis the Guardians you taught us to keep," Olaf replied, alarm apparent in his face. "There must be a problem."

Bairn followed Olaf and Hervis up the stairs.

Guardians? he thought. These people were learning fast. Of course, they'd had a moon since his last visit to implement what he'd told them and what he'd written in his first letter to them.

Olaf opened the door a crack and peered out. Then he opened the door, and what Bairn saw made his heart sink. Suspended, unconscious, between two men was his friend, Raoul. Like Bairn, he was wearing common street clothing.

"Magus," one of the men said. "This man followed you here."

Oh, Raoul! Bairn thought. *Why did you have to do this?*

"There's your answer, Hervis," he said quietly.

"Magus?"

"Today we are going to learn how to deal with unwanted guests," Bairn replied.

Raoul woke to the shock of water in his face. The back of his head ached tremendously. Where was he?

Memory returned and he jerked upright, opening his eyes. That was a mistake. The ache in his skull exploded into agony, forcing him to close his eyes again.

He felt a hand on the back of his head and a curious, warm sensation that seemed to dull the pain.

"Better?" Bairn's voice asked softly.

"Bairn!" he said, opening his eyes. He was in a small room—a cellar of some sort. It smelled very much like the herb cellar in the palace, although it was completely bare except for a large tub full of water in the center of the room.

Raoul was tied to a hard wooden chair with coarse rope. Bairn knelt before him. There were three people behind Bairn wearing black hoods over their faces. Bairn's face was not hidden.

"Bairn?" Raoul said. "What is happening?"

"Why did you have to follow me, Raoul?" Bairn asked.

"I was curious," Raoul replied. "I thought you were seeing a woman, was all!"

Bairn smiled sadly.

"I meant no harm," Raoul continued. "I swear. By the gods, I swear! Bairn—we're friends!"

"Yes," Bairn said. "We are. But these people depend on me for protection. I cannot put them at risk."

Raoul looked up at the hooded people behind Bairn. Each of them had faint auras, not quite as strong as Bairn's. Renegade magi. Raoul knew of others like them in Soren. What had he gotten himself into? What had Bairn gotten himself into?

"I won't betray you!" Raoul said. "I swear it!"

"Good," Bairn replied. "Then there is hope." He rose from his knees in front of Raoul and turned to face the renegades.

"Leave us," he said. "I have much to explain to Raoul. I will summon you when we are done."

"Yes, Magus," they replied. Raoul watched as the hooded figures silently left the room.

"What is happening?" he asked when he and Bairn were alone.

"I have questions for you, my friend," he said. Raoul felt something strange, as if his mind were being touched. *Bairn?*

"Do you like the world the way it is, Raoul?" Bairn asked.

"What . . . do you mean?"

"Do you like the fact that the Lords rule over all and that all humanity has to serve their whims?"

"I . . . suppose not," Raoul answered. He had never thought about it. That was just how things were.

"Do you like the fact that if one of Rylur's women displeases him, he turns her into a mindless fish-creature capable only of lust and dumps her in the ponds of his gardens?"

"No!" Raoul said. "That's horrible!"

"Do you like the fact that the women of the Golden Hare are nothing more than slaves to sate the appetites of Rylur's apprentices? Or your appetites, if you so choose?"

"I don't go there!" Raoul objected. "You know that!"

"Do you like the fact that you *really* don't have to pay for anything if you don't want to?" Bairn asked. "That you can just take it if you want and no one in town will stop you? That no one will dare?"

"I don't do that," Raoul said.

"Good," Bairn said. "Do you like the way the townspeople look at you when you walk past in your apprentice's uniform? Does their fear make you feel powerful?"

"No," Raoul replied, surprised at the pain in his own voice. "I hate it."

"Would you like to change *all* of it?" Bairn asked.

Raoul snorted derisively. Bairn was a fool if he believed that he could change things.

"That's impossible," he said.

"Look at me, Raoul," Bairn said. Raoul looked up, and the breath caught in his throat. Bairn's aura sheathed him like the sun. It was almost as powerful as Rylur's aura.

"Would you like to change *all* of it?" Bairn asked again.

"Yes," Raoul whispered. "I would. But how?"

" 'How' is *my* concern," Bairn replied.

"Are . . . you a Lord?" Raoul asked.

"No," Bairn replied. "I am an untrained apprentice. Will you join us?"

"I . . . will," Raoul said. An *apprentice?* With an aura *that* powerful?

"You will have to pass the Rite of Acceptance," Bairn told him. "If you fail the test, you will be killed."

"But if you kill me, Rylur will discover you," Raoul said. Not to mention, he really didn't want to die. How had he gotten himself into this?

"No," Bairn replied. "He won't. If you fail the test, you will be drowned in this tub of water. Then, tonight, I will take your body over the wall into the garden and leave it in the mermaid pool. No one will suspect that you were murdered."

"Oh, gods," Raoul said. Bairn was right. Everyone would assume that he had tried to take one of the mermaids and had died in the attempt.

"Will you join us?" Bairn asked. "Truly join us?"

"I will," Raoul said. "I hate them too." And he did. He had never considered it before, but he hated the Lords. Once one looked past the fear, it was there to be seen.

Bairn nodded, smiling. He rose to his feet and went up the stairs, leaving Raoul alone to stare at the tub of water before him.

Idiot! Raoul thought. He should *never* have followed Bairn. If these people did not kill him, Rylur would do worse.

The three hooded men returned with Bairn. One stood on each side of Raoul as the third knelt behind him to untie the ropes. Raoul almost did not notice—he was watching Bairn.

A glowing sphere of Power began to fill the room, emanating from Bairn. The two men lifted Raoul to his feet and then forced him to his knees. The third man took the chair over to Bairn, who sat in it. The third man returned to his place behind Raoul.

Raoul felt the third man grab his ankles, and the three of them lifted him into the air over the tub of water. He began to struggle uselessly against their grip on his arms and legs.

"No!" Raoul cried. "Please!"

"Raoul!" Bairn called sharply. "You are not going to die—unless you fail the test."

Raoul calmed, at least outwardly. It was hard to remain calm inwardly with a watery death a footspan below your face. Again, Raoul felt that strange touch in his mind.

"Raoul," Bairn began, "do you join our ranks willingly in full knowledge of who we are?"

"I . . . I do," Raoul replied, never taking his eyes from the tub below him.

"Do you swear to protect any of our secrets you may learn with your very life? To take your own life, if you must, to keep them?"

"I do." Death would be preferable to what Rylur would do to him if they were discovered.

"Do you swear to protect the identity of any member of the Circle with your life?"

"I do." There was a pause. Raoul held his breath, but he was not plunged into the tub to be drowned.

"So be it," Bairn said. "We accept you into our fold. Be it known that if you betray any part of this oath, your life will be forfeit to us."

"I know," Raoul said, trembling in relief. He was going to *live*!

"Set him on his feet," Bairn said. The three men set Raoul gently onto his feet. When they released him, he swayed with a sudden wave of dizziness. Someone steadied him.

"When next we meet," Bairn said, "I will teach all of you the means by which I was able to feel his thoughts as I questioned him. This is how we deal with those who discover us."

"Yes, Magus," the hooded figures replied.

"Return to your business," Bairn said. "Our new brother and I have much to discuss."

Raoul breathed a sigh of relief as the hooded men left the cellar. Bairn rose from his chair.

''We can continue this better in private,'' he said.

''At your inn?'' Raoul asked. Bairn gave him a sharp glance.

''Is there anything you *don't* know about what I've been doing?'' he asked.

''Much,'' Raoul replied, nodding.

Hervis returned to the apothecary after Bairn and the other apprentice had left. The situation was getting out of hand. He had actually been prepared to kill one of Rylur's apprentices!

Of course, Bairn's plan had been sound. It was highly unlikely that anyone would have suspected the murder. Even so—the *risk*!

He walked into the shop. There were no customers.

''What do you want, Hervis?'' Olaf asked.

''I don't like this,'' Hervis said. He did not need to explain. They both knew what ''this'' was.

''I don't either, Hervis,'' Olaf said. ''But we have little choice. And Bairn was prepared to kill that man to protect us.''

''Do you really think he would have?'' Hervis asked.

Olaf paused a moment before answering. It had been in Bairn's eyes. Grim determination poorly concealing his anxiety, and then the obvious relief when the other had passed his test.

''Yes,'' he said. ''I do.''

''Bairn?'' Raoul whispered. Bairn sighed in relief. He had sent Raoul, dressed in his apprentice's tunic, into the inn to get his own uniform. There was no way that Bjorn and Raoul could walk into the inn together unnoticed. Raoul was too . . . distinctive for that. He'd had no choice but to trust his friend.

''Here,'' Bairn whispered back. Raoul stepped into the alley and handed Bairn the package that was his apprentice's uniform.

''Thanks,'' Bairn said. Now he would be sharing his room on holiday with Raoul. That gave him an idea.

''Raoul, do you have six . . . no, seven silver you can spare?'' he asked.

''Of course,'' Raoul replied. He drew out a bulging purse and counted out seven silver.

''How much do you *have* in there?'' Bairn asked.

"A little less than thirty," Raoul replied. "I have not spent much of my stipend."

"Raoul," Bairn said, "could I trouble you for another five? What is bought is going to be partly yours."

"What is it?"

"A writing desk for our room, here," Bairn explained.

"*Our* room?"

"I was assuming you would share the room with me on holidays now that you knew what I was doing," Bairn said. "Am I wrong?"

"No!" Raoul said. "I would be happy to . . . not have to go back to the palace at night."

"That's what the seven is for, your share of the room price," Bairn said. "The other five would be for the desk."

"That's what you were doing with the furniture maker!" Raoul said.

"Right," Bairn said. "Come on, let's go talk to the innkeeper and then go to the craftsman's shop."

"Very well," Raoul said, handing Bairn twelve silver. It was beginning to look like what happened today was a good thing. It certainly helped with the problem of Bairn's limited resources.

"And remember," Bairn added, "we have to be every bit the superior asses the other apprentices are when we deal with these people. Otherwise we will arouse suspicion."

"Yes," Raoul agreed.

The innkeeper looked up in surprise as the two of them walked in. Conversation in the inn died. The patrons had gotten accustomed to seeing Bairn, or as accustomed as anyone could. Now there were *two* apprentices walking in together.

"Good afternoon . . . Lords," the innkeeper said. "How may I help ye?"

"Two things," Bairn told him. He laid six silver on the counter.

"I believe that is the balance of the amount we discussed," Bairn said. Bairn hoped the man was up to adding six and eight in his currently unsettled state.

"Aye, Lord!" the innkeeper said, scooping up the coins. "Thank ye, Lord."

"It comes at a price," Bairn said.

"A . . . price, Lord?"

"I need a second bed moved into that room," Bairn explained. "See to it while I'm gone."

"Aye, Lord!" the innkeeper replied. " 'Twill be done."

"Good," Bairn said. "Let's go, Raoul. We have business elsewhere."

Bairn did not see the innkeeper pour himself a mug of ale behind them. Nor did he see the man drain the mug in a single draught. However, it would not have surprised him.

They made it back to the inn a few hours later. Raoul was carrying the trunk that Bairn had suggested he buy. Apparently, the innkeeper cleaned the room during the moon between holidays, and anything you wanted kept private had best stay locked up.

Raoul had already spent half of the silver he had saved. Fortunately, there wasn't anything else they needed to buy. Besides, after this morning, he was happy simply to be alive.

The patrons watched them walk up the stairs. Conversation started back up again once they were out of sight. Raoul hated that.

Bairn turned his key in the lock and opened the door. The second bed had been put into the room while they were gone.

"This isn't going to work," Bairn said. "Help me move these things, Raoul."

They moved the beds so that the ends met in one corner of the room. That left room along one wall for the desk and chair Bairn was going to have brought in.

"What do you think?" Bairn asked.

"It is . . . small," Raoul replied.

"Yes, well 'tis just a place to sleep, after all," Bairn said.

"It is . . . nice," Raoul said. "Somehow it seems . . . I do not know."

"Private?" Bairn suggested.

"Yes, that's it," Raoul agreed. "This is . . . ours."

"I'll tell you this," Bairn said. "It beats the barracks."

"Bairn?"

"Yes?"

"Will you please tell me why we are taking such terrible risks?" Raoul asked.

"Yes," Bairn said, sitting on his bed. "And then I will teach you how to lie to a MageLord."

• • •

Raoul lay awake in the room he now shared with Bairn, staring up at the dark ceiling above. If anyone but Bairn had told him the story he had heard tonight, he would have believed them mad. Before this morning, he would have thought the same of Bairn, in fact.

After this morning, after seeing the incredibly powerful aura that surrounded Bairn, he was more inclined to believe. Otherwise how could someone like Bairn, someone who was having genuine difficulty in his mathematics studies, possess such Power? This also explained Bairn's strange appearance in the House of Soren as well as Soren's disappearance.

Could it all be true? The great war, the Power wasted, the MageLords destroyed, humanity almost destroyed with them? Could it be?

It could. If the MageLords went to war against one another, anything could happen. They wielded enough Power to do horrendous things. The only part that Raoul found difficult to believe was that the Power could be exhausted. Even with, as Bairn had put it, every Lord, every journeyman and every apprentice using the Power as quickly as they could, he could not see how it could be used up.

But Bairn said that it could. And Bairn knew more, much more, about the Power than Raoul.

Try as he might, Raoul could find no flaw in Bairn's tale. Therefore, for now, he had little choice but to believe it.

Again, Bairn sat at a table in the common room writing another epistle to the magi. It would be nice next moon when he had his desk.

No, when *they* had *their* desk. Raoul, his new partner, was upstairs sleeping. Bairn was glad that it had not been necessary to kill Raoul, but this was going to complicate things. Raoul was . . . unusual. It would be next to impossible for him to move about town unnoticed. Bairn was amazed that Raoul had managed to follow him to the apothecary.

No, Bairn would have to find other ways to make use of Raoul—other tasks with which to keep him busy on holiday.

Bairn finished the letter and carefully folded the sheets of parchment into thirds. He hadn't been given the opportunity to teach his Circle anything new this holiday, so this letter simply dealt with the role of the magi.

He knew most of the epistles of Bairn, but, save for the first, it was uncertain in what order they had been written. This one was generally accepted as the second, but no one had known for certain—until now.

They would meet Hervis on the way back to the palace tomorrow, and Bairn would give this to him. Hervis was shaping up into a fine Guardian. In a few years Bairn might have managed to teach the magi everything he needed to.

The pace was maddeningly slow. However, time was the one thing he held in plenty. Bairn extinguished his candle and went upstairs to bed.

Hervis walked into the apothecary and handed the sealed parchment to Olaf.

"Our latest orders," he said sarcastically.

"These are good things, Hervis," Olaf said in Bairn's defense. "We all benefit from Bairn's teachings."

That was true, Hervis had to agree. Without Bairn's lesson of the Guardians, they might never have known that another had discovered them. So what, exactly, was he upset about?

"I suppose," Hervis said. "I never planned on serving a Lord, though."

"We don't serve a Lord," Olaf replied. "We serve Bairn."

"So now we are the House of Bairn," Hervis said, smiling sadly.

"I suppose we are," Olaf agreed. Hervis turned and walked out of the shop as Olaf broke the seal and read Bairn's letter.

We are called renegades, it said. *However, it is not we who are the renegades. It is those called the MageLords who have lost their way and who are the true renegades.*

We are the secret guardians of mankind. The healers and the teachers and the protectors who work to lessen the ravages of those who abuse the Power. And, at all costs, we must remain secret . . .

Chapter Nine

"Do you, Bairn, swear to use the Arts you are to be taught in my service and no other?" Rylur asked him. He and three other first-order apprentices, including Raoul, were being advanced to second order today.

"I do," Bairn said. He certainly had no intention of serving any other Lord. However, he was concerned for Raoul. Raoul had already sworn to Bairn as Magus. How would he answer this oath? Until now, Raoul had not betrayed him. Would he do so now?

The off-white sash was removed from Bairn's waist, and Valerian tied the silver sash in its place. The First met his eyes with a fleeting glare.

"Well done, Bairn," Rylur said below the hearing of the assembly. "I knew you would do well—if you wanted to."

"Thank you, Lord," Bairn replied softly, enjoying the look of surprise that briefly crossed Valerian's face. Praise from Rylur was not something that was freely given. Rylur stepped over to Raoul, and Valerian favored Bairn with a look of open curiosity before joining the Lord.

Bairn forced himself to breathe evenly as Rylur prepared to give Raoul the oath. *This,* more than any other, would be the moment of truth.

"Do you, Raoul, swear to use the Arts you are to be taught in my service and no other?" Rylur asked.

"I do," Raoul replied without pause.

There was no outburst from Rylur. He merely removed Raoul's white sash as Valerian replaced it with silver. Bairn *knew* that Rylur was taking their oaths under truthspell. How had Raoul managed to avoid detection?

"Congratulations on your ascension," Rylur told them. "You are dismissed. Chief First?"

"Apprentices," Valerian said, "report to the barracks."

Once Bairn and Raoul were out of the throne room, Bairn walked with his friend.

"How did you beat the truthspell?" Bairn whispered.

"He only asked if I swore the oath," Raoul replied. "He did not ask if I intended to honor it as well."

Bairn looked at Raoul in surprise. Apparently evasion was another subject in which Raoul excelled. Raoul smiled.

"So, you've ascended," Valerian said to the four apprentices who had advanced to the second order. "Now you need to know what that means.

"Essentially, it means that all of you are starting over. Bairn and Raoul, that means you no longer hold the lead in your lessons. In fact, you will probably not for quite some time. The lessons get much more difficult from here on up.

"However, not to worry," Valerian continued. "Your monthly stipend has been increased to twelve pieces of silver.

"Your holidays will be taken on the twenty-first day of the moon from now until you reach second rank. Which will be *quite* some time from now."

He directed that last comment at Bairn.

I accept your challenge, Bairn thought.

"And yes, this means that you get another holiday this moon," Valerian said. "With a full stipend. Consider it a bonus for advancing past a point which many apprentices never reach."

That was good news. Bairn and Raoul could use the extra money for the desk. They might even be able to get another change of clothes.

"It also means that your chores will change," Valerian added. "Except for you, Bairn. You will continue in the gardens. However, you will have no other duties."

"Now, go get your things from the barracks," Valerian said. "You'll be moving to the advanced barracks with the second- and third-order firsts."

"Yes, Chief First," Bairn said in unison with Raoul and the other two apprentices who had been advanced.

Olaf was surprised by the knock on his alley door. It could not be Bairn—only two quarters had passed since his last visit. Olaf opened the shutter over the small window in the door itself.

It was Bairn with another man. The hood of the other's cloak was pulled up to cover his face. No doubt this was the man the Guardians had caught spying on them two quarters ago. Olaf opened the door. They stepped in, and he glanced down the alley before closing the door behind them.

"What is amiss?" he asked.

"Nothing," Bjorn replied. "Our holiday has been changed. From now on, I will come on the twenty-first day of the moon."

"Yes, Magus," Olaf replied.

"Can you gather the others?" Bjorn asked.

"Ingrid has not yet left on her errands," Olaf said. "I can send word to Hervis, but it might take some time."

"Do so," Bjorn said. "We have much to do before I leave tonight."

"Yes, Magus," Olaf replied.

The five of them sat on the floor in the cellar of Olaf's apothecary. It had taken less than an hour for Hervis to arrive. Bjorn was glad for that. There was much to be done today.

While they waited, Bairn had learned that the magi of this time knew neither the Circle nor Communion. At the very least today, he had to teach them Communion. He hoped that he could teach them the Call as well. On those two things, and the raising of the Circle, hung all the teachings of the magi in his own time.

"The Circle unites us," Bairn explained. "It brings us together with our brothers and sisters in a way that the ungifted cannot know. It makes us whole rather than apart."

"I know that you still do not fully trust me," Bairn added. "I do not blame you for that. However, trust is the cornerstone upon which the Circle is built. Without perfect trust, the Circle is meaningless."

"I trust no one completely," Hervis said. "Least of all you." Bairn smiled. Olaf and Ingrid looked at Hervis in surprise. He ignored them, keeping his gaze fixed on Bjorn.

"The Guardian does not trust anyone *outside* of the raised Circle," Bairn replied. "It is the role of the Guardian to protect the Circle from its enemies, be they from without or within. Once your training is complete, you will make a fine Guardian, Hervis."

"To generate that trust, it is necessary for you to know the hearts of those with whom you share the Circle,'' Bairn continued. ''To Commune with them as one. That is what we shall learn today.''

''How?'' Olaf asked.

''We begin by raising the Circle around us,'' Bairn explained. ''For within the Circle all guards must be dropped. I shall do this today, as you have not yet been taught.''

Bairn closed his eyes and raised the Circle around them in the form in which it was known to the magi of his own time. He did not put much Power into it in order to avoid notice. Once the Circle had been raised, Bairn opened his eyes.

''Olaf, let's begin with you,'' Bairn said. ''Take my hands.'' Olaf timidly reached out and took Bairn's hands.

''With practice, physical contact will not be necessary,'' Bairn said. ''With those you know well, even distance is not a factor. Now open your heart—cast aside your barriers, and I shall do likewise.''

Olaf closed his eyes and relaxed with what was, to Bairn, obvious effort. With practiced ease, Bairn reached out to Olaf's mind and drew them both together. He felt the tension dissolve from Olaf's grasp. Bairn released the old man's hands and opened his eyes. They were still bound together in Communion.

Olaf's eyes were likewise open, looking into Bairn's.

''Do you see?'' Bairn asked.

''I do,'' Olaf said, nodding. ''I never imagined . . .''

''Be silent for now,'' Bairn said. ''While I show the others. I am going to let go now.''

''Yes, Magus,'' Olaf said. Bairn stepped away from the contact he had held with Olaf and turned to Ingrid.

''Give me your hands,'' he said.

Hervis watched while Bairn first took Olaf's hands and then Ingrid's in his own. After he was finished, the old couple had a curious look in their eyes. A . . . peaceful look. Then Bairn turned to Hervis.

''Are you ready?'' Bairn asked.

''What did you do to them?'' he asked.

''I did nothing *to* them,'' Bairn replied. ''I allowed them to peer inside my soul. I laid myself bare to them—and they to me.''

''I'm not certain I like the sound of that,'' Hervis said. Was

Bairn reading their minds? Had this all been an elaborate scheme to uncover their friends as well as themselves?

"Are there not things about me that you would like to know, Hervis?" Bairn asked. "This is your opportunity to have all your questions about me answered, once and for all. Will you turn away from that?"

I laid myself bare to them, Hervis thought. Was it true?

"Very well," Hervis said. Olaf and Ingrid knew more of the magi than he. If Bairn was seeking for their friends, he would learn nothing from Hervis at this point that he had not learned from the others.

"Take my hands," Bairn said.

Hervis reached out and took Bairn's hands. They were not the soft hands of a pampered Lord, as Hervis had expected.

"Open your heart," Bairn said. "Cast aside your barriers."

Hervis closed his eyes and relaxed. What barriers? Something stirred in his mind. He had the disconcerting feeling of being in two places at once. Of being . . . someone else. Bairn released his hands.

With a gasp, Hervis opened his eyes. He looked into Bairn's eyes. At the same time, he looked into his own eyes, through Bairn's. And he remembered.

He remembered playing as a child in a small village, among people he had never known, yet somehow knew now. He remembered friends and loved ones who had never shared his life. A woman, a wife, a father, a son. A simple life—lost forever. The pain of that loss made him want to weep.

"Do you see?" Bairn asked.

"I do," Hervis replied, breathless with astonishment.

"Do you trust me, Hervis?" Bairn asked.

"I . . . do," Hervis said.

"Good. Wait while I bring in Raoul, and then we shall talk."

Hervis stayed to talk with Olaf and Ingrid after Bairn had left for the night.

"I have never experienced anything like that," Olaf said. "It was . . ."

"Unbelievable," Hervis said.

"Aye, that it was," Olaf agreed.

Hervis looked out the window at the nighttime street. Unbelievable. To know another that intimately for even a brief period as they had tonight. To *know* that you could trust another individual completely, for however short a time, simply because for a short time you *were* that person as well as yourself. Unbelievable.

Part of him still wondered. Bairn was apprentice to a Lord. Could he have enchanted them? Spelled them into believing he could be trusted?

If I controlled your mind, would you doubt me? Bairn had asked him. Hervis could only come up with one answer to that question. No.

"It's time to bring the rest of us into this," Hervis said. Olaf and Ingrid looked at Hervis with surprise plain in their faces. Then they smiled knowingly.

"Aye," Olaf agreed.

Over the next few moons Bairn began to grow accustomed to his routine as a first-rank, second-order apprentice. He was no longer required to do the menial morning chores of the House. That work was the sole domain of the first-order firsts. Instead, the early morning was given over to study time in the first-rank library.

The higher-ranking firsts had the library to themselves during this time, as the lower order was busy preparing the palace for the coming day. After breakfast, Bjorn went to lessons, including a private session with one of the second-order apprentices for instruction in the Art. Bairn's instructor turned out to be Jorgen, the former Chief First.

In the afternoons, he was allowed to continue his work in the gardens. Raoul was assigned to teach mathematics to the first-order apprentices. The evenings were theirs. Most of the second- and third-order firsts spent their evenings in their rooms or in the common room they shared. Each pair of apprentices had a room of their own and, by good fate, Bairn and Raoul shared a room.

However, Bairn and Raoul spent their evenings as they always had—in the library among the lower-order firsts. The second- and third-order firsts rarely spent any time in the library during the lower-order free period. They were already assuming the superior attitudes that would follow them through life as Lords. After all, why should *they* associate with the lower ranks? They were allowed to remove any books they required, up to three, from the library to study during the night and return the next morning.

The three-book limit kept Bairn and Raoul in the library, however, where they had access to the entire selection. When the library closed for the night, they would then each pick three books in which they wished to continue studying and return to their room.

In this manner they began to pull ahead of the other students in their lessons. By the time the winter solstice had come along, Bairn and Raoul were beginning to come within sight of the lead in a few of their subjects. Raoul, of course, in mathematics.

Their holidays were also busy. With the coming of winter, Raoul was able to accompany Bairn to his meetings with the magi. With the hood of his commoner's cloak raised, Raoul was able to move about town without attracting notice.

Those lessons were proceeding well, too. It almost seemed as if the magi had simply been awaiting a teacher all these years.

The most difficult task facing Bairn was his study with Jorgen in the Art. Not that he had difficulty with what the former Chief First was teaching. Rather, he was having difficulty in appearing inept at techniques with which he had been familiar for years.

Even with his feigned ignorance, Bairn made progress in those lessons quickly enough to remain ahead of his contemporaries and gain ground on the more seasoned students. Jorgen frequently complimented him on the speed of his progress.

Thus, it came as little surprise when, just before the spring equinox, he was advanced to first rank, third order ahead of Raoul. The surprise was that he was also named to the position of Chief First at the same time, while Valerian was advanced to the first order of the second rank. He was now exactly one order behind Valerian—a fact that seemed to annoy his former superior.

Bairn found that amusing.

As Chief First, Bairn was issued private quarters. He was also given the same holiday schedule as both the first-order firsts and the higher-order firsts, giving him two holidays per moon. His stipend of twenty silver was divided between the two holidays.

He no longer worked in the gardens. His duties as Chief First kept him far too busy for that. However, his position allowed him to visit them during his leisure hours. When not studying,

Bairn would visit the gardens to run with the wolves or groom the unicorns. These activities helped him to keep fit even though he no longer worked the gardens.

Unfortunately, his new position also required that he deal with Rylur on a regular basis. Whenever the Lord had questions regarding the progress or discipline of one of Bairn's subordinates, he would summon Bairn to his quarters.

Bairn found he was able to use this threat to keep such problems to a minimum, however. All he had to do was let drop to his problem apprentices that Rylur occasionally summoned him to review the records of each apprentice to bring them rapidly back into line. Most of the time.

The few times that threat was not immediately sufficient, one visit to the gardens, and the mermaid ponds, was enough to convert even the most recalcitrant offender. Especially when they learned that, while the pond harbored Rylur's lovers who had displeased him, the surrounding groves consisted of those apprentices who had displeased him.

So it was that, for two full seasons, Bairn served as the chief of Lord Rylur's first-rank apprentices with few incidents. Even Rylur complimented him on how smoothly things were running under his supervision.

At the end of that time, just after the autumn equinox, Bairn was advanced to second rank, first order.

"Now your lessons will truly begin," Rylur said to him after Bairn had donned the silver robe and the white sash. Bairn smiled. He would see about that.

"Thank you, Lord," he replied.

Bairn stood in a place he knew well. A place in his mind where Power twinkled like stars in the background and the three Cords of Power undulated like snakes around him.

He had already "mastered" the background Power. That was necessary before one was allowed to advance to the second rank. It had been no problem for Bairn. After all, he had done that long ago, as he also had with the Cords. Now, however, he must face the Cords as though he had never learned their mastery. He must remember all the mistakes he had made in trying to claim them and make them all again. It was not going to be easy.

"Call the red Cord toward you," Aivald, the third-rank apprentice assigned to his instruction, told him. "Let it come to you and wash over you. Do not fight it."

Aivald was considered to be one of the best instructors among the thirds. He was dark of hair and clean-shaven with dark eyes. Unlike most of the lesser apprentices he was, like all of the upper-ranking thirds, lean and well muscled.

Bairn reached out and took hold of the Cord firmly—too firmly, as he had the first time he had made this attempt. It fought him, and Bairn tightened his hold, trying to force the Cord to him. The Power burned through him as it resisted its efforts.

"No!" Aivald cried, but it was too late. The Power blasted through Bairn, hurling him from his stool. Bairn discarded the Cord before it could do true damage to him.

Bairn had forgotten how violent the Cord's reaction could be to such mishandling. Every part of his body stung as if burned. He tried to pick himself up from the floor and felt a hand on his right arm helping him up.

"I did not say to wrestle it like a bear!" Aivald chided him.

"I'm . . . sorry, Master Aivald," Bairn said. He actually was—sorry that he had to go through all this again. To graduate from first rank to second, he had been required to master the Stars of Power, as the Lords referred to the background Power outside the Cords. Of course, he had first had to learn warding and how to raise a lattice of Power and innumerable mental disciplines.

Some of those had been familiar from his studies of the Silver Book back when he had been Bjorn. Other lessons had been new, but Bairn had learned them all quickly.

Although his lessons in other subjects continued, the *only* requirement for progressing in orders within the second rank was the mastery of the Cords. Once he claimed the red Cord, he would be advanced to the second order. Mastery of the yellow Cord would see him to the third order, and mastery of the final, violet Cord would graduate him into the third rank.

Bairn could graduate tomorrow, if he chose. However, that would draw a great deal of unwanted attention to himself. So he struggled as though he had never seen the Cords before, let alone mastered them.

"It is a common mistake," Aivald assured him. "You are fortunate. Some die from it."

Which explains why there are so few apprentices of the third rank, Bairn thought.

"The secret is not to fight the Cords," Aivald explained. "You must call them to you gently and surrender to their Power as they wash over you. That is the key."

"Shall . . . we try again?" Bairn asked.

"Not today," Aivald explained. "You need time to recover. We will make the attempt again within the quarter. You are dismissed. Go to your quarters and rest for the remainder of the day."

"Yes, Master Aivald," Bairn said.

Three days later, Bairn claimed the red Cord. After another quarter of preparation, he allowed himself to take the yellow on the first attempt, after only affecting minor difficulty. On impulse, Aivald had him attempt the violet during the same session. Bairn mastered it as he had the first time—effortlessly.

Thus he went from second rank to third rank within a moon. This was unprecedented among Rylur's apprentices, although Rylur himself had done similarly well in his own training, he confided in Bairn later.

"I knew you held promise, Bairn," he said over brandy after the advancement ceremony. Bairn had been the only second advancing to third today.

"Thank you, Lord," Bairn replied.

"Do not expect to make journeyman as quickly," Rylur cautioned him.

"No, Lord," Bairn said.

"There are seasons of study awaiting you as a third," Rylur explained. "Your lessons from here on will become *much* more difficult."

Bairn nodded in agreement. He had been told that exact statement each time he had advanced in rank. "The lessons get much more difficult from here on." Each time it had been true.

"As a third you will now begin to truly learn the Art," Rylur added. "The wonders of the universe will be yours to command."

"I am looking forward to it, Lord," Bairn replied.

"Valerian!" Bairn called to the lean, second-rank apprentice walking down the corridor. Valerian turned as Bairn walked up.

"Congratulations on making third order," Bairn said, indicating Valerian's gold sash. For a brief moment Valerian said nothing. He had recognized the compliment for the insult that it was, coming, as it did, from a former subordinate.

"Thank you . . . Master Bairn," he replied.

"Lord Rylur has assigned me to take over your instruction," Bairn continued. Valerian's surprise, and then dismay, were obvious. However, they were quickly concealed.

You never did learn to cover those flashes of emotion, did you? Bairn thought. Now he knew why he had seen a flash of recognition in Valerian's eyes so many years from now when the former apprentice had met Bjorn the hunt master.

"I will expect to see you this afternoon," Bairn continued. "Hopefully, we can get you to third rank in less time than it took you to reach third order. Good day."

"Yes, Master Bairn," Valerian replied. He could barely conceal the anger in his voice. As his father's yet-to-be murderer turned and strode stiffly down the hall, Bairn smiled.

That was petty, Bairn thought, chiding himself. Still—it had felt good.

CHAPTER
------- TEN -----------

HERVIS PULLED THE fur cloak tighter about his body with one hand as he used the other to drive his team. The winter wind whipped through him as though he were unclad. By nightfall he should have returned to Rylur after visiting with the Circle in Hart.

The Circle. How quickly that name had grafted itself into their thoughts. They no longer thought of themselves as renegades or outlaws. Bairn had given them that sense of identity.

And more. Hervis would never have dared to travel openly between cities before. His weak aura would have made him an immediate target by any Lord or journeyman he might encounter. Now he made this journey to Hart once a moon without fear to carry the teachings of Bairn to their brothers and sisters in the Circle there.

Bairn's teachings were spreading quickly. Passed from Circle to Circle—from city to town and from town to village. The House of Bairn, as Hervis had once dubbed it, was spreading even further than Lord Rylur's influence could reach.

Every moon, new Circles were formed as the established Circles sent messengers to the towns and villages outside of Bairn's teachings. Bairn's letters were copied and carried to new students eager to learn the new law.

In this manner, Bairn's followers had spread beyond the confines of Rylur's lands in less than a year. Hervis shook his head. The world was changing—quickly. It was an exciting time to be alive.

That worried him.

Bairn pulled the hood of his apprentice's cloak more tightly around his neck. As an apprentice of the third rank, he was given a holiday each quarter. Today, in the height of winter, just over a moon past the solstice, it was *cold*.

Ice crunched under his boots in the street, and his breath

frosted on the frigid air. On days like today, Bairn cursed the eternal spring of the palace grounds. It did nothing to prepare him for the true weather out in the city.

Next to him, Raoul, in the silver robes of the second order, said little, as if the cold had taken the will for speech from him. In his home far to the south, Bairn's friend had never experienced cold of this nature. Even the desert nights were not so cold as the days of Rylur's winters.

As usual, conversation in the inn died when the two apprentices entered the common room. Conversation had resumed by the time Bairn and Raoul left the bar to head upstairs for their room. The patrons had finally become accustomed to their presence.

Moments later, when they both came downstairs in their commoner's clothing, no one noticed them. They returned to the cold outside the inn, still without speaking. The commoner's cloaks did not provide as much warmth as their apprentice cloaks. Almost without thought Bairn called on the Power, drawing a blanket of warmth around himself and Raoul.

He had learned much in the past year since his ascension to third rank. In a few moons, he would rise to the rank of journeyman. Then his life would change yet again. The journeymen were exactly that. They travelled throughout Rylur's lands with contingents of his soldiers, maintaining order throughout his vast domain.

Raoul put out a hand to stop him. Startled from his thoughts, Bairn saw that he had been about to pass the alley behind Olaf's shop.

He turned into the alley, sending the Call to Olaf as he did so. He felt Olaf's answering touch in his own mind. The Circle was waiting. Today he would leave them.

''I have taught you all that you need to know,'' Bairn told them. Hervis could not believe his ears.

''Today will be my last time to lead this Circle as your High Magus,'' he continued. ''It will be your duty to select one from among you who will take my place. Whoever becomes your Magus, let him wear this.''

Bairn laid a golden medallion on the floor at his feet. It was a duplicate of the one he wore about his own neck. He had fashioned it last quarter in his room at the inn.

"Whoever wears this medallion and calls upon me will be answered," Bairn told them. "I will supply others for the High Magi of each Circle. You will distribute them."

"Magus, why must you leave us?" Olaf asked.

"Because you are ready," Bairn replied. "I have given you all of my teachings. Taught you all of our Laws. Now I give you your freedom. Use what I have taught you in the service of your fellow man. Abuse these teachings, and you will answer to your brothers. Call on me only when you must."

"I will have need of your Circle again," Bairn continued. "I will call on you when it is time to flee the wrath of the Lords. Be prepared."

"Yes, Magus," the Circle answered.

"So we part," Bairn said.

"Until we meet again," almost a score of voices replied. Without another word Bairn turned and walked out of the Circle, withdrawing his Power from it as he went. Once Bairn had gone, Hervis was surprised to find that his cheeks were wet from tears.

"What will we do now?" Raoul asked once they had left Olaf's shop.

"We shall continue our studies," Bairn said.

"What of the magi?"

"They now know enough to take care of themselves," Bairn assured him. "They will be ready when we again have need of them."

"But what is the next step?" Raoul asked. Bairn stopped and turned to face his friend.

"I don't know, Raoul," he said.

Indeed, Bairn did not know. The Bairn of legend had prepared deep places in the earth to shelter humanity from the wrath of the Lords. He had stocked these places with enough food and supplies to endure for generations.

Bairn could not do these things. Not even with the full Art of the Lords at his disposal, for he dared not use those teachings. Workings of great Power created changes in the flow of Power within the vicinity. This was one reason the journeymen were scattered throughout the kingdom. Any use of the Cords would alert them to the presence of one with Power. Only the barest amount of Power could be used without notice.

Bairn buried himself in his studies, hoping to learn some means by which his goals could be accomplished. On a few occasions, the magi Called upon him. As time passed, these Calls became more and more rare as they learned to rely on themselves. Moons passed.

One day, Bairn was summoned to Rylur's throne room. Six first-order journeymen came to his quarters and escorted him to the Lord. They strode silently alongside him.

What is this about? Bairn wondered. The journeymen had told him only that he was summoned to Rylur's presence. They had not told him why.

The great, gilded doors to the throne room swung open as they approached, and Bairn entered Rylur's presence. The journeymen continued to the dais, where all of the other journeymen currently in the palace waited behind their Lord.

Bairn was left facing Rylur as the journeymen who had escorted him here took their place behind their Lord and their higher-ranking fellows.

"I discharge you as my apprentice," Rylur said.

"L-Lord?" Bairn asked. What had he done to displease Rylur?

"Remove your robes," Rylur commanded. Bairn's hands shook as he untied the sash around his waist. Had Rylur learned of his ties with the magi? Had he been discovered after all this time?

Soon he stood naked on the steps to the dais. His gold medallion burned cold on his bare chest.

"Take him," Rylur commanded. The journeymen stepped forward past Bairn and formed a double line in front of the dais. Bairn looked up at Rylur. The Lord's face was cold and dispassionate, revealing nothing. Bairn turned and walked between the rows of waiting journeymen. There was nothing he could do. Even with all he had learned of the Art, he was no match for the twenty men who surrounded him.

They led him out a side door of the throne room near the dais. The door opened on a short hallway that ended in another door. Behind this door was a large room. In the center sat an ornate wooden tub, filled with steaming water. Two women waited in the room.

What? Bairn thought. The journeymen took up positions around the room as the women stepped forward and led him to the tub. Bairn stepped into the scented water and sat.

They bathed him, scrubbing at his flesh with soap and stiff sponges. Even the soles of his feet were washed. Bairn began to relax. One did not order beautiful women to bathe someone they were about to kill. At least, he hoped not.

When they had finished, the women silently led him from the tub, where they towelled him dry. Once they had finished, they folded up the towels and handed them, along with the sponges, to one of the journeymen. Then they left the room through the door by which Bairn had entered.

The journeymen led him to another room. This room was empty save for two women and a wooden stool. Here, they shaved him. His beard fell to the floor, followed by his hair and eyebrows, and then all of his body hair was removed. The women carefully gathered up the hair into a large bag, which they gave to another of the journeymen.

The third room contained a large firepit. The journeymen handed the towels and the bag of Bairn's hair to two women who waited in this room. As Bairn watched, they consigned all of these items to the fire. Once the hair and towels had been consumed, the journeymen led Bairn from the room.

In the next room was a cot, and again two women waited within. They led Bairn to the cot, upon which they urged him to lie. Then they massaged him with warmed and scented oil, again even to the soles of his feet. Once they had finished, the women helped him to his feet and left the room.

From this room he was led back into the throne room, naked, before Rylur. The journeymen formed a corridor leading to the dais along which Bairn passed. He mounted the steps and knelt in front of Rylur.

"Do you swear yourself into my service," Rylur began, "until such time as I release you? Do you swear to accept my rule and to use your Art in the defense of my person and my lands for so long as I retain your service?"

"I do," Bairn replied. Bairn felt Rylur invoke the Power.

"Then rise, Journeyman Bairn," Rylur commanded. As Bairn rose he felt cloth form around his body. When he again stood on his feet, he was clad in the black boots, trousers and tunic of a journeyman. Rylur's crest, he knew, was emblazoned on the left breast and on the back in gold. Rylur stepped forward and fastened a white leather belt around Bairn's waist and over his right shoulder.

More surprising was what was *taken* from him. The spells and compulsions that bound him to Rylur were lifted, evaporating from him like mist. The journeymen were free men. It was no wonder that so few were elevated to this station.

"Congratulations, Bairn," Rylur said.

"Thank you, Lord," Bairn replied.

"Prepare him for tonight," Rylur commanded. Bairn followed the other journeymen from the room.

"Tonight" meant the presentation ceremony, when the new journeyman was presented to the other apprentices at banquet. This ceremony he had seen before. He had not been aware of the preceding rite until today.

His preparation consisted mainly of growing his hair and beard back. Some time ago, he had noticed that the apprentices' tendency toward corpulence vanished at third rank. The reason for this had surprised him, although it should not have.

At that rank an apprentice had learned enough of the Art to control his appearance, his age—everything about his body. If Bairn wanted to be a seven-foot redhead, muscled like a bear, he could be so by morning. For that matter, he could even be an actual bear if he wished.

And he could live forever, barring accidental death or murder. Murder would be no mean feat, however. Protection spells surrounded him like armor. If a drop of poison passed his lips, he knew of it before it had reached his tongue. He should know, he had drunk enough of it. Part of his training as third rank, third order was to have his food and drink randomly poisoned with various substances. If he lived, he passed the test.

He had no doubt that his meal at table tonight would have been so treated. This would be a natural time for one to relax one's guard. Bairn was not about to make that mistake.

He and the other journeymen waited outside the great hall as Rylur addressed the apprentices. The other part of his preparation for tonight had been coaching in the ceremony itself.

"No House in the Northern Alliance is more powerful than the House of Rylur," Rylur was saying. "Today, we add to that strength. A Lord is powerful, but his Power is nothing without that of the journeymen in his service. A Lord is the foundation of his House. His journeymen are the pillars that give it shape.

"Tonight we add a new pillar to our House," Rylur finished.

That was their cue. The senior journeymen opened the doors to the great hall and passed through, forming a double rank all the way to the High Table. Bairn waited until they were in position and then entered the hall.

As he passed between the double rank of journeymen, he looked straight ahead to where Rylur stood, awaiting him. He stopped at the foot of the dais surrounding the High Table and knelt.

Rylur descended to him, carrying a sheathed sword across his arms. The scabbard was fashioned of gold and leather, and the hilt of the sword was gilded and set with amethysts. This, as much as the black robes, was the journeyman's symbolic badge of authority.

"Do you, Bairn, swear to bear this sword faithfully in my service until such day as I release you?" Rylur asked.

"I do," Bairn replied.

"Do you swear by it to enforce my laws and my judgements in all of the lands that I control?"

"I do."

"Then I grant you the Power to speak with my voice in all of the lands that I control," Rylur said. "Rise, Journeyman Bairn."

Bairn rose to his feet, and two journeymen with gold belts took the sword from Rylur. Bairn raised his left arm, and they fastened it to his sword belt. Once it was in place, Bairn turned to face the assembled apprentices.

They rose to cheer him. Bairn studied the faces of the apprentices closest to him—the thirds. While they cheered him with the rest, their faces betrayed a variety of emotions other than joy.

Most were simply envious. A few were scornful. Only Raoul's face bore an expression of genuine happiness at Bairn's ascension. Valerian looked on him with a mix of scorn and anger—almost revulsion. No doubt, still at first order among the thirds, he felt that Bairn had somehow taken a place that was rightly his. Bairn met his eyes and smiled. A trace of fear crossed Valerian's face before all expression was wiped away.

The seconds and firsts were more enthusiastic. Most of these had joined Rylur's house long after Bairn and so did not know him personally. They only saw that it was possible to rise to greatness within Rylur's House. They cheered their own hope—not Bairn.

"Let the feast begin," Rylur shouted above the roar. Bairn turned and took his place among the first-order journeymen at the High Table.

Bairn learned, to his surprise and relief, that the occupants of the High Table left the celebrations shortly after the evening's debauchery had begun. Rylur dismissed the other journeymen and asked that Bairn accompany him to his chambers.

"It is customary," Rylur said, taking a glass of his beloved brandy from the woman who proffered it to him, "for a journeyman to have a page. The Chief First will assign an apprentice to you. You will be responsible for his training."

"Yes, Lord," Bairn replied, accepting a brandy of his own from Rylur's latest woman. A blonde with large, blue eyes and full lips.

"Here at Rylur we have another custom," Rylur added. "One that presents us with a minor problem."

"Lord?"

"I allow all of my journeymen, upon their initiation, to select one woman from my harem as their own," Rylur said. "Normally, they select their favorite from the feasts. *You*, however, never remain at the feasts. I doubt that you could name even one of my women. Could you, Bairn?"

"No, Lord," Bairn agreed. "I do not need . . ."

"No," Rylur interrupted. "You must have one. I care little whether or not you bed her, although why you would refuse to is, and has been, beyond me. You will need her to tend to other needs besides the physical, and there are also appearances to consider."

"Yes, Lord," Bairn replied.

"Is there, perhaps, a woman in town you have been seeing?" Rylur suggested. "One that you could bring to the palace as your own?"

"Not . . . any particular one, Lord," Bairn said. Not any, actually, but he felt it best to give a different impression.

"How shall we proceed, then?"

"I have a thought, Lord," Bairn replied.

"Yes?"

"There is one among your women I would choose."

"Oh?" Rylur said. "And how have you come to select her? Certainly not during the feasts." Rylur's tone was quiet. Bairn well knew the penalty for infidelity with one of Rylur's women outside the feasts.

"Actually, it *was* at a feast, Lord," Bairn replied. "If it pleases you, Lord, I choose the Lady Rowena."

Rylur blinked in surprise. Bairn said nothing. He was taking a small risk making this request. However, he owed Rowena that much. After all, it was her infatuation with him that had sentenced her to that fate.

"Rowena," Rylur said. "I have not thought of her in moons." The Lord took a sip of his brandy and thought for a moment longer.

"Very well," he said. "I suppose that almost three years is enough punishment for her. Once your quarters have been assigned, you may remove her from the pond. Assuming she still lives."

"Thank you, Lord."

"It will be interesting to see if you can restore her to her normal self," Rylur added, smiling.

The light of the half moon reflected from the waters of the pond. The mermaids slept on their backs, floating on the surface, bobbing gently with the motion of the water and their own breathing. This was probably the only time they were at peace, if at peace they were. The gods only knew what dreams tortured them.

Bairn reached out with the Power and deepened their sleep. Then he separated Rowena out from the group. She floated toward the bank where he waited. Even with water plants tangled in her hair, she was incredibly beautiful. More so, in an odd way.

Only one spell was visible to his magesight. Bairn examined it carefully. It was trapped—heavily. The signs and symbols of the spell were those dealing with the mind.

This was the true prison. Her body had been changed, but this was what imprisoned her mind. Made her a creature of blind lust. But the real Rowena was still trapped within. After all, if Rylur had destroyed her, where would be the punishment? No, she had to still be able to appreciate the horror of what had happened to her.

Bairn studied and analyzed the spell carefully. The traps were hideous. If the wrong lead were activated, or if the spell were itself removed in the wrong way, it would kill him—or Rowena.

Bairn closed his eyes and, with a deep breath, moved into the spell. Here, the signs and symbols were gone, replaced with the Cords and nodes of Power that they represented. Bairn reached out with his mind and took hold of what he hoped would be the first node he needed to remove. If he had chosen incorrectly, they could both die.

One by one, he removed the nodes of Power from Rowena's mind. When he finally cast away the last piece of the spell, he opened his eyes with a shuddering breath. Rowena still slept before him. Bairn removed his enchantment from her.

Her eyelids fluttered as she moved toward wakefulness. They opened, and her brilliant green eyes met his.

"Bairn . . ." she said softly. Then she became aware of her surroundings. She raised up on her elbows and looked around at the pond. Her eyes widened in fear.

With a splash, her tail lifted out of the water. For a time, she stared at it without speaking.

Then she screamed.

"Rowena!" Bairn shouted, throwing his arms around her. "Rowena!"

She continued to scream, punctuated only by gasps for breath. Bairn touched her mind with his, projecting calm and assurance.

"Rowena," he said softly. "Rowena."

Slowly her screams subsided, to be replaced with sobs.

"It's going to be all right," Bairn told her. "I've come to save you. It will be all right."

"But we will never escape from . . . from . . . *him*," Rowena objected, still sobbing.

"Rowena," Bairn whispered. "Rylur has given you to me. You are free."

"Given me?" she asked, breaking free and turning to face him. For the first time she seemed to see him.

"*Master* Bairn?" she said.

"Aye."

"How . . . how long?"

"Almost three years," Bairn replied.

"But I . . . I . . ." She turned and looked back at her tail. She looked completely aghast when she turned back.

"I'm . . . a monster," she said.

"Hardly," Bairn assured her. "Rowena, I can change you back—once I've rested. Tomorrow. But even if I could not, you are no monster. You are beautiful."

"You find me attractive?" Rowena asked.

"I do."

"Even like this?" she asked, again lifting her tail from the water.

"In some ways, more so this way," Bairn admitted. "But I will be able to change you back to your old self tomorrow."

"Will you swim with me, Master?" she asked, smiling coyly.

"Well . . . I mean . . ." Bairn stammered. "Well, why not? But don't call me Master. At least, not when we're alone."

"I won't," she promised. She turned and swam out to the middle of the pond with two powerful strokes of her tail. Then she turned to face him.

Bairn dove into the water after laying his clothes on the bank and ensuring that the sleeping mermaids would continue to do so. What had taken her only two strokes of her tail to cross took Bairn several moments.

She had taken the time to clear the plants from her hair. Her red mane floated around her on the water like a flower. She held out her arms, and Bairn swam into them.

Her lips were cold, but her passions were not. Bairn kissed her long before she broke away from him with a laugh. She swam away from him with lazy flips of her tail. It was all Bairn could do to keep up with her. He caught her to pull him toward her for another kiss, but she just laughed and broke away from him, splashing water in his face.

Bairn laughed and splashed back. For a few moments they fought like happy children. Then Rowena threw herself back. Before Bairn could attempt to follow, her tail flipped out of the water inches in front of his face, drenching him completely.

"Aagh!" Bairn cried out, flinching back and laughing. "I surrender!" There was no response. Bairn wiped the water from his eyes and looked around.

"Rowena?" he asked. He felt something break the water behind him and turned around to find her inches from him. Before he could put his arms around her, she dove back under the water, slapping the surface with her tail.

"This isn't fair," he laughed. "Rowena!"

She shot out of the water less than a foot in front of him. Bairn flinched back involuntarily as she arced over him to dive into the water again behind him. For a moment he just stared at the water where she had disappeared—awed by her beauty.

"Gods," he breathed.

"Rowena?" he said, regaining a little of his composure. "Rowena?" He could not see through the surface of the pond in the night. Of course, he could use his Art to find her, but that would be cheating.

Well, she's cheating, too, he thought. He had just made up his mind to find her when he felt something grab him by the ankles.

"*Wha . . . ?*" he cried out just before he was dragged beneath the surface.

Chapter Eleven

To Bairn's surprise, he was expected to learn how to use the sword he wore at his side. A second-order journeyman was assigned to instruct him in the art of its use. It was an art unto itself. It took Bairn moons just to *begin* to master its use.

Once he had learned how to fight with just the sword, he had to learn to use it in concert with his Art. He had to learn how to channel Power through the blade as he fought with it. To make it stronger, to make it keener and to shatter the blade of his opponent's sword when they met.

Then he had to learn how to fight using the Power and then to coordinate the two styles of combat together. Many a journeyman had died from a sword wound inflicted by an enemy while he was focused solely on his use of the Power. A journeyman had to be able to use both simultaneously.

Thank the gods Valerian had never passed beyond third rank. Had he received the training Bairn was now being given, Magnus would never have been able to plant his dagger in the monster's chest. Gavin's stroke, which had severed the false MageLord's head, would never have landed.

Despite all this training, Bairn seemed no closer to a solution of his problems than he had been as an apprentice. He was in no better position to topple the MageLords from power than he had been on the day of his arrival in the House of Soren.

Soren. It had been moons—seasons—since Bairn had even thought of Soren. Or Gavin, for that matter. He had become so focused on his short-term goals that he had almost forgotten the original reasons that had brought him here.

It was not enough to topple the Lords from power. He must survive to face and defeat Lord Soren in Bjorn's time. After that, he would have to save his people from Gavin's army.

His people—including Helga. Helga. Bairn rolled over in the bed and looked down to where Rowena slept beside him. Her red hair had fallen to cover her face. Bairn gently brushed it aside, and she stirred in her sleep, snuggling against his side and putting her arm across his chest.

He loved this woman. But his heart still ached for the one he had left behind—and for his son. If he survived into his own time to face Soren, then he would be reunited with both. But at what cost? Would he then have to forsake Rowena? A woman who, by then, would have been his wife for a thousand years?

Bairn sighed. Best to walk those trails when he came upon them. For now, it was time to rest. He had much to do on the morrow.

Bairn awoke just before dawn to the Call. A brief use of the Power completed his morning grooming. He put on clean robes and buckled on his sword belt before stepping out into the hallway.

The palace had not yet begun to wake for the day. The halls were quiet. Only silent sentries shared the empty corridors with him. There seemed to be no state of alarm, yet still the Call summoned him. What did Rylur want with him at this hour?

The Call led him to the throne room. As Bairn approached, the golden doors swung open. He stepped through and began to walk toward the throne.

He felt the use of Power before he saw its effects. A journeyman of the second order appeared before him, sword drawn, and attacked.

Without thought, Bairn drew his own sword and countered the attack. The attack was not limited to the physical, however. A bolt of Power struck his wards and Bairn reinforced them, even as he focused Power through his sword for his own counterattack.

His opponent was not flesh and blood. Rather, this was the shade of another journeyman, given solidity by the Power. That gave Bairn the advantage. He was not forced to expend Power on a simulacrum. The battle was over quickly.

The journeyman he had just defeated stepped out from behind the throne and stood next to his Lord as another appeared before Bairn. Again Bairn was forced to fight.

This battle went almost as quickly as the first. Another journeyman took his place beside Rylur, and a third appeared before him.

Another damned test, Bairn thought, as he engaged his fresh opponent. Was he going to have to fight every journeyman in Rylur's service? If so, he could not hope to defeat them all. But he must—so much more than his own life or station depended on his advancement, and his survival.

By the time Bairn had faced his ninth opponent, the effort was beginning to tax him. How many more could he defeat? How many more *were* there?

For Helga! he thought as he dispatched this latest opponent. The thought of Helga and his son gave him fresh strength. His tenth opponent was defeated almost as quickly as his first.

By the time he had faced his twelfth opponent, his renewed strength was waning. Flesh and bone could only be pushed so far—even with the Power. Bairn found himself faltering against his thirteenth opponent. With a final desperate attack, Bairn dispatched him.

The battle against his fourteenth opponent was over quickly. Bairn could barely lift his own sword, could barely hold his wards intact. One burst of Power shattered them as the journeyman knocked aside Bairn's guard and drove his sword two-handed through Bairn's chest.

Pain burned through him like fire as the empowered blade sliced through his flesh.

Oh, gods, I've failed! was his only thought.

Bairn fell to his knees as his opponent ripped the sword from his flesh. The pain faded quickly and Bairn fell to his hands, shaking, but still alive. No blood stained the floor beneath him.

The sword had been as much a shade as the journeyman who had faced him. Their intent had not been to kill him, but to test him.

A test which I have failed, Bairn thought. He felt a hand touch his shoulder and felt strength flow into him, easing his fatigue. He rose from his hands to his knees to see Rylur standing over him.

"Rise and walk with me, Bairn," he said. Bairn rose to his feet and walked beside Rylur. The fourteen he had faced, and another nine besides, stood behind Rylur's throne. As a man, they all drew their swords and placed their sword hands over their hearts in salute. Bairn saw something in their eyes he had never expected to see from another in the palace.

Respect.

"You had only to defeat six of them to pass your test," Rylur said softly as they walked. "The best among them has only defeated eleven. I defeated twelve on my advancement to second order. I am impressed."

Bairn felt relief flood over him. When he reached the dais, the journeymen resheathed their weapons and descended to him as Rylur mounted the steps and took his throne.

They removed his sword belt. In its place they put one fashioned of woven silver mesh. Then they all moved to stand behind him, facing Rylur. Rylur rose from his throne.

"Your training has been completed," Rylur said. "You have today shown mastery of all the Arts which are known to the Lords. Take your place among my House forever, Master Bairn."

"I take it with pride, Lord," Bairn replied.

"From this day forth you answer only to yourself and to me," Rylur said. "No other in this House has mastery over you."

Fully half of the other journeymen disappeared, including all four of the third order. They had been present in shade only, no doubt from distant regions of the kingdom. The others gathered around and offered their congratulations.

"Come, Bairn," one said. "I know a tavern in town where the wine is excellent and the women do not scar their faces."

Bairn thought to refuse, then thought better of it. He was now a figure of importance within the House. If he were to topple the empire of the Lords, it was time to start learning the politics.

"Sounds good," he replied, smiling.

It was long after dark when Bairn returned to his chambers. He had learned much, speaking with the other journeymen tonight.

The first question that had been answered for him was one of organization. Rylur had said that Bairn was finished with his training, yet he had only attained second order. If there was no more for them to be taught, how did the journeymen attain the gold belt?

"By dying in battle," Master Ivan had replied. "Or killing an enemy journeyman."

"Or a Lord," Master Herris had added which had prompted a great deal of laughter around the table.

"Aye, they'll hang you with it," another journeyman had added.

"Who are our enemies?" Bairn had then asked. The laughter around the table had died immediately.

"Everyone," Ivan had answered.

Apparently the Alliance was not as strongly cemented as everyone believed. Border skirmishes between the Lords were almost an everyday occurrence. It was not uncommon for journeymen to die in these conflicts.

However, killing an opposing Lord was never tolerated. If a Lord appeared on a border skirmish, the journeymen were to withdraw, and the matter would be taken up in the Court of Lords. For one Lord to directly oppose another in the Alliance was considered the most severe offense possible for a Lord to commit. Once, it was rumored, a Lord had even been stripped of his title and lands because of several such repeated offenses.

Bairn had been surprised to learn that there was actually an authority to which Rylur was forced to answer. An authority of which he was a part, to be sure, but an authority nevertheless.

Bairn opened the door to his quarters to find Rowena waiting up for him.

"Hello, dearest," Bairn said, closing the door behind him. "You didn't have to wait up for me."

Her eyes took in the new belt around his waist. She looked up to meet his eyes.

"You have been celebrating your new station?" she asked.

"It was necessary," Bairn replied, reaching for her. She stepped into his arms, but Bairn could tell there was something wrong. He held her and looked down at her bowed head.

"No doubt," she said quietly, after a moment, "there were many beautiful women there, Master."

"There were," Bairn admitted. "But none that interested me."

Rowena looked up at him and smiled sadly.

"Thank you, Master," she replied before closing her eyes and resting her head on his shoulder. It was obvious that she did not believe him.

Why should she? No other man in her world, with the Power that Bairn possessed, would have troubled himself with loyalty to a woman. The concept would likely never have occurred to them.

"Rowena, look at me," Bairn said. Rowena looked up into his eyes. Bairn touched her mind and drew her into union with his own. It was not a complete union for she had no defenses with which to protect his secrets. Nor would she know the difference.

I love you. Bairn's thought passed through their minds. Rowena's eyes widened, and Bairn felt the wonder she felt at this joining.

I will never betray you, he assured her.

Then he felt something odd within her. Rowena felt his change in mood and pulled away from him. Bairn broke the connection between them.

"You have the Gift," he said. It was weak—very weak. Rowena did not even have a noticeable aura unless one specifically thought to look. Still, it was there to be felt if you touched her mind.

"No!" Rowena protested. "No, Master, I do not!"

"Yes!" Bairn said. "You do!"

Rowena fell to her knees and clutched at his tunic, weeping. "No, Master!" she cried. "Please. I love you!"

Bairn knelt down in front of her.

"And I you," he said. "But you *do* have it."

"Then we are lost," she said.

"How so?"

"Rylur will take me," Rowena said. "He will shackle me in his Power and use me to bear his sons."

"Then we won't tell him," Bairn said.

"Master?"

"Please don't call me that," Bairn said.

"I am sorry . . . husband," she said.

"That's better," Bairn said. "We just won't tell him about it."

"But how will we hide it?"

"You seem to have hidden it quite well for some time," Bairn pointed out.

"I did not know of it myself," Rowena said. "And he never . . . touched my mind."

"I doubt he ever had any interest in it."

"Aye, his only interest was three feet lower."

"You are also under my protection now," Bairn added. "Rylur will not enter your mind so long as I am loyal to him."

Or as long as he thinks *I am loyal to him,* Bairn thought.

"Yes, Mas . . . husband," Rowena said.

"Still, I think this has served to convince you that I did not spend the evening whoring in town," Bairn added.

"Aye," Rowena agreed, smiling. "That means you've still some left for me."

"That I do," Bairn agreed, rising to his feet and lifting her in his arms.

The doors to Rylur's chambers opened for him as he approached. Bairn entered to find Rylur sitting at the council table with journeymen Ivan and Herris. A large map was spread on the table before them.

"You summoned me, Lord?" Bairn said.

"Yes, Bairn," Rylur replied. "Tell me, have you commissioned your coach?"

"Not yet, Lord," Bairn said.

"You will need to do so," Rylur informed him. "I have a . . . situation that I want you to deal with. You need to leave within the moon. Sit down."

Rylur indicated a nearby chair, and Bairn walked over to the table and sat.

"This piece of land here has been under dispute between myself and Lord Cambien for some time," Rylur explained, indicating a location on the map almost due south of Rylur. Bairn examined the map. The land under dispute was over four hundred miles from the city. Bairn could find no villages within the region.

"No one lives there?" he asked.

"Not anymore," Rylur said. "The land has been ravaged by combat. It will be a simple matter to replenish it once we have secured it."

Not anymore? Bairn thought. How many people had died in these battles? Hundreds? Thousands? All dismissed by Rylur with two words—not anymore.

"Who now holds the land?" Bairn asked.

"Neither of us," Rylur said. "Cambien will almost certainly move against you once he realizes what we're about. You must have your defenses in place before he realizes you are there."

"I will not be able to draw on the Power," Bairn observed.

"Correct," Rylur said. "You will have to lay the spells for your fortress without activating them. By the time you have done that, Ivan and Herris should have joined you. Together, the three of you will raise the fortress and defend it. If you can hold for ten days, Lord Cambien will be forced to cede his claim to that territory—for now."

"Your fortress must be able to barracks a thousand troops during that time," Rylur added. "They will leave on foot when you depart by coach.

"Once you have secured the land, you will be charged with defending and governing that land in my name," Rylur concluded.

"Thank you, Lord," Bairn replied. "I shall have my coach commissioned at once."

"I can help you with that, if you like," Ivan offered.

"I would be grateful, Master Ivan," Bairn said.

"By your leave, Lord," Ivan said. Rylur nodded, rolling up the map. Ivan took Bairn by the arm.

"I know an excellent wainwright in town . . ."

The coach was easy to drive, despite its size. Unlike Rylur's coach, Bairn's kept to the ground, as did the coaches of all the journeymen. The coach rode on thick wheels fashioned of a black, leathery substance called rubber. This was supposedly a natural substance, from far to the south, but Bairn had fashioned the coach's eight wheels entirely by the Power from vats of pine tar.

Four evenly spaced axles supported the body on heavy leaves of spring steel. Bairn had hired the best craftsmen in Rylur to fashion the body of aged walnut. The coach was a full seven feet in width and thirty in length, divided into four compartments. The exterior was beautifully stained and polished with Bairn's name symbol carved into the wood and filled with gold on each side as well as on the bow, stern and roof of the coach.

The foremost five feet of the coach was the control compartment. It was surrounded on all sides by glass made stronger than steel through the Power. In it two comfortable, overstuffed chairs sat side by side with the control ball between them.

The coach could be driven by either Bairn or his aide, Owyn. Later, Bairn intended to link Raoul and Rowena to the security spell as well, thus allowing them to drive the coach. He would have to teach them secretly, but that would not be difficult.

Aft of the control compartment was a lounge containing a sofa and two chairs. This room also contained bookcases and a wine cabinet. In another life, Bjorn had once chided a young prince for travelling with a tent the size of a lodge. At least Gavin had not carried his library and wine cellar with him.

The same could not be said for the men-at-arms who travelled with him. The rearmost compartment contained two benches where ten armored men could ride shoulder to shoulder. Between the lounge and the troop compartment was a storage compartment that held all of Bairn's personal belongings with room to spare.

"Do you think you can handle it, Owyn?" Bairn asked.

"Yes, Master," Owyn replied. Bairn removed his hand from the control ball, and Owyn reached out to place his own there instead. The coach drew its Power, as well as its direction, from the driver, with a large reserve of Power stored in the motive spells themselves.

If Bairn did teach Rowena to drive the coach, she would not be able to drive it very far before depleting the reserve. Her Power was almost nonexistent. It was growing as he trained her, but it was still minimal.

Training her was a serious risk. The laws of the Court of Lords forbade the training of women in the Art. Women with the Gift were to be either killed or bound by Power and used for breeding purposes. To do otherwise was to risk death at the hands of the combined Lords.

Of course, Bairn had no intention of training her beyond the level of the common magi. If Rowena had true Power, she might be tempted to use it and thereby give them both away.

Once he was satisfied that Owyn had the coach under his control, Bairn rose from his seat and left the control compartment for the lounge. Rowena looked toward him from the seat where she lounged, looking out the window. She smiled and rose to embrace him as he closed the door.

"I was beginning to think you would never come back here," she said. "Is Owyn's company so much better than mine?"

"Hardly," Bairn replied, smiling. "But I had to take over for a while before the coach ran out of Power."

"You should put another ball back here so you can feed it while someone else drives," Rowena said. She nibbled on his earlobe. "I missed you."

Bairn blinked in surprise.

"I hadn't thought of that," he said. "That's an excellent idea."

It would not be difficult to tie in a second control point. In fact, it could be tied in solely to the reserve so as not to interfere with the driver. Since it would have no ability to control the coach, it would not be necessary to bar access to the device. Then, literally anybody could fill the reserve.

Rowena pushed Bairn down onto the sofa, startling him from his thoughts. She climbed onto his lap, facing him.

"Let me show you *why* it is such a good idea," she offered.

Bairn had to agree. It was an excellent suggestion.

By mid-morning of the second day, they reached the edge of the contested territory. Bairn stopped the coach and stared out the window. Then he rose and went into the lounge to exit the coach and stand on the soil for himself.

The air was cold, with the first warning breath of winter. Before Bairn, no living thing stirred. The thick forest they had travelled through now faded into barren rock and sand.

Not anymore, Bairn thought.

"It is horrible," Rowena whispered beside him.

"This is what happens when Lords battle," Bairn said. "Remember this."

"Shall we make camp here, Master?" Bairn's sergeant asked from behind him.

"No, Lars," Bairn replied. "We will be pushing on. I want to make the construction site by noon."

"Yes, Master Bairn," Lars acknowledged.

"Come, Rowena," Bairn said.

"Yes, Master," Rowena said, using his title in the presence of others.

Bairn took one last look at the blasted land before boarding the coach.

Chapter
------ Twelve ----------

The site Bairn selected for his fortress was near the center of the disputed lands. A barren hill flanked on one side by a moderately wide river. The river was not wide enough for traffic, but it would supply his future city with water if he managed to claim this territory.

From atop this hill, Bairn could see miles of barren land in all directions. If he could claim this land, then he would also have the task of restoring it to health. That would almost be as difficult as winning it in the first place.

"Rowena, stay in the coach," Bairn ordered. "Keep the door sealed. I will join you tonight."

"Yes, Master," she said. Once she had boarded the coach and closed the door behind her, Bairn started up the hill.

"Come, Owyn," he said. There was much to be done.

The sun had set long before Bairn felt he could stop for the day. Given the constraints under which he was forced to operate, Bairn had opted for a simple fortress design.

A large, round tower would form the central keep where he and, later, Journeymen Ivan and Herris would dwell. Four smaller towers would flank the central tower and would be joined by walls. A roof from those walls to the central tower would give Bairn the barracks space he needed.

An odd thought had occurred to Bairn regarding the raising of the fortress. At the ruins of the House of Soren, each feature of the fortress had been composed of a single spell, separate from all others.

With a simpler fortress design, Bairn could improve upon that method. Once he had crafted all of the component spells, he could tie them together to a single Power reservoir, enabling the entire small fortress to be raised at once. The reservoir would contain enough storage to automatically raise the structure once it was filled. In this manner, the fortress could be raised without having to draw enough Power at one time to attract notice.

The next morning, Bairn brought forth the first portion of his fortress. Not a tower, but a cellar, beneath where the central tower would eventually stand. This would be the location of the Power reservoir.

Stairs wound down the outer wall of the circular room from above. In the center of the room sat a triangular table. Three chairs sat at each face before a control ball. These would automatically draw Power from whomever laid their hands upon the balls. This would enable anybody to fill the reservoir.

Bairn had been careful not to charge the spell for this chamber fast enough for the use of Power to be noticed. That, combined with the fact that this was a cellar, should prevent discovery. No other portion of the fortress would be built until all of the spells were laid.

It took Bairn the rest of the day to build the reservoir. Once it was finished, however, he could set Owyn to work filling it while he worked on crafting the spells for the rest of the fortress. At the rate at which Owyn could fill the reservoir, even someone standing next to him would not detect the flow of Power.

More important, this project had suggested a solution to a larger problem facing Bairn. If a reservoir could be designed for a mage to draw from directly, one could perform works of Power within another's lands without detection. Such reservoirs could also be used to provide one with Power after the great war.

Bairn had finally discovered his secret weapon.

Nine days of hard work later, the spells for the fortress were finished, including spells that would provide food for the inhabitants so long as they were kept active. Walls, stairs, battlements, arrow slits, furnishings, all had been crafted. Now they only awaited the touch of Power to spring forth.

Power that would be easily available. Already, Owyn had filled over half the reservoir. The poor apprentice was exhausted from the constant drain on his limited supply, but it had paid off. Tomorrow, Bairn would let him rest while he, himself, took over at the table. By the time Ivan and Herris arrived, the reservoir would be almost full. Then, with a single touch, Bairn would raise the entire fortress.

He smiled at the thought. That should impress them.

Bairn watched the two coaches climb the hill toward his fortress. Ivan and Herris were a day late. The troops had arrived last night, on schedule. The reservoir was filled—Bairn was only awaiting the journeymen's arrival.

Once they had gained the top of the hill, Bairn directed them into the places he had designed into the fortress to hold the coaches—first Ivan and then Herris. Three coaches sat abreast in the midst of the camp.

"Sergeant," Bairn said to Lars, "inform the captain to get his men into position."

"Yes, Master Bairn!" Lars replied, hurrying off to relay Bairn's orders.

"Greetings, Master Bairn!" Ivan said as he and Herris walked up. As Bairn did, they had brought their women and their aides with them.

"Master Ivan, Master Herris," Bairn replied. "I trust your journey was uneventful."

"It was," Ivan replied.

"Most pleasant," Herris agreed.

"Are you ready to raise the fortress?" Ivan asked.

"Yes," Bairn said. "If you'll come with me?"

As Bairn led them to the location of the central keep, he noticed that they studied the patterns of his spells as they passed.

"Lords, Bairn!" Ivan finally said. "Did you fashion this as one huge work?"

"I fashioned the component spells separately," Bairn replied. "Then I linked them all to a central activation spell."

"It will take forever to raise the fortress that way!" Herris said.

"I think not," Bairn replied, smiling. "Master Ivan, will you please stand here with your lady and your aide?"

"Very well," Ivan said, puzzlement in his voice.

"Master Herris?" Bairn said, indicating another location within the confines of the central tower. Herris took his place silently, although he exchanged a puzzled look with Ivan. Bairn took a position a third of the way around the central tower from each of them. Together they formed a perfect triangle.

"Shall we begin?" Ivan asked.

"Yes," Bairn said. With the barest touch of Power, he opened the flow of the reservoir to the construction spells.

"I don't see how you expect to raise the whole fortress at once . . ." Herris began. He fell silent abruptly when the ground began to tremble.

Around them the battlement of the central tower rose from the ground, and then the roof itself began to rise beneath their feet. Both Ivan and Herris turned to look over the new battlement as the growing tower lifted them into the air. Bairn did likewise, although less hurriedly.

The central tower rose beneath them. A hundred and fifty feet from the central tower, the four flanking towers rose from the ground with their connecting walls. Once these had risen, pillars sprouted from the ground inside the walls on a fifty-foot-grid pattern. At a height of twenty feet, the pillars began to spread out like flat flowers, forming the stone roof of the outer keep.

Finally, from the central keep and the flanking towers, poles rose, and then the banner of Rylur unfurled itself onto the wind from each. The entire process had taken only moments. Below, the soldiers, who had known what to expect, filed onto the roof to take their positions. Bairn turned back to face Ivan and Herris.

They stared out at the fortress for a moment before they turned back to face him. Their faces were noticeably paler than they had been a few moments before.

"Lords!" Ivan breathed in astonishment.

"Shall I show you to your rooms?" Bairn asked pleasantly.

Bairn approached a shimmering barrier of Power. He touched his fingers to the gold amulet. Before his perceptions, an opening appeared in the barrier. He passed through.

He found himself standing in a small chamber off the throne room. There was no door. One wall had two words carved into the gray stone and filled with gold: "Wait here." The room contained a single chair, and Bairn sat down to wait.

He did not have to wait long. A small hole appeared in the center of the wall with the sign, spreading until it had formed a narrow archway in the wall. Bairn rose to his feet and walked into the throne room.

"Ah Bairn!" Rylur said pleasantly. "What is your progress? Do you need more time?"

"No, Lord," Bairn replied. "The fortress has been raised."

"It has?"

"Yes, Lord."

"I felt no use of Power," Rylur said, puzzled. Bairn smiled.

"No, Lord," he replied.

"You look insufferably pleased with yourself, Bairn," Rylur said, also smiling. "How did you do it?"

"Lord, the first spell I crafted was a reservoir large enough to empower all of the creation spells," Bairn explained. "Then, for nine days, I had Owyn empower it while I finished the other spells."

Rylur's eyes had widened as Bairn had explained the process. He almost looked frightened.

"This reservoir is now drained?" he asked.

"Yes, Lord," Bairn replied. "Is there something wrong?"

"Large reservoirs such as that can sometimes become unstable, Bairn," Rylur explained. "No one is certain why, but the larger the reservoir, the more likely it is to . . . discharge. With a reservoir of that size, you could have destroyed yourself and everything within a league of your fortress."

"I . . . see," Bairn replied.

"You are fortunate," Rylur added. Then, more cheerfully: "However, the gamble paid off, didn't it? I'm certain that Lord Cambien has no idea that you're there."

"I do not see how he could, Lord," Bairn said.

"Excellent!" Rylur said. "We shall begin this battle with a completed fortress. I shall summon the Court of Lords on the morrow and lay formal claim to the lands you occupy. Rest for the remainder of today and tonight, but remain vigilant. On the morrow you will almost certainly fall under attack. Good fortune, Bairn."

"Yes, Lord," Bairn replied. Back at his fortress, Bairn recalled his shade and opened his eyes. Downstairs, the aides of the three journeymen were refilling the reservoir. Should he stop them?

No. That reservoir was integral to their strategy, and it had held before. Its presence would free the journeymen from the necessity of maintaining the physical structure of the fortress and would help to maintain the wards. Once the attack had begun, Bairn doubted that it would remain filled.

However, if he hoped to use reservoirs of Power in the manner that had occurred to him for his other purposes, he was going to have to find a way to make them stable.

Rylur entered the Chamber of Lords and stood before the assembled Court. Four score and eight in all; only one seat stood empty—his.

"Why have you assembled us, Lord Rylur?" Lord Janis, the High Lord, asked. His dark eyes and lean, dark-complexioned features gave no clues to what thoughts passed through the mind behind them.

"To present the Court with a formal claim," Rylur replied. "I hereby lay claim to all lands within fifty miles of a fortress that I have established on the border between myself and Lord Cambien."

"What!" Lord Cambien shouted, rising to his feet. His fiery temperament had always matched the red of his hair. His fair skin was rapidly approaching the same shade.

"You have brought the appropriate documents?" Lord Janis asked, as unperturbed as stone.

"I have, Lord," Rylur replied. "The lands are accurately described within, as is the location of the fortress."

"Lord Cambien, do you intend to contest this claim?" Janis asked.

"I most certainly do!" Cambien replied.

"You will find that difficult, Lord," Rylur explained. "My fortress is well established and defended."

"There has been no indication of that level of Power in use on my borders," Cambien countered. "You are bluffing."

"Not according to these documents, Lord Cambien," Janis interrupted. "This structure *is* in place, Lord Rylur?"

"It is," Rylur assured him.

"Esteemed Lords," Janis said, "this dispute between you has lasted for nigh on three centuries. During that time, this land has lain unused and desolate. We cannot afford such a waste of resources. Not with the Southern Alliance searching for any weakness they can find in us. May I request that you settle this dispute quickly and *finally*?"

"I will *not* cede my right to these lands!" Cambien shouted.

"Nor shall I," Rylur replied.

"Very well," Lord Janis said. "If, after ten days, Lord Rylur's forces still occupy these lands, title will be ceded to him. Is there anything else before this Court?"

No one spoke.

"Then I declare us adjourned," Lord Janis said.

The Lords vanished, leaving the seats empty. Only Rylur and Cambien remained.

"You will never take Horacehold," Cambien promised.

"In ten days, *Lord* Cambien, it will no longer be Horacehold, but Bairnshold," Rylur replied. "And take it I shall. Good day."

The two Lords disappeared, leaving the Court room empty.

A wall of mirrors stood before Lord Cambien. In each of them was reflected a fortress. It was not large—barely two hundred feet wide. The outer towers rose thirty feet. The central turret rose another thirty above that.

One could tell a lot about a man from the design of his House. This one spoke volumes. The fortress had no door. No window, save for narrow slits through which to fire weapons, pierced its stone walls. There was no embellishment. Nothing but solid, unadorned stone.

The design of this fortress intimidated *him*! This Bairn had no intention of retreating. He had left himself *no* avenue of escape. He was not interested in luxury or comfort. He had come here to do battle—nothing else.

I will not be moved, that fortress said to Cambien.

And, somehow, it had been erected without *anyone* being aware of it. It took days to erect a fortress of even this small size. In that time, some of his journeyman would have had to have noticed. Yet no one had. It had appeared without warning, without a single ripple in the flow of Power.

Whoever this man Bairn was, he was certainly not someone to be trifled with. Cambien would have to be very careful in planning this battle.

Bairn stood on the battlements of the central keep. Ivan and Herris preferred to watch from their chambers, through their mirrors. Once the battle had begun, Bairn would do so as well. But for now, he preferred to watch with his own eyes.

All day long, since early this morning, Bairn and the others had felt vibrations along the Cords. Large rumblings—

unceasing. Power was being used in the area. Vast amounts of it.

"Are they coming, Master Bairn?" Captain Johann asked.

"They are, Captain," Bairn replied. "They most certainly are."

Just over the horizon, Bairn could see the source of the disturbances in the Power. Not with his eyes, but with his Art. Thousands of men gathered to march against them. They marched through mystic portals from some faraway place.

Alone, the men were no threat. As Valerian had done in his tower a thousand years from now, Bairn could simply ignore them, had they been alone.

They were not alone. Bairn counted five journeymen and twice that many third-rank apprentices among them. Lord Cambien must be leaving himself weak on other fronts to send a force of this size against them. Why? As Bairn watched, the portals closed. Cambien had gathered his army.

"Tell your men to be ready," Bairn told the captain. "They will be here well before nightfall."

"How . . . many, Master?" Johann asked.

Bairn looked at him.

"Ten thousand," he replied. Johann's eyes widened. He, too, realized that Cambien was throwing more at them than he should.

"And?" Johann asked quietly.

"Five journeymen," Bairn said. "And ten of the third rank. But they are *my* problem."

"Y-yes, Master," Johann said.

Bairn unsealed the door to his chambers. Each journeyman occupied a full floor of the tower. However, Bairn's quarters had one added touch—a linking ball connected to the reservoir. Rowena looked up from the chair where she sat with her hand on the ball.

He had placed it here hoping to make her feel as though she were contributing. Now he was glad that he had. They would need every ounce of Power at their disposal to survive this assault. Bairn sealed the door behind him.

"Have they arrived?"

"Not yet," Bairn assured her. "But it will be soon, now."

"How many?"

"Five journeymen," Bairn said. "Ten of the third rank."

"Can . . . can we . . . ?"

"Yes," Bairn said. "We can—and we will. We are well situated. I must take my position."

"Husband?"

"Yes, Rowena?"

"I love you," she said. Bairn smiled and leaned over to embrace her. She put one arm around him, refusing to take her hand from the ball.

"And I you," Bairn said. "We will survive. I promise. Meditate as I taught you—it will help."

"Yes, husband."

Bairn went into an adjoining chamber and sealed the door. A chair sat in the room, designed to support whoever sat upon it, regardless of that person's state of consciousness. It was oddly comfortable. At his right and left hands were control balls. Every spell in the fortress was routed through these controls. Wards, structures, food and water suppliers, sewage—everything.

Ivan and Herris had been impressed by the arrangement. They had identical stations in their quarters. Any one of them could muster all the defenses of the fortress. Bairn placed his hands on the balls and activated the reservoir, allowing his Power to be drawn into it while he waited.

It was not even a fifth filled. There would be little danger of the reservoir becoming unstable at this rate.

The wall across from him was covered with mirrors. Bairn activated them. Five showed him the fortress—one view from each of the four sides and another from above. Another four looked out from the fortress in all directions. One in the center showed whatever view he desired.

Bairn looked to the south, moving his point of view until he could see the force approaching them. Ten thousand men marched through the barren land toward their position, followed by fifteen magi. Despite his words to Rowena, Bairn was not at all certain of the outcome of this battle.

A purely defensive strategy was doomed to failure. Far too much Power was arrayed against them. Sheer brute force would eventually break down their defenses. It was going to be necessary to kill some of Cambien's apprentices.

Once their forces were even, Bairn's position would enable him to wait out the ten days of the siege.

''Ivan! Herris!'' Bairn said.

''Here,'' Ivan responded. Voice spells transferred their words between one another.

''We need to take the offensive,'' Bairn said. ''There are too many of them for us to simply hold our wards.'' There was a pause.

''Bairn, I'm not quite that anxious to be buried in a gold belt,'' Ivan finally said.

''Aye,'' Herris agreed. Bairn smiled. Whoever placed the attack would likewise expose themselves to attack.

''Then I take it you've no objection to remaining here while I carry the battle to our opponents?'' he said.

''None at all,'' Ivan said. ''We will reinforce you.''

Rylur watched from his throne room as the enemy forces advanced on Bairn's fortress. Had Cambien lost his mind? He had committed almost a quarter of his journeymen and his upper-ranking thirds to this battle, not to mention the bulk of his army. If he lost . . .

Of course, it was not likely that he would lose, Rylur was forced to admit. Not against three lone journeymen and their aides.

This was unfortunate. Rylur had placed great hope in Bairn, which was why he had sent him on this campaign. If anyone had the potential to wrest this land from Cambien, it would have been him.

It was not too late. Rylur could cede his claim to these lands and recall Bairn. Cambien would never let him forget it, but it would save him three good journeymen.

A bright flash on the mirror broke Rylur from this line of thought. A single journeyman in the opposing force was immolated in a blast of pure Power. His charred corpse toppled to the ground.

Now it was too late . . .

Their combined Power had easily blasted through the lone defenses of one journeyman. On the march, it was not possible to muster heavy defenses. Now, however, the journeymen would be gathering their Power and reinforcing their wards.

So Bairn did not attack any of them. His next bolt of Power claimed one of the thirds. He threw the bolts as quickly as he could, aiming at one gold robe after another. Three, four, five, six of the thirds perished. His seventh stroke rebounded from combined wards.

It was time to withdraw.

"To the wards!" Bairn commanded. He felt Ivan's and Herris's Power leave him. There was time for one last attack. White-hot Power blasted into the ground among the troops, hurling earth and bodies into the air.

Gods forgive me, Bairn thought as he withdrew behind the protection of the wards and added his own Power to them. The journeymen and thirds were MageLords. He felt no regret for their deaths.

The soldiers, however, were mere men. Although corrupt and arrogant like their masters, they still did not deserve slaughter by a Power against which they had no defense.

The counterattack struck the wards. Bairn had no more time for regret.

Rylur smiled. Now only four journeymen and four thirds opposed his forces. Bairn also appeared to have slain at least a thousand of the opposing men-at-arms as well, but that would have little effect on the battle.

The attack had been brilliant. Another might have attacked the journeymen, but Bairn had only opened with such an attack, correctly deducing that the remaining journeymen would marshal their defenses quickly enough to save themselves.

The third-rank apprentices were not combat-trained, however. Although just as powerful, they were much slower to react and so had died easily. The parting stroke against the troops had been a good touch. It would demoralize the remaining men.

Rylur had underestimated Bairn. He was much more vicious than Rylur had realized. He would have to remember that.

Lord Cambien stood before the mirrors, not even realizing that he had risen to his feet. Seven of his best, dead! In as many heartbeats.

Should he withdraw? Cut his losses? Cambien ground his teeth together.

No, by the Lords! This land was his! It had been for centuries. He would not allow Rylur, and some upstart journeyman he had never even heard of before this, to wrest them from him!

No, Bairn's attack had been spent. Now he was on the defensive. It would be only a matter of time before those defenses were breached and Bairn's fortress fell. Cambien still had eight of his most powerful men arrayed against him. Bairn had nowhere near the resources to stand against that in a long siege.

No, there would be *no* surrender.

Chapter Thirteen

The battering against the wards was constant—unceasing. Bairn poured his Power into them as he watched the mirrors.

The soldiers were now carrying the third-rank apprentices on makeshift litters, freeing them to use their Art as the army moved. Bairn was glad the enemy had not thought of this earlier. Even with their losses, the enemy force was still too large for the three of them to defend against.

It was time for a change in tactics.

"Ivan," Bairn said, "can you and Herris handle the wards for a while?"

"Don't be long," Ivan replied.

"I'm going to try and take some of the pressure off," Bairn said.

One spell was routed through Bairn's chair. He had not entrusted this to his allies—had hoped not to use it. He removed himself from the wards and activated the spell.

He drew Power from the Cords as quickly as possible and fed it into the spell. On the southern wall, in shallow alcoves, metal figures began to grow. These were similar to the golems that Bairn had discovered in the ruins of the House of Soren in his own time. Only one command burned in their empty minds—*kill.*

They would travel southward until they sighted a target, and then they would move to attack it. Each golem carried a reservoir with enough Power to last it a day—less if they were attacked with Power, for they were also warded. If the opposing force had to defend against them, they would not be able to attack the fortress.

Ten iron men stepped from the fortress wall. Bairn began the creation of ten more. The fortress wards seemed to be holding. The more he could create, the more damage would be done. Another ten went forth, then another.

"Bairn!" Ivan called. His voice was shaky. Bairn left the

fourth batch of golems unfinished and returned to the wards.

"Yes, Ivan?" Bairn asked.

"Thanks," Ivan said. "I don't see how we're going to keep this up for ten days."

"Neither can they," Bairn said. "I *will not* fall before they do! Neither will you. How are you holding up, Herris?"

"Well enough," Herris replied. "Go back to your attack."

"Ivan?"

"Yes," Ivan said. "I have recovered."

In the mirror before him, the first batch of golems reached the enemy force. At first, there was no reaction. The enemy took them for opposing soldiers as Bairn had hoped. They dispatched a small force, fifty men, to deal with them.

The ten golems killed the small force quickly. By the time they had finished, the second group of ten had caught up to them. Bairn continued to create more.

A bolt of Power enveloped one of the golems. It survived, although it had almost certainly lost a good deal of its reserve. Another bolt of Power struck it, melting the golem to slag. Several more bolts struck among the golems, but they had reached the front line of the enemy's forces.

Bairn felt the bombardment on the wards lessen. The third group of golems reached the enemy. Bolts of Power crackled among the iron men, reducing them to slag. But it was better for the enemy attack to be directed here than at his fortress. The attack against their wards had reduced to almost nothing.

"Ivan, feed the reservoir," Bairn ordered.

"Aye," Ivan said. That would give him the opportunity to rest a little.

Bairn continued to manufacture mindless soldiers. Over a hundred now crossed the land toward their enemy. Bairn returned his attention to the wards.

In the mirror, he could see that the enemy force had halted its advance. Bairn watched as the golems pounded their fists against an invisible wall. Bolts of Power melted them to slag. The attack against the fortress had ceased.

Bairn noticed that the four third-rank apprentices were still being carried on the litters. Protected from the battle behind the wards, they were able to concentrate on their Art.

Who's attacking and who's warding? Bairn wondered. He smiled. *If it were the unseasoned third-rank apprentices . . .*

"Ivan, Herris, reinforce me!" Bairn ordered. "I'm going out!"

Bairn felt their Power join with his as he cast his consciousness outside the wards. Down into the stone he looked, studying weaknesses, cracks, stresses. Looking . . . searching . . . *found!*

Bairn directed his Power into the small magma pocket far beneath them. It was old, cooling—had been dormant for centuries. Bairn woke it.

Bairn returned his attention to the enemy force. Any moment now . . .

The ground shook. The journeymen reacted with trained precision, working to still the earth. The apprentices, however . . .

With their concentration broken, the wards over the enemy force wavered for just a second. It was all Bairn needed.

A bolt of pure Power claimed another journeyman, and then two more of the thirds. Bairn's fourth strike was blocked by powerful wards.

He saw the attack mere instants before it struck.

"Wards!" Bairn shouted, but Ivan and Herris had anticipated him.

He did not withdraw quickly enough. He threw up his own wards as the psychic bolt struck him. They shattered.

Brilliant light blinded his senses as his mind burned beneath the onslaught.

Bairn screamed.

"Bairn!" Ivan shouted. "Bairn!"

There was no response.

"Herris," Ivan said, "take the wards." The enemy force was still dealing with Bairn's toys. Ivan could spare a moment from the wards.

"Is he dead?" Herris asked.

"I don't know!" Ivan replied. "Take the damned wards!"

Ivan's shade appeared in Bairn's combat chamber. He looked down at the chair in which Bairn lay. The journeyman's eyes were open, sightlessly, and blood trickled from his nose and mouth.

Ivan knelt by the chair and reached out for Bairn with his senses. He was dying. That was good. Dying could be fixed—dead was another matter.

Ivan built a cage of Power and imprisoned Bairn's soul within it. So long as Bairn's soul was within, Bairn could be revived.

"Sorry, Bairn, but you're *not* leaving us here to deal with this!" Ivan muttered as he set to work repairing the damage to the unoccupied body before him.

Fortunately, the damage was minor. The brain had escaped most of it—the heart had not been so fortunate. It had ruptured completely.

But the heart was merely muscle. Muscle could be rebuilt. The brain would have been another matter. Bairn could have been rendered Power-less if the damage had been severe enough. Or mindless. In either case, it was kinder to let death claim such a person.

But Bairn would live. With the damage repaired, Ivan guided Bairn's soul back into the living body. It fought him.

"*No,* damn you!" Ivan shouted. "Live, you miserable son of a whore!"

The flesh grabbed hold of the soul, and it settled back into Bairn's body. A low moan escaped from Bairn's lips. Instants later, Bairn's personal wards reformed and his eyes fluttered open.

"Ivan?" he asked weakly.

"You died," Ivan explained. "Rest for a while. But not *too* long! We're going to be under attack again in a few minutes."

"Thank you," Bairn said. Ivan snorted.

"I wasn't about to let you leave *us* with this battle," Ivan said. Then he was gone.

Bairn linked to the controls at his chair again. He could taste blood in his mouth. Bairn summoned the Power, directing his senses inward.

Ivan had been thorough. All of the critical damage had been repaired. Bairn found only a few minor injuries that still required attention.

In the mirror, he watched as the enemy force dispatched the last of his golems. Cleaned, and all of his injuries healed, Bairn allowed the reservoir to siphon his energies as he watched and rested.

"Bairn?" Ivan asked.

"Here," Bairn replied. "It looks like our forces are more even now."

"You call three against five even?" Ivan said.

"More so than three against fifteen," Bairn countered. "I

doubt they'll make any more mistakes at this point. We're going to have to outlast them.''

''For ten days?'' Ivan said.

''Nine and a half,'' Bairn replied pleasantly.

''Smart-ass,'' Ivan grumbled. Bairn chuckled.

Three days of constant siege had taken its toll on the three journeymen. Bairn had not slept since the beginning of the battle. He was able to keep his body refreshed with his Art, but his mind craved the release of sleep.

As Bairn had predicted, the enemy made no more mistakes. They kept themselves defended at all times and used the third-rank apprentices they had left as reinforcement for the journeymen who were the true orchestrators of the battle.

As best Bairn could figure, one enemy journeyman maintained a constant barrage against their wards. Another, probably with the reinforcement of the two thirds, kept the enemy's wards solid. The third journeyman tried more . . . inventive tactics.

Likewise, Bairn's forces had settled into a defensive pattern. Herris held their own wards solid, with the help of the Power from the reservoir, while Ivan battered the enemy's defenses incessantly. This left Bairn free to deal with the surprises.

He summoned dragons to fight similar creatures summoned against them. He stilled the magma pocket beneath them countless times, it seemed, when the enemy tried to waken it against them. He sent forth hordes of metal warriors to harass the enemy lines and to prevent attempts by the enemy at physical assaults on the fortress. Between these events he poured Power into the reservoir.

That had saved them. The ability to use every source of Power at their disposal, no matter how weak, and to save unused Power for when it would be needed had proven invaluable.

With the wards tied to the reservoir, Herris's task was made possible. If the enemy tried to suddenly punch through their wards, the reservoir would automatically reinforce them until Bairn could come to his aid.

But the constant warfare was telling on them. Ivan and Herris had become irritable, as had he. Mental exhaustion was encroaching on them. Soon they would begin to make mistakes—fatal ones.

Surely this had to be true for the enemy as well. How much

longer could they maintain this constant barrage? How much longer could they go without rest?

No longer than I, Bairn decided.

On the evening of the fourth day, the attack lessened. It took a while for Bairn to realize, but the more creative attacks had stopped. Only the endless battering of the wards continued.

"Ivan," Bairn called.

"Yes," Ivan said. "They've given out."

"Take a rest," Bairn ordered. "I'll maintain the barrage while you . . ."

"No," Ivan interrupted.

"What?"

"You take first rest," Ivan said. "You've carried most of this battle. I will take second rest. I will wake you in one sleep cycle."

"Very well," Bairn agreed. He *was* tired. "I will link with the reservoir as I sleep."

"Good idea," Ivan agreed. "Get some rest."

Bairn activated his connection to the reservoir and settled back in his chair. The mirrors went blank, and the lights in the room dimmed. It felt *so* good to just lie back . . .

"Bairn!" Ivan called. Bairn's eyes snapped open. In some ways he felt less rested than before he had gone to sleep three hours ago. His sleep had been haunted by dreams of dragons and MageLords. In the dream, his fortress had been replaced by Bjornshall and the army against him had been Gavin's—led by Valerian and Soren.

"Report," Bairn said.

"No change," Ivan said. "My turn."

Bairn raised the lights in his chamber and activated the mirrors. As Ivan had said, there was little change.

"All right," Bairn said. "Link with the reservoir as you sleep."

"Right," Ivan agreed.

"Herris, how are you holding up?" Bairn asked.

"Well enough," Herris said.

The reservoir was almost a tenth full—the highest it had been since the siege had begun. This break in the combat was serving them well.

Bairn assumed Ivan's task of maintaining a constant barrage against the enemy's wards. He hurled bolt after bolt of pure Power against them. Even so, this did not require all his concentration. He was free to think—to search for weaknesses in their opponent's strategy.

He diverted some of his Power into the golem-creation spells. Not much—the majority was being expended against the wards. Still, they should serve as a nuisance.

There did not seem to be any weaknesses in the strategy of the opposing force. It was damnably simple. Hold their ground and attack. It was the same strategy that Bairn was using. If the last four days were any indication, *he* would win that contest. As the last days of the contest approached, that might make them desperate. Desperate men were dangerous, but desperate men also made mistakes.

On impulse, Bairn focused the central mirror into his chambers. Rowena sat in the control chair, apparently asleep. Her hand remained on the control ball, feeding the reservoir with the barest trickle of Power.

Bairn looked closer. The belt from her silken gown had been used to tie her hand to the ball. Bairn smiled. So brave, for such a tiny thing as she was. She had tied herself to the ball, determined that nothing would move her from her duty to him.

I love you, he thought.

He changed the image in the mirror back to the enemy camp. The dome of their ward was clearly visible, outlined by the flashes of Power that Bairn continued to hurl against it. The other mirrors showed a similar dome over the fortress, illuminated by bursts of Power.

The golems reached the enemy camp. They began striking the wards with their metal fists. Small flashes of Power illuminated the ward where they struck.

Bolts of Power assaulted the golems. Simultaneously, the assault on the fortress ended.

"Herris, feed the reservoir," Bairn ordered. The wards would take care of themselves without attack.

"Yes, Bairn," Herris replied.

"Stand ready to take the wards," Bairn cautioned.

"I shall," Herris assured him.

So, a change had been effected. A minor one, but it freed Herris to build up their reserves even further. Bairn continued to manufacture the golems. After all, he had nothing better to do.

The situation had not changed by the time Bairn woke Ivan from his sleep. Herris took his turn at rest while Ivan continued to feed the reservoir, which was now almost a quarter full.

"When this is over," Ivan grumbled, "I am going to spend a *week* in the Golden Hare."

Bairn smiled. He could agree with the sentiment, if not the intent.

"I think I'll just sleep that long," Bairn said.

"Nope, you don't get to," Ivan said.

"What do you mean?"

"You get to start building on this oversized sandbox," Ivan explained. "The battle's the *easy* part! Herris and I get to go home—you've got to cultivate this land."

"Thank you *so* much," Bairn replied, laughing.

"We'll come visit when you're done," Ivan promised.

"Freeloader!" Bairn said.

"The polite term is 'guest,' " Ivan replied.

"Oh, I see . . ." Bairn began. He was interrupted by a massive attack on the wards. The reservoir automatically reinforced the ward with a massive amount of Power. Bairn actually felt the attack physically as the fortress shuddered.

"Ivan!" Bairn shouted, throwing his Power into the wards.

"I'm on it!" Ivan replied.

"Herris!" Bairn called. "Herris, wake up!"

"I'm here!" Herris replied.

"Get on the wards!"

"I have them!" Herris replied.

With Ivan and Herris reinforcing the wards, Bairn resumed his attacks against the enemy wards. To his surprise, he almost broke through. They had combined all of their force into their renewed attack. If it had not been for the reservoir . . .

Bairn shuddered to think of it. His second attack on the enemy's wards did not come close to breaking through.

"The attack has lessened," Ivan informed him.

"They put everything into it, hoping to break through," Bairn explained. "I almost broke through their wards by myself."

"I'll take the attack," Ivan said.

"Good," Bairn replied. "Herris, how are you holding out?"

"I'm tired," Herris said. "But I'll hang on."

"You'll get first rest, next break," Bairn promised.

"That would be advisable," Herris said.

In the mirrors, dawn broke over the horizon.

"Good morning, everybody," Ivan said sarcastically.

"Six days to go," Bairn said. Herris groaned.

They got another break the next night. Herris took the first rest. It was the only one they got.

That was not enough time for the enemy to cycle through for rest, either. What were they doing?

They're trying to wear us down, Bairn realized. In one sleep cycle, the enemy could sleep three—one journeyman and the two third-rank apprentices. Just as their attack pattern was dictated by the presence of three journeymen, so was the defensive pattern that Bairn and his allies had adopted. The enemy had deduced their numbers.

If that were their strategy—a slow wearing down of their enemy through sleep deprivation—they would repeat this pattern tomorrow night. Could Bairn find some way to put that to use?

"Ivan?" Bairn said. "Herris?"

"Yes?" Ivan replied. Bairn began to explain his deductions. Hopefully they could come up with some way to take advantage of this knowledge.

The sun went down on the sixth day of the siege. Soon, if the enemy was going to pursue the strategy that Bairn thought they were using, the attack would let up.

It did, about an hour after sunset. Bairn waited for a few minutes, but the lull seemed genuine.

"Herris, take over the attack," Bairn ordered. The enemy would notice a change in the style of attack and think one of their number had gone to rest.

"Ivan, take the wards for now," Bairn ordered. For this tactic to work, they needed to keep the reservoir, now nearly a quarter full, as full as possible. To that end, Bairn allowed Power to flow into the reservoir, but at a reduced rate to avoid detection. The enemy needed to believe that one of them was asleep.

"I think the wards have softened a little," Herris reported.

"All right, let's give it time," Bairn said. If he were correct, that "softening" would have been the third-rank apprentices withdrawing from the wards. Bairn wanted to give them time to fall asleep.

"Bairn?" Ivan prompted.

"Just a little longer," Bairn said.

"Say the word," Ivan said. They waited. It should not take long if the thirds used their Art to induce sleep . . .

"Now!" Bairn said. He drew Power as quickly as he could while Ivan and Herris both did likewise, channelling their Power into him.

Bairn launched a massive assault against the enemy wards. They shattered on the first blow. Bairn felt Herris withdraw to take up the wards, and Bairn aimed another blow into the enemy camp. Another of the enemy journeymen died.

Bairn did not test their wards with a third blow. He had learned the lesson of tarrying too long on the last sortie. Instead, both he and Ivan withdrew behind the wards and reinforced them.

In the short time that they had been left unattended, the wards had drained the reservoir from a quarter full to less than a tenth. Even so, with one less journeyman arrayed against them, the reservoir would refill more quickly.

They had all but won, at this point. The enemy battered at their wards with the short strength of anger, but they held.

"Congratulations, Master Bairn," Ivan said, evidently echoing Bairn's thoughts.

"We haven't won yet," Bairn cautioned. "We're still outnumbered."

"No," Ivan said. "We're even. Two third-ranks don't outnumber one journeyman."

"Don't get careless!" Bairn said. "Remember, we took them from fifteen to four because *they* were careless."

"Bairn is right," Herris said. "It is not over until it is over."

"Four more days," Ivan said cheerfully.

"Four and a *half*," Bairn replied.

"Spoilsport."

Cambien listened to the report grimly. Another journeyman had died in the siege against Bairn. Now there were only two, with the support of two third-rank apprentices. He was fairly certain that three journeymen, and at least an equal number of third-rank apprentices, were inside the fortress.

It was time to yield. He sent out the Call to all the members of his House.

The movement of Power woke Bairn even before Ivan called to him with panic clear in his voice.

"Bairn!" he shouted. "Lords, Bairn! Wake up!"

"I'm awake!" Bairn shouted. "Let me think!"

The amount of Power he felt was staggering. Far more than the mere force arrayed against them could manage. Bairn scanned his mirrors.

The ward over the enemy camp was visible, even without the brief flashes from Ivan's attack.

"Feed the reservoir!" Bairn ordered. No attack they could muster would damage that ward in the slightest. What was happening? Only an entire House could summon this much Power.

A face appeared in Bairn's central mirror, wiping the image of the battlefield from view. Beardless, with close-cropped red hair. Heavy red brows frowned over ice-blue eyes.

"I hereby cede my claim to these lands," the face in the mirror said. Lord Cambien.

"On the condition," Cambien continued, "that my men be allowed to withdraw without harassment."

"Certainly, Lord Cambien," Bairn said, allowing the mirror to transmit his own voice and image. "Your men may withdraw in peace."

"Thank you, Master Bairn," Cambien replied. "It is good to finally meet you. You have proven an . . . able opponent."

"Thank you, Lord," Bairn said. From his tone, Bairn doubted that respect was truly what Cambien felt toward him. His tone also suggested that Cambien would very much like to meet him—alone and without witnesses.

"Farewell," Cambien said, and his visage vanished from the mirror. Bairn focused the image onto the enemy camp.

"We've won!" Ivan said.

"Maintain the wards until they are clear from these lands," Bairn said. "They don't have to leave until that surrender is official in the Court."

"Of course," Ivan said. "Still, we've won!"

"It would appear so," Bairn conceded. "It would appear so."

Chapter Fourteen

"I MUST SAY, I am *very* impressed," Rylur said. "Not only did you face a force over five times as powerful as your own, you defeated it without loss."

"Thank you, Lord," Bairn said. "However, the enemy defeated themselves. They were overconfident."

"They had reason to be," Rylur granted. "I admit, when I saw what Cambien was committing to this battle, I thought of recalling you. I am glad, now, that you committed us to the battle before I had the opportunity to do so."

"Thank you, Lord," Bairn said.

"Ivan tells me that you died once during the battle," Rylur said.

"Yes, Lord," Bairn admitted. "He pulled me from the brink."

"Did the thought of retreat occur to you?"

"You commanded me to hold this land, Lord," Bairn said. "You did not tell me that I had the option to withdraw. The thought never occurred to me."

"Well said," Rylur told him. "I need you back in Rylur for your ceremony tonight. You may translocate there and back."

"Ceremony?"

"Yes. You will be instated as the governor of these lands and given your gold belt. You have your work cut out for you here."

"So I have been told," Bairn replied.

"Until tonight, then," Rylur said, and then he was gone.

The lands of Bairnshold had been repeatedly scoured by battle for centuries as both Rylur and Cambien failed to win clear title to the land. All trace of arable soil, of life, had been eradicated long ago.

It was Bairn's duty to undo those centuries of damage now that the land belonged to Rylur. To help in establishing the new territory, he was granted the right to select two third-rank apprentices, four second-rank and sixteen first-rank from Rylur's staff.

Of course, he chose Raoul to become one of his third-rank apprentices. On impulse, he had chosen Valerian as the second. How better to keep an eye on the apprentice and to retard his progress through the ranks?

Bairn began his work by rebuilding the fortress. He left the reservoir chamber intact, but reduced the reservoir itself in size by half. It had proven too valuable in his battle against Lord Cambien to do away with completely.

Borrowing from his memories of Reykvid, Bairn designed a square central keep with an inner courtyard garden. As in Reykvid, the outer walls of the keep were heavily fortified, but the inner wall surrounding the garden was only light stonework. A hundred feet from the central palace, barracks, stables and smithies lined the inside of an outer defensive wall.

In addition to the thousand infantry that had been sent with him to hold this land, Bairn had received a thousand cavalry to patrol his new holdings. He kept a hundred of his cavalry on the palace grounds, and the other nine hundred he housed in the outer wall of what would eventually become his city.

The structures were the easy part of his task. Healing all of the land within fifty miles of his fortress proved to be the most difficult chore facing him. It was painfully obvious that this task would require years of work before it could be completed.

Life had to be painstakingly introduced back into the barren rock. Bairn could cover a mile square in soil in the blink of an eye. But it was dead soil—lifeless and barren. Nothing would grow within it.

Life sprang from life. Nothing else would serve. Into the barren soil of each square mile he had to mix a quarter moon's waste from two thousand men and a thousand horses. Once the fertilized ground had been seeded with grass, Bairn would then use his Power to bring green to the entire field in the twinkling of an eye.

However, even this was not sufficient. It took more than manure and grass to restore a land. Once the grass was in place, thousands of earthworms, ants and other insects had to be placed in order for the land to thrive. Even with the Power, it was tedious work. At his present rate, Bairn calculated that it would take one hundred and sixty years to reclaim all the land under his rule working alone.

True to their word, Ivan and Herris arrived after the winter solstice to visit him in Bairnshold. Bairn stood on the battlements of the outer palace wall and watched as their coaches approached. This was . . . inconvenient. Bairn had hoped to spend the winter studying and experimenting with reservoir spells. Now he would have to take greater pains to keep those studies secret.

The inner gatehouse doors opened to admit the coaches, and Bairn headed down the stairs to greet his guests.

"Well," Ivan said, looking about the garden, "this is *much* more comfortable than when we were last here."

"Interesting design," Herris said. "Why is the palace so . . . fortified? If anyone gets past your outer wall, you've lost already. You might as well make the palace more pleasant."

"I like this design," Bairn said. "It gives me the option of sacrificing the outer grounds if I choose. *Before* they get past my outer wall."

"Do you still have the reservoir?" Ivan asked.

"Yes, but it is much smaller," Bairn replied. "And it is only tied in with the wards."

"Good," Ivan said. "It won us the battle, but those things are dangerous."

"So I have been informed," Bairn said. "Are you planning on staying the winter?"

"I doubt it," Ivan replied. "We wanted to come pay our respects and see how you were coming. This is a little off the trail for an entire season, however."

"It is that," Bairn agreed, relieved that they would not be staying long. "But it will grow."

"Yes," Ivan agreed. "It will. I shall be interested to see it again in a year or two. You've done good work here."

"Thank you," Bairn replied. "It has been . . . tedious."

Ivan laughed.

"I imagine so," he said. "Shoveling shit and planting worms is never agreeable work—even if one can do it without ever touching either. But it is important work. These lands will make us stronger once they are fully inhabited."

"That they will," Bairn said.

• • •

It was a full two quarters before Ivan and Herris left to return to Rylur. Once their coaches had travelled out of sight, Bairn turned and left the battlements.

He had only two moons left before spring, when he would have to begin the work of reclaiming his land anew. There was much to be done in that time.

Rylur's library contained five full volumes on the subject of reservoir spells. Bairn had ordered copies of these made by the palace scribes and had added them to his own library in Bairnshold.

What he learned had convinced him that his reservoir chamber needed extensive redesign. That is, if he wanted to keep it at all after what he had learned.

The stability of a Power reservoir was dependent on three things: the foundation material upon which it was built, its size and its age. Bairn had not picked the best material for his reservoir when he had laid it upon the native stone. Iron was considered the best material, although opinions on other materials varied between the authors of the various books.

Regardless of the material, the larger the reservoir, the faster it became unstable. If it was large enough, it would discharge explosively almost at once. It was also possible for a seemingly stable reservoir to explode if the foundation material were physically damaged. Bairn had been extremely fortunate during the siege.

Even if a reservoir were laid upon a foundation of pure iron, over time it would become increasingly unstable. The signs that a reservoir was losing its stability included loss of Power stored within the reservoir as well as strange burns and sicknesses evident in whoever came in contact with it.

Once such a reservoir became unstable, it was not sufficient to merely remove and replace the reservoir spell to restore it to stability. It was necessary to remove the spells, transmute the foundation to its original material and then replace the spells. The various texts did not know why such transmutation was necessary, for the material had not changed in any obvious way.

It seemed to Bairn that the foundation material was being changed in some way by the presence of the reservoir. If it were not, then transmutation of the foundation would not be necessary. It was also apparent that this change, whatever it might be, was linked to the cause of the deterioration. The questions were, in precisely what manner was the foundation material affected, and how did this change cause the reservoir to become unstable?

The tomes that Bairn had read made the assumption that the Power stored in the reservoir damaged the foundation material over time. If that were so, it was possible that the Power was, in fact, consuming the foundation upon which it was laid. That was something that Bairn could test.

He fashioned two identical cylinders of iron, with two-inch-thick walls approximately five feet tall and three feet in diameter. Each cylinder had a four-inch slot cut along its entire length and hooks lining the rim at each end of the cylinder.

On both the inner and outer surfaces of one of the cylinders, Bairn fashioned a Power reservoir as large as the cylinder could safely hold, according to his studies. Once that was done he suspended both cylinders from a heavy steel rocker bar, creating a giant set of scales.

It took him the remainder of that evening and another three days to fill the reservoir. By the time he had finished, something surprising had occurred. Instead of getting lighter, as Bairn had assumed would happen if the iron were being destroyed, the cylinder containing the reservoir had gotten *heavier*.

Bairn slowly added weights to the barren cylinder. Just under forty measures of weight, a little less than two pounds, had been added to the cylinder containing the reservoir. Two pounds *added* to four thousand pounds of iron. Where had the extra weight come from? What was it? What had been added to the iron?

With the onset of spring, Bairn was forced to abandon his experiments and focus on the task of reclaiming his lands. In the first half moon of spring, Bairn was able to reclaim fourteen more square miles of land. Once his winter stockpile of human waste was exhausted, his progress slowed to the more familiar square mile per quarter moon.

This gave him three square miles of established land for crops and fourteen square miles of newly reclaimed land for hay. Ruling Bairnshold was similar to what it had been like leading Bjornshall, only on a larger scale. In Bjornshall, he had been concerned with how many acres to plant for crops and how many acres to plant for fodder. Here, he planned in miles.

With the planting season also came the first of his subjects: one hundred families of farmers and an equal number of townsmen of various crafts. With no trees for fifty miles and no established stone quarries, Bairn was expected to provide housing, shops and food for these people.

Housing for the farmers was the simplest of these problems. Each farm could be identical. Bairn crafted the spell to create each farm onto a staff, which he gave to Valerian. All the third-rank apprentice had to do was proceed to the locations shown on his map, activate the spells, and the house, barn and well would form from the ground itself.

The shops for the townsmen proved more difficult. Each shop was different according to the requirements for the particular trade that would be practiced therein. Whereas Valerian could build ten farms a day with the enspelled staff, Bairn and Raoul could only construct four shops between the two of them.

Food was a simple matter of building warehouses with enspelled bins and small Power reservoirs and then assigning second-rank apprentices to run them. Bairn built bins that would produce potatoes, carrots, onions, beans, flour and every other type of produce and grain imaginable. Of course, none of this produce would grow if you planted it in the ground, but they were just as edible as their living counterparts.

Spring and summer passed far too quickly and autumn was almost over before Bairn had a chance to return to his work with the reservoir spells. However, he had reclaimed fifty square miles of land around his city during that time. It would have been rewarding work—if he hadn't known that it would all be destroyed in a few more years.

Bairn had replaced the massive iron cylinders of his first scale with a smaller test reservoir. A hundred-pound disc of iron had replaced the four thousand pounds of his previous reservoir. This disc hung from a rocker arm fifteen feet long. Three feet past the pivot, a five-hundred-pound iron sphere balanced both the hundred-pound disc and the weight of the rocker arm.

Halfway between the counterbalance and the pivot was suspended a tray for adding weight to the scale. This arrangement would magnify the weight changes in the reservoir disc by ten.

If the weight of the disc increased by a measure, Bairn would have to add ten measures to the tray to bring the scale back into balance. This enabled him to make fine measurements of the weight changes in the reservoir disc.

Those measurements had surprised him. Over the last few quarters, Bairn had filled and drained the smaller reservoir literally hundreds of times. He had expected to learn that repeated use of the reservoir slowly destroyed the iron.

Again, he had learned the exact opposite. Over time the empty weight of the reservoir had gradually increased. After hundreds of uses, Bairn had succeeded in adding a full measure to the weight of the disc when the reservoir was empty. The disc was gradually getting heavier over time.

The reservoir had begun to leak as well. Not much, but Bairn had noticed a definite loss of Power stored in the reservoir. Somehow this change in weight was tied to degradation of the reservoir. But how?

More farmers and townsmen arrived in the spring—two hundred and fifty families of farmers and another hundred families of townsmen. Bairn would have been hard-pressed to provide them all with shelter and still restore new land, had not Ivan and Herris arrived as well.

This time they had not come to visit. Rylur had assigned them to erect and man two outposts on Bairn's southern border with Cambien. They formally swore allegiance to him upon their arrival as his subordinates. Although Bairn was glad for the assistance with his land, their presence presented him with a problem.

Bairn did not want them to have too many of his people under their rule. Actually, he did not want them to have *any* of his people under their rule, but that was not going to be possible. So, how to utilize them, yet keep the number of people living in their territory to a minimum?

The answer was fairly simple. With only a hundred infantry and a hundred cavalry assigned to each of them, they would not need extensive farmland to support their strongholds. Beyond their needs, Bairn would see to it that the land they held was not heavily settled. They would plant forests.

Bairn showed them the territory they would be governing on

a large map in the council chambers. It consisted of roughly five hundred square miles for each of them.

"These are the lands that I want forested," Bairn explained. "I have indicated on the map roughly where I want heavier concentrations of pine, oak, maple and other trees.

"Keep approximately two miles around your fortress cleared for cropland," Bairn said. "That should give you more than enough cropland to support your fortress and the village that will eventually grow around it. I will give each of you fifty families of farmers to cultivate this land and, of course, enough craftsmen to support them and your fortress."

"Sounds good," Herris said.

"If you can call being stuck in the middle of the backwoods good," Ivan replied. Bairn shrugged.

"We all go where we are sent, Ivan," Bairn said.

"Aye, that we do," Ivan agreed.

"Forestation is a slow process," Bairn continued. "Once you plant trees, you can use the Power to mature them past the first five years of their life span. After that, however, you have to allow them to grow naturally, or the forest will not survive."

"But that will take decades!" Ivan protested. "Rylur grows his trees to maturity in a single day!"

"Those are trees in his garden, constantly tended by his groundskeepers and apprentices," Bairn said. "We are not concerned so much with the health of individual trees as we are the health of the forest as a whole. These books explain the process."

Bairn indicated two small stacks of books next to him on the table.

"I have had the scribes make copies for each of you. Good luck with your lands."

With the help of Ivan and Herris, Bairn was able to reclaim well over a hundred square miles of land that year. Things were looking better.

Bairn studied the image on the mirror before him. Thousands of spheres vibrated in the image. According to the texts of the Lords, these were the smallest things in existence. The MageLords called them elementals. There were a hundred known types of elementals. Alone they formed substances such as lead, gold, quicksilver, and so forth. The remainder of the entirety of the universe was fashioned of myriad combinations of these pure elements. Interestingly, iron, the best substance for reservoir foundations, was one of the pure elements.

It had taken Bairn all winter to refine the magnification spells to show him this image. Bairn had thought to see if new elementals were being added to the material. One might as well try to count the stars in the heavens. It would be an easier task.

Bairn had proceeded as far as he could on his own. He would have to ask Raoul to assist him with these experiments. Perhaps, at this scale, he could see changes as they occurred if he were to watch while Raoul filled and emptied the reservoir.

That would have to wait until next winter, however. Spring was almost upon them yet again, and the planting had to resume.

"Begin filling the reservoir," Bairn said. Raoul began feeding Power into the iron disc. Bairn watched the mirror closely. So far as he could tell, no new elementals were added to the ranks of dancing balls in the image before him. There was no apparent change.

But there *was* a change. The iron disc slowly dropped, lifting its counterweight, as Raoul filled the reservoir scribed onto it with Power. Where was the extra weight coming from?

A flash of light from the mirror caught Bairn's attention. He saw nothing. It must have been his . . .

Another small flash of light drew his attention to another section of the mirror. After a moment there was yet another. As the reservoir filled, the tiny flashes became more numerous. This behavior had not been evident before. Was Bairn seeing one of the leaks in the reservoir?

"Keep feeding it," Bairn said. He shifted the image in the mirror to an area where the flashes seemed to be more frequent and increased the magnification of the image. As the reservoir became closer to full, the flashes occurred more and more frequently until one was appearing every ten or twelve heartbeats.

Bairn saw something strange and froze the image on the mirror. He leaned forward to look more closely at what had caught his attention and increased the magnification until a single elemental filled the entire mirror. The image could be made no larger.

A tiny sphere, much smaller than the elemental shown in the mirror, had emerged from *inside* the elemental. The Lords were mistaken—the elementals were not the smallest particles of matter in the universe. There was clearly something much, much smaller that existed. *This* must be where the extra weight was coming from. Subelemental particles were being added to the elementals. As the reservoir degraded, these particles began to escape.

"Thank you, Raoul," Bairn said. "You may go now."

"What did you find?" Raoul asked.

"Nothing of consequence," Bairn lied, clearing the image from the mirror. "It appears that I will have to take a new approach to this problem. Thank you."

"Yes, Magus," Raoul said.

By the time next spring arrived, Bairn knew much more about the nature of elementals than anyone else. Each elemental was composed of one or more shells around an inner core. That core was composed of two distinct types of subelemental particles. A given element, iron for example, contained elementals composed of a fixed number of one type of particle and a variable number of the other type.

The first type he called *identicles*, as they determined the identity of the elemental—whether it was iron or lead or gold. The second type he called *bondicles*, because they seemed to hold the identicles in the elemental together.

When Power was added to a reservoir, extra *bondicles* were added to the elementals of the foundation material. Apparently, Power could be converted directly into material, and vice versa. The degradation occurred because not all of the new *bondicles* were removed when the reservoir was drained.

Over time, more and more extra *bondicles* were added to the elementals of the foundation material. Eventually, there were too many *bondicles* inside the elemental and they would begin to escape. In some cases of failure, more energy could be released than was originally stored within the reservoir. Bairn suspected that, in those cases, some of the original material of the foundation was also being converted into Power.

This was all very fascinating, but Bairn was not certain exactly how to put this knowledge to use. It was possible that, given time, he could refine the reservoir spells to convert all of the extra *bondicles* back into Power, but there had to be another way to put this knowledge to work on his behalf.

Could he possibly devise a way to take material and extract *all* of the Power within it, leaving nothing behind? Judging by how little weight a truly stupendous amount of Power added to a reservoir, the ability to do that would release staggering amounts of Power.

More so than all the Great Houses of the world combined. Enough to destroy a world.

Two

Chapter Fifteen

Hervis walked up to the gates of the city. Bairnshold. It had been ten years since they had last heard from Bairn. Some said that he had abandoned them—that he now pursued the path of Power, as did all of the other Lords.

Hervis did not believe that—he had shared the man's soul. Hervis was slow to trust, but he had trusted Bairn with his whole heart after that day. Still, a man *could* change in ten years. Had Bairn changed?

That was what Hervis was here to discover. He had not been sent, save by his own heart. The magi spoke among themselves, but none had the courage to summon Bairn—to face him. So Hervis had come to learn the truth for himself.

Hervis was the first among them to speak with Bairn. The first to be chosen by him. And he was Guardian. If any man had the right, the duty, to demand answers of Lord Magus Bairn, it was Hervis.

Bairn sat in court as the people of his land brought their petitions to him. Raoul had already sifted through the ranks of petitioners, ensuring that Bairn's time was devoted to those with the greatest need.

Over the years, Bairnshold had grown to a land of ten thousand souls. For an hour each day, Bairn held court to hear the pleas of his people—a practice that had surprised Rylur. Bairn had explained that the information he gathered in this way made it worth his time, as if that were the only reason.

Indeed, he had uncovered several agents sent into his lands by Lord Cambien in this manner. While no great work of Power could be performed in Bairn's lands without his knowledge, an enemy could work small magics undetected. A village swept with disease, crops ruined by pests, and other small troubles had uncovered three of Cambien's journeymen in his lands. Bairn had defeated them and sent them to Rylur.

He dismissed the last petitioner with a promise to visit his village on the following day. An outbreak of influenza, not uncommon in the winter, was threatening to destroy the village. A few hours' work should solve that problem handily. He wished that all his tasks were so simple.

"So, that's the last of them," Bairn said.

"No, Master," Raoul replied. Bairn glanced around at the empty throne room.

"There is a another petitioner waiting in your chambers," Raoul explained. "I thought it best for you to receive him in private."

"Who is it?"Bairn asked.

"I think you should see for yourself, Master," Raoul said.

Bairn rose from his seat, curious at Raoul's mysteriousness.

"Lead on," he said.

Hervis looked up as the door opened and Bairn stepped into the room. Bairn's black journeyman's uniform was belted in gold. Hervis automatically looked to the black marks that were spaced evenly across the front of the belt. Seven.

"Hervis?" Bairn said. "Gods, man! It is good to see you!" Bairn walked toward him and held out his hands. Hervis rose and clasped Bairn's wrists as the Lord Magus did likewise.

"Is it?" Hervis asked.

"Is something wrong?" Bairn asked. "Why have you come?"

"To find out why our Lord Magus has abandoned us," Hervis replied.

Bairn released Hervis's hands and gestured toward the table.

"Please sit," Bairn said. "Abandoned you? I have not abandoned you, Hervis. No one has Called on me. Has there been need?"

"No, Lord Magus," Hervis said. "No need but for us to hear answers to our doubts. The High Magi are afraid to call on you. Afraid that you have turned to the path of the Lords and have forsaken us. Should they call on you if that is what they fear?"

"They should," Bairn answered. "But I can understand why they would not. What of the medallions? Are they still in use?"

"They are still worn," Hervis said.

"I will soon have need of all of you," Bairn told him. "I

need to know that the magi will be there when it is time to lead humanity to safety.''

''And we need to know that you have not forgotten us,'' Hervis replied.

''I have not,'' Bairn assured him. Hervis held out his hand.

''Show me,'' he said. For a moment Bairn simply stared at his hand as if he did not know what Hervis was requesting. Then he reached out and clasped Hervis's hand in his own.

''Very well,'' Bairn said.

Hervis rode from the gates of Bairnshold and out into the farmland surrounding the city. Communion had told him much. Bairn had changed, but what man would not after ten years? He was more at peace, less consumed with the pain of the loss of his family.

He had *not* changed in the ways that were important, however. He still sought the destruction of the Lords and the deliverance of humanity. He had never abandoned his quest—he had simply entered an area where his path did not cross with theirs. He had become so immersed in his goals that he had forgotten to take time for his people.

That would not happen again. Hervis rode to the city of Rylur with a message—the first letter they had received from Bairn in ten years. One quarter after the winter solstice, the High Magi were to gather with their Circles. Bairn would reach out to them at that time, every year. He would reassure them, all of them, that they had not been forgotten.

A great burden had lifted from Hervis's heart at the touch of Bairn's mind. He had *known* that Bairn would not forsake them. Now he had to take that message to his Circle, and from there spread it to all the Circles in the world. He hoped that two seasons would be enough time.

The sterile soil crunched beneath Bairn's feet in the absolute silence. No living thing stirred, no wind blew, no sound travelled save that which travelled through his own bones.

There was no Power here. Here the Cords did not exist. Only the Stars of Power were available to him, and what Power he carried with him in the reservoir built into the airtight iron suit he wore. For here, no living thing had ever existed.

He looked to the horizon, where his world hung blue and

beautiful before him. He had lost himself in that view for almost an hour when he had first arrived on this gray, airless, alien landscape. But there was work to be done. Bairn turned his attention to the device he had brought with him.

He fitted a gold bar into the slot of the iron staff he carried. If his mathematics were correct, there was enough Power in this small bar of gold to shatter the entire world. He dared not make this first attempt on his own world.

He fed Power into the small reservoir on the staff. It filled quickly. Once it was filled, Bairn connected the reservoir to the activation point of the conversion spell.

In his mind's eye, the staff was surrounded by a golden sphere of Power. Bairn reached out and took hold of it as he would have the Cords. Power, unimaginable Power, flowed into him.

Bairn knelt and scribed the pattern of a spell into the ground before him. The Power flowed easily into the arcs and symbols of the pattern, as if an entire House stood behind him feeding the Power to him.

Bairn stepped back as a stone monolith rose from the soil of the moon. It had worked. Bairn had wielded Power where there was none to be wielded. Had raised a structure on the lifeless moon, where no Lord had ever before been able to work with the Power.

According to some legends from Bjorn's own time, Bairn lived on the moon in a great castle of his own creation. These were told as children's stories and were not given much credence. But here—here Bairn could survive the centuries untouched by the war of the MageLords.

Here, he would build his true House.

Seven days after the winter solstice, Bairn felt the Call. Instead of going forth to them, Bairn reached out and drew them to him. This was a work of immense Power, but no one would feel his work. No Lord or journeyman would be alarmed by such a movement of Power in his lands, for the Power came from a tiny golden bar in his staff.

They arrived in the immense amphitheater he had prepared for them a day's ride outside Bairnshold. High Magi from all over the world. Some were of an appearance familiar to Bairn. Others he had never seen the like of before. Some were dark of feature, like Raoul's people. Others were dark as mahogany.

Some were strangely golden in color, with eyes the shape of almonds and the color of obsidian.

His people—all of them. The magi from all over the Northern Alliance. So far, no one had been able to penetrate into the Southern Alliance. Somehow, Bairn was going to have to change that.

"So we meet," Bairn said to them.

"So we meet," more than a thousand voices proclaimed in unison.

"My people," Bairn said, "I beg your forgiveness for having been away from you for so long. But there will be a time, after the fall of the Lords, when I will depart for much longer. But while I am with you, I will always be available to you."

There was a murmuring among the High Magi. Some apparently knew one another. Others had never before met those who sat beside them. All seemed reassured by his words.

"Let us join in the Circle," Bairn said. "So that in our hearts we may know one another and be one. I have much to tell you and much to explain. Join with me."

Bairn sat in his chambers after returning from the gathering. Holding a thousand minds joined into one Circle had taken its toll on even him.

The magi would now begin their task of searching their lands for the caverns that Bairn would need to house the remnants of humanity after the war. No doubt it would take years to prepare the caverns. Food bins would have to be built into them, activated by the new elementally fueled Power reservoirs he had devised. These would last through the centuries to come, even after the collapse of Power.

All of his problems had been solved save one. How was he to incite this war between the two Alliances?

A few moons after the first Feast of Bairn, as Bairn knew it would eventually come to be known, he was awakened during the night by the Call. Not from the magi—this was from Rylur.

Bairn rose from his bed, careful not to disturb Rowena, and dressed himself by the Art before entering his sitting room. He sat in the chair before the blank mirror and acknowledged the Call. Rylur appeared in the mirror. He looked frightened—Bairn shuddered to think what could frighten Rylur.

"Is something amiss, Lord?" Bairn asked.

"I have been summoned to an emergency meeting of the Court of Lords," Rylur explained. "As my highest-ranking journeyman, I want you to attend with me."

"Of course, Lord," Bairn said. "What has happened?"

"The Southern Alliance has attacked one of our southern kingdoms," Rylur said. Bairn felt the blood drain from his own face.

No! he thought. *It is too soon!*

"Translocate to my throne room at once!" Rylur commanded.

"Yes, Lord!" Bairn replied. Less than a heartbeat later, he appeared in Rylur's throne room.

"Come quickly," Rylur said. Bairn moved to stand beside him as Rylur opened a portal to the secret location of the Lords' Court. They stepped through together.

Most of the other Lords had already assembled, including Cambien, Bairn noted. Behind each stood a journeyman of the third order. Notably, the seat of the High Lord sat empty. A confused and panicked babble filled the room. Bairn moved to stand behind Rylur as the Lord took his seat among his peers.

Bairn could gather little from the commotion in the room. Apparently, one of the kingdoms in the Southern Alliance had attacked one of the bordering kingdoms in the Northern Alliance.

The High Lord entered the room from a door behind the great hall. He took his seat, and the babble in the room died quickly.

"I have spoken with the High Lord of the Southern Alliance," he began. "I have been assured that this attack was not sanctioned by their Council and that the individual responsible will be . . . chastised."

Several of the Lords grumbled their disbelief of that statement.

"It is the best we can do," the High Lord said, "unless you would prefer that we simply go to war with them, Lord Shaun?"

"No, High Lord!" a dark-haired Lord, presumably Shaun, said. Bairn wondered why the High Lord had singled him out.

"The High Lord of the Southern Alliance claims that you attempted to send spies into their lands," the High Lord added, answering Bairn's unspoken question. "One journeyman and a third-rank apprentice, to be precise."

If Bairn had thought the earlier discussion heated before the arrival of the High Lord, then the ensuing eruption could only be called murderous.

"Silence!" the High Lord shouted, his voice carrying above the bedlam. The cries of outrage quieted almost instantly. Bairn was impressed. Here was the one man who could presume to command the Lords.

"Allow Lord Shaun to answer the charge," the High Lord said once quiet had returned.

"It . . . is true," Shaun said. "Fellow Lords, I had no choice! I have felt great movements of Power south of my lands in the last few days. They were preparing for just such an attack!"

"You have no way of knowing that," the High Lord said. "You could have plunged us all into a disastrous war. For all you knew, they were simply reclaiming dead fields. The proper response was for you to *notify this Court*!"

"Yes, High Lord," Shaun agreed. It was bizarre to hear a MageLord sound as cowed as a whipped puppy.

"I move that Lord Shaun be stripped of the privilege of casting his lot in this Court for a period of ten years," the High Lord said. "Is there a second?"

Several Lords, including Rylur, indicated their support of the motion. It was passed without dissent—Lord Shaun did not cast his vote.

"High Lord," one of the other Lords said once Lord Shaun had been stripped of his vote, "we need to find some means to keep this from happening again."

"What would you suggest, Lord Chen?" the High Lord asked.

"Is there not some agreement we can reach with the Southern Alliance?" Chen suggested. "Perhaps if we were to agree to inform one another when large amounts of Power are to be used within each other's lands?"

"I can suggest that," the High Lord said.

"Have we no ambassador to the Southern Alliance?" Bairn asked. All eyes in the room, including Rylur's, turned to him.

"Forgive me, Lords," Bairn said. "I . . . did not mean to interrupt."

"Do you think you have a solution to our problem, Journeyman?" the High Lord asked. Bairn looked askance at Rylur.

The MageLord smiled, amusedly, at him and nodded his permission.

"Perhaps, High Lord," Bairn said. "If I could clarify a few things?"

"If you wish to address the Court, you must do so from the petitioner's box," the High Lord informed him.

"Go," Rylur said quietly. "Do not speak until given permission. I hope you know what you are doing, Bairn."

Bairn hoped so as well. He made his way down the stairs to the petitioner's box in front of the assembled Lords.

"Who brings this man before us?" the High Lord asked when Bairn had taken his place on the railed platform.

"I do, esteemed Lords," Rylur said, rising to his feet.

"Identify him."

"This is Master Bairn," Rylur said, "my highest-ranking journeyman. He is third order, seventh grade."

Some surprised murmurs greeted that announcement. Seven kills was apparently an unusually high number in any land.

"He is the conqueror of Bairnshold," Rylur continued, "which he took against a force of five third-order journeymen and ten third-rank apprentices with only two second-order journeymen at his command. He has served me faithfully as the ruler of Bairnshold for over ten years."

"Well!" the High Lord said. "You are certainly qualified to speak before this body, Master Bairn."

"Thank you, High Lord," Bairn said, "and esteemed Lords."

"What do you have to say to us?"

"Am I correct to understand that we have no ambassador to the Southern Alliance?" Bairn asked.

"You are," the High Lord replied. "After all, whom could we send? And whom would they send in return?"

"It would have to be a Lord, I suppose," Bairn said.

"Exactly," the High Lord replied. "What Lord would choose to live among the enemy, unable to tend to his lands and people?"

"Would it be possible to appoint a Lord without lands?" Bairn asked.

"Who would accept such a post?" the High Lord asked. "Would *you* accept the mantle of Lord with none of the privileges to serve in such a dangerous post?"

"If it pleased my Lord, and this esteemed Court, I would do

so,'' Bairn replied. Bairn saw a smile on Rylur's face.

''You would agree to be a Lord in name only?'' the High Lord said. ''Without lands or people? To live among the Lords of the Southern Alliance, where your life would be at risk, to serve this Court?''

''If it pleased my Lord and this esteemed Court,'' Bairn said again.

''Well, your loyalty is commendable, Master Bairn,'' the High Lord said. ''And you have certainly given us something to think about. If you are willing to accept such a thankless post, then doubtless others would be as well. You may return to your Lord.''

''Lords, Bairn!'' Rylur said to him as they sat in his chambers after the meeting.

''Lord?''

''I'll give you credit,'' Rylur said. ''You must have nickel-plated, solid steel balls to have pulled that stunt tonight.''

''Not courage, Lord,'' Bairn said. ''Just an amazing ability to place my foot in my mouth.''

Rylur laughed and took another sip of his brandy.

''I was just surprised to learn that we have no ambassador to the Southern Alliance,'' Bairn added.

''And so you thought to use that vacuum to carve yourself a Lordship?'' Rylur said smiling.

''You credit me with too much advance planning, Lord,'' Bairn replied. ''The initial question popped out before I could think. At that point, I had no choice but to play the board.''

''Indeed,'' Rylur said. ''We shall have to see where this all turns out.''

''My Lord, I am sorry if I have embarrassed you . . .'' Bairn began.

''Nonsense,'' Rylur said. ''Your apparent loyalty and devotion to both myself and the Alliance made me look very good tonight. Hopefully, it won't cost me my best journeyman. If it does, however, at least it will gain me a friend in the ambassador to the Southern Alliance.''

''You don't think . . . ?'' Bairn said, letting his words trail off.

''Stranger things have happened,'' Rylur said.

• • •

It came as little surprise to Rylur when he was summoned to meet with the High Lord a few days later. It did surprise him that Lord Cambien was there as well.

"Lords," Lord Janis said. "Thank you for coming. I wish to speak with both of you regarding a matter that personally concerns you."

"And this is . . . ?" Cambien asked.

"The Southern Alliance has agreed to accept an ambassador from us," Janis explained, "so long as we accept an ambassador from them in return."

"Are you going to appoint this journeyman of Rylur's to that post?" Cambien asked.

"Bairn was questioned under truthspell," Janis said. "His words were genuine. Do you have a man who would pass this test, Cambien? One you would be willing to lose?"

"No," Cambien said. "I do not."

"Rylur, will you allow your journeyman to accept this post?" Janis asked.

"I would be honored, High Lord," Rylur replied.

"Excellent," Janis said.

"You said you had a matter that concerned both of us," Cambien said.

"Yes," Janis said. "I wish to discuss the land of Bairnshold with you. I think it would be fitting if those lands were assigned to Bairn if he is given this post. After all, a Lord cannot be wholly without land. This land would enjoy the same protections that are afforded the lands of the High Lord as long as Bairn remains our ambassador."

"I . . . see," Cambien said. The lands of the High Lord could not be attacked or claimed so long as their Lord held the post of High Lord. Similarly, the High Lord could not attempt to claim the lands of another so long as he held the post.

"Unless both of you voluntarily relinquish your claim to those lands, this cannot be, of course," Janis said.

"Bairn rules those lands already," Rylur said. "I would have no reservations about ceding them to him."

"I don't know . . ." Cambien said.

"With your depleted strength, it is the only means you have to deny them to me, Cambien," Rylur pointed out. "Not to mention that Bairn would be forbidden to attack you."

"Very well," Cambien said. "I will surrender any future

claim to those lands so long as Bairn serves as ambassador."

"Excellent," Janis said. "Then I can now bring this matter to the Court as a whole. My thanks to both of you."

"I await your will, High Lord," Rylur said, bowing his head briefly.

He pulled it off! Rylur thought, almost surprised. *Bairn actually created a new Lordship for himself.* It was a most impressive feat.

Chapter

------ Sixteen ----------

Bairn wore the white robes of initiation. Today, on the first full moon after the spring equinox, he would become a Lord.

More important, he would become the ambassador to the Southern Alliance. It seemed so very ironic that the MageLords themselves had given him everything he needed to destroy them. They had taught him the Art, and now they were sending him to their enemies.

He walked through the petitioner's doors into the lower arena of the Court. The petitioner's box stood before him, and Bairn climbed the few steps to stand within it. He placed his hands on the railing, linking himself to the truthspell that was laid upon it.

"Who comes?" Lord Janis, the High Lord, asked.

"Master Bairn," Bairn replied. "Journeyman of the third order, seventh grade." He had been rehearsed on this ceremony by Rylur.

"Why have you come?"

"To take my place among you," Bairn said.

"Do you willingly submit to the authority of this Court?" Janis asked.

"I do."

"Will you abide by its rulings over your lands and actions?"

"I will."

"Have you been given copies of the laws and rulings of this Court that will apply to you as one of us?"

"I have," Bairn replied.

"Do you swear to abide by all the articles contained therein to the best of your ability?"

"I do."

"Do you accept the consequences described therein should you fail to abide by these decrees?"

"I do."

"Esteemed Lords," Janis said, "we have one before us who

seeks to join our ranks on this Court. It has been over five hundred years since a new seat has been added to this Court. How say you today?''

One by one the Lords cast their lots while Bairn waited. One of the High Lord's journeymen carried a sealed box to each seated Lord, and the Lords dropped the tiles containing their votes within. Finally the box was returned to Lord Janis, and he broke the seal on the box and glanced within.

''All are in favor,'' he announced. ''Welcome to our Court, Lord Bairn.''

''Thank you, High Lord,'' Bairn replied.

''You will submit your amulet to us,'' Janis commanded. Bairn removed the golden amulet from his neck and raised it above his head. Janis took hold of it with the Power, and the amulet floated across the chamber to the Lords.

The amulet was consigned to an iron pot and melted. Soon, a new amulet bearing his name was taken from the pot and sent back to him. Unlike his apprentice's amulet, this was ringed in obsidian to denote his new status.

''This amulet, keyed only to you, will now grant you access to this chamber,'' Janis told him. ''Protect it with your life.''

''I shall,'' Bairn promised.

''Now, to other matters,'' Janis said. ''Lord Bairn, this Court now offers to you the post of Ambassador to the Southern Alliance. Do you accept?''

''It is my honor to accept this post, High Lord,'' Bairn replied.

''Then it is the will of this Court that you be appointed our ambassador,'' Janis said. ''You will be granted title to the ambassadorial lands as long as you serve in this post.''

''Ambassadorial lands?'' Bairn said.

''Those lands formerly known as Bairnshold have been donated by Lord Rylur and Lord Cambien to house our ambassador,'' Janis explained. ''From this day forward, they will enjoy protected status as part of the lands of the High Lord. Do you accept these lands as your kingdom, Lord Bairn?''

''I do, High Lord!'' Bairn replied.

''Good,'' Janis replied. ''You will be given one season to establish your House before you take your post in the Southern Alliance. You may work out the particulars with Lord Rylur. I believe that some of his journeymen are stationed on those lands. He will undoubtedly want them back."

"Undoubtedly," Bairn agreed.

"Come take your seat among us, Lord Bairn," Janis said.

Bairn descended from the petitioner's box and walked up the steps to the Lord's table to take a seat at the right hand of the High Lord.

"I move that this assembly be dismissed," Lord Janis said once Bairn had taken his seat. "Are all in favor?"

All were.

"Then this gathering is adjourned," Janis said. "Lord Bairn, Lord Rylur, if I may see you in my chambers before you depart?"

"Congratulations, Lord Bairn," Lord Janis said as he handed Bairn a glass of burgundy.

"Thank you, High Lord," Bairn said.

"Lord Rylur has volunteered to help you get your House in order," Janis said. "One season is a very short time."

"If anyone can get a House running in one season, it is my Lor . . . it is Lord Rylur," Bairn said, deliberately faltering over Rylur's title. Rylur smiled.

"That's right," he agreed. "I am your Lord no longer. You may keep the apprentices you selected for your holding as part of your House, but I will want Ivan and Herris to return."

"Thank you, Lord Rylur. However, if it pleases you, I would like to return Valerian to your House."

"Has he displeased you?" Rylur asked.

"Not greatly," Bairn said. "However, he would resent serving me as his Lord. That is not a healthy situation. Especially since I shall be away from my lands for long periods at a time."

"I see," Rylur said thoughtfully. "Do you think I will have any difficulty with him?"

"No, Lord Rylur," Bairn replied, smiling. "You were never subordinate to him."

"That's right," Rylur said. "He was over you as Chief First, was he not?"

"Exactly."

"No wonder you have had problems with him," Rylur said. "Very well."

"Esteemed Lords," Janis interrupted. "Could you continue these discussions later?"

"Of course, High Lord," Bairn replied.

"Lord Rylur, would you please excuse the ambassador and myself?" Janis asked. "I promise not to delay him long."

"Certainly, High Lord," Rylur said. He rose and bowed to the High Lord. "Until later, Ambassador."

"Until later, Lord Rylur," Bairn said. Rylur turned and left the High Lord's chambers.

"I wanted to discuss your post with you for a moment, Bairn," Lord Janis said.

"Yes, High Lord?"

"Please, Janis is sufficient at this point," Lord Janis said.

"Very well," Bairn said.

"The Lords of the Southern Alliance have agreed to allow you into their lands as well as a single first-rank apprentice to serve as your aide," Janis said. "You may, of course, take as many ungifted servants as you like."

"Servants?"

"Yes," Janis said. "You will be given a single square mile of land on which to build a stronghold. We shall grant their ambassador the same privilege."

"That sounds more than acceptable," Bairn said.

"Bairn," he said, "you must never forget that you are among the enemy. They will, no doubt, present their most charming appearance to you. *Never* fall into the trap of thinking you are among friends."

"I shall not, High Lord," Bairn replied. "I am well aware of the danger in which I am placing myself."

"Which brings me to my next question," Janis said. "*Why* are you willing to accept this post? None have been before you, although you were not the first to make the proposal."

Bairn paused. Did Janis have him under truthspell at this point?

"Because it is more dangerous *not* to accept this post, Janis," Bairn said. "Not only to myself but to all of us. We must have lines of communication between ourselves and the Southern Alliance. And, as a virtually landless Lord, I have much less to lose."

"Very good," Janis replied. "After the summer solstice, we

will be allowed to translocate you into the lands of the Southern Alliance.

"You will come to this Court exactly seven days after the summer solstice," Janis added. "I do not have to emphasize how important it is that you not miss this appointment."

"Of course not," Bairn replied.

"Excellent," Janis said. "I shall see you in a season, Lord Bairn."

"Lord Janis," Bairn said, rising to his feet and bowing briefly to Lord Janis. He turned and left the room. There was *much* to be done in one season. Not all of it in keeping with the plans of the High Lord.

Hervis awoke at the urging of the Call. He rose from his bed and donned the black cloak that would help to hide him from the watch.

He needn't have bothered. The Call led him to his own front room and stopped there. Bairn stood before him.

"Lord Magus!" he said. "How may I be of service?"

"That is exactly what I am here to discuss, Hervis," Bairn told him. "I need you to resign as Guardian of the Circle here in Rylur and come to Bairnshold."

"Why, Lord Magus?"

"I am going on a dangerous journey to foreign lands," Bairn explained. "And I want you by my side."

"Yes, Lord Magus," Hervis answered without hesitation. Bairn vanished, and Hervis sat in his favorite chair to ponder what had just happened.

Bairn was going away? And the Lord Magus wanted *him* at his side on this journey?

Hervis was not certain whether to feel proud or afraid. The solution was simple—he felt both.

Bairn clasped Raoul's hands before leaving. All was in readiness. Raoul had reached journeyman second order long ago. Bairn had given him charge of Bairnshold in his absence.

"I shall miss you, Lord," Raoul said to him.

"And I you, Raoul," Bairn said. "Take good care of my people while I am gone."

"I shall, Lord," Raoul assured him.

Bairn's party was small. Himself and Rowena, his valets, her maids and Hervis. Raoul had given the former Guardian what was probably the most intensive instruction that any new first-rank apprentice had ever received—an entire season of education under Communion. Hervis would continue his studies at a more sedate pace under Bairn in the Southern Alliance.

Bairn needed apprentices for his true House, and Hervis was a logical choice. Anyone who had the courage to face Bairn himself down when they feared that he might have turned was of the caliber that Bairn wanted among his people.

"Is everyone ready?" Bairn asked. Everyone in his party nodded assent. Bairn offered his arm to Rowena and opened the portal to the Court of Lords after she had accepted it.

Together, they stepped through into the arena before the assembly. All of the Lords had been gathered here for this moment.

"Greetings, Lord Bairn!" Janis called to him.

"Greetings, High Lord," Bairn replied. "Esteemed Lords."

"Are you prepared to take your post among the Southern Alliance?" Janis asked.

"I am," Bairn replied.

"Then so be it," Janis said. Bairn felt a vast flow of Power as all of the assembled Lords focused on opening a portal to the lands of the Southern Alliance.

"Go in health, Lord Bairn," Janis said once the portal had formed.

"Thank you, High Lord," Bairn said. "You shall receive my first report this evening."

With that he turned and led his people through the portal. He felt Rowena hesitate at the mouth of the swirling maelstrom of Power.

"It is all right," he whispered to her. She took a deep breath and followed beside him.

An astonishing sight greeted Bairn on the far side of the portal. He had emerged in what was the equivalent of the Court of Lords in the Southern Alliance. A domed ceiling of solid gold supported by marble pillars formed the meeting hall.

Instead of a single Great Table, the Lords surrounded the hall. Each member of the court had a table where the Lord sat with what were presumably members of the Lord's House. Each table and seat was of hand-carved mahogany, polished to a clear shine. Behind each area was a silk banner carrying the symbol of the Lord of that House.

One seat in particular was elevated above the others, as were all of the seats of that House. An immense crystal chandelier hung from the ceiling, casting glittering light throughout the chamber.

Although much more ornate than its counterpart in the north, it was not the Council chamber that astonished Bairn. It was those who filled it.

In every seat of the southern Court sat a woman.

They could have at least warned me, Bairn thought.

A stunningly beautiful woman with dark features and hair, wearing a strange robelike garment that fell off one shoulder, rose from the High Chair before him. Her head bore a wreath of green, waxy leaves.

"I am Ethenia," she said, "High Lord of the Southern Alliance. We bid you welcome, Lord Bairn."

Bairn swallowed to clear his throat before answering. He had clearly underestimated the danger of his new post.

"Thank you . . . High Lord," he said. "It is my hope that this exchange of representatives will herald a new era of stability between our people."

Ethenia's smile was as cold as a serpent's kiss.

"We hope so as well," Ethenia said. "You will be a guest in my House, Lord Bairn, until you can prepare your own palace to your liking."

Out of the cooking pot . . . Bairn thought.

"My thanks for your hospitality, Lady Ethenia," Bairn said. There was a collective gasp from the assembly. Clearly Bairn had just done something wrong.

"My title is *Lord*, Lord Bairn," Ethenia informed him. "You will not refer to me by the same title which you bestow upon your *toy* again!"

Her hand gestured toward Rowena at the word "toy." Rowena flushed a deep red, and Bairn could feel her anger, but she remained silent, thank the gods!

"My sincerest apologies, Lord Ethenia," Bairn said. "I assure you, I truly meant no disrespect."

Again Ethenia smiled that frozen smile.

"You will be forgiven this one error," she said. "My fellow Lords and I have some questions for you, Lord Bairn."

"Certainly, High Lord," Bairn replied, grateful for the change in subject. He might survive until tonight after all.

Lord Ethenia's guest house turned out to be a commandeered inn just outside her palace. Aside from being a bit nervous, the family that owned the inn was not too unhappy with the arrangement. Ethenia had ordered the inn modified to accommodate an individual of Bairn's station and had let it be known that the innkeeper would be allowed to retain the improvements to his facility once Bairn had left.

An entire floor had been added to the formerly two-story inn. Over three quarters of the third floor was devoted entirely to Bairn's lodging: a bedroom that would be considered spacious for an inn, a sitting room, a dining room and a bath. Hervis, as his aide, was also given a bedroom on the upper floor.

The few servants that Bairn had brought with him were housed on the inn's unmodified second floor. Bairn spent most of the afternoon searching the inn for any spells that might have been placed by his hostess. Once he was satisfied that there were none to be found, Bairn warded the inn to prevent uninvited eavesdropping.

"Why don't you go enjoy a nice hot bath, before dinner, while Hervis and I talk?" Bairn suggested to Rowena once they were finally settled in.

"Yes, Lord," Rowena said, smiling. She disappeared into the bedroom, leaving Bairn and Hervis alone to talk. Bairn raised a special ward intended to muffle his conversation with Hervis, just in case there were nonmagical eavesdroppers about. It was surely not beyond Ethenia to replace the true owners of the inn with convincing spies.

"We have not had much time to talk since you entered my service," Bairn said.

"No," Hervis agreed.

"What have you thought of your studies?" Bairn asked.

"They do not seem to have much to do with magic," Hervis said. Bairn laughed at his answer.

"I didn't think so, either," Bairn told him. "They have more to do with it than you realize, however."

"Lord Bairn, why am I here?" Hervis asked.

"You are here for a number of reasons," Bairn replied. "But mainly you are here because I trust you. My House has but one journeyman. I trust him implicitly, but I need more. I have to be extremely careful in selecting those whom I train. I have to be certain that they are people who will not misuse their Power as the MageLords have. Does that help you understand?"

"Yes, Lord," Hervis said. "I am honored by your trust in me."

"Just today, it has occurred to me that there is one other whom I could make into one of my journeymen," Bairn added.

"Who is that, Lord?"

"The Lady Rowena," Bairn said.

"Rowena?" Hervis asked in surprise.

"She has the Gift," Bairn assured him. "Given our present environment, I think it would be advantageous to have her trained."

"Why is that?"

"Think of it," Bairn said. "Ironically, she is the last person among us that they would expect to be skilled in the Art."

"It is forbidden, you realize," Hervis pointed out.

"So is dealing with or training rogue mages," Bairn countered.

"That is true," Hervis said. "Can she be trusted with such Power?"

"That is what I am going to have to determine," Bairn said. "But first I must report our status to High Lord Janis, and then we must attend dinner with Lord Ethenia."

Bairn's report to Lord Janis was short, essentially consisting of "They haven't killed me yet." The High Lord had been amused to learn that Bairn had not known that the southern Lords were all women. Still, despite a few minor blunders, the day had gone well, both had to agree.

Dinner with Lord Ethenia went much more smoothly than their initial meeting, although Bairn clearly felt that his presence was tolerated as a necessity, not a pleasure. The fact that the Lords of the Southern Alliance were all women explained much that Bairn had never understood. The two factions would never unite, solely because of the treatment of women at the hands of the Northern Alliance. Bairn found himself wondering how men with the Gift were treated in the Southern Alliance. He didn't ask.

This was another reason he now wanted to train Rowena in

the Art. Here, in this time, the classic conflict between men and women had manifested in this divided society—a division that would ultimately, with Bairn's help, destroy this world. When his House finally survived into Bjorn's time, Bairn did not want to perpetuate that division. His House would be united with both men and women.

Hervis had raised a valid point, however. Could Rowena be trusted with this sort of Power? Absolute power could corrupt anybody—even himself. Only through constant self-vigilance could it be prevented. Did Rowena have the character that would enable her to wield such Power justly?

For that matter, did Hervis? Or Raoul? When they found themselves alone on a world with no other Lords, would they be tempted to use their Power for their own ends? Almost certainly. Anybody would be tempted by that prospect. The true question was whether or not they would succumb.

For that reason, Bairn had not shared the final results of his experiments with anyone. No one knew of the immense Power that was stored in everything around them. Only Bairn had access to that Power. Raoul knew only that Bairn had discovered a way to make stable reservoirs.

Once his true House had been established, Bairn would demonstrate his superior strength. He would prove to them that he, alone and without aid, could stand against their combined might. That would reduce the temptation of going renegade.

Then he would only have to worry about himself.

"Why so solemn, my husband?" Rowena asked, interrupting his thoughts.

"What do you think of these southern Lords, Rowena?" Bairn asked.

"I can still hardly believe that they are all women," Rowena said. "I had no idea that a woman could become a Lord."

"Do you find that appealing?"

Rowena looked surprised at the question. To her credit, she thought for a long time before answering.

"It would be . . . nice not to have to be . . . afraid anymore," she finally said. Her answer surprised him.

"What are you afraid of, beloved?" he asked.

"That you will grow weary of me," she said. "That, when I start to grow old, you will discard me for a younger woman and I will be left to beg on the streets."

Bairn smiled and caressed her face.

"My love," he said, "even if you were as wrinkled as an old prune, I would still love you. However, I shall tell you a secret. We have been together for over ten years now. Would you say that you look ten years older than when we met?"

Again, Rowena was surprised by his question. After a moment, she rose from the sofa where they were sitting and walked into the bedroom. When she came out, she was clad in a night-robe. She had obviously been examining herself in the mirror.

"No," she said, "I do not. Are you . . . ?"

Bairn nodded.

"I could not bear to spend the centuries ahead of me without you," he said. "You will never grow old, my love."

"That is not all I fear," she confessed.

"What else?" Bairn asked.

"That something will happen to you," she said. "That I will again be a slave, a toy, in some other Lord's House. Or that I will be sold to a brothel to pleasure another Lord's guards and apprentices."

"So the thought of becoming a Lord appeals to you?"

"I'm not sure," Rowena said.

"What of the other benefits?" Bairn asked.

"What do you mean?"

"The ability to have your own House," Bairn said. "To rule a land of thousands of people and to fill your palace with slaves to fulfill your every desire."

Rowena's mouth fell open in shock. Her mouth snapped shut, and Bairn saw anger flare in her eyes. Without warning, she slapped him and then turned and fled into the bedroom.

On the one hand, her reaction made him feel very proud of her. Bairn raised his hand to his face where she had slapped him. To strike a Lord, even him, went against a lifetime of conditioning.

He had been right—Rowena would not be likely to misuse her Power. However, his heart ached at the pain he had just caused her. He told himself that it had been necessary, but that did not make him feel better about it. He rose to his feet and walked over to the bedroom.

"Rowena," he said softly, opening the door to the bedroom. She turned from where she lay face down on the bed. Her face was streaked with tears.

"How could you *say* that to me?" she shrieked at him. Bairn quickly raised a silencing ward around the room.

"You *know* I was a slave!" she continued. "I was passed among the apprentices like a whore—I *was* a whore! Do you honestly think I would ever do that to somebody else? I *hate* you!"

"Rowena . . ." Bairn began.

"Do you think I *admire* that bitch Ethenia?" Rowena interrupted. "She makes me sick. She's no better than Rylur or any of the others. How could you *say* that to me?"

"Rowena, I'm sorry," Bairn said. "I didn't think you could do something like that, but I had to be absolutely certain."

"Why?" she asked. Her initial outrage had finally passed and she was left with only the hurt he had caused her.

"Because I want to train you as one of my journeymen," Bairn said. "But I couldn't do that if you would misuse that training."

"Train . . . me?"

"Yes," Bairn said. "The journeymen are just as powerful as the Lords. I had to be *certain* of your feelings."

"But . . . why?" she asked. "If the others find out . . ."

"They won't," Bairn assured her.

"But *why*?" she said again.

"Rowena, there are many things about me that you do not know," Bairn said. "And it is time for you to learn about them."

Rowena sat up in bed watching Bairn as he slept beside her. If anyone but her husband had told her the things he had just told her, she would have thought him mad.

But he had shared his mind with her. Not with sections walled off, as he had before, but totally. Well, almost. There was still one small place he had kept hidden, but it was recent. If what he had told her was true, she understood that he had secrets that must be kept.

She knew it was true. She had seen everything and she knew his ultimate goals. What she had seen had frightened her, but it also made her love him even more. He lived his whole life for his people. Nothing he did was done solely for himself.

He had told her that she could take all the time she needed

to think over her answer. She already knew what that answer was going to be.

"You may teach me," she said quietly, as she stroked his hair. "I will serve you, Lord."

Chapter Seventeen

Bairn did not think that he had ever seen a more useless piece of land. Of course, he had not expected Ethenia to give him a square mile of her prime cropland. Even so, the barren, windswept and fractured land before him was quite forbidding.

Large boulders littered the landscape as if they had been thrust up through the ground itself. Which they had, he learned once he extended his mystical senses into the earth below him. The bedrock had been shattered and fractured by some ancient cataclysm—probably an earthquake.

This site had been chosen for its lack of defensibility. Once Bairn had leveled the site, it would be surrounded by large stone hills from which a physical attack could be mounted. The shattered bedrock beneath him would be extremely susceptible to the inducement of earthquakes.

"Lord Ethenia has chosen this site carefully," Bairn noted.

"Indeed, Lord," Hervis agreed.

"We will have to demonstrate to her that we can rise above such things," Bairn added.

"Lord?"

"Leave it to me, Hervis," Bairn said. "See that the others are taken care of for the next few days."

"Yes, Lord," Hervis said.

The "next few days" turned out to be almost an entire moon as Bairn reshaped the land he had been given. The first step was to repair the shattered bedrock below him. He fused the stone into an inverted dome, a mile in diameter and half a mile deep at the center.

With a firm foundation upon which to build, Bairn gathered the separate, upthrust rocks into a single, monolithic bluff whose flat top he made four hundred feet square. A hundred feet below, at its base, the sides of the bluff were fifty feet longer.

Atop the bluff, he built a duplicate of his fortress at Bairnshold. Fountains built into the palace grounds extracted water from deep beneath the shattered rock. Their output gathered into a single small waterfall that cascaded down the face of the bluff.

A lake surrounded the bluff for roughly a hundred feet in all directions. A single stone bridge led to a spiral trail made to appear as if it had been carved into the natural-looking rock of the bluff.

Bairn surrounded his lands with a modest wall. Inside the walls, all was made green. Grass, trees, and various berry and flowering bushes filled the land. The seed stock for all of these was imported from his lands in the north. Water flowed from the central lake to fill small ponds that supplied his lands with water.

When he had finished, a desolate piece of land had been transformed into a nearly impenetrable fortress surrounded by an idyllic countryside. Bairn smiled. He was certain that Ethenia would not be pleased.

Indeed, she was not, although she hid her dismay well when Bairn finally invited her and the other southern Lords to his first formal dinner.

"You did all of this in one moon?" she asked. "I am . . . impressed, Lord Bairn."

"For the past ten years, I have done nothing *but* reclaim lands for my former Lord," Bairn replied. "At the risk of sounding presumptuous, I have gotten quite good at it, I believe."

"I would say that is a safe boast," Ethenia agreed.

"I am surprised at the . . . art of your lands," Lord Izabel added. Like Ethenia, she was dark of hair and olive-complexioned—and beautiful, of course. "I had expected something . . ." Izabel paused uncomfortably.

"Dismal?" Bairn suggested.

"Yes," Izabel said, smiling. "I did not expect to see anything green, much less lakes and waterfalls. It is quite beautiful."

"From what I have heard of your gardens, Lord Izabel," Bairn said, "I shall take that as extraordinary praise."

"You must visit sometime and see them," Izabel suggested.

"I would be honored."

Conversation continued in this vein throughout dinner. Trivial pleasantries and thinly veiled distrust of both himself and one another. It was maddeningly . . . female. Even as duplicitous as the northern Lords could be, they were infinitely more direct than these women.

Dinner was finally over, and Bairn suggested they retire to the inner garden. Izabel immediately took to suggesting changes to his arrangements and designs. Bairn affected to listen intently to her suggestions and even decided to implement a few. After all, it would not hurt to court her favor. It might come in handy sometime in the future.

"High Lord Ethenia," Bairn said, after promising Lord Izabel that he would visit her lands within the next moon, "I was wondering if we could discuss my staff, now that my House is complete."

"Your staff?" Ethenia said.

"Yes," Bairn said. "Obviously I cannot run such a place with only one first-rank apprentice."

"What did you have in mind?" Ethenia asked.

"Not much," Bairn said. "I was thinking a single journeyman and a fourfold pyramid beneath him. Four third-rank, sixteen second . . ."

"Absolutely not," Ethenia said, interrupting him.

"But, High Lord, that is a small House indeed," Bairn said. "It would be too small to be a threat."

"I do not call six men of Lord strength too small to be a threat," Ethenia countered. "Especially not when supported by another sixteen who wield nearly as much Power."

"What would you allow, then?" Bairn asked. "I must expand my staff simply to deal with the day-to-day operations of the House."

"You may add nine more first-rank apprentices," Ethenia said.

"High Lord," Bairn pleaded, "I need at least one journeyman to leave in charge of these lands when I travel among you."

"I will discuss that with the Council at our next meeting," Ethenia promised. "That is all I can do. Whatever is decided, your people will have to agree to allow an equal-sized force in *your* lands. I suggest you speak with them on this issue as well."

"I shall," Bairn said. "Thank you, High Lord."

"What is the *minimum* you will need to operate your estate there?" Lord Janis asked him.

"I must have at least one journeyman," Bairn replied.

"You currently have only one journeyman in your entire House," Janis said. "Are you going to remove him from his post here?"

"It would be better to have him here, where security is more important," Bairn said. "I am not as doubtful regarding the safety of my lands back home."

"True," Janis said. "However, whatever we give you, we shall have to agree to give your counterpart here as well."

"I could get by with the one journeyman and a handful of second-rank apprentices," Bairn said. "Perhaps four?"

"With sixteen first-rank below them?" Janis asked.

"Of course," Bairn said. "I would also like to house three hundred troops here."

"I will make your proposal to the Court," Janis said. "I will advise you of the meeting so that you may attend, of course."

"Thank you, Lord Janis," Bairn said. "However, until I have someone I trust here, it would be better for me to remain on my lands. Until then, you may cast my lot for me in Court as you judge best."

"As you wish," Janis said. "You have done us a great service there, Bairn. Already our communications with the Southern Alliance are better than they have ever been."

"Thank you, High Lord."

"I will inform you of the decision of the Court," Janis concluded.

It was almost a moon before Bairn was allowed to bring his new staff to the southern fortress of Bairnskeep, as it had become known to the southern Lords. Whenever Bairn was away from Bairnskeep, Raoul would take his place and leave William, Bairn's Chief First, in charge of Bairnshold.

As yet, Bairn did not have any second-rank apprentices to fill vacant posts here. Instead, he added four first-rank apprentices to fill those vacancies. It would not be long before Hervis reached the second rank, and others would graduate soon after that. Bairn would slowly bring up his staff to the allowed levels—plus one.

Of course, no one would know of his wild card. Rowena's studies were progressing well, under Communion. She showed a gift with mathematics almost as great as Raoul's. Unlike Raoul had been at her level of training, however, she also showed a ready understanding with matters of Power.

"Must you go see that woman?" Rowena was asking him as he prepared for his promised visit to Lord Izabel's gardens.

"Diplomatic contact *is* my assigned duty here, beloved," Bairn replied. "Besides, I promised Lord Izabel that I would visit her gardens before the moon was out. It would damage my credibility with them if I were to renege.

"At any rate, Lord Izabel is one of the less unfriendly ones," Bairn pointed out.

"I know," Rowena said. "That is what concerns me."

"What do you . . . ?" Bairn began to ask, but the question brought its own answer.

"Are you . . . jealous, Rowena?" he asked.

"I am concerned," she said. "I think that Lord Izabel is more interested in showing you her bed than her garden."

"Well, if you are correct, I can assure you that her interest is not returned," Bairn said.

Rowena smiled mischievously.

"Liar," she said. "How could anyone not be interested in a woman as beautiful as any of the southern Lords?"

"Oh, I don't know about that," Bairn replied. "Any man who saw Ethenia smile would have no interest whatsoever."

Rowena laughed.

"Granted," she said. Then more seriously, "Would you not lie with Izabel to gain her as an ally in the Council?"

"No," Bairn said. "Besides, I doubt that she is at all interested. Such a . . . dalliance could very easily hurt her position in the council. The southern Lords do not like the northern Lords very much at all."

"Then why does she want you to visit her?"

"Well," Bairn said, "that is . . ." Bairn turned to face Rowena, realizing that he did not have an answer to that question.

"I don't know," he said.

"My point exactly," Rowena said, smiling triumphantly.

"I suppose she might hope to learn some useful piece of information from me," Bairn suggested.

"That is possible, I suppose," Rowena said. Her tone expressed doubt.

"Even if she does have . . . designs on me," Bairn said, "you have no cause for concern."

"Be careful with this one," Rowena said. "I do not trust her."

"Who would trust *any* of them?" Bairn asked, laughing.

"I would trust Ethenia more than I would Izabel," Rowena said. "Izabel is far better at concealing her true feelings. Be wary."

"I shall, love," Bairn promised. He turned and held out his arms to her.

"I have to go now," he said. Rowena stepped into his arms.

"Goodbye," she said. She gave him a long kiss.

"Hurry home," she said.

"I shall," Bairn promised.

Lord Izabel's gardens put Rylur's gardens to shame. Acres of sculpted flower bushes were arranged by size and color into a natural tapestry of beauty. Birds sang in flowering trees or on marble fountains splashing with crystal clear water. As in Rylur's gardens, small herds of deer grazed throughout the garden. Unlike in Rylur's garden, there were no predators other than a few dens of foxes to control the rodents.

Open-walled buildings, far too large to be called gazebos, with marble roofs supported by ornate pillars protected one from the sun while still allowing all the sounds and smells of the garden to be experienced by those within. Bairn shared a glass of wine in one such edifice with Izabel as they watched the sun set.

The day had been spent in trivial conversation about the gardens, other gardens that Bairn had seen before and general aspects of life in both empires. As Bairn had suspected, men with the Gift were treated almost exactly as were women in the north. However, men in general seemed to be better treated.

"I suppose it is as necessary for your Lords to bind women with the Gift as it is for us to bind men with the Gift," Izabel said.

"Do you mean to say that it does not bother you?" Bairn asked.

"I did not say *that*," Izabel replied.

"Forgive me," Bairn said. "I was baiting you—that was ungracious of me."

"Of course, Bairn," Izabel said. Titles had been dropped from their conversation much earlier.

"Still," Bairn said, braving a further step, "I wonder how necessary it truly is."

"What do you mean?"

"Our . . . methods divide us," Bairn said. "What would it be like if our Houses apprenticed *both* men and women—trained them as equals? Then north and south could unite, peacefully, into one world-spanning empire. Peace between us would be assured forever."

Izabel was silent for a moment.

"Is this the view of your Court?" she finally asked. Bairn laughed.

"Hardly," he said. "I could be stripped of my status for even suggesting that we apprentice women. I imagine the reverse would be true for you as well."

Izabel smiled, her dark red lips parting to reveal teeth that were shockingly white in contrast with her dark complexion.

"You imagine correctly," she said. "Even so, my thoughts have strayed in that direction from time to time as well. More so, since you have come to live among us."

"Indeed?" Bairn said.

"Yes," Izabel said. Then, changing the subject, she added, "The moon is out. There is a part of the garden I would like you to see in the moonlight."

"Lead on," Bairn said.

She led him to a nearby glen where a few low hills surrounded a silver pond. Beyond the pond lay a field of white flowers. The white flowers shone like silver in the dark grass. It was as though the stars had come to rest on the ground. A warm breeze stirred the fields, making the flowers twinkle like the stars they resembled.

"It is . . . magnificent," Bairn said. It was ironic that such beauty could be created by the same hands that could also turn and bring so much misery to the world.

"Bairn?"

"Yes?" Bairn said, turning to face her. Izabel stepped close to him and looked up into his eyes.

Gods! he thought. *Rowena was right!*

"Have you ever wondered," she asked, "what it would be like to love someone who was not obliged to your will?"

"Lady Izabel," Bairn began, "I-I mean, Lord Izabel . . ."

"You may call me Lady," Izabel said, placing her hand on

his chest. "I hear the respect in your voice when you say it."

Bairn's head swam. Was Izabel enhancing her proposition with the Power? It did not seem likely. Bairn would have detected its use, and his wards would protect him. No, Izabel used only the magic that all women possessed against men.

"Have you?" she asked again.

"I have no need to wonder, my Lady," Bairn said. "I have loved someone who was my equal."

"You have?"

"Long ago, before I was apprenticed," Bairn said, taking a short step back. "I lost her, and my son, before Rylur found me."

"How long ago?"

"Fourteen years," Bairn said.

"And I can still hear the pain in your voice when you speak of it," Izabel said.

"Yes," Bairn said.

"Let me help," Izabel whispered. "The woman you are with now is not your equal. She cannot ease your pain as an equal."

I plan to correct that, Bairn thought.

Both of Izabel's hands were sliding up Bairn's chest toward his shoulders. Bairn grabbed her hands in his own and squeezed them gently, stopping them from going further.

"Lady Izabel," Bairn said, "this is . . . ill-advised. I cannot say that the thought is unappealing. In fact, the thought has crossed my own mind more than once, today. But the risk, to both of us, is simply too great."

"What is life without risk?" she asked.

"Longer," Bairn replied.

"So," she said, looking down and away from him, "you reject me."

"No, Lady Izabel," Bairn said. "I could never reject you. I am . . . declining your . . . offer, but it is by no means an easy thing to do. Your beauty is beyond imagination."

"A parting kiss, Lord Bairn?" she asked.

"I suppose there would be little harm in that," Bairn agreed. The truth was that he could see no way to easily refuse that much.

Her lips were warm and sweet and gently drew his tongue into her mouth. The kiss lasted far too long, and Bairn eventually broke away gently.

"I think I must leave now," Bairn whispered.

"Must you?"

"If I do not, I fear I will stay far *too* long," Bairn said. "I am sorry, Lady Izabel."

"Do not be, Lord Bairn," Izabel said. "You have given me a new experience, after all."

"What is that?"

"Refusal," Izabel said, smiling sadly.

"Goodnight, my Lady," Bairn said.

"Goodnight, my Lord," she whispered in reply.

Once Bairn had left, Izabel returned to the palace and her chambers. Alone, she turned to her mirror and Called to the High Lord. Ethenia's face appeared in the mirror.

"Izabel!" Ethenia said, smiling. "How was your visit today?"

"Very nice," Izabel said.

"Were you able . . . ?"

"No," Izabel sighed. "He has remarkable self-control. It's a pity—I was actually looking forward to it. I did learn one thing, though."

"What is that?"

"He is a wonderful liar," Izabel said, smiling. "He mixes in enough sincere flattery that you don't mind."

Ethenia and Izabel's laughter echoed through the halls of two palaces.

"Who seeks to enter Circle?" Raoul asked as Bairn watched from his seat as High Magus. Bairn winced as the point of Raoul's sword touched Rowena's breast.

"A student," Rowena answered. Her wards had been released, and Raoul held her mind in his. Through the Circle, Bairn and all others of the House could feel her thoughts. Her fear, her anticipation and her determination.

"Do you swear to preserve the sanctity of this Circle and the identities of its members with your life?" Raoul asked.

"I do," Rowena answered. There was a pause as Raoul evaluated her response, peering deep inside her mind. Bairn held his breath. Raoul had already killed once during the challenge, several moons ago. Bairn had no doubt that, if he found Rowena's answer false, he would do so again.

"You may enter Circle," Raoul said, drawing his sword away

and stepping back. He took his position behind and to the left of Bairn. Rowena stepped through the circle of apprentices that surrounded the High Magus and the Guardian.

All of Bairn's apprentices had been selected from among various Circles throughout Rylur's lands. They were people who had already sworn themselves to secrecy and to the Law of Bairn. People who could be trusted, who had no desire to rule over others.

"Why does our sister come to us tonight?" Bairn asked.

"I come to take my place as a member of the second rank," Rowena answered.

"Are you prepared to submit to the Rite of Advancement?" Bairn asked.

"I am," Rowena answered confidently.

"Guardian, administer the Rite," Bairn commanded. Raoul stepped behind Rowena. He gently pulled her arms behind her and bound her wrists together. Then he placed a black sack over her head and tied its drawstring about her neck.

"Kneel," Raoul commanded, "and bow to the High Magus."

Rowena did so, settling to her knees, sitting back and then leaning forward. Raoul adjusted her hood and drew his sword. He let her feel the cold steel on the back of her neck as he gathered the Power and entered her mind. Then he lifted the sword over his head and held it still.

"Do you swear to use the Arts you will be taught in the service of the Circle and your brethren?" Bairn asked.

"I do," Rowena's muffled voice replied. Raoul's sword held steady.

"Do you swear to protect the secrets of our Art from all who would steal them, even if it costs you your life?"

"I do."

"Do you seek this Power to gain mastery over others?"

"I do not," Rowena replied. Raoul's sword did not waver.

"Guardian, release our sister from her bonds," Bairn commanded. Raoul lowered and sheathed his sword. Then he knelt down to untie Rowena's hands and remove her hood.

"Rise," Bairn commanded. Bairn approached her as Raoul retrieved a cloth bundle from another member of the Circle and carried it to Bairn.

"Raise your arms," Bairn said. Rowena did so, lifting her arms straight above her head. Bairn removed the golden sash from her waist, and the white cotton robe she wore fell loose around her. Then he and Raoul slipped the silver silk overtunic over her head. Bairn tied the white sash of the first order around her waist.

"As your High Magus, I welcome you to the second rank of our Circle," Bairn said.

"And as your husband, I am very proud of you," he added, smiling. Rowena smiled, and Bairn took her in his arms. Then he turned to face the Circle.

"And now we part," he said.

"Until we meet again," the Circle responded.

Chapter Eighteen

Hervis marvelled at the difference between this market and those he had seen before. Bairn had altered Hervis's appearance to match the rich brown hues of the local populace. With almost all of his Power discarded, he was safe from notice.

What amazed him was the number of young women travelling freely about the city. Beautiful women, walking freely through the market without fear of being scooped up by the Lord's guardsmen.

Even so, life was no safer here. The apprentices and journeymen were free to take whatever liberties they pleased, as in the north. In the market they paid for nothing, merely taking what pleased them. Shoppers would vacate a stall as soon as one of the women from the palace arrived, leaving it to her alone. That fear spoke of a tyranny just as firm as in any of the northern lands.

Hervis had been unable to find any sign of rogue magi in Lord Naomi's capital city. Of course, that was what he would expect on an apprentice's holiday, which this appeared to be. Bairn wanted to spread his teachings among the rogues of the southern lands as he had in the north. It would be necessary if he was to save any of the people from these lands when the war began.

This was their first attempt at contact. Bairn had chosen to send him to one of the lands far removed from his fortress. It was beginning to look as though Hervis would have to return at some other time, however. The magi, if they were here, had gone to ground during the holiday.

"You!" a woman's voice said as a hand touched his back. Hervis turned to see one of the apprentices, a first-rank third-order, from the palace. Had he somehow been discovered?

"Yes, Lord," he said, kneeling before the woman, as he had seen others do when addressed by the apprentices.

"Rise," she said. Hervis stood. The woman looked him over

carefully. Hervis tried not to look at her. She was heavy, as the junior apprentices tended to be, and fairly plain.

"You'll do," she finally said. "What is your name?"

"Nibal, Lord," Hervis said, using a name he had heard someone called by earlier.

"Hold this," she said, handing him a bundle of things she was carrying. "Come, Nibal."

Hervis fell into step beside her. As they walked among the stalls, her hand idly caressed his upper arm. He had not been discovered, although this was almost as bad.

Couldn't it at least have been one of the pretty *ones?* he thought.

Bairn was concerned. Hervis should have Called to him long ago. He had been instructed to return by sunset. The sun was now near to rising and still Bairn had not heard from him.

Rowena waited with him. Bairn could tell that she too was alarmed. Had their first attempt to contact the magi in the south met with disaster? Had Lord Naomi captured Hervis in her capital?

Just after dawn, Bairn felt the Call. Hervis was still alive! The Call was weak and ragged, however. Bairn activated the spell in the translocation chamber and reached out to Hervis.

A heartbeat later, Hervis stood before him. He seemed unsteady on his feet.

"Hervis, are you all right?" Bairn asked.

"I am . . . well," Hervis replied. Already he was regathering his Power and rebuilding his wards. Bairn led him to a chair.

"What happened?" Bairn asked. "Were you discovered?"

"No," Hervis replied. Then he glanced over to Rowena.

"Lady Rowena," he said, "could you . . . excuse us?"

Bairn nodded to her, and Rowena rose to leave. She threw one last, concerned glance in their direction before leaving the room.

"What happened?" Bairn asked, once she had gone.

"I was . . . abducted," Hervis said.

"Abducted?"

"Today was apparently the first rank holiday," Hervis said. "Apparently, their apprentices have . . . appetites similar to those of the north."

"You mean . . . ?"

"Aye," Hervis said.

Bairn had to stifle an impulse to laugh. Here he and Rowena had been worried to distraction about Hervis, and it turned out that one of Naomi's apprentices had merely been riding him like a prize stallion all night!

"Hervis," Bairn said. "I'm sorry. I never meant for you to . . ."

"I know," Hervis said. He sounded more embarrassed than upset.

"Was she pretty?" Bairn asked, unable to resist the impulse.

"No!" Hervis said. "That would not have been so bad, but she was fat and ugly in with it all. And those whores can use the Power to turn you into enough of an animal to forget what they look like."

"I know," Bairn said.

"You do?"

"Yes," Bairn said. "Lord Izabel tried something like that with me a few seasons ago, I think."

"At least your wards were intact," Hervis said. "And she *is* beautiful."

"So," Bairn asked, "will you be all right?"

"Oh, yes," Hervis said. "It really . . . wasn't too bad . . ."

Bairn could contain his laughter no longer.

Rowena was waiting for him when he returned to their room.

"Is Hervis all right?" she asked. Her concern shattered Bairn's composure and triggered another round of laughter.

"What is so funny?" she asked.

"We sent him on holiday," Bairn said.

"What do you mean?"

"Lord Naomi's first-rank apprentices were on holiday," Bairn explained. "One of her fat, ugly firsts got her hands on Hervis."

"That's terrible!" Rowena said. "How can you laugh about this? You don't know what that's like! To . . . to be . . . *used* that way! Poor Hervis! And you laughing about it! You should be ashamed!"

"Rowena!" Bairn said, interrupting her tirade.

"What?"

"Hervis enjoyed it."

Rowena just looked at him for a moment. Then a look of pure disgust crossed her face.

"Men!" she said.

Bairn collapsed onto the bed, laughing so hard his sides hurt. After a moment, Rowena joined him in laughter.

Rowena reached out gingerly to touch the purple Cord with her mind. Just ten days ago, she had tried to claim the Power of this Cord and had been injured in the attempt. She was not anxious to repeat the experience.

She remained still as the Cord swung toward her. Purple filled her mind as the Power began to hum through her. She felt panic start to rise within her, as it had the last time, but she forced herself to relax.

Don't run, she told herself. That was what had happened the last time. She had been frightened by the sudden flow of Power and had panicked. The result had nearly cost her her life.

Gradually, the purple cleared from her mind and the angry buzz of Power faded into the background. To her mind's eye, it seemed as though the three Cords of Power united at her breast into a single blazing white Cord that passed through her.

She had done it!

"Congratulations, beloved," her husband said to her. Rowena opened her eyes, awed by the new flow of Power through her body.

"Almost frightening, isn't it?" Bairn said.

"Yes!" she whispered.

"Now we can begin your *real* training," he told her.

Hervis passed through the streets of Naomi cautiously. It was unlikely that one of Naomi's apprentices would accost him, if any were about. On all of his trips since the first, Bairn had changed him to resemble an old man, rather than a young man such women might find attractive.

Still, what he carried could gain him a much worse fate than a night's exertions. Concealed in a bag, he carried a book containing the teachings of Bairn. As he had suspected, the magi had been in hiding during the holiday. The next day, they had been much easier to find.

In the moons since then, Hervis had passed on to them all of the teachings that Bairn had given the Circle in Rylur. This book would enable them to carry Bairn's teachings to those beyond this city. As in the north, Bairn's words would spread quickly.

But not quickly enough. Now that his work here was done, Hervis was to repeat his performance in Lord Ethenia's lands. That would give them two widely separated points from which Bairn's teachings would spread. In a few years, all of the rogue magi would have been brought into the Circle.

And then the world will end, Hervis thought.

Bairn stood on the battlements of his fortress, looking out over the mile of garden surrounding him. The winter solstice had passed less than a moon ago—not that one could tell. In this land, so close to the world's girdle, the seasons mattered very little.

On top of that, here in the south the seasons were reversed. When he had first arrived here, it had been summer in the Northern Alliance but winter here. Now, a year later, it was nearing summer back home.

Home? Bairn thought. Home was *not* in the Northern Alliance. Home was a lodge in the far north, a thousand years from now. He seemed no closer to it now than when he had first arrived in the House of Soren fifteen years ago.

His ambassadorial duties had given him no insight as to how to bring these opposing factions into battle with each other. Ethenia channelled messages to him regarding large workings of Power near the borders. Bairn relayed these messages to Lord Janis, and that comprised the entirety of his duties. The two alliances had nothing beyond that to negotiate. There was *no* traffic between them.

Bairn smiled. He was probably the only *bored* MageLord in the world.

No, he realized. They were *all* bored. That was why the Lords of the north pursued their little vendettas against one another. To relieve the monotony. That could even be why Lord Izabel had attempted to seduce him that night almost a year ago in her gardens. Boredom.

Bairn chuckled. *That* was certainly a flattering thought. That her advances to Bairn had been nothing more than an attempt to relieve her boredom by lying with an enemy of her people. A dangerous risk to quicken the heart.

What is life without risk? Izabel had asked him that night. Her own words.

Would Bairn grow as bored, over time? Did immortality and omnipotence rob life of its pleasure? When was there nothing new to see or do? How *long* did it take to exhaust the possibilities of a lifetime? A century? Two? Would one begin to long for death?

Bairn sighed. This line of thought was depressing. He suddenly felt the need for Rowena's company. Perhaps a solution would occur to him on the morrow.

The mental blast knocked Rowena across the training hall. She lay on the floor for a moment before struggling to her hands and knees. Raoul stood over her, waiting for her to regain her feet.

"An enemy will not give you the time to recover," he said. Rowena glared up at him. She had always liked Raoul. Now, less than a moon after becoming a journeyman, she was beginning to hate him.

"You may hate me if you like," Raoul said, "if it keeps you alive."

He's listening to my thoughts! she thought. *How dare he*?

"It hasn't even been a moon!" Rowena said, beginning to rise to her feet. "Ease up, Raoul."

"You are in the wrong place if it is ease that you wish," Raoul said. "Perhaps you should content yourself with the Lord's bed if ease is your desire."

Rowena fell back as if he'd struck her. Her mouth gaped in surprise.

"How *dare* you!" she said. She was Bairn's *wife*! How dare Raoul speak to her like this?

"I would not care if you were his mother," Raoul said.

"Get out of my mind!" Rowena shouted, slamming up her wards.

"Still, that *is* what you are best at, is it not?" Raoul said. "Spreading your thighs to get by with ease? I've watched you do it enough times . . ."

Rowena put Power into the fist she slammed backwards against his face. Raoul rolled to his feet as soon as he hit the floor.

"Damn you!" Rowena screamed, charging at him. Raoul

sidestepped her neatly, ramming his sword through her chest. Fire flared through her entire body. He ripped the steel bloodlessly from her chest.

"Bastard!" she shouted, ignoring the pain to slice across his throat. He staggered back, raising his sword unsteadily to block her next attack.

His next attack was blocked by her wards. The steel rang harmlessly against them as she attacked.

"I . . . am . . . your . . . equal!" she shouted, punctuating each word with a blast of Power and a stroke of her sword. "You have *no right* to speak to me that way, you pig!"

Raoul caught her sword with his own and, with a flip of his wrist, disarmed her. Fear made her hesitate as he rammed his own blade through her wavering wards. Another blast of Power flung her from his blade. She lay on the floor, burning in agony over her entire body.

"Get up, whore," Raoul commanded. The anger that burned through her changed—settled into a cold rage. She was doing this all wrong. She *was* Raoul's equal—in Power. She could make him pay for this!

"*Damn* you," Rowena said, rising to her feet. She reached out, and her sword flew to her hand from across the room. Raoul raised his sword to guard.

Rowena drew from the Cords. Power burned through her as had her anger earlier. She directed it at Raoul in a continuous barrage as she attacked. His blade met hers in a shower of sparks as Power flowed through each sword.

While their swords were locked, Rowena struck his face with the back of her fist. Raoul staggered back a step from the blow that would have removed his head, had he not been warded.

"Pig!" Rowena shouted as she brought her sword down overhand at his head. Raoul blocked it with his own. Rowena stepped forward and kicked up between his legs. She gave him no time to recover. The barrage of Power did not waver, her attacks did not slow.

She forced Raoul across the room, inch by inch. The Power flowed through her like a raging river, maddening her. *Now* she was a goddess—an angry goddess, full of her Power.

"*DIE!*" she screamed, ramming her sword through his torso and into the stone wall behind him. Raoul cried out in pain, but Rowena did not relent. Through the metal blade now buried in his flesh, she poured all the Power she could draw. Raoul screamed in agony and his own sword fell from his grasp.

Then his form vanished like smoke. After all, this had only been a projection. Rowena released the Power, and exhaustion rolled over her. She turned and fell back against the wall, sliding to a sitting position. Then she began to weep.

"That was . . . *much* . . . better," she heard Raoul say. She looked up. Raoul this time—not a shade. He leaned against the doorway, his face ashen. Rowena smiled briefly—she had hurt him.

"I hate you," she said quietly. She turned her face to the corner to hide her tears. She hated Bairn too, for putting her through this—for turning her over to this horrible man.

"I am sorry," Raoul said. "But I had to get you angry. If it means anything, I *never* watched you at Rylur's court."

Rowena turned back to face him. He had walked over and knelt before her. Now he looked more like the Raoul she remembered—tender and concerned.

"It does," Rowena said. "At least there's *one* of Rylur's apprentices I've never whored for."

"Rowena," Raoul said, "if you face another journeyman, an enemy, he will do much worse to you than this."

"I know," Rowena said, turning back to the corner. For a moment, neither spoke as Rowena's tears slowly passed. Finally, she turned back to face him.

"Raoul, how did you get your gold?" she asked. Raoul paused for a moment, surprised by the sudden change in topic.

"I killed a man," he finally said. "One of Cambien's journeymen challenged me to a duel. Why?"

"Before you began training me, I never could have imagined you as a killer," she said. "You always seemed too gentle."

"And now?"

"Now?" Rowena said, smiling wickedly as she climbed to her feet. "Now I can imagine you on a *spit*!"

Raoul smiled, rising to his own feet with the help of the wall. Her earlier pleasure at seeing his weakness was replaced with concern. She reached out to help steady him.

"That shall have to wait for tomorrow, I fear," Raoul said, accepting her assistance. "If you can maintain this level of performance, I shall be recommending you for silver in a few more moons."

"I don't know if I can survive a few more moons," Rowena said.

"Ha!" Raoul exclaimed. "You don't know if *you* will survive?"

Rowena laughed and helped Raoul from the training hall. She looked forward to returning to her husband tonight. He would be proud of her.

"Is Lord Bairn available?" Izabel asked.

"No, Lord Izabel," Hervis replied to the image in the mirror. "He is not in the palace at the moment."

"Have him contact me at his earliest convenience, Journeyman," Izabel said.

"Yes, Lor . . ." Hervis began, but Izabel had already terminated the sending.

Bairn had been gone more often than not during the last year. Even Rowena did not know where he was or what he was about. This worried Hervis, although he was certain there was no cause for alarm. Bairn was undoubtedly about the business of preparing for the coming war.

Hervis and Raoul had each converted scores of caverns into sanctuaries for the populace as part of that preparation. Thousands would be able to escape the devastation within the shelters. Hundreds of thousands would not.

Hervis cleared his mind of such thoughts and focused on the mirror. He formed an image of Bairn in his mind as he directed his Power into the spell on the mirror.

Bairn! he thought, directing his thought into the matrix of Power. He felt a remote, impossibly distant touch with his mind.

"What is it, Hervis?" Bairn's voice asked. Hervis opened his eyes to see Bairn's face in the mirror. Bairn was in what looked like a sitting room, but Hervis did not recognize the furnishings. It was not from Bairnshold unless Bairn had redesigned that palace.

"Lord Izabel has called for you," Hervis said. "She wishes for you to contact her as soon as you are able."

"I shall return immediately," Bairn said. "Thank you, Hervis."

"Yes, Lord," Hervis replied. Bairn's image disappeared from the mirror. Hervis felt the use of Power behind him and rose to face his Lord Magus.

"Did she say what this is about?" Bairn asked.

"She did not say," Hervis replied.

"Very well," Bairn sighed. "Thank you, Hervis."

Hervis bowed and left the room. Bairn had been strange this last year—melancholy. It was almost as if some fire had gone out inside him. He felt it sometimes in Circle when Bairn joined with them. The Lady Rowena, of course, noticed it even more often, but seemed able to offer little solace to her husband.

Hervis needed to speak with Raoul. If anyone besides Rowena could convince Bairn to speak about this, it would be him.

CHAPTER
------- NINETEEN -----------

"MUST WE GO?" Rowena asked.

"You still don't care for Lord Izabel, do you?" Bairn said.

"I do not trust her," Rowena said. "Remember, I know what she wants."

"She didn't get it, though," Bairn said.

"Even so, this is the winter solstice," Rowena said. "If it's anything like Rylur's celebrations . . ."

"I doubt that it will be," Bairn said. "If you become uncomfortable, we will leave."

"Thank you," Rowena said. Bairn reached out and Called to Izabel. He felt the female Lord reach out to him. Bairn reached out to complete the link, and he and Rowena were translocated to her palace.

"Lord Bairn," she said, walking up and embracing him briefly, "how good of you to accept my invitation. Greetings, Lady Rowena."

"Greetings . . . Lord," Rowena said.

"That is a beautiful gown," Izabel said, taking Rowena's arm and leading her from the room as Bairn followed. "Did your master fashion it for you?"

"No, Lord Izabel," Rowena said. "My Lord commissioned his ten best tailors to create it only yesterday."

"Handmade?" Izabel said. "My. So, how does it feel to have a Lord wrapped around your finger?"

"What do you mean?" Rowena said.

"I think she has us on that one, beloved," Bairn said.

"I can tell when a man has lost himself to a woman," Izabel said. "Admit it—he denies you nothing."

"No, he does not," Rowena said, smiling back at Bairn.

"And you are . . . what? Twenty-two? Three?" Izabel said.

"Thirty-eight," Rowena replied. Izabel stopped in the hallway and turned to face Rowena.

"He's keeping you young," Izabel finally said.

"Yes," Rowena replied.

"So much for hoping to outlast you," Izabel said, smiling and taking Rowena's arm again.

"What do you mean?" Rowena said, evenly.

"You *know* he rejected me in favor of you, do you not?" Izabel asked.

"I shamelessly attempted to seduce him on his first visit," she added, dropping her voice to a whisper loud enough for Bairn to hear.

"No, I did not know," Rowena lied, scowling back at Bairn.

"I thought it best not to worry you," Bairn explained. Actually he had told her of the incident, but Rowena apparently did not wish to reveal that to Izabel.

"He thought it best not to get you angry with him, he means," Izabel said.

"Or with you, perhaps," Rowena suggested. Izabel glanced sharply at her. Then she smiled, genuinely amused.

"She is a spirited one, Bairn," Izabel said. "I'm beginning to understand your feelings for her."

"I can only say that you are mistaken as to who is the master," Bairn said, "and who the slave."

"No," Izabel said, smiling back at him, "I think I have deduced who holds what position, if not the title. Come, the feast is waiting."

Bairn had been correct. Lord Izabel's midwinter feast bore little resemblance to similar events at the House of Rylur. Not that there were not plenty of men in attendance. However, over time, the great hall slowly emptied as the men and the apprentices paired off and left for more private environs.

"Well, it seems that we are the only ones remaining," Izabel noted. Only the High Table was still occupied.

"Would you and the Lady Rowena care to join me in the gardens?" Izabel asked.

"I would like to see them," Rowena said. She had become less uncomfortable as the evening had progressed.

"Lord Bairn?" Izabel asked.

"Of course," Bairn replied. They rose from their seats, and Izabel's journeymen took their leave, giving Bairn suspicious glances as they left.

The evening was cool, but not cold. Unlike Rylur's gardens,

Izabel's were exposed to the natural seasons, mild as they were in these lands. Inside the marble pavilion, however, the temperature was quite warm, although the breezes were still cool.

To the west, the sky burned the brilliant red of sunset. Shadows fell across the garden as the sun slipped below the horizon and the stars slowly appeared in the sky.

"Your gardens are very beautiful, Lord Izabel," Rowena said.

"Thank you," Izabel said. "They are beautiful at night, too, when the moon is out. Unfortunately, there is no moon tonight. Perhaps your Lord will bring you back to see them."

"If she wishes," Bairn said.

"Next full moon, then?" Izabel said to Rowena.

"If my Lord is not busy," Rowena said.

"Can you two ever make a decision, or do you just constantly defer to one another?" Izabel asked. Bairn laughed.

"Next full moon is fine," he said.

"Excellent," Izabel said. "Shall we retire to my sitting room for some mulled wine before you leave?"

"That sounds perfect," Bairn said.

"I had this one commissioned over a hundred years ago," Izabel said. She was showing off the tapestries in her sitting room to Rowena. This one was of Izabel's palace as seen from the gardens.

"It's beautiful," Rowena said.

"He was a wonderful artisan," Izabel said. "I have some more by him in my chambers. Would you like to see them?"

"I suppose," Rowena said.

"This way," Izabel said. Bairn began to follow them.

"No," Izabel said, turning and placing a hand on his chest. "You do not get to see these, my Lord. Not unless you change your mind regarding my offer. Stay here and enjoy your wine. We'll be back in a moment. Come, Rowena."

Rowena glanced back to Bairn, who smiled and nodded to her. She followed Izabel into her chambers. The Lord's bed was immense. Her eye fell on the tapestries adorning the room. All were rather . . . erotic depictions of the Lord herself.

"Oh, my," Rowena said.

"Now you know why I didn't want Bairn to see them," Izabel said. Rowena walked up to the closest one and studied it for a moment. In the tapestry, Izabel reclined back among cushions on the bed, nude, while nude male servants served her wine and grapes. The Lord was undeniably beautiful, as was the workmanship itself.

"What are you thinking?" Izabel asked.

"I am thinking how much my Lord must love me," Rowena answered, "to have refused someone so beautiful."

"Oh," Izabel said. Something in her voice made Rowena turn to look at her. The Lord's olive skin had flushed dark.

"You know," Izabel said, stammering a little at first, "I've been admiring that gown all night. Green is most definitely your color. I have something that would go *very* well with that." She went over to a large chest against one of the walls.

"Oh, I couldn't," Rowena began.

"Nonsense!" Izabel said. "Of course you can."

She removed a necklace fashioned of emeralds from the bureau. The center stone, cut flat, was easily the size of a hen's egg.

"Oh!" Rowena said.

"Still want to say no?" Izabel said, smiling mischievously. "This should look wonderful on that creamy skin of yours. Let me fasten it."

She stepped forward and reached around Rowena to fasten the necklace. It was practically an embrace, as the Lord looked behind Rowena's shoulder to fasten the clasp. Rowena trembled only partly from fear as Izabel's fingers caressed her neck.

"Of course," Izabel whispered in her ear, "it would be more beautiful if you were . . ."

Izabel's words stopped abruptly as she stepped back and stared at the necklace. Her expression was one of astonishment. Rowena glanced down at the necklace. It was beautiful, and glowed with its own green light—magic.

". . . gifted," Izabel finished. Astonishment was replaced with anger. Eyes burning with rage, Izabel turned and stormed from the room.

"Lord Izabel?" Rowena called, running after her.

Bairn looked up to see Lord Izabel march into the sitting room, followed by Rowena. Izabel headed directly for him, sheer hatred burning in her eyes. He hurriedly rose to his feet.

"Lord Izabel?" he said. "What is wrong . . . ?"

She slapped him across the face—hard.

"You bastard!" she said. "How *dare* you?"

"How dare I *what*?" Bairn asked. "What has happened?"

"How *dare* you enslave one of the gifted to sate your male desires *in our lands*?" Izabel demanded. "How *dare* you parade *my sister* in chains in *my House*? How *dare* you *flaunt* her in my presence? I should kill you where you stand, you *animal*!"

"*No*!" Rowena shouted, throwing herself between Izabel and Bairn.

"Rowena!" Bairn said, trying to push her away. "Don't . . ."

Rowena wrapped her arms around Bairn with the strength of desperation. She glared back at Izabel.

"You shall have to kill me as well!" Rowena said.

"Don't you see that he has you spelled?" Izabel said. "Bound to his will. Is that not your law, Bairn?"

"There are no spells on Rowena," Bairn said. "Her mind is her own."

"*Liar*!"

"It is true," Bairn said. "See for yourself. I only ask that you do not read her thoughts."

Izabel looked at Rowena, and Bairn felt the Lord probe her mind, searching for signs of tampering. After a moment, Izabel looked back to Bairn.

"It is true," she said. "You have kept this secret?"

"No one else knows," Bairn replied.

"You defy your own laws?"

"I could not do that to her," Bairn explained.

"You love her?"

"I do."

"If you truly love her," Izabel said, "you will give her to me and let me teach her. Let her have her destiny."

"No!" Rowena said.

"If she chooses to stay with you, I will not refuse her," Bairn said.

"Bairn!" Rowena said. "No! I love you. Do not send me away."

"I will not if you do not want to go," Bairn said.

"I don't!"

"Lord Izabel," Bairn said, "I insist that you honor Rowena's desires in this matter."

"I insist the same," Izabel said. "If she changes her mind in the future, will you give her to me then?"

"I will."

"You love him enough to throw away your future?" Izabel asked.

"He *is* my future," Rowena replied.

Izabel looked to Bairn, something akin to sorrow in her eyes.

"Lord Bairn, I apologize for striking you," she said.

"It is forgotten," Bairn said.

"I am . . . very tired," Izabel said. "Please . . . excuse me."

"Izabel," Bairn said, letting go of Rowena and reaching out.

"*Please*," Izabel said, throwing up her hands. "Just . . . go."

"Bairn," Rowena said in a whisper. "You cannot help her. We should go."

"Goodbye, Lord Izabel," Bairn said.

"Don't forget," Izabel said, regaining a little of her composure. "You are coming back on the moon."

"We won't forget," Rowena assured her. Then Bairn translocated them both home.

"I don't understand why she was so upset at the end," Bairn said once they were alone in their own rooms. "She knew you were free."

"We showed her what love is," Rowena explained. "And she now knows that she has no one who loves her."

Izabel spent midwinter's night alone. At a snap of her fingers, she could have any number of men, or women, to service her. But which among them would throw themselves between her and another Lord in a useless gesture of defiance? Which among them would die *eagerly* in her defense? Not one.

And which one of them would she hand over to another Lord if he wished it? Would she step aside to give one of them a life of his own choosing? Would she defy the laws of her own Council on their behalf?

She would not. They were possessions, not equals. But Bairn had taken a possession and made her an equal.

I have loved someone who was my equal, he had said one night, almost two years ago. He had been speaking of another, long lost, but it was true of Rowena as well. She was not his equal in Power, but he was still enslaved to her charms.

Izabel had tasted his lips that night, two years ago. She had felt his heart pound against her breast. She had felt her own heart pound in response to his kiss. The forbidden kiss of an equal, freely given.

To love him, could she walk away from everything? Turn down the Power that she had offered Rowena without even a moment's hesitation? To simply say, "No, this is more important?"

To her surprise, part of her claimed that it could do exactly that. That *any* price would be worth it if he looked into her eyes just once the way he had looked into Rowena's.

"Damn you, Bairn!" she whispered to her empty room.

"We welcome our sister on this night," Bairn said to the gathered apprentices. "To bestow upon her the final badge of rank that may be earned through study. Know all in this room that this woman speaks with my voice. She is my right hand, my shield and my sword. To defy her is to defy me."

Rowena stood before the assembled apprentices in her new silver belt. Bairn had hurriedly gathered the House to witness Rowena's ascension to second order. It seemed prudent after the events at Lord Izabel's House earlier this evening.

"Let all swear allegiance to my journeyman as they have to me," Bairn commanded. One at a time, the other apprentices filed past, kneeling before Rowena and pledging their loyalty to her as they had before to Bairn.

"Congratulations, beloved," Bairn told her.

"Thank you," Rowena said. "I know we had to do this tonight, but can we go to bed now?"

"We can," Bairn said.

"Izabel, you should have told me of this *immediately*!" Ethenia said.

"I know," Izabel said. "I was too upset, Ethenia."

"I understand," she said, more softly. "It is *very* upsetting news. To think of that . . . *man* keeping one of us prisoner in our own lands!"

"He did not know, Ethenia," Izabel lied. "*I* did not know until I put the necklace on her."

"He did not surrender her, either, though," Ethenia said. "You should *never* have let him take her back to his fortress."

"Are you telling me that I should have attacked a northern Lord without permission?" Izabel asked.

"I . . . suppose not," Ethenia said. "You are right. I wish you had thought to contact me last night."

"Ethenia, she told him that she wanted to stay with him," Izabel said. "He offered to leave her with me *if* she wanted to stay. She did not."

"Do you expect a child to understand what's at stake here?" Ethenia asked.

"What are you going to do?" Izabel asked.

"He thinks the matter is settled?" Ethenia asked.

"He does."

"In that case, I have time to call an emergency meeting of the Council," Ethenia said. "We are going to *demand* that he surrender Rowena to us."

"And if he refuses?"

"Then we shall take her by force," Ethenia said. "I will see you in Council."

Ethenia's image vanished from the mirror. Izabel bit her lower lip. She had not expected this. She should have, however. Her own reaction last night should have told her what to expect. Oh, Lords! What was she going to do?

There was only one thing she *could* do. She faced the mirror and focused her Power.

Bairn!

"Lord," Hervis called through the door. "Lord Izabel is asking to speak with you and the Lady Rowena."

"Oh, gods," Bairn said, forcing his eyes open. It had been a long night.

Is it even dawn yet? he wondered.

"Yes, Lord," Hervis replied.

"Quit eavesdropping," Bairn grumbled, climbing from bed. Rowena was already up and dressing. Bairn simply used the Power to gather his clothes and groom himself, as well as to wipe the fuzziness from his mind. Rowena followed him out into the sitting room.

"Bairn, Rowena!" Izabel said from the mirror. "I'm so sorry!"

"That's all right," Bairn said. "I needed to get up anyway."

"No!" Izabel said. "I told Ethenia about Rowena."

"What?" Bairn said.

"I'm taking a terrible risk, talking to you," Izabel said. "Ethenia is calling an emergency meeting of the Council. They're going to take Rowena by force."

"No!" Bairn said.

"I'm sorry," Izabel said. She was actually crying. "I didn't know Ethenia would react this way."

"I believe you, Izabel," Bairn assured her.

"You have to leave."

"I can't do that."

"You have to!" Izabel said. "At least send Rowena back north. You can't fight all of us."

"I'll try to send her to safety," Bairn lied.

"Bairn?"

"Yes?"

"I . . . I have to leave now."

"Go," Bairn said. "Don't risk discovery. Thank you for your help."

Izabel hesitated.

"Is there something else?" Bairn asked.

"Yes," Izabel said.

"What?"

"I . . . I think I love you," she said. Then she was gone, leaving Bairn staring slack-jawed at his own reflection.

"Considering the risk she just took, I think she's right," Rowena said coolly. Bairn laughed, eliciting a glare from Rowena.

"It's *funny* that she loves you?" Rowena asked icily. "That she just risked her life for you?"

"No!" Bairn said. "This is *it*!"

"What?" Rowena asked.

"*This* is what starts it all!" Bairn said. "*I* don't start the war—*you* do! They're going to war over you."

"I'm not leaving without you," Rowena said.

"No," Bairn said, "you have to stay for this to work. I have to contact Raoul."

Bairn focused on the mirror. Soon Raoul's image appeared within.

"Yes, Lord," Raoul said.

"It is time," Bairn said. Raoul paled visibly in the mirror.

"Make *all* of the arrangements," Bairn continued. "I'm counting on you."

"Yes, Lord!" Raoul said. His image vanished from the mirror.

"We . . . are not leaving?" Hervis asked.

"No, Hervis, we are not," Bairn said. "We are going to blow this incident completely out of proportion. Contrary to Lord Izabel's belief, we *can* withstand the entire Southern Alliance—at least for a few days."

"We can?" Hervis said.

"We can," Bairn assured him.

"What do we do now?" Rowena asked.

"We wait," Bairn replied. "When Ethenia sends for us, remember that we know nothing of what is happening."

"I wish that were true," Hervis said.

All over the world, they slipped quietly from the cities and towns. A few at a time, gathering in the secret places that had been prepared for them. They brought nothing but what they could carry, secure in the knowledge that everything else would be provided for them.

Soon, the MageLords would go to war. The end of the world was at hand. However, they did not fear—Bairn would watch over them. Forever.

"Lord Bairn," Hervis said. "High Lord Ethenia wishes to speak with you at once."

"Thank you, Hervis," Bairn replied. He walked into the sitting room and sat down in the sending chair. He took a deep breath before he activated the mirror. This conversation would demand a performance equal to that of the best player of Rylur's court.

Ethenia did not look at all pleased when Bairn activated the mirror.

"Good morning, High Lord," Bairn said. "How may I be of service?"

"Lord Bairn," Ethenia said, "you are to surrender the woman Rowena into my custody immediately."

Bairn allowed the smile to vanish from his face.

"I beg your pardon?" he replied icily.

"I realize that you were not aware that she was gifted when

you brought her to our lands,'' Ethenia said. Apparently Izabel had not told Ethenia *everything* she had learned.

''However,'' Ethenia continued, ''it is unconscionable for you to keep one of our sisters as a *pet* in our own lands.''

''I thought this matter was settled between Lord Izabel and myself last night,'' Bairn said. ''I see that I was mistaken.''

''Will you surrender Rowena to us?'' Ethenia asked.

''I will not,'' Bairn replied. ''She does not wish to leave. I promised Izabel that if Rowena ever changed her mind, I would allow her to leave. That will have to be sufficient.''

''Lord Bairn,'' Ethenia said, ''if you do not surrender our sister to us, we shall have no choice but to take her from you by force.''

''Are you *truly* prepared to go to war over this matter, High Lord?'' Bairn asked. ''That *is* what you are risking here.''

''Together we are powerful enough to destroy your wards and take the woman without causing serious harm to your person,'' Ethenia said. ''I doubt your northern masters will go to war with us over that. I give you one last opportunity to release her willingly.''

''I refuse,'' Bairn said. ''Rowena and I would rather die than be separated.''

Bairn terminated the link and activated the spell that would bring the gold reservoir into contact with the defenses of his palace. A translucent silver sphere formed instantly around the entirety of his lands.

Seconds after the wards were erected, they were bombarded with considerable force. Bairn estimated that at least three, perhaps more, of the Great Houses had joined in this attack. With what the Southern Alliance knew of his resources, his wards should have collapsed instantly. They did not so much as waver.

There was a pause after the attack. No doubt the southern Lords were taking new stock of the situation. Bairn should *not* have been able to resist such an attack.

A moment later, another stronger attack struck his wards with an equal lack of effect. There was no pause this time. Another bolt struck, followed by another and yet another. For almost an hour the barrage continued. Then, as suddenly as it had begun, the attack was over.

Bairn felt a sending. He activated the mirror. Ethenia glared at him.

"What do you have in there?" she demanded. "You were only authorized *one* journeyman."

"And that is all I have," Bairn lied. Ethenia could not truth-spell him over a sending.

"That and the largest Power reservoir you have ever seen," Bairn added. "My staff and I have been filling it *for two years*!"

This was, of course, not true. However, it was a plausible explanation. Ethenia would believe him.

"That is impossible!" Ethenia said, but Bairn noted that she had paled at his announcement. "Such a reservoir would overload!"

"Not if you spread it out over half a square mile," Bairn countered. "Ask Lord Cambien how I used such a reservoir to erect a fortress within his lands with no detectable use of the Power. Do you *still* believe you can break through my wards, High Lord?"

"You are forcing us to destroy you!" Ethenia said.

"You are welcome to try, High Lord," Bairn said.

"Fool!" Ethenia shouted. "This could cost Rowena her life as well!"

"Rowena has told me that she would rather die than be taken from me," Bairn said. "Even if you take her, she will probably take her own life."

"On your own head be it," Ethenia said, breaking the link.

Bairn used the mirror to observe outside his palace. A ward around his own wards prevented him from seeing beyond them. The Southern Alliance had cut him off from the outside world. The attack resumed, but much reduced in Power. Only one House, Bairn guessed—trying to slowly wear down his wards. No doubt the other Houses would relieve each other during the attack.

That was fine with Bairn. At this rate, it would take them *moons* to break through. There was a standard reservoir that acted as a buffer between the gold reservoir and the defenses. That reservoir was now being fed by Hervis, Rowena and his entire staff, extending his reserves.

Bairn rose from the sending chair. It was time for him to take his post in the war room. Three combat couches, each with its own array of observation mirrors, shared the war room. As in his original fortress, each chair contained control balls that linked to the defensive spells of the fortress and to the reservoir.

In this battle, though, they only had to feed the reservoir and wait. Bairn settled into his chair and smiled over at Rowena. She smiled back, worry plain in her face.

The waiting would be the hard part.

Chapter
------- Twenty -----------

Lord Janis was concerned. In two years, Lord Bairn had never missed a daily report. Janis was given notice of Bairn's reports every day by his personal staff.

Today, instead, he had received notice that Bairn had *not* reported yesterday. Furthermore, this morning, when the third-rank apprentice in charge had realized that a report was overdue, he had attempted to contact Bairn's House in the Southern Alliance. There had been no response.

There *was* a response from Lord Imelia's House, however. The ambassador from the Southern Alliance greeted him warmly.

"Good morning, High Lord," Imelia said. "How may I be of service to you?"

"Good morrow, Lord Imelia," Janis said. "I am hoping that you can explain to me why I have been unable to contact Lord Bairn. He did not report in yesterday, nor have we heard from him today. Our sendings go unanswered."

"Oh dear," Imelia said. "I . . . do not know, High Lord." She *sounded* concerned, but the bitch was a better player than many who had performed in Janis's own court.

"Will you please make inquiries and report back to me?" Janis said. "If I have not heard from you in one hour, I shall contact you again."

"Of course, High Lord," Imelia replied.

Janis did not have to wait long. Scarcely five minutes had passed when Imelia sent back to him. Janis activated the sending mirror.

"I am afraid that I have . . . bad news, High Lord," Imelia began.

"What is it?" Janis asked.

"Lord Bairn is . . . under siege," Imelia said. Janis waited for a moment before replying.

"I sincerely hope that you have an explanation for this," he said calmly and evenly. Many had come to learn that this tone, more than any other, heralded the High Lord's anger.

"I do," Imelia said. "Lord Bairn is holding one of our sisters in bondage within his fortress. We have demanded that he release her to us, and he has refused."

"Are you saying that Lord Bairn has kidnapped one of your women?" Janis asked. He would not have thought Bairn that stupid.

"No," Imelia said. "He brought the woman from his own lands. However, it was discovered that she has the Gift. Our laws do not permit her to be held against her will. She must be apprenticed."

"So you told Lord Bairn that he had to give his woman to you, and when he refused to turn over his property, you *attacked* him?" Janis asked.

"She is *not* property!" Imelia said. "She is gifted."

"And she is his legal property under our laws!" Janis shouted.

"Not under ours!" Imelia said. "And this is occurring within our lands."

"*You* reside in our lands," Janis said. "It is our law that all gifted females must be bound to a Lord or killed. Would *you* submit to *that* law?"

"I most certainly would not!" Imelia said.

"Then I suggest that you contact your High Lord and rethink your position on this matter," Janis said. "We have both made exceptions to our laws to allow our ambassadors to reside in one another's lands."

"You have a point," Imelia said. "I will do so at once, High Lord."

"In the meantime," Janis added, "I demand that communication between Lord Bairn and myself be restored at once. Do not force us to take action on this matter, Lord Imelia."

"I shall have an answer for you within the hour, High Lord," Imelia replied coolly.

"See that you do," Janis said, breaking the link.

Only women would start a war over something as ridiculous *as this*, Janis thought. Still, it was impressive that Bairn had held out for two days against the entire Southern Alliance. He was going to have to learn how Bairn had managed this.

• • •

Bairn felt the telltale call of a sending. He directed it to the central mirror of his battle couch. Lord Janis's face filled the mirror.

"Lord Janis!" Bairn said. "I have been unable to reach you."

"Bairn, what the *hell* is going on down there?" Janis demanded.

"I am under attack," Bairn said.

"I *know* that!" Janis said. "How did this happen?"

"Lord Izabel discovered that Rowena was gifted," Bairn said. "Quite by accident, I must add. I did not know of it myself. Her Gift is *extremely* weak."

"And you refused to surrender her?" Janis asked.

"Actually, I offered to give her to them if *she* were willing to go," Bairn replied. "She stated that she preferred to remain with me. In my mind, that settles the matter. Rowena is my property."

"Rowena turned down an apprenticeship to stay with you?" Janis asked.

"She did," Bairn said.

"I can certainly understand why you would want to keep that one, then," Janis said. "Still, would it not be wiser to surrender her? Is any female worth starting a war over?"

"Of course not," Bairn replied. "But they did not give me the luxury of debate. They demanded that I turn her over, and when I refused, they attacked without delay."

"So, you *are* willing to give her up?" Janis asked.

"I do not think that we should capitulate at this point, Lord," Bairn said.

"Why not?"

"If this matter had been handled civilly, I would have been amenable to surrendering Rowena to them," Bairn explained. "It was not, however. Do we truly want to establish a precedent of yielding to force?"

"No," Janis said without pause. "We most certainly do not."

"Before this matter escalated, I agreed that, if Rowena should ever change her mind, I would give her up to them," Bairn added. "I think that should be our position at this point, which would mean not binding her as our law normally requires. I believe that is all the compromise we can afford now that they have attacked our sovereignty."

"I knew I shouldn't have listened to what these idiot women

were telling me,'' Janis said. ''They had me half convinced that you had gone mad and were being completely unreasonable.''

''I have refrained from counterattack to prevent this matter from escalating further,'' Bairn replied. ''I think that goes *beyond* reasonableness.''

''It does indeed,'' Janis agreed.

''What are your orders, High Lord?'' Bairn asked.

''Can you hold out for much longer?'' Janis asked.

''At this rate, I could hold out for another moon,'' Bairn said.

''You jest.''

''I am quite serious, High Lord,'' Bairn assured him. ''Their attack is not intense. I would estimate that only a single House is attacking my wards.''

''Would you care to explain how you can hold out so easily against an entire House?'' Janis said.

''It is simplicity itself, High Lord,'' Bairn said. ''Knowing that I was among enemies, I built a reservoir beneath all of my lands here. My staff and I have been quietly filling it for these past two years.''

Janis's eyes widened, and then a slow smile crept across his face.

''Lords, Bairn!'' he said. ''Rylur told me you were a cunning bastard. Well done!''

''Thank you, High Lord.''

''Since you are in no immediate danger, which must infuriate them to no end, I will convene the Court and we will decide how to proceed on this matter,'' Lord Janis said. ''Carry on, Lord Bairn.''

''As you command, High Lord,'' Bairn said.

Once Janis had terminated the link, Bairn, Hervis and Rowena were free to finally laugh. Both alliances were playing directly into their plan.

''We are one step closer,'' Bairn said. ''It should not be long now.''

That thought brought an end to their laughter.

Lord Janis again sent to Lord Imelia. He had a move to play that might gain Bairn some more time before he called the Court together.

''Yes, High Lord?'' Imelia said.

''Lord Bairn is not merely under siege,'' Lord Janis said to her. "He is under *attack*! I demand that the barrage be halted while our respective Courts negotiate on this matter. Otherwise, we have nothing to negotiate and this will be considered an act of war."

"I will get back with you, *immediately*, High Lord," Imelia assured him. She broke the link. Almost immediately she contacted him again.

"The attack has been halted, High Lord," Lord Imelia told him. "But the wards remain in place. High Lord Ethenia says that she is very pleased that you are willing to discuss this matter."

"Tell Lord Ethenia that I am extremely *displeased* that she authorized an attack against our ambassador without attempting to negotiate with us first," Janis told her. "This entire incident could have been avoided with a little thought. I am convening the Court. Please be prepared to join us if necessary."

"I await your convenience, High Lord," Lord Imelia said.

That's one *good thing about all this,* Janis thought. *The damned bitch is showing some respect for a change.*

"They have done *what*?" Rylur shouted above the din of the assembled Lords.

"Please!" Lord Janis shouted. "Please! Let me speak!"

The commotion in the courtroom slowly subsided. Janis spoke once order had been restored.

"Lord Bairn is in no immediate danger," Lord Janis assured them.

"Only because he is a brilliant strategist," Rylur said. "If he had not crafted that immense reservoir, they would have overwhelmed him. Lord Janis, this is nothing short of an outright act of war against a member of our Alliance!"

"We *knew* that we were placing Lord Bairn at risk," Janis reminded the assembled Lords. "He knew this as well. *He* is not demanding that we go to war in his rescue. He has suggested what I feel is an acceptable compromise, *if* we can convince the Southern Alliance to accept his proposal."

"What is this compromise?" Rylur asked.

"That the Lady Rowena be given the right to choose whether or not she wishes to become an apprentice in the Southern Alliance," Lord Janis said. "She has *already* chosen not to do so."

"In that case, how will the Southern Alliance see this as a compromise?" Lord Shaun asked.

"We will propose that Rowena be exempted from the law requiring her to be bound to Bairn's will," Janis explained. "If, in the future, she decides to accept their offer after all, she will be allowed to do so. We will also assure them that no other women with the Gift will be taken into their lands."

"Lord Bairn proposed this?" Rylur asked.

"He did," Janis replied.

"Well, it *is* his property that is in question," Rylur said. "If he finds such a situation acceptable, I will support such a proposal. However, I think we should also demand reparations for the attack itself."

"What kind of reparations do you have in mind?" Janis asked.

"Perhaps we should demand an increase in the size of Bairn's staff with no corresponding increase in the staff of their ambassador," Rylur suggested. "After all, *we* have not attacked their ambassador. Perhaps two third-rank apprentices?"

"I do not think they will agree to that," Janis said.

"Well, just tell them we want reparations," Rylur said. "Let *them* suggest something."

"Then let us vote on the matter," Janis said. "All in favor of this position?"

The vote was unanimous. Rowena would be left with the freedom of choice—something unprecedented in their history. Still, it was only one woman, and one with a rather weak Gift at that, if Bairn were correct.

"Thank you, Lords," Janis said to them. "I will summon you again if the situation changes. Return to your kingdoms and prepare for the worst."

"This is unacceptable!" Ethenia told the assembly of Lords. "The woman Rowena must be freed. We have agreed to stop the barrage, but we must not allow these men to keep our sister imprisoned! The siege must continue until our sister is released!"

"High Lord, she does not *want* to be released!" Izabel said. "If the Northern Alliance has offered to give her the freedom to choose now, and in the future, I think we should accept that rather than risk war with the North!"

"Despite their posturing, they will not go to war over this," Ethenia said.

"Are you so certain?" Izabel asked.

"Yes!" Ethenia said. "Lord Imelia has assured me that they are as anxious to avoid war as we. So long as we do not actually *harm* Lord Bairn, they should refrain from outright attack. Let us see how long he can bear his confinement."

"That could take years!" Izabel said. "Is the House of Naomi prepared to spend all of its resources maintaining the ward around Lord Bairn's estate for so long?"

"We are not," Naomi responded. "High Lord, some compromise must be reached."

"We must maintain the siege during our negotiations, at the very least," Ethenia said. "Each Great House can maintain the ward for one day, in order of rank. Lords, would that be acceptable until this situation is resolved?"

"I would find that acceptable," Naomi said.

"Lord Izabel," Ethenia said, "will your House assume the task of maintaining the wards surrounding the estate of Lord Bairn for the next day?"

"I would remind the High Lord that we have not yet voted on the proposal from the Northern Alliance," Izabel said. "If it is accepted by this Council, there will be no need to maintain the ward, and this dangerous situation will have passed. I call for a vote!"

Ethenia glared at Izabel. Izabel returned her gaze unflinching. No matter what came of this vote, Izabel had lost a friend, and an ally, here today.

"I too, call for a vote," Naomi said. "However, I wish to vote on the two portions of their proposal separately. I do not like this talk of 'reparations.' "

"We must vote on the entire proposal," Ethenia said. "They will not give us one without the other. All Houses in favor of acceptance, so signify."

Izabel's heart fell at the response. The voting globes illuminated above far less than half the assembly. She noted that Naomi did not vote in favor of acceptance. How many others had been swayed by that one point in the proposal? Ethenia had played this board well.

"All Houses opposed?" Ethenia asked, smiling. It was clear that the proposal had been rejected.

"The vote is taken," Ethenia said. "Twenty-three Houses in favor of acceptance. Sixty-one opposed. The proposal from the Northern Alliance is rejected."

Ethenia turned to face Izabel, smiling.

"I ask again, Lord Izabel," Ethenia said. "Will your House assume the task of maintaining the siege for another day?"

"We shall," Izabel said, "if the House of Lilith will pledge to assume that task at the end of that time."

"We will so pledge," Lord Lilith announced.

"Lord Naomi," Ethenia said, "the House of Izabel will take over the siege at midnight tonight. This Council is dismissed."

Izabel took careful note of which Houses had voted in favor of the proposal. They did not have much time to reverse this decision. Unlike Ethenia, Izabel was not so confident this would not lead to war.

"They rejected the proposal?" Rylur asked. The Lords had been reassembled less than twelve hours after their last session.

"Completely," Lord Janis replied. "They will settle for nothing less than the surrender of the woman."

"Who do these women think they are dealing with?" Rylur said. "We offered them a *significant* compromise! They do *not* dictate terms to us!"

"Rylur, please calm yourself," Janis said.

"*Calm* myself?" Rylur said. "These women are holding one of us prisoner, and they ignore us as if we were of no consequence. Each moment we allow them to attack us in this manner tells them we are weak and will not act to defend one of our own."

"Do you want to go to *war* over this, Rylur?" Janis asked.

"I doubt they would go to war if we were to simply rescue our people," Rylur said.

"What are you suggesting?"

"We know that only one House is holding Bairn imprisoned in his fortress," Rylur said. "It would be a simple matter for our combined Power to break that ward. That would allow Bairn to escape to his lands within our borders and put an *end* to this crisis."

"They might counterattack without realizing that Lord Bairn's estate was our only target," Janis said. "After all, they would only know that a powerful attack was being launched—not at *whom.*''

''Perhaps the *threat* of such action would be sufficient,'' Lord Cambien suggested. ''We could tell them that unless Lord Bairn and his house are released within twenty-four hours, we will act to rescue him.''

''That could work,'' Rylur said. ''High Lord, what do you think?''

''I think we should not make threats that we are not prepared to back up,'' Janis said. ''Are we prepared to *take* such action after the elapsed time?''

''They would know where the attack was directed,'' Rylur said. ''It would be better than making the attack without warning.''

''I think this course of action is ill-advised,'' Janis warned. ''This could trigger a full war with the Southern Alliance. Are we prepared for that?''

''We cannot do *nothing*!'' Rylur said. ''If we do nothing, they will assault us the next time it suits their whim. We will have shown them that they can do so without consequence. We *must* act!''

''I agree with Lord Rylur,'' Cambien said. ''Put it to vote, High Lord.''

''Very well,'' Janis sighed. ''All those in favor of threatening action against the siege, please signify.''

Janis counted the vote. Fifty-seven Houses voted in favor of the proposition, carrying it easily. Only thirty-one, including Bairn's lot which Janis cast himself, were opposed.

''The proposal is accepted,'' Janis said. ''Lords, may I ask you to remain in attendance while I confer with Lord Ethenia of the Southern Alliance?''

Gradually, the information came back to Izabel. Enough Houses would change their vote, *if* the Northern Alliance would drop its demand of reparations, to accept the proposal. The margin was narrow—two Houses—but it was enough.

Now the problem was how to get this information to the Northern Alliance. She could contact Imelia, but Izabel was doubtful of the ambassador's assistance. Imelia was very much Ethenia's creature. Rumor had it that the two had even been lovers while Imelia had been apprenticed to the High Lord. Izabel dared not trust her.

Nor did she know how to contact the Northern Alliance directly. That knowledge was limited to the High Lord alone. Whom could she trust?

"My Lord," her ranking journeyman said, interrupting her thoughts, "it is almost time for us to assume the wards."

"What?" Izabel said. "Oh, of course! See to it, Felicia."

"Yes, Lord," Felicia replied.

That was her answer. Bairn could tell her how to contact his High Lord directly.

Bairn directed the sending to his central mirror and was very surprised to see Izabel's face appear within it.

"Lord Izabel?" he asked.

"Bairn!" she said. "We have arrived at a compromise that the Council will accept. But I have to contact your High Lord secretly to let him know exactly *which* compromise he should propose for us to vote upon. Ethenia has gone mad. She's leading us right into war. Can you tell me how to contact your Council?"

"I . . . can," Bairn replied. For the life of him, he could think of no plausible means to avoid granting her request. *Damn!*

"You have secretly gathered the support for this compromise?" he asked.

"I have," Izabel said.

"I am . . . impressed," Bairn said. Dismayed was more like it.

"You can tell me how impressed you are later," Izabel replied, smiling. "How do I contact them?"

Bairn gave her the sending codes to communicate directly with Lord Janis. Once she had broken the link, he was silent for a moment.

"That woman might destroy everything we're trying to do," he said.

"She means well," Rowena assured him.

"High Lord," Journeyman Evan said.

"What is it, Evan?" Janis asked. He had long ago given up on getting any rest tonight. The situation was far too tense. He had long forgotten the taste of fear, but was learning it all over again. Ethenia had blatantly stated that any attempt to free Bairn would be treated as a direct attack against their lands and responded to accordingly.

War. It was beginning to seem as though there would be no way out of it, and once it occurred, none of them would survive it—North or South.

"A Lord Izabel of the Southern Alliance wishes to speak with you," Evan replied. Janis looked up in surprise. Had Ethenia been removed?

"Izabel?" Janis asked. Wasn't that the woman who had started this whole mess? Hadn't Bairn said that she was amenable to compromise?

"High Lord," Evan said, "she called using Lord Bairn's code. She says that it is *most* urgent."

She was using Bairn's identification code? That had to mean this communication was unofficial. Janis quickly rose to his feet, hoping against hope that he was about to be given a way out.

Lord Izabel leaned back in her sending chair. It was done. High Lord Janis had been almost eager to accept her proposal. It would be transmitted, via Imelia, and then Ethenia would have to call them to vote on the proposal. Then this madness would finally be over.

The summons came within the hour. Izabel checked herself in the mirror and quickly translocated to the Council chamber.

"Forty-one Houses vote in favor of the proposal," Ethenia announced. "Forty-three are opposed. The proposal is rejected!"

Izabel felt as though a giant hand were squeezing her chest. They had rejected the proposal? She looked over to the tables of the four Lords who had switched their votes. None met her gaze.

Why? Izabel wondered.

"Now *I* have a matter to bring before this body," Ethenia announced. "It seems that at least one of us is collaborating with the enemy!"

Lords! Izabel thought, as a gasp of astonishment swept the Council chamber. Surely Ethenia was not *serious*?

"Lord Izabel!" Ethenia said. "Lord Naomi! The two of you spent the entire night gathering support for this proposal—*before it was proposed!* I, and I'm certain this Council, would be *very* interested in learning how you knew of this."

Izabel rose to her feet.

"Since when does negotiation constitute collaboration?" she asked.

"Do you have something to tell us, Lord Izabel?" Ethenia asked.

"I do," Izabel said. "You can leave Lord Naomi out of this. *I* contacted the Northern Alliance."

"You contacted the Northern Alliance in violation of *my* authority!" Ethenia accused.

"Yes!" Izabel said. "It seemed prudent since you seem determined to go to war over a woman who *does not want our help*!"

"Since Lord Izabel does not seem to have any desire to hide her offense," Ethenia said, "I propose to this Council that she be barred from casting her lot among us for a period of one year."

Izabel reeled from the proposal. Barred from voting in the Council? This could not be happening!

Could I walk away from everything? she remembered thinking. It seemed that she just had.

"Does anyone have anything to say before we vote on this censure?" Ethenia asked.

"I do!" Izabel said.

"What, Lord Izabel?" Ethenia said, with a groan. She was playing this for blood. However, so was Izabel at this point.

"*I challenge you!*" Izabel shouted.

"W-what?" Ethenia said.

"I challenge you for the High Seat!" Izabel repeated. "All voting, all actions from this Council are hereby suspended until the outcome of my challenge!"

"You cannot challenge me during a crisis!" Ethenia objected. Lord Naomi stood to interrupt.

"Our law does not state such," she said. "You must accept the challenge or step down as High Lord. Are you prepared to step down, Lord Ethenia?"

"I most certainly am *not*!" Ethenia replied.

"Then you must accept Lord Izabel's challenge," Naomi insisted.

"Very well," Ethenia said. "This Council will reconvene in twelve hours to witness the challenge."

Ethenia walked over to Izabel's table as the other Lords departed. Izabel fought not to tremble as the High Lord approached. When they had battled as friends, Ethenia had *always* won. The High Lord leaned over the rail to whisper to Izabel.

"I," Ethenia whispered, "am going to strip you of Power and turn you into a sex-crazed harlot. Then I'm going to send you north. We'll see how much you like these northern Lords then."

"Thank you for the idea, Ethenia," Izabel hissed in response. Ethenia smiled coldly and then turned to walk away.

"You will triumph, Lord," Felicia assured her.

"I fear not," Izabel said. "But I have bought us some time. Felicia, promise me something."

"What?"

"If I lose," Izabel said, "promise me that you will kill me before she has a chance to do otherwise."

"Lord!"

"Promise me!"

"I . . . I swear it, Lord."

Chapter
------ Twenty-One ----------

"Is the challenger present?" Lord Naomi asked. As Lord of the highest-ranking House in the Council, it had fallen to her to oversee the challenge.

"I am," Izabel replied.

"Is the High Lord prepared to meet the challenger?" Naomi asked.

"I am prepared," Ethenia said.

"Select the form of combat," Naomi said.

"I choose live combat," Ethenia replied. There did not seem to be too much surprise at this announcement. Too much ill will existed between Ethenia and Izabel at this point for the High Lord to have chosen combat between projections.

"Lord Izabel, do you wish to withdraw your challenge?" Naomi asked.

"I do not," Izabel replied.

"To the victor will go the High Seat," Lord Naomi informed them, needlessly, "as well as the right to determine the fate of the loser. The combatants will now enter the arena."

Felicia took the cloak from Izabel's shoulders to reveal the gold inlaid breastplate and boiled leather kilt that she wore. Sandals, with thongs laced up to the knees, completed the traditional combatant's uniform. Felicia handed Izabel her round, bronze shield and her short sword.

"Fight well, Lord," Felicia said.

As the two combatants entered the center of the room, the remaining Lords raised a ward about them to protect the Council chamber from the Power that would be used within.

Izabel's heart pounded as she faced her former friend across the sand floor of the chamber. She had never defeated Ethenia during their sparring sessions. However, never before had the stakes been so high.

Izabel drew Power from the Cords, letting it build within her to the point where she thought it would burst from her and beyond. She and Ethenia circled each other warily, watching for an opening. Sparkles began to dance in front of Izabel's eyes as the Power continued to flow into her.

She released the Power in a single attack of staggering strength as she charged across the sand toward her opponent. Ethenia's wards buckled as Izabel drove her sword toward the High Lord's breast. Ethenia blocked the thrust with her shield, but the blade slid off and sliced deeply into her shield arm.

Izabel blocked Ethenia's attacks easily and continued a relentless assault against the High Lord. She had scored first blood! If Izabel could press her advantage, Ethenia would begin to weaken as she lost blood. Izabel could not afford to give Ethenia the opportunity to heal that wound—she had to keep the High Lord on the defensive.

If nothing else, Izabel thought, *I have wiped the arrogance from her face.*

Ethenia's expression had gone from one of supreme confidence to surprise and now showed the beginnings of fear. Izabel felt that her own features were twisted into a mask of rage as she drove Ethenia back across the arena. Around them, the Lords watched attentively. This was not the battle they had expected to see.

With each blow that fell against her shield and her wards, Ethenia's eyes widened further in fear. She had never seen Izabel fight like this—had never felt this level of hatred and viciousness in her attacks. As the sands of the arena became spotted with her own blood, Ethenia finally realized that the outcome of this contest was far from certain.

She diverted all of her Power to her wards and leaped back from Izabel's attack. Izabel continued to batter her wards, but was forced to defend as well, lest Ethenia return to the attack.

The two circled each other in the sand as Ethenia healed the wound in her arm.

"Yield, Ethenia!" Izabel said. "Yield and I shall leave you your House."

"*Never!*" Ethenia said.

"Then die!" Izabel shouted, followed instantly by another blow of more Power than Ethenia had thought possible. She staggered back and fell to one knee as she fought to keep her wards intact.

Izabel charged toward her. Ethenia caught the downward

blow on her shield and her wards as she thrust upward beneath Izabel's breastplate. Ethenia felt the blade bite into flesh, and then bone.

Izabel staggered back off the blade, but did not fall. Nor did her wards collapse. Ethenia rose to her feet and smiled coldly. Izabel's face was ashen and her lips were pale. Blood streamed down her legs from her wound.

"Trying to heal your wounds, Izabel?" Ethenia asked, lashing out with the Power. Izabel staggered back from the impact, but still did not fall.

"Can you do it with me battering at your wards?" Ethenia asked, lashing out once again. Again Izabel did not fall.

"*Can you?*" Ethenia shouted, striking harder. Izabel finally fell back, but she caught herself in the sand by her elbows.

"Will you just *give up*?" Ethenia shouted, striking out again.

Izabel cried out in pain, but still did not fall completely prone.

"Give up!"

Izabel finally collapsed to the sand, unconscious. Ethenia released the Power as Izabel's wards evaporated. She turned to face the Lords surrounding her, her bloody sword raised high above her head.

"All hail Ethenia," Naomi said in a flat voice, "the High Lord."

As soon as the wards fell, Felicia summoned the Power and pulled on the Cords as hard and as quickly as she could. All in the chamber felt the Power and acted to ward themselves. All but one, of course.

The bolt of Power that struck the center of the arena reduced Izabel's unconscious body to ash in the twinkling of an eye. Felicia released the Power as all eyes in the room turned to her.

"What have you *done*?" Ethenia shouted.

"I have carried out my Lord's final order," Felicia replied. "If she lost, I was commanded to destroy her."

"Her fate was *mine* to decide!" Ethenia shouted.

"No longer," Felicia said. "Now you will not be able to carry out your threat of sending her to the north as a whore."

"*What?*" Naomi asked, her voice full of menace.

"It was an empty threat!" Ethenia said. "I had no intention of actually doing that."

"It did not sound that way to me," Felicia said. "Nor to my Lord. Hence my orders."

"You have violated our laws!" Ethenia shouted.

"I would not press the issue," Lord Naomi said.

"I beg your pardon?"

"I would not press the issue, High Lord," Naomi repeated. "Your 'empty threat' could also be considered a violation of our laws."

"I . . . see your point," Ethenia said.

"Then shall we return to the deliberations which were interrupted by this challenge?" Naomi suggested.

"High Lord," Evan said. "Lord Ethenia of the Southern Alliance wishes to speak with you."

"Finally!" Janis said, rising to his feet. Perhaps this matter was finally about to draw to a close.

"Good afternoon, High Lord," he said. "What news do you have for me?"

"Your most recent proposal has been rejected," Ethenia told him, instantly dashing his hopes. "And your pet collaborator, Lord Izabel, has been killed."

"She was hardly a collaborator," Janis said. "All she did was to propose a compromise that could have ended this dangerous situation. Which, I might add, is more than *you* have accomplished in this matter."

"We will be satisfied with nothing less than the release of the woman Rowena to our custody," Ethenia told him. "There is no room for compromise beyond this point."

"I demand to speak with Lord Bairn," Janis said.

"You *demand* nothing from *me*!" Ethenia said.

"Very well," Janis conceded. "Then I request to speak with Lord Bairn immediately, or I am going to declare war. Is that better?"

"You would not!"

"Then call my bluff, Lord Ethenia," Janis said. "Before you do, however, let me tell you that you have just about exhausted our patience in this matter. It is all I have been able to do to *prevent* the declaration of war. That declaration comes closer with each proposal you reject."

"Are you threatening us?"

"Most definitely," Janis said. "Now are you going to let me speak with my ambassador?"

"Very *well*," Ethenia said.

"Thank you, High Lord," Janis said, but Ethenia had already broken the link.

Izabel's eyes fluttered open. She was sitting in a small room in a comfortable seat. Her abdomen ached for some reason. And then she remembered.

I'm alive? she thought. She sat up and looked around. She was in the front compartment of her own airborne coach. Through the window she could see that she was inside a barn. How?

"My Lord," Felicia's voice said, and her image appeared in the small sending mirror.

"Felicia!" Izabel said.

"If you are hearing this message, then I am sorry to say that you are my Lord no longer," the recorded message continued. "Ethenia believes that you are dead, but that mistake will not last for long. I am acting as Lord of our House at this point. I will try to delay Ethenia as long as possible in Council, but you must flee at once."

Flee? Izabel thought. *Where?* No one would take her in, in defiance of the Council.

"The House of Lilith has agreed to let you pass through the ward surrounding Lord Bairn's estate," Felicia continued. "Forgive me, Lord, but that is the only place where you can be safe now. Hurry before our deception is discovered."

Izabel smiled. Her House was in good hands. Felicia had obviously used the Power of her attack to mask a small translocation. Furthermore, she had arranged with the House of Lilith for her escape. Felicia would do well for herself.

I wish I could collect my things, Izabel thought. Still, she should be grateful merely to have her life—and her Power.

Using as little Power as possible, she reached out with her mind and swung open the doors of the barn. Noon sunlight shone in.

She was at full speed before she cleared the barn.

Bairn directed the sending to the central mirror. Izabel's face appeared in the mirror.

"Lord Izabel," Bairn said.

"Not any longer," Izabel said.

"I beg your pardon?"

"The proposal was rejected," Izabel explained. "I have been stripped of my House."

"What?"

"Bairn, will you grant me sanctuary?" Izabel asked. "Please, I beg you. There is nowhere else I can turn. Please!"

"In case you have not noticed, I am under siege," Bairn said. "How are you going to get past the ward?"

"I am already past our ward," Izabel said. "Will you allow me through yours? I am in my coach. I'm sure you can use another of Lord strength in your situation."

Bairn glanced over to Rowena. She merely nodded at him, her expression grim. Bairn turned back to the mirror.

"Lord Izabel," Bairn said, "if I grant you sanctuary, will you submit to examination by . . ."

"Yes!" Izabel said, interrupting him. "I will do anything! Please!"

"Very well, I will retract the ward behind my main gate," Bairn told her. "Once you have landed, I will sweep the ward past you again. I will send someone to meet you."

"Thank you," Izabel said.

Bairn terminated the link. This was certainly an unexpected twist—and contrary to his plans. He was either going to have to kill Izabel or render her Power-less.

Or give her the Rite of Acceptance. Would she—*could* she pass? Bairn did not think so, but then he would not have thought her capable of begging, either.

"Hervis, Rowena," Bairn said, "go meet Izabel. Let me know when you are ready. Be careful—this could easily be a trap."

"Yes, Lord," Hervis said.

"Rowena, get into your uniform first."

"Yes, Lord," Rowena replied, smiling.

As they left to meet Izabel, Bairn received another sending. He accepted it, and the face of Lord Janis filled the mirror.

"Lord Janis," Bairn said, "it is good to hear from you."

"What is your situation, Bairn?" Janis asked.

"Unchanged," Bairn told him. "Save for one . . . unusual detail."

"What is that?"

"Lord Izabel has requested that I give her sanctuary," Bairn said.

"Ethenia just told me that Izabel is dead!" Janis said. "This could be a trap, Bairn."

"I am taking precautions," Bairn said. "She has agreed to any examination of her that I care to make."

"So you have agreed to grant her sanctuary?" Janis said.

"I have," Bairn said. "Although I have no idea what to do with her after that. However, she has been a valuable ally thus far, and, as she pointed out, right now I can certainly use someone of her level of Power. I figure that 'later' will take care of itself, for now."

"True," Janis said. "I assume you know that our latest proposal has been rejected."

"I do," Bairn said.

"Bairn, I fear this is going to end badly," Janis said. "These women are completely unreasonable."

"No, Lord," Bairn said. "Merely one of them. Izabel gathered support for a compromise once. I think that Ethenia is our problem."

"What are you suggesting?" Janis asked.

"Nothing," Bairn said. "However, Izabel *might* have some ideas on what we can try next. She knows their politics better than we."

"This is true," Janis said. "If nothing else, perhaps we can use her as a bargaining piece."

You'll never get the chance, Bairn thought.

"It is a possibility," he said.

"I shall be back in touch with you as soon as I can," Janis said.

"Thank you, High Lord," Bairn said.

Izabel set the coach down just outside the ward, but inside Bairn's outer wall. Two people in journeyman uniforms waited for her. Bairn had two journeymen here? He was allowed only one. She could not see them clearly, as they stood on the other side of Bairn's wards. He was being cautious.

What do I *care?* Izabel thought. Right now, she would have been happy to see a dozen of Bairn's journeymen. It would make their position better.

The ward swept forward, passing over her and her coach, making the hairs on her arm and neck rise as it passed. Izabel opened the door to her coach and stepped out into Bairn's gardens.

As the two journeymen approached, Izabel noted that one was blond and heavy of build. Both were second order, as the northerners kept rank. The other was red of hair and *very* slight of build. Almost . . . feminine . . .

"*Rowena*?" Izabel said. It *was* Rowena, with her red hair pulled back into a horse's tail.

"As you said," Rowena replied, smiling, "he denies me nothing."

"I . . . I . . . how long?" Izabel asked.

"I have been a journeyman just over a year," Rowena replied. "I have been in training much longer, of course."

"Of . . . course," Izabel said.

"We wish to inspect your coach," Rowena said.

"Of course," Izabel said.

"Hervis, will you check the coach?" Rowena asked.

"Yes, my Lady," Hervis said.

"Lord Izabel, I must ask you to lower your wards," Rowena said. "Lord Bairn is expecting us, but we are not returning until *I* am satisfied with your intentions."

"As . . . you wish," Izabel said.

Lord Felicia watched the High Table as Ethenia leaned over to listen to the journeyman who had just come in. It had almost been an hour since the challenge. Izabel should be safely in Bairn's fortress by now.

"Lords," Ethenia said, rising to her feet, "I have just been told something strange. It seems that a flying coach was seen leaving this area a little less than an hour ago. However, we are all present in this room."

"Whose coach was it?" Lord Naomi asked.

"We do not know," Ethenia replied. "Unfortunately, those who saw it were not able to discern that. Lord Lilith, are you certain that Lord Bairn is still imprisoned within his fortress?"

"Absolutely," Lilith responded.

"I would not be concerned, High Lord," Felicia said.

"What do *you* know of this?" Ethenia asked.

"That it was Lord Izabel's coach which was seen leaving this area," Felicia replied.

"Izabel?" Ethenia asked. "She is *alive*?" The murmur of

shocked conversation rose into the chamber from the surrounding tables.

"And, hopefully, well beyond your reach by this time," Felicia added.

"You little *bitch*!" Ethenia shouted. "Where is she?"

"I do not actually know for certain," Felicia said.

"She is safe," Lilith interrupted.

"*What?*" Ethenia said, turning to face Lilith. "*You* have her?"

"No," Lilith replied. "If I gave her sanctuary, I could be forced to surrender her. She entered Lord Bairn's fortress some time ago. He was able to admit her without lowering his wards, so I was unable to act, unfortunately."

Ethenia had taken her seat, stunned by the news that Lilith had been a part of all this.

"Is that . . . why you did this?" Ethenia asked. "To get the woman?"

"No," Lilith replied. "Because Izabel has been a trusted ally to my House. However, if the opportunity had presented itself . . ." Lilith spread her hands, palms upward.

"So now he has *both* of them!" Ethenia realized. "Not only does he have our sister Rowena, but now he has possession of Izabel and, with her, all of our secrets! This is *treason*!"

"You *could* accuse Izabel of that crime, yes," Lilith agreed.

"I can accuse *you* of that crime!" Ethenia shouted.

"No, you cannot," Lilith said. "I have no knowledge whether Izabel's intentions are treasonous or not. Neither does Lord Felicia."

"You are *traitors*!" Ethenia said. "Conspiring to betray this Council!"

"No allegations of treason will be supported," Lord Naomi stated.

"*Damn* you, Naomi!" Ethenia said. "I will make whatever allegations I please!"

"Are you prepared to face me in challenge as well?" Naomi asked.

Ethenia fell silent. Naomi had never before shown interest in the High Seat. Everyone, including Ethenia, knew, however, that if she ever wanted it, it would be hers.

"No," Ethenia finally said.

"Then this matter is settled," Naomi said.

"This bickering has divided us," Ethenia said. "I ask the Council to grant me emergency authority to deal with the North."

The Council fell silent. Emergency authority had *never* been invoked. It gave the High Lord absolute power over the Alliance until it was rescinded.

"Have we come to this?" Naomi asked.

"I believe we have," Ethenia said.

"Then should we not consider accepting the latest proposal from the Northern Alliance instead?" Naomi suggested. "I, for one, do not wish to face a war in the next few days."

"That proposal does not deal with the matter of Izabel," Ethenia pointed out. "We shall take the vote. All of those in favor of a declaration of emergency, so signify."

Felicia's watched in dismay. Over two-thirds of the Houses voted in favor of the declaration. Ethenia now held absolute power over them all.

"This Council is dismissed," Ethenia announced. "Thank you for your confidence, esteemed Lords."

Somehow, Felicia did not feel too confident at the moment.

High Lord Janis sat before the sending mirror himself. He had been authorized by the Court to offer varying levels of compromise using the woman Izabel as a bargaining factor. Somehow, he knew that none of them would be accepted. Ethenia would not be happy with anything less than full capitulation—something they dared not give in this situation. *Damn* the woman!

He was about to activate the mirror when he received a sending. He accepted the image—it was Ethenia.

"High Lord!" Janis said. "I was just about to contact you."

"Regarding?"

"It seems that one of your people has taken sanctuary in Bairn's fortress," Janis began.

"He must return her to us immediately," Ethenia said.

"I am amenable to that," Janis said. "*If* you will reconsider your acceptance of our earlier proposal . . ."

"No," Ethenia said.

"That was . . . a bit sudden, don't you think?" Janis said. "Should you not discuss this with your Council?"

"The Council has declared a state of emergency and granted me full emergency powers until this matter is settled," Ethenia told him. "I alone make the decisions for our Alliance at this point."

Then we are all doomed, Janis thought.

"Ethenia, you have been completely unwilling to negotiate or to compromise throughout this entire incident," Janis said. "And yet it was your Council who attacked one of our Lords without provocation."

"You will surrender both the woman Rowena and the traitor to us," Ethenia said. "If you have not done so in one quarter moon, we will take them from Lord Bairn's estate by force."

"Is there nothing I can say to convince you to reconsider our offer?" Janis asked.

"Nothing," Ethenia replied.

"I am very sorry to hear that," Janis said. "If you will excuse me, I must convene the Court."

"One quarter, Janis!" Ethenia said.

Janis broke the link. Nothing could save them now.

Imelia felt the Power—a massive movement just outside her ambassadorial estate. She also felt the defenses of the estate rise in response. She hurried into the front chamber.

"What is happening?" she asked.

"Lord Imelia!" Journeyman Elspeth said. There was obvious fear in her eyes.

"What *is* it?" Imelia asked again.

"We have been besieged," Elspeth replied. "They have sealed us behind a ward. We . . . we estimate that three Houses support it."

"Lords!" Imelia said. "Let me see." Elspeth moved from before the sending mirror, and Imelia took her seat.

Outside her lands, an opaque barrier of Power shimmered. As Elspeth said, they were under siege. Thus far there had been no attack. When it finally came, there would be no stopping it.

"Damn you, Ethenia!" Imelia hissed.

She felt a sending arrive. Imelia accepted the image quickly. The face of High Lord Janis appeared in the mirror.

"High Lord!" Imelia said. "What is the *meaning* of . . ."

"Silence," Janis commanded. Imelia fell silent. The High Lord seemed different. A cold fury burned in his eyes unlike anything Imelia had yet seen.

"I am sorry, Ambassador," he said, "but you are now a

hostage. I have a message for you to convey to High Lord Ethenia. You might also want to convey it to others of your Alliance, but that is your decision. Listen carefully."

"High Lord," one of her journeymen said.

"What is it, Caspia?" Ethenia asked.

"Lord Imelia wishes to speak with you," Caspia said. "She seems most upset."

Ethenia hurried into the sitting room. Imelia's face in the mirror showed considerable strain. There were even signs that she might have been crying.

"Imelia, what is it?" Ethenia asked.

"I am under siege," she replied.

"*What?*"

"I have been given a message," Imelia continued. "If . . . if you attack Lord Bairn, I . . . I and my staff will be taken captive and t-tortured to death."

"They would not *dare*!" Ethenia said.

"*Yes, they would*!" Imelia shouted. "You did not s-see him! They will *kill* me!"

"Calm down, Imelia," Ethenia said. "I won't let that happen. I will speak with Lord Janis immediately."

"All right," Imelia said. Ethenia broke the link and immediately issued a sending to Lord Janis. How dare those northern bastards *do* this!

Janis himself answered the sending.

"Ah, Lord Ethenia," he said. "You must have spoken with your ambassador."

"I have indeed," Ethenia said. "How *dare* you threaten our ambassador?"

"How dare you attack ours?" Janis asked. "We have tolerated all of this situation that we intend. If you attack Lord Bairn, Lord Imelia will die most unpleasantly. Do you understand me, Ethenia?"

"I do," Ethenia said.

"I am prepared to return to negotiation, if you are prepared to compromise," Janis said. "Otherwise, I am prepared to let you drag us into war, and may the best . . . man win."

"You are bluffing," Ethenia said. "You are not going to go to war over this woman . . ."

"It is *not* over 'this woman'!" Janis shouted. "This is over your unprovoked attack of one of our Lords. This is over your refusal to compromise and your attempts to force us to comply to your demands through force! I would go to war for any *one* of those reasons! *You* are the one who is going to war over 'this woman'!"

"I . . . see," Ethenia said.

"I am still willing to offer you Lord Izabel *and* our sworn pledge to allow Rowena freedom of choice *if you end this*," Janis said. "If that is not acceptable to you, then suggest something else and I will be *most* happy to discuss it."

"And our ambassador?" Ethenia asked.

"She will be freed as soon as you and I reach an agreement," Janis said. "Until then, she is hostage to your good intentions, Lord Ethenia."

"If you harm her, it will mean war," Ethenia said.

"I know that," Janis replied. "I suggest you do not cause that to happen. Oh, and the Court has granted me emergency powers as well. It's down to you and me, Ethenia. We decide if the world lives or dies between us. Either of us can destroy it. Only both of us together can save it. Choose wisely."

"I will consider what you have said," Ethenia said.

"Good," Janis replied, and broke the link.

Ethenia stared at her reflection in the mirror for a time after the link had been broken.

"Lord?" Caspia asked.

"He's bluffing," Ethenia assured her journeyman.

"I . . . do not think so," Caspia replied.

CHAPTER
------ TWENTY-TWO ----------

THE DAYS PASSED with agonizing slowness. Lord Janis waited. He had resorted to using the Power to force himself to sleep at night.

During the day, he took long walks in his gardens, but only by projection. He remained in front of the sending mirror while his mind enjoyed the tranquility of his gardens. It had occurred to Janis that he might never see them again.

How have we come to this? he wondered. In an attempt to ensure peace, they had sown the seeds of their own destruction. If they had never sent Bairn to the Southern Alliance, none of this would have happened.

But it would have happened another way, eventually. It had almost happened when Lord Shaun had sent his agents into the South. Over a century ago, it had almost happened when Lord Damien had taken a fancy to a southern Lord. His passion had cost him his life and the life of the woman who had seduced him. They had come close to destruction in the past, but never this close.

If Ethenia followed through on her threat to take Bairn's stronghold by force tomorrow, Janis doubted that anything could save them.

Ethenia, too, did not stray too far from the sending mirror. Why couldn't those idiot men see how *simple* the solution to this problem was? All they had to do was turn over one woman, one insignificant woman, to end all of this!

But their arrogant pride would not let them do that. No, they had to crow over their prize like a cock in a barnyard.

And Bairn! *He* had turned out to be the worst of the lot! Ethenia had no doubt that he was feeling quite full of himself at this point. Not only had he brought his gifted prize with him, but he had managed to claim another, a full Lord, from beneath their very noses!

The northerners had done this before. That northern Lord had tried to claim Lord Consuela as his property only a century before this. Only then, their two Alliances had been united. Consuela and her captor had united their Houses in a pitiful attempt to hold off both Alliances.

Thank the Power that he *was not as cunning as this man Bairn,* Ethenia thought. No one could have suspected that Bairn was hoarding enough Power to hold all of them at bay as he had.

Well, Ethenia doubted that Bairn would be quite so full of himself in a few days. Not when his wards began to crack beneath the assault of the entire Southern Alliance. She only wished she could be there to see his face when he realized that his precious allies were not going to rush to his rescue.

Bairn awoke on the last morning of the grace period set by Ethenia. Today at noon the assault would begin, unless Ethenia suddenly decided to listen to reason. Bairn did not think that likely. The North and the South had arrayed themselves against one another like rutting bulls and, like bulls, neither could afford to back down.

The destruction of the world was practically assured.

Izabel awaited them outside the war room. Her anxiety was obvious. She knew nothing of what was truly happening here. As far as she knew, their lives were at risk. Hervis and Rowena did not know Bairn's capabilities, but they trusted him.

"Is there nothing we can do?" she asked. "Ethenia *will* attack, and when she does . . ."

"When she does, we shall all die, regardless of the final outcome," Bairn said.

"But everyone else will, too," Izabel said. "It will mean war! It will kill everyone!"

"Who do you mourn for, Izabel?" Bairn asked.

"I-I . . . don't know," Izabel said. "Felicia, I suppose. Others—Lilith, Naomi."

"What of your people?" Bairn asked.

"What?"

"Your people," Bairn repeated. "The carpenters who build the houses of your cities. The farmers who want nothing more than to plow their fields next spring and to see their children grow up. The artists who make your beloved tapestries for you.

What of all of them? All of the people who have no hope at all of surviving this. What of them?''

''I . . . I never thought of that,'' Izabel said.

''That's the problem with you people,'' Bairn said bitterly. ''You *never* think of them. You fight your wars, ravage their land, destroy their lives, and you *never* think of them!''

''Bairn, stop,'' Rowena said.

Izabel had stepped back as Bairn moved closer to her during his tirade. Her eyes were wide with a mixture of surprise and fear.

''You steal their sons for your harems and their daughters to be your apprentices without *once* asking whether they *want* to be taken!'' Bairn said. His voice was rising as almost sixteen years of frustration and anger suddenly boiled to the surface.

''You do the same!'' Izabel cried. She had backed up against a wall, and now Bairn towered over her. His fists were white-knuckled with rage and his eyes burned through her.

''*I* do not!'' Bairn shouted, and Izabel flinched. ''The other male Lords—yes, *they* do. But I *protect* my people. You see the entirety of my collection of women in this room!''

''Bairn, *stop*!'' Rowena said.

''All of *my* apprentices are apprenticed by their choice,'' Bairn continued. ''*None* have been forced to join me!''

Rowena grabbed Bairn by the shoulder and pulled him around to slap him hard across the face.

''*Stop it*!'' she shouted. ''Izabel is not our enemy!''

''But . . .'' Bairn began.

''No!'' Rowena shouted. ''She threw everything away to help us. Is *this* how you reward her? She walked away from her title to *protect her people*! She is no longer one of them!''

''She was trying to protect only herself!'' Bairn said.

''No, she was not,'' Rowena said. ''She walked away from everything she had because she loves you. She loves her people, too. She just does not understand them the way you do.''

''Your family,'' Izabel whispered, as realization sunk in. ''You lost them because of a Lord?''

''Yes,'' Bairn said.

''Oh, Bairn!'' Izabel said, ''I am so sorry.'' She reached out to him, but he recoiled from her touch. For a moment they just stood there as the rage slowly faded from his face, leaving only emptiness and pain.

"Please . . . forgive me," he said. "I am . . . not myself today."

With that, he simply turned and left the room, returning to the war room. Izabel collapsed against the wall and began to weep.

"Izabel, come," Rowena said.

"He's right," Izabel said.

"No, for once he is not," Rowena told her. "Come, let me take you to your quarters."

"No, the attack will come soon," Izabel said. "I must be here to help."

"Ethenia's deadline is not over until noon," Rowena said. "We will return. Come."

Izabel nodded and allowed Rowena to lead her from the room.

Janis accepted the sending, and Ethenia's face filled the mirror.

"The time is up," Ethenia said. "Are you prepared to surrender Izabel and Rowena?"

"We are not," Janis replied. "Our proposal still stands. I urge you to accept it."

"Your proposal is unacceptable!" Ethenia said.

"Do not do this, Ethenia," Janis said.

"Then surrender the women," Ethenia said.

"Only one of them," Janis replied. Ethenia broke the link.

Janis focused the mirror to a view well outside Bairn's lands in the Southern Alliance. An opaque wall of Power blocked his view of the fortress and the gardens.

The ward surrounding Bairn's defenses vanished. A bolt of Power that could only have been produced by the combined might of the Southern Alliance struck Bairn's wards. Miraculously, they held. After a short pause, another bolt struck the wards. Still they held.

Janis turned to another mirror and sent to Lord Rylur. Rylur's faced, lined with fatigue, filled the mirror.

"Take Lord Imelia captive," Janis ordered.

"Yes, High Lord," Rylur replied. Janis terminated the sending and turned back to the scene of the battle.

Even the wards, backed by the Power drawn from the gold beneath the fortress, could not keep out the full fury of the attack. The war room trembled noticeably with each attack. The four of them struggled to refill the reservoir with each attack, drawing out their survival as long as possible.

Bairn had spent the last quarter moon adding a fourth battle couch to the war room. Izabel only had access to the reservoir. If the occupants of the other three couches lost consciousness, her couch would then, and only then, give her access to the remainder of the defensive spells of the fortress.

With the enemy's wards gone, Bairn could again see beyond his borders. The sand and tumbled rock of the surrounding terrain had vanished, melted into slag by the fury of the attack. With each blow, molten earth splashed against his wards like ocean breakers against a cliff.

Bairn paid little attention to the turmoil without. In his central mirror eight pillars of gold, six feet tall and three wide, were displayed. With each stroke of the enemy's Power, veins of black travelled up each of the pillars as the gold was consumed into iron.

At this rate, they would not be able to withstand a single day of the barrage. Was it possible that Bairn had not survived the war he had begun? Was he going to die here today?

No, it was said that Bairn had led the magi to places of safety after they had been banished from the sanctuaries, centuries *after* the war. Somehow, he was going to survive this. He continued to watch as the black veins travelled up the pillars of gold like a cancer.

Whatever is going to save us had best happen soon, he thought.

Ethenia watched in the mirror as the barrage against Lord Bairn's fortress continued. Those wards had held against almost an hour of the combined might of all the Great Houses. Such was the Power of the attack that the earth for over a mile around Bairn's lands had been completely melted.

If nothing else, it was good that they had discovered this. Bairn had *no right* to build such an impregnable fortress in the midst of their lands. Especially not by means of something as dangerous to all concerned as a Power reservoir of this size. What if the reservoir had become unstable? At this size, it could have destroyed all of Ethenia's lands and possibly done severe damage to her neighbors as well.

That was how these men did things—with no regard for anyone or anything but their own plans.

She felt a sending and directed it to one of the side mirrors. Lord Janis's face filled the smaller mirror.

"You were warned, Ethenia," he said.

"What do you . . ." she began, but he was gone. In his place was an image of Imelia, standing on a platform with her arms tied to a bar above her head.

Ethenia redirected the sending to the central mirror. Two journeymen stood on the dais with Imelia. No doubt there were others out of sight preventing her from using the Power.

As Ethenia watched, the journeymen began peeling the skin from Imelia's body. At first she begged, but it was not long before her cries for mercy dissolved into screams of agony. Ethenia watched, unable to turn away—mesmerized by the sheer horror of what she was seeing.

When Ethenia thought they could do no more, the journeymen began to disembowel Imelia. The ambassador's screams reached a new pitch of agony as they cut her open. Ethenia terminated the image, finally able to tear herself away.

"*No-ooooo!*" she screamed. Damn them! Damn them all!

She reached out, and the Power of her House answered her Call as the journeymen and apprentices fed their Power into her. Ethenia reached out and claimed the Power of the other Houses, directing it away from the attack on Bairn.

She had never before wielded the Power of the entire Alliance. It intoxicated her—fueled her rage to inhuman levels. She no longer *was* human. Now she was truly an angry goddess, and she would rain destruction upon her enemies.

"High Lord!" Evan said, shouting in alarm as he charged in through the door to the sitting room.

"I *know*!" Janis replied as he sent out the Call. The damned woman had done it! She had loosed annihilation upon them all.

He gathered the Power of his House and then proceeded to gather up the Power of the other Great Houses. It took precious seconds to organize the defense.

Lord Shaun had already been lost. By the time Janis had marshalled their defense, Lords Chen, Diego and Abdul had been lost as well. The next blast fell on wards backed by the entire strength of the Northern Alliance.

In his mind, he could see Ethenia as a towering figure of Power looming over the South, hurling bolts of destruction at them. He knew that she could see him as well.

"Damn you, you stupid bitch!" he shouted at her. "You have brought us to destruction!"

"You have brought us to this, you arrogant pig!" she answered. He blocked another bolt of unimaginable Power and hurled one of his own. She blocked with her own wards, diverting the Power aside. Entire acres of land erupted skyward where it struck.

Neither noticed.

"Shh-shh," Olga cooed to her infant. The walls of the great cavern shook and trembled, but did not collapse.

"What *is* it?" someone cried out.

"The MageLords battle, as has been foretold," one of the magi told them. "Do not fear, we shall be safe. Bairn shall watch over us. Forever."

In Bairn's stronghold, the sudden cessation of the attack was a welcome relief. Something had brought the barrage to a sudden halt. Had the two Alliances arrived at a solution?

Bairn need not have feared. When Raoul's face appeared in the mirror, it told him the story. The journeyman remained calm, but the relief in his eyes told Bairn that Raoul had feared the worst.

"Thank the gods you are all right!" Raoul said. "When the attack came, I feared that you had been destroyed."

Bairn glanced into the side mirror that showed the golden pillars. The bottom two-thirds of each was solid, black iron. The remaining third was veined through with more black than gold. It had been a near thing.

"Almost," Bairn said, "but we live. Gather the House in your courtyard. Prepare to evacuate. You will know the time."

"Yes, Lord," Raoul said. "Where are we going?"

"You will see," Bairn replied. "Farewell."

"Hervis, Rowena—gather the entire staff in the courtyard, quickly!" Bairn said. "We have to leave here before they decide to turn their attention back to us. For the gods' sake, do not use any Power!"

"Yes, Lord," Hervis said. He knew, as well as Bairn, that

any use of the Power could draw the attention of the Southern Alliance back upon them.

"Izabel, you shall come with me," Bairn said.

"Yes, Lord," Izabel replied. Bairn paused and looked at her in surprise.

"I am Lord no longer," she said to him. "I guess that makes me . . . one of yours."

"Not yet, it does not," Bairn replied. "But there is no time to discuss that now. Come. Stand by me."

Izabel moved over to his battle couch and rested a hand on his shoulder.

"What do you want me to . . ." she began. Then they were in another room, with Izabel standing next to Bairn, who lay upon another battle couch.

This couch was fashioned more like a throne and sat upon a dais overlooking a vast hall filled with row upon row of benches. The battle mirrors were arrayed behind the throne, which was currently turned to face them. Two smaller seats flanked the main couch, facing the room.

"By the Power!" she said. "I . . . I felt . . . *nothing*!"

"I have Power you do not understand," Bairn said as he activated the defenses of his new fortress.

"It feels as though we are sinking, yet we remain still," Izabel said. "And . . . oh, great Lords! There is no Power here! There are no Cords!"

"Silence!" Bairn said. "You can panic later, Lady Izabel."

Izabel fell silent. She had not been entirely correct. The Stars of Power still existed, but that was so meager as to be ludicrous. Yet Bairn still shone like the sun, as though he still held his full Power in this place.

Indeed, it seemed that he did. His mirrors showed images of twin palaces: Bairn's fortress among the Southern Alliance and, presumably, his palace in his own lands. The central mirror showed a great hall, much like the one in Izabel's palace, yet more spartan in furnishing.

Before her eyes twin portals opened in that room. People began to enter the hall through them. Izabel recognized Rowena and Hervis as they arrived through one. Another journeyman, as dark of hue as herself, emerged from the second portal, followed by a far vaster number of people.

After a time, the flow of people stopped and the portals vanished. In the side mirrors, Izabel watched as the twin fortresses were both destroyed by powerful bolts of Power. Had Bairn done this himself? The timing certainly made it seem likely.

"Take a seat in the front row," Bairn commanded.

"Y-yes, Lord," Izabel said. Walking was not easy. Each step tried to carry her higher and further than she wished to go. She seemed to float down to the floor below.

"You'll get used to it," Bairn assured her. "It will take some time."

"Where *are* we?" Izabel asked.

"The moon," Bairn replied. "No more questions. I am very busy."

The moon? Izabel thought. How had Bairn managed to build anything *here*? No Lord had ever been able to extend his reach beyond the planet itself.

No Lord but Bairn, Izabel corrected herself.

For a time, Bairn seemed to do nothing. But then Izabel heard something and turned to see the golden doors of the throne room swing open and Rowena enter through them.

Izabel was oddly relieved to see that Rowena had no easier time walking in the strange lightness than Izabel and that the confusion in her eyes seemed just as great as that which Izabel felt. Rowena ignored Izabel and walked in that strange bouncing gait up the steps to the throne.

"Bairn, I am frightened," she said. "Where are we?"

"There is nothing to fear, beloved," Bairn said. "I will explain in detail when the others have arrived. Here, sit next to me." Bairn reached over and squeezed Rowena's hand briefly when she sat in her throne next to him.

Izabel felt the Call that he then sent out to the rest of the House. Slowly, they all filed into the throne room, moving awkwardly in the low gravity. All wore similar expressions of relief when they took their seats and no longer had to try to walk. No one spoke. The dark-skinned journeyman moved to stand behind Bairn's throne as if that were his place.

"I believe the predominant question on everyone's mind is 'Where are we?' " Bairn began. "We are far from the reach of any Lord from either Alliance. We are safe. We are on the moon."

Bairn waited for the surprised conversation to die around the room before continuing.

"Only I wield Power here," he told them. "The Cords of Power do not exist here. Here we shall wait while the world heals from the insane war that now consumes it."

Izabel had never seen this side of Bairn. Strong, confident, commanding and yet still kind and gentle, taking the time to soothe his people.

"Our work is done," Bairn said to them. "The war that I foretold has finally come to pass."

Foretold? Izabel wondered. Bairn had *known* this was going to happen? A chill settled across her shoulders. Had Bairn *caused* this to happen in vengeance for his wife and son?

"Our brothers and sisters wait out the battle in the refuges we have prepared," he continued. "Decades from now, when life has returned to the world, they will emerge to build a new world. A world in which all men and women can be free of the tyranny that has ended on this day."

"My work, however, has just begun," Bairn said. "This war must be managed to bring about the end of all of the Lords. Not one MageLord can be allowed to survive this catastrophe. Not one apprentice can be allowed to survive to carry their knowledge forward, or the tyranny of the MageLords will surely return."

What about me? Izabel thought. *Oh, Lords, is he going to kill me?* If that was his intent, there was certainly nothing she could do to stop him. Here, she was as Power-less as . . .

As Power-less as the farmers who want nothing more than to plow their fields, next spring, she realized. This was how *they* felt in the presence of a Lord. Impotent and unsure of their lives.

"For the next few days, I invite you to explore your new home," Bairn suggested. "Raoul is the Guardian of our Circle in this place. Look to him for guidance. Raoul, you will find documents in the council chamber off this room detailing room assignments and other information you will need to know."

"Yes, Lord," the dark-skinned apprentice replied.

"I apologize, but I will be unavailable during this crisis," Bairn told them. "You are dismissed. Settle into your new home and relax. Enjoy the gardens. Your work is done for now."

Izabel started to rise with the others.

"Lady Izabel, will you remain for a while?" Bairn asked.

"Y-yes, Lord," she said. She waited uncomfortably as the others left the room. Finally she was alone with Bairn and Rowena. Surely Rowena would not let Bairn kill her. Bairn rose from the throne that also served as his battle couch in this palace and descended the dais toward her.

"My quarters are off this room," he said. "It is time for you and I to have a long talk. Rowena? Will you join us?"

"I think that would be best," Rowena replied.

CHAPTER
------ TWENTY-THREE ----------

THE IMAGE IN the mirrors no longer resembled the world that Izabel remembered. Vast areas had been laid waste. Whole forests had been consumed by fire. Where once had stood glorious cities, volcanoes belched fire and ash into the air. Great lakes had been boiled away to leave behind plains of dry, cracked mud.

Darkness covered the face of the world. No sun could penetrate the clouds of water, ash and dust that covered the world. Monsters, conjured from other realms of reality, ravaged the land with their fury.

Still the war raged. Few of the Lords had died. In the first day of the war the North had begun to take the advantage, but Bairn had intervened. He reached out from his throne and struck down a Great House as Izabel would have swatted a fly. Balance was restored.

Through it all, he monitored the war, the Great Houses and his precious refuges as though he were the conductor of a vast symphony. He worked to keep the two Alliances in balance as a master mason would work to keep a roof beam level. When the fighting threatened to destroy one of the many caverns where hundreds of thousands of people waited for the madness to end, Bairn acted to shield it.

I have Power you do not understand, he had said. *This* was the true High Lord, sitting in judgement over his erring world—and weeping for its pain. Izabel and Rowena worked to keep him sane through the madness—to prevent the grief and horror from overwhelming his conscience.

It was one thing to plan the destruction of the world. It was another to witness it and to lay the blame for it upon one's own soul. Between the two of them, they could keep the madness at bay within his mind—could convince him that it was not truly *he* who had caused this, but the greed and arrogance of those who now battled.

"How much longer?" Izabel asked.

"Legend says that the war lasted only a single moon," Bairn replied. "And that, at the end, nothing lived on the face of the world."

"Lords!" Izabel said. An entire *moon*? It had been only seven days since the war had begun.

Izabel had changed almost as drastically as the world she saw before her. Part of it was the knowledge of Bairn's true nature and what his purpose here had been for these past sixteen years, but not all.

She had witnessed how Bairn's people executed workings of Power. She had thought it odd, the raising of the ward and the challenge to enter the matrix. However, only a few days ago she had been allowed to join a smaller Circle consisting of Rowena, Hervis and Raoul. They had thought it important for her to experience it firsthand.

It were as though she had been blind all her life and then had her sight restored by magic. She had never imagined such unity among the gifted—had never thought such absolute trust possible.

She had wept at that experience. Wept with gratitude at the gift they had given to her and with grief that she had lived so long and yet had never felt such peace. Raoul had said that it was a promising sign.

"What is to become of me, Bairn?" Izabel asked.

"I have not decided," he replied. "Nor do I have time to think about that now. I'm sorry, Izabel."

Izabel nodded. According to Rowena, there were three possibilities. If Izabel could pass the Rite of Acceptance and show that she had truly changed, she would be accepted into the House of Bairn. Otherwise she would either be killed or have her ability to use the Power destroyed along with her knowledge of the Art. Bairn would leave no opportunity for the MageLords to return to power.

"The Southern Alliance is gaining ground on the North," Bairn said. "Which surviving House is the smallest?"

"That would be the House of Watimi, in the eastern isles," Izabel said, knowing that her words meant Watimi's doom. More than anything else, Bairn strove to maintain the balance in this war, dragging it out as long as possible.

She watched as Bairn gathered his Power. The House of Watimi appeared in the central mirror. Soon a bolt of Power struck from the sky. It punched through the wards surrounding the House of Watimi without pause. As Izabel watched, a shock wave travelled toward the viewpoint that Bairn had selected, blasting trees, buildings and everything else in its wake. After it had passed, nothing was left standing.

Izabel stared at the mirror in disbelief, even after it had become blank, showing only their own reflections. Bairn had only struck twice before, against the North. This was the first attack that Izabel had witnessed.

How can one man wield such Power? Izabel wondered. Especially here, where there was *no* Power?

"Thank you, Izabel," Bairn said.

"Yes . . . Lord," Izabel said in a hushed voice.

"You may go," Bairn told her. "I will Call if I have need of you again."

"Y-yes, Lord," Izabel said.

The Power died without warning. One moment, High Lord Janis was coordinating the attacks and defenses of the entire Alliance and the next he sat before his sending mirror, Power-less.

The war had lasted for seventeen days, with neither side gaining the upper hand. And now, as quickly as it had begun, it was over.

How could the Power just . . . end? Janis wondered. He rose from his seat and wandered over to the window that overlooked his gardens.

The gardens remained intact, protected by his wards during the war. Beyond the outermost wall, however, nothing remained. Nothing.

Of the city surrounding the House of Janis, there was no sign. Only desolate and blasted terrain was visible as far as the eye could see through the dim light that the ominous clouds admitted.

A hot, dry wind blew in through the window now that the spells that kept the palace environment comfortable had died with the passing of the Power.

Is the whole world like this? Janis wondered. Dry, desolate—dead.

"Janis, what in the Power is going on?" a voice said behind him. Janis turned to see Rylur standing in his sitting room.

"Lord Rylur!" Janis said. "How do you come to be here?"

"There is still enough Power for me to send a shade," Rylur said. "Barely. Is this some trick of the Southern Alliance?"

"I think not," Janis said. "If they still had control of Power, we would all be dead by now. I can only assume this is . . . global."

"How?" Rylur asked. Other shades were beginning to join his—Cambien, LoSing, Vlad. All of the Lords were arriving to find out what was happening.

"Perhaps we . . . used it up," Janis suggested.

"Used it . . . up?" Rylur asked.

"Perhaps the Power was not the inexhaustible river we all believed it to be," Janis said. "In fact, that seems certain now."

"What shall we do?" Cambien asked.

"Return to your palaces," Janis said. "Those of you with reservoirs, put them to use. There is not much Power, but what little you have can be combined into something . . . almost reasonable."

"If we can hold out long enough, the Power may return," Rylur suggested.

"I shall contact the Southern Alliance," Janis said. "Do I have everyone's support in asking for a cessation of hostilities?"

"Aye," Rylur said. The other Lords agreed as well.

"Then return to your Houses," Janis told them. "I shall contact Ethenia."

"It is over," Bairn said. He had Called his journeymen, and Izabel, to the throne room.

"Over?" Raoul asked.

"Yes, the Power has failed them," he said. "They are now defenseless."

"We have won," Hervis said.

"Not yet," Bairn told him. "There is still much to be done. Tell the others to prepare for the long sleep. Rowena, Izabel, please remain."

Once the others had left, Bairn summoned the image of the world in his mirror. Most of the MageLords still lived, stripped of most of their Power, but still deadly. Left alone, many of them would probably die in the aftermath of the war.

Bairn had to make certain they all died. Points of light on the globe showed the locations of all the Great Houses and their known outposts.

"What are you doing?" Izabel asked.

"Destroying those who caused all of this," Bairn replied. He gathered the Power. One by one, the points of light on the globe began to wink out of existence. Soon, all but four had been destroyed.

"Why have you left these?" Izabel asked. One of those spared was the House of Ethenia.

"I must tend to these personally," Bairn said. "I cannot simply destroy them. Events must be prepared."

"But you cannot go back!" Rowena said. "There is no Power, and horrible monsters still roam the world!"

"I shall wield Power there as I do here," Bairn assured her. "Rowena, Izabel, I would like you to accompany me on my first stop."

"Ethenia?" Izabel asked.

"Exactly," Bairn said.

"We shall agree to end the war," Ethenia told Janis. It took all of the meager Power she could muster to maintain the sending. Presumably that was true for Janis as well.

"It is unfortunate that it took this to bring us to our senses," Janis replied.

"Indeed," Ethenia said. "We should have accepted your offer. It was just. If you will excuse me, there are matters to which I must attend."

"I as well," Janis said. "Farewell, Ethenia."

The mirror went blank and Ethenia collapsed back in her chair, staring at her own reflection.

"Too little, too late," the familiar voice of a man said behind her. Ethenia jumped up from her chair and whirled around. Behind her, just out of sight from the mirror, stood Lord Bairn and Lord Izabel. The woman Rowena was with them, in the uniform of a northern journeyman.

Bairn's aura was brighter than the sun.

"You wield *Power*?" Ethenia said.

"I do," Bairn replied.

"W-why are you . . . here?" she asked.

"In your arrogance you have destroyed this world," Bairn replied. "You have slaughtered billions of innocents. Mothers and daughters, fathers and sons, all dead because of your presumption. I am here to pass judgement."

"What right do *you* have to judge *me*?" Ethenia demanded.

"The one right you understand," Bairn said. "The right of Power."

"No!" Ethenia said. "You cannot! I beg of you! Izabel, do not let him do this. We were friends!"

"Were we?" Izabel asked. "I think not. Allies, perhaps, but no more than that. Bairn is right, Ethenia. You must die—we must *all* die so that this can never happen again."

"You . . . you're *insane*!"

"Goodbye, Ethenia," Izabel said. Then she turned and left the room, leaving Ethenia alone with Bairn and Rowena.

"Judgement has been passed," Bairn said.

Lord Janis stared out his window at the sunset on a dying world. It was the darkest sunset he had ever seen, barely burning through the clouds of smoke and ash that surrounded the globe. If the Power did not return, they would never be able to restore this world. They would all die.

"Admiring your handiwork, Lord Janis?" someone asked behind him.

"It was all madness," Janis replied, turning to face the voice.

"Bairn!" he said. Then he noticed something more.

"You . . . you still wield Power!"

"I do," Bairn said.

"*How*?"

"That is my secret," Bairn told him.

"Lords, Bairn!" Janis said. "You must help us! Help us to save what we can!"

"I already have," Bairn said. "Before you began this madness I prepared places of safety for the people of the world. Hundreds of thousands now live in these refuges. Billions more are dead at your hands."

"Do you seek to blame *me* for this?" Janis asked.

"Whom else should I blame?" Bairn asked. Janis did not answer immediately.

"I . . . suppose I do bear the blame," Janis said. "But Ethenia does as well."

"Ethenia has paid the final price for her actions," Bairn said.

"You have . . . ?"

"Yes," Bairn said. "She is dead."

"And now you have come for me?" Janis asked.

"Yes."

"Then do it," Janis said, turning back to the window. "Do not draw it out—just end it."

"As you wish, High Lord," Bairn replied.

Bairn looked at the grounds of the former House of Soren. After Soren's disappearance, this had become the House of Hashim. Bairn's fingers touched the amulet he wore around his neck.

This says his name is Bairn, he remembered. Here—here was where it had all begun, a thousand years from now. Spells on the amulet received Power sent from his stronghold on the moon. Enough Power to level this place without a trace, but that could not be. This House had to be left standing.

This, and the House of Rylur, must be left standing. Both must be allowed to survive, in part, into his own time.

After all of this, I still *have to spare Valerian,* he thought bitterly. That was later, however. There was no person here he must spare.

He gathered the Power and sent it out in a wave toward the palace. Where it passed, everything living died. Stone, brick, glass and mortar were untouched, but everything that carried life gave it up.

He walked into the palace. He had to find the books. Soren had scattered numerous copies of his preserved book around the world. Bairn would have to find them all and destroy them, save one. That one he would keep until it was time for it to find its way into the possession of his family. No one could be allowed to find and use one before that could occur.

Rylur looked up from his books as a journeyman barged into his chambers without knocking. Rylur rose to his feet, his rebuke silenced at one look in Olaf's eyes.

"Lord!" Olaf said. "We are under siege!"

"What?" Rylur said.

"It is true!" Olaf insisted. "A ward has been raised around the palace grounds."

Rylur walked over to the window and threw the heavy velvet drapes aside. It was true. A shimmering, transparent silver dome surrounded the palace. Someone had enough Power to besiege him.

"Who is doing this?" Rylur asked.

"I am," replied a voice that he knew well. Rylur turned to face Bairn, who was smiling.

"Bairn, thank the Power you still live!" Rylur said as he turned. "I am glad that . . ."

Rylur's words died in his throat. Olaf lay dead at Bairn's feet. Bairn himself was surrounded by an aura more powerful than Rylur had ever seen.

"What are you doing?" Rylur asked.

"Setting things in order," Bairn replied. "This is the last Great House. The others have been destroyed."

"By you?" Rylur said. "*Why?*"

"To make certain *this* never happens again," Bairn said, gesturing out the window. "To make certain that humanity has a chance to live without the oppression caused by you and others like you."

"So, you want the entire world to yourself," Rylur said. "But who will serve you in this empty world you are going to rule, Bairn?"

"I suppose you are incapable of understanding," Bairn said. "I do not intend to rule at all. Also, there are more people who survive this than you realize. However, none of this is important. Goodbye, Lord Rylur."

One by one Bairn Called the inhabitants of the House of Rylur to him. Journeymen, apprentices, guards and servants were all subjected to his inspection. Most were found unworthy and killed.

Those few who passed his examinations, Bairn placed in the east wing of the palace. When he was done here, they would be absorbed into his House.

Finally, he Called Valerian into his presence. Valerian walked into the throne room and knelt before him.

"Please, Lord Bairn," he said, almost weeping. "Spare me. I have served you well in the past."

So you are a coward as well, Bairn thought. He was not surprised.

"It is time for you to serve me again, Valerian," Bairn said to him. "Come with me."

"Yes, Lord!" Valerian said, rising to his feet. Bairn rose from the throne and led him through the palace to a tower on the north end of the west wing.

"Follow," Bairn commanded. Valerian did so. As they descended, Bairn invoked the illumination spells along the tower walls. Finally they emerged into a long hallway, a tunnel carved through the stone.

"Where . . . are we?" Valerian asked.

"You will see," Bairn said.

The hallway ended in a natural cavern—a small one. Doors of solid stone barred their way. Bairn fed Power into the spells upon them, and the stone doors swung open silently. Inside was a small cavern with a stone bier in the center of it.

"What is this place?" Valerian asked.

"All of the Lords have secret places of refuge," Bairn said. "Places in which they can seal themselves in a state of enchanted sleep. Here you will sleep, Valerian. When you awake, centuries from now, the world will again be green and whole."

"Why?" Valerian asked.

"Do you remember where my stronghold lies?" Bairn asked.

"You mean where it used to lie," Valerian said. "I heard that it was destroyed early in the war."

"It was," Bairn said. "By me. Centuries from now when you awake, travel to my stronghold. You will find a cavern there as well. On the floor you will find my symbol bearing an untrapped spell. Empower that spell, and I and my House will return. You will find me *most* grateful at that point."

Of course, the story was a complete fabrication. Valerian would never know that, however.

"I am honored, Lord," Valerian said. "I will not fail you!"

"I know you will not," Bairn said. "Lie down."

"Yes, Lord," Valerian said, climbing onto the stone bier. Bairn placed his hand on the charge point for the reservoir that was built beneath the bier. Once filled, Bairn activated the link that bound the reservoir to the spell of stasis. Valerian's body instantly changed to resemble a shining silver statue of himself.

"Sleep well, Valerian," Bairn said. "When you next see me, you will die."

Bairn was amazed at how quickly time could pass. Instead of being the interminable wait he had thought, the years were filled with activity. Additional refuges had to be prepared for the magi when they were driven from those prepared before the war.

The world itself had to be healed, and that was no small task. Life still existed, deep within the oceans, and in a few sheltered places on the land. Bairn found that he needed all four of his journeymen to aid him in its recultivation.

With the Power slowly returning over the centuries, Raoul, Hervis, Izabel and Rowena were able to work with him, reclaiming and planting what arable land could be found. The former gardens of the MageLords became preserves of wildlife, waiting to be transplanted across the world. Rylur's unicorns once again bred foals as true horses. Deer and wolves, mice, rabbits and cattle once again wandered wild across the world. Forests rose with the passage of time and spread their canopies across the world.

Over all of this, Bairn watched, tending his immense garden—leading the world back from the brink of destruction that had almost claimed it against the day when men finally emerged from their sunless prisons into the light of day.

When they did, mankind ran afoul of those monsters that still remained from the Great War so long ago. Chief among these was the dragon, Arcalion—the sole surviving Great Dragon from the war.

The dragon ravaged the northlands, threatening to drive humanity from that part of the world forever. It was clear that action was required.

Bairn waited outside the cavern in the cliffs where Arcalion had made his lair. From here, the dragon ravaged the countryside for hundreds of miles.

Bairn wielded the Power from his fortress and none of the Cords. Drawing on the Cords would have warned the dragon of his presence. Bairn wished his assault to be a complete surprise. Arcalion did not know that a MageLord still walked the world.

Dawn broke over the horizon. If the dragon followed his normal pattern, he should emerge soon after sunrise, when the rising air would support him as he leaped from the cliff.

Bairn was not disappointed. Less than an hour after sunrise, Arcalion emerged onto the ledge of the cavern. He was as beautiful as Bairn remembered him. Arcalion spread his massive black wings and leaped from the cliff.

A bolt of Power struck the dragon squarely in the chest. With a scream of anguish, its wings folded and the magnificent creature plummeted to the ground. Bairn translocated to the site in time to witness Arcalion's impact on the stones below. The monster was dazed, both by the attack and the fall. Bairn reached out with the Power.

Invisible bonds pinned Arcalion to the ground as Bairn climbed up onto the armored belly of the monster. Black scales scintillated with all the colors of the rainbow. A creature of Power, but with no sense of the Art. Impervious to physical attack and nearly so to magical assault. No other but Bairn could have brought him down so easily.

Already the dragon was rousing from his stupor. Bairn walked up to the broad chest as the dragon raised its head to look at him.

Without warning the massive maw was racing to engulf him. A proud creature—fearless and defiant.

A single burst of Power threw Arcalion's head back to smash into the cliff face. Rock shattered and crumbled to rain down upon them. Bairn diverted the avalanche to either side.

He found himself engulfed in flames roaring from the mighty gullet of the dragon. Bairn waited. Eventually the flames subsided, and Bairn looked into the alien eyes of the dragon.

Are you finished? Bairn asked, communicating directly with the dragon's mind.

Who are you? the strong mental voice of Arcalion demanded.

I am Lord Bairn, of the House of Bairn, Bairn replied.

No Lords survived the Great War, Arcalion said.

Then I suppose I do not exist, Bairn said. Arcalion stared at him for a moment.

You exist, Arcalion said. *Therefore you must speak the truth. What do you want?*

Your destruction of my people must cease, Bairn told him.

Who are your people?

All people on this world are under my protection, Bairn said. *This is their world, not yours.*

I must survive, Arcalion said. *Unless it is your intent to destroy me.*

I would prefer not to do so, Bairn told the dragon. *Not only do I have a purpose for you, but it would be tragic to destroy such a magnificent creature as yourself.*

I will never *serve you!* Arcalion's voice shouted in his mind. Again the flames engulfed him. This time, however, Arcalion also attempted to eat him. Another bolt of Power brought an end to the assault.

You cannot harm me, Bairn said once the dragon had regained his senses.

So it would appear, Arcalion grumbled. *Bind me to your service, then, Lord Bairn.*

I would prefer not to do that as well, Bairn said. *So, I propose a bargain.*

A . . . bargain?

I have prepared a lair for you, far north of here, Bairn said. *There you will sleep. You will awake once a decade to go forth and feed. Centuries from now a man will come to you. He will resemble me, but he will not be me. He will have a request to make of you. Your service to me is to grant his request.*

How will I know him? Arcalion asked. *All of you apes look similar to me.*

You will know him by this mark, Bairn said, mentally showing the dragon his name symbol. *It will be cast in gold and imbued with Power.*

You mentioned a bargain? Arcalion said.

Perform this task for me, and I shall return you to your own world at the time which you were taken from it, Bairn told him.

How do I know you will honor this bargain? Arcalion asked.

You do not, Bairn said. *However, what would be the point of deceiving you when I could simply bind you to me?*

Very well, Arcalion said. *Show me this lair you have prepared for me.*

Three

Chapter
------ Twenty-Four ----------

Once Arcalion had withdrawn from the world, Bairn did so as well, allowing the people to build and shape their own world. That was when the wait became tedious and the time began to crawl slowly by. Raoul, Hervis, Rowena and Izabel waited out the decades in their enchanted sleep, but Bairn sat and watched.

He filled his days watching the world and recording the events that occurred without judgement or involvement. A true, permanent history of all the lands of the world. Sometimes he would travel among them, disguised often as an old man of whichever land he visited.

Once he visited his own home, long before his birth. He gave the Sign and contacted the local Circle. He told them that he was from the South, fleeing the Hunt to resettle further north. He stayed in the home of the High Magus, Eric.

"A sad business," Eric said. "I grieve for your loss, Lars."

"Thank you," Bairn replied. He had arrived in the guise of a man of middle years. Not young, but not too old to move on and start a new life.

"What are your plans?" Eric asked him.

"I will head a little further north," Bairn said. "Live by trapping and selling my prizes."

"That sounds like a lonely life," Eric's wife said. She was pregnant with their first child—Rolf, Bairn's father.

"It will keep me safe," Bairn said. "But it will leave me without heir, and so I have one additional request to make of you."

"What is that?"

"I have something very old," Bairn replied, "that has been passed down in my Circle from one High Magus to the next for generations. When I die, I will have no one to entrust with its guard."

"What . . . is it?" Eric asked.

"This," Bairn replied, pulling the Silver Book from his pack.

"It is said to be from the Time of Lords. Keep it safe for me—for all of us."

"Is it truly a book?" Eric asked.

"We believe that it is," Bairn said. "A book of Forbidden Knowledge, perhaps. We have no way of knowing. I only know that my Circle has kept it safe for generations. It cannot be destroyed—we have tried. So we keep it safe and guarded, that it might never fall into misguided hands. I regret having to pass such a task on to you . . ."

"Nonsense," Eric said, gingerly taking the book from him. "We shall be honored to accept this burden from you. It shall remain safe."

"Thank you, Eric."

"You must be tired," Eric said. "It is late. My wife will show you to your bed."

"My thanks, High Magus," Bairn replied.

The woman on the bed screamed in pain as the child was delivered. Bairn watched as Freida and the other women of the Circle tended to her. This was Sylph, *his* mother. This was where she had died, during *his* birth.

Bairn stepped out of Freida's way. He was not actually invisible to them. Rather, they did not notice that he was there. They saw him, and would move to avoid him, but nothing more than that registered in their minds.

His mother would not die here today. She would appear to, but she would not. Bairn was here to prevent that. He had never known his mother, but had watched her these past few years since she had married his father.

He had visited once, long ago, and taken a lock of her hair and some tissue from inside her mouth. She had thought it just a mouth sore the next morning. Using these, he had crafted a body identical to the one that now writhed on the bed.

Creating a body was simple. After all, it was just meat, blood and bone. Not even Bairn could breathe life into that construct, however. But it *would* live, once he had captured the fleeing soul of his mother and placed it in the new flesh that waited for her.

The child was finally delivered, but the woman's cries did not stop. Bairn knelt down near her head, weaving the matrix of Power that would house her soul.

"In Bairn's name!" Aunt Freida shouted. "She's bleeding to death!" Aunt Freida reached into the womb, trying to massage the hemorrhaging tissues in a vain attempt to stop the bleeding.

Sylph's cries subsided as the life flowed out of her. Bairn was ready. As the spirit fled her body, he drew it into the matrix of Power that he had built. There was little time. He had to get his mother into her new body quickly, or even he would not be able to save her.

He translocated away from the weeping women.

Bairn stood outside the cabin they had built in the far north. It was a peaceful winter night, bitterly cold, but the cold did not touch him. All inside were asleep.

This was going to be much easier than saving Sylph. No one had been present when Rolf had died, save Freida, and she was asleep. Bairn reached out with the Power and deepened the sleep of all within the cabin before he entered.

This had been their home for such a short time. Valerian had destroyed it as soon as Bjorn had been wrested from his control.

Bairn carried the bag containing the body he had created over his shoulder. He walked into his father's small room behind the fireplace. The heat would have been oppressive had it been able to penetrate his barriers. Bairn laid the body beside Rolf's bed and pushed it beneath the cot before examining his father in his sleep.

The infection had spread far through Rolf's lungs. Pneumonia. A thousand years ago, as he remembered time, Bjorn had been unable to help his father. That was no longer true. Bairn extended his Power into the old man's body, first destroying the infection and then healing the tissues that had been damaged by the disease. As Bairn worked, his father's breathing cleared noticeably and his sleep became more peaceful.

"Father," Bairn said, gently shaking his father's shoulder. "Father, wake up."

"Wha . . . Bjorn?" Rolf said. "What is it, son?"

"Father, I need to speak with you," Bairn said. "How are you feeling?"

"Well . . . I-I feel quite good, actually!" Rolf said.

"Will you go in the sitting room and wait for me while I cover Aunt Freida?" Bairn asked.

"Of course, son," Rolf said. Once he had left, Bairn removed the bag and laid the lifeless duplicate of his father in the bed. Then he went into the sitting room, where his father stood by the fire.

"How is it I am feeling so much better?" Rolf asked. "I was certain that . . ."

His words stopped as he turned to face Bairn.

"Your . . . aura," Rolf said.

"Do not be afraid," Bairn said.

"Who are you?" Rolf shouted. "Theodr! Angus!"

"They will not wake," Bairn said.

"How *dare* you take the form of my son!" Rolf said. "I *know* who you are! You are that villain Valerian!"

"I am Bairn," Bairn said. Rolf fell silent.

"Bairn?" he finally asked.

"Yes," Bairn said. "And I am also your son."

"This is . . . not . . . possible," Rolf said.

"I fear it is," Bairn said. "Come with me, father. You, mother and I have much to discuss."

"M-mother?" Rolf asked. "Do you mean . . . ?"

"Yes," Bairn said. "Sylph, your wife, is waiting for you. Come with me."

Bairn held out his hand, and Rolf stepped forward to take it.

Bairn stepped carefully over the rubble. Fire raged throughout the palace, but the heavy rain of the storm summoned by Valerian was quickly extinguishing the flames.

The Great Dragon lay broken and dying in the garden. Bairn watched as Bjorn knelt down near the dying dragon's head. Bairn walked up and knelt down once Bjorn had left. No one noticed him as he placed his hand on the dragon's enormous brow.

Greetings, mighty Arcalion, Bairn thought to him.

You have . . . lied to me . . . Lord Bairn, Arcalion said. *I . . . die.*

You shall not die, Bairn assured him. *Are you ready to go home?*

I . . . am, Arcalion said.

Then sleep, Bairn said. *You shall awake in your own lair.*

Bairn watched as his journeymen assembled in the throne room. The time had finally arrived. Even now, on the world below them, Bjorn activated the spell that would summon Soren from the distant past.

"Raoul, you shall take Hervis and Izabel to this camp west of Soren's palace," Bairn said. "Tell those within to flee. They will die if they remain. Join your Power with mine when they are safe."

"Yes, Lord," Raoul said.

"Rowena, Sylph, you will accompany me into Soren's stronghold," Bairn said. "I think I can defeat him alone, but he is cunning. He may have reserves of Power of which I am unaware."

"Yes, Lord," Rowena said.

"What about me, son?" Rolf asked.

"Your training is not far enough along for this battle, father," Bairn said. "I want you to take a position here. Theodr and his companion will flee in this direction. You must intercept them. Are you certain that Theodr will recognize you?"

Rolf smiled. He had been restored to his prime. He was no longer the old man of Bjorn's manhood, but the strong young man that Bairn remembered from childhood.

"Theodr will recognize me," Rolf assured him. "I will stimulate his memory, if necessary."

"Good," Bairn said. He opened the portal that would take Raoul to Theodr's camp outside the ruins of the House of Soren.

"Raoul, Hervis, Izabel!" Bairn called. "Go!" As soon as they were through, Bairn closed that portal to open another.

"Rolf, take your position," Bairn said.

"Yes, Lord," Rolf replied.

Bairn turned to his battle mirrors. In the central mirror he saw a much younger version of himself in the process of activating the spell that would summon Soren and hurl himself back into the past.

The circle is complete, Bairn thought. *You are in for a surprise, Lord Soren.*

"Rowena, Sylph, with me," Bairn said, rising from his throne. His wife and his mother stepped to his sides as Bairn began the spell that would translocate them to the cellar of the House of Soren.

Soren walked over and opened the door that led from the Circle chamber. Someone stood on the other side. As Soren stepped back in surprise, the other entered the room. He recognized the man who followed him back into the central chamber. It was the man he had just condemned to the doomed past, but wearing the badge of a Lord and displaying an aura vastly more powerful than any Soren had ever seen.

"Greetings, Lord Soren," Bairn said.

"No!" Soren cried. "You *cannot* still live!"

"But I do," Bairn said to him. Two women in the uniforms of journeymen entered the room behind him. The three were linked, warded together. The women drew their swords.

Soren felt Power from three others somewhere beyond this room join with the force opposing him. Six to one.

Soren drew from the Cords, raising his wards. He might be doomed, but they would not take him without a fight.

Theodr and Abdul rode hard to the west. They had been forced to leave most of their supplies behind. It was doubtful that they would survive the desert to reach Valencia.

"Theodr!" a strangely familiar voice called to him. Theodr reined his horse to a stop and turned toward the sound of the voice. Abdul stopped as well.

A man in a gold robe stood atop a nearby sand dune. He was blond of hair and fully bearded. He walked down the side of the dune toward them. His aura was clearly as powerful as those they had seen earlier. As with them, the symbol of Bairn was emblazoned on his left breast.

"Theodr, you must turn around and go back," this strangely familiar man told him.

"Who are you?" Theodr demanded. "How do you know my name?"

"I know that it has been several years since you have seen me," the man said. "Surely, you have not forgotten your old friend Rolf so soon."

"Rolf?" Theodr asked. Then he recognized this strangely familiar man standing before him. It *was* Rolf, but Rolf in his prime, not as Theodr had last seen him.

"But . . . *how*?" Theodr asked.

"With Bairn, many things are possible," Rolf said.

"Bairn?"

"Whom do you think is battling back there?" Rolf asked. "Bairn is destroying the only MageLord that escaped him during the Time of Madness. One who fled through Time itself to escape.''

''We were . . . told to leave,'' Theodr said.

''I have been sent to turn you back,'' Rolf said. ''The battle is nearly over. Come, old friend. Sylph will be happy to see you. Your companion may go on.''

''Sylph?'' Theodr said. ''Sylph is . . . alive?''

''As alive as I,'' Rolf said. Theodr was not certain how to take that response. He had buried Rolf in the frozen lands of the north himself.

''My friend here will perish without supplies,'' Theodr said. At that Rolf turned and began speaking with Abdul in his own language. After a time, Abdul turned and rode away, leading the camel.

''Where is he going?'' Theodr asked.

''I told him to go over there about a mile,'' Rolf said. ''There is a camp with supplies waiting for him. Come, Theodr. It is almost time.''

''Time for what?''

''The return of the House of Bairn,'' Rolf replied.

Rolf turned and walked back east, toward the cloud of smoke that rose from the horizon. With one last glance back at Abdul, Theodr turned to follow.

Again, Raoul followed the Call to the throne room. Hervis and Izabel joined him in the Grand Hall leading to the golden doors. It had been two days since the defeat of Lord Soren. As they entered the throne room, they saw that a new apprentice had been added to the ranks. He wore the white robes of the first rank, but his aura was that of one much more advanced.

''Greetings, Raoul,'' Bairn said as he walked into the room. ''Hervis, Izabel.''

''So we meet, Lord,'' Raoul replied. ''What do you desire of us?''

''One last work lies before us, Raoul,'' Bairn said. ''We must raise our House in the northlands. This is the site I have selected, just south of Hunter's Glen. Here we shall build our House and here we shall face the armies of Reykvid.''

''Yes, Lord,'' Raoul replied.

''Here are the plans I have made,'' Bairn continued, indicating a roll of documents on the table before him. ''I want you three to take all of the apprentices and begin work on the construction at once. Gavin has already left Reykvid. We have less than two moons to finish the construction."

"It shall be done," Raoul assured him.

"I know it shall, Raoul," Bairn said. "I shall join you within the moon when I have finished removing this House."

"Until we meet again, Lord," Raoul replied, gathering up the plans.

Ian examined the fortress from the vantage of a nearby hilltop. Even from more than two miles away, he could clearly make out the symbol of Bairn that flew on all the banners of the palace. He had almost not believed Arik when he had brought word of this place, but here it was.

The palace was immense, occupying an entire large hill just over a day's ride south of Hunters Glen. The central building was a circular keep, large enough to easily encompass the keep of Reykvid. Surrounding the central keep for roughly a hundred feet was what appeared to be a forest or perhaps a large garden. There was no sign of snow within, although the terrain around them was still in the loosening grip of winter.

Surrounding the central keep and its garden was another, larger building. This outer keep was somewhat egg-shaped as it followed the contour of the hill around the central keep. The central keep and its surrounding garden were cut from the large end of the egg, with some type of outbuilding connecting the two structures together.

At the base of the hill, the two structures were surrounded by what could inadequately be described as an outer wall. From this distance the structure appeared to be fifty or sixty feet thick. On the inside of the wall, which Ian could see in places from his elevated vantage point, were what appeared to be windows, stable doors and other such structures built into the outer wall. These were presumably the barracks and stables of the palace. The front bailey between the outer wall and the outer keep was easily four hundred feet across and also devoid of snow. The entire fortress bore an aura of Power.

Guards patrolled the battlements of the outer wall. Even from this distance, Ian could make out the gray of steel armor. Steel, not bronze as Ian himself wore. To use so much steel in the making of armor spoke of great wealth on the part of whoever occupied the fortress.

This place was directly on the route between Hunter's Glen and Pine Grove. There was no way that Gavin would not find it. Nor was there any way that he could hope to defeat it.

"Let's go," he said, mounting his horse. With him, Ivanel and Arik and the three guardsmen mounted their horses. They rode from the cover of the forested hill down onto the grassy plain surrounding the fortress.

There was no challenge or attack as they rode up to the fortress. They rode up to the only gate, which swung silently open as they approached. Ian stopped. No challenge, no hail—just admittance.

One of the guards called down to them when they did not immediately pass through the gate.

"You may pass!" he called. "Lord Bairn is expecting you!"

"Gods above!" Ivanel whispered. Ian agreed with the sentiment, although he remained silent as he spurred his horse forward into the entry tunnel. The walls were lined with arrow slits, and the ceiling was pierced with murder holes.

At the end of the tunnel they emerged into the forward bailey. Gone was the cold of winter. Ian threw back his heavy cloak. It was as though they had just ridden into spring.

Men and women in white robes came to take their horses. A woman, also in a white robe, waited patiently for Ian and his party to dismount. She wore a belt of silver cloth in place of the white belts the others wore. Apparently this was a badge of rank.

"Come with me," she said. "Lord Bairn is eager to see you."

Ian, Ivanel and Arik exchanged alarmed glances at that statement. Why would Bairn be interested in seeing *them*?

The woman led them into the outer keep. Ian's breath caught at the splendor of the palace. Pillars of carved marble supported the ceiling high overhead. The walls and ceilings were decorated in ornate gold trim. Tapestries and paintings adorned the walls, and ornate carpets were laid across the inlaid marble floors.

Despite the lack of windows on the outer wall of the keep, light flooded all the rooms from ornate structures of hanging crystal set into the ceiling. Ian could not find the source of the light—neither candles nor lamps were visible. The light was simply there, as though it sprang forth from the crystal itself.

Their guide led them from the vast entrance foyer into a wide corridor. Ian counted over a hundred paces before they reached the connecting building between the inner and outer keeps. The inner wall of the outer keep was formed of open archways, much as the wall surrounding the courtyard at Reykvid.

They walked from the outer keep into the arched corridor that connected the two keeps. Through the glass archways, Ian could see that the forested area between the two keeps was indeed a cultivated garden. Gravel paths wound between the trees, and flowering bushes abounded within. One hundred and fifty feet separated the two structures. The inner keep was heavily fortified except for several open archways leading into the garden.

They passed through another entrance tunnel lined with arrow slits into the inner keep. The corridor continued past the entrance tunnel, past smaller side corridors until it ended in a pair of solid gold doors. The mark of Bairn was set into these doors in obsidian.

They passed through as the doors swung silently open. The throne room was immense. It radiated out in a quarter circle around the dais at the far end. Rows upon rows of benches filled the room. Ian guessed that one could easily seat five hundred in this room—perhaps more.

Four thrones sat on the dais, two of equal size and two of lesser size. A man with golden hair and beard sat in the larger throne on Ian's right hand. Bairn?

A woman with blonde hair and wearing a white robe sat in the other large throne to the man's right. Two other women sat in the smaller thrones on either side. Both wore black trousers and tunics.

The woman on the man's left wore a silver sword belt that circled her waist and crossed over her right shoulder. She had brilliant red hair and cream-white skin. The woman to the right of the woman in the white robe wore a gold sword belt. Her hair was raven black, and her skin was as dark as polished bronze.

In front of the thrones stood another man in the same black trousers and tunic as worn by the women on the lesser thrones. His belt was also gold, and he was colored much like the darker woman. His face was beardless.

Also in black uniforms, behind the thrones, were another man and woman. These were both fair-haired. With them stood a blond man in a gold robe tied with a silver sash and another blond-haired man in a white robe. All of those in either black or gold bore auras of incredible Power.

"Bjorn!" Ivanel said when they had approached closer. Ian's father was correct. The man who sat on the throne *was* Bjorn, just as the woman who sat in the throne next to him was his wife Helga.

"I have not been called Bjorn in over a thousand years," Bjorn said. "Now I am Bairn."

"What are you talking about?" Ivanel asked.

"When I left in search of the House of Soren, I was warned that it might be a trap," Bjorn explained. "It was."

Ian listened as Bjorn explained how Soren had used him to travel through Time from before the Time of Madness to the present and how Bjorn had been sent back in place of the ancient MageLord. Bjorn claimed that he had been apprenticed to another MageLord and had risen through the ranks until he had obtained a position where he could start the war that had led to the downfall of all the MageLords. When he was finished, the throne room was silent as all with Ian's party considered Bjorn's words.

"Do you expect us to *believe* all of this?" Arik finally asked.

"I had hoped that you would," the man who now called himself Bairn said to them, "but your belief is irrelevant at this time. Gavin's forces are less than two quarters from here."

"Two what?" Ian asked.

"My apologies—a fortnight," Bairn replied. "Two quarter moons."

"Do you fear Gavin's forces?" Ivanel asked. The dark woman snorted derisively. The others in black only smiled. Clearly they had found what Ivanel had said amusing.

"I do not fear them for myself," Bairn said. "I am concerned that, if they do not withdraw, I may have to destroy them. Despite his recent actions, Gavin is a good man. Ivanel, you among all of us know him best. Will you Commune with me on this subject? It may be that, between us, we can find the means to a peaceful resolution of this matter."

"I fear that is unlikely," Ivanel said.

"We must at least try," Bairn said.

''I agree,'' Ivanel said. ''But I have never been able to Commune before now . . .''

''That will not be a problem,'' Bairn assured him. He rose from his throne and Ivanel left the room with him, leaving Ian and the others idle.

''Helga,'' Ian said, beginning to step forward onto the dais. The dark man moved to block him, his hand on the hilt of the sword he carried on his gold belt. Ian stepped back, his hand falling to the hilt of his own sword.

''It is all right, Raoul,'' Helga said. ''He is a friend.''

''As you wish, Lady Helga,'' Raoul said, stepping aside. Ian climbed the dais to stand beside Helga.

''Helga,'' Ian said again, ''is all of this true?''

''It seems so,'' Helga said. ''I have Communed much with my husband since his return. I have shared his memories of these events myself.''

''If that is true,'' Ian said, ''then he really *is* Bairn.''

''Yes, he is,'' Helga agreed. ''Many of the people here are also from the Time of the MageLords. Their memories support his claims as well.''

''How many?''

''I have only entered Circle with those in this room,'' Helga replied. ''Lord Ian, this is the Lady Rowena.''

Helga gestured to the red-haired woman who occupied the throne to Bairn's left. Ian bowed to the woman. She was stunningly beautiful.

''Lord Ian,'' Rowena replied, nodding toward him.

''She is my husband's second wife,'' Helga added. Ian blinked in surprise.

''Lady Izabel is my husband's third wife,'' Helga added. ''Izabel was once a Lord herself. She abandoned her station to side with Bairn.''

''Lady . . . Izabel,'' Ian said hesitantly. A MageLord serving Bairn?

''Master Raoul is our Guardian,'' Helga said, indicating the dark man who had attempted to block Ian's entry onto the dais. Raoul nodded at Ian at the mention of his name. If he was Guardian, that would explain his actions when Ian had first attempted to mount the dais.

''He apprenticed with Bairn in the House of Rylur,'' Helga

added. "Master Hervis was one of the common mages in Rylur's lands. He is our Guardian of the South."

Ian waited, but the introductions seemed to be over.

"And these are?" he asked, indicating the others in the room.

"Oh," Helga said. "I was introducing those who have come with Bairn from the Time of Lords. I believe you already know Theodr."

Ian blinked in surprise. Helga had indicated the man in the white robe when she said this, but this man was *much* too young to be Theodr.

" 'Tis me, lad," the man said. "How is the lodge coming?"

It *was* Theodr. Ian knew the voice if not the man, and he could see a ghost of the old man's face in the face of this younger man.

"It is . . . as you saw it last," Ian said shakily.

"This is Master Rolf, Bjorn's father," Helga added, "and the Lady Sylph, his mother."

"It is a . . . pleasure to meet all of you," Ian said.

"Bairn and your father are likely to be a while," Helga said. "Would you like to see more of the palace?"

"I would," Ian said.

"Theodr," Helga said, "would you like to show Ian the palace? I'm sure the two of you have much to talk about."

"I would like that," Theodr said, smiling. "Come, everyone, 'tis quite a sight."

Chapter
------- Twenty-Five -----------

"Where in Frigga's hell did *this* come from?" King Gavin said as he examined the fortress before him. He had ridden ahead of the main body of his force to inspect this discovery of his scouts. This fortress had certainly not been here three years ago when Gavin had last travelled to Hunter's Glen.

Gavin was unable to discern any apparent *reason* for it to be here now. This fortress, larger by far than his own palace at Reykvid, was completely alone in the wilderness. There was no town to protect, no inhabitants to support such a structure. Yet here it was, half a mile long and apparently fully manned.

"Majesty," Mathen said.

"What is it, First Knight?" Gavin asked.

"I have seen this mark before," Mathen told him. Gavin was certain that he had seen the symbol that flew from the banners of the palace as well, but he could not recall where.

"This mark is common among the mages," Mathen explained. "It is worn by the leaders of their foul bands. It is supposed to represent their patron MageLord, Bairn."

Bairn! Gavin remembered. That was where he had seen this symbol before. On the amulet that had been around Bjorn's neck when he had brought Arcalion to Reykvid. If this fortress flew Bairn's banner, then it must have been built by the magi, much as Valerian had raised his tower in the lands of the Star clan.

This was no mere tower, however. This was a mighty fortress sprawling over hundreds of acres and fully manned. However, one thing was clear. Valerian had not raised this fortress. No MageLord would fly *this* banner over his stronghold.

"I did not bring enough men to take *this* fortress," Gavin said.

"No, majesty," Mathen agreed.

"There are not enough men in the world to take this fortress," someone said behind him. Gavin and Mathen spun to face the man who now stood behind them.

"Bjorn!" Gavin said.

"Not anymore," Bjorn replied.

"Die, MageLord!" Mathen shouted as he drew and drove his sword through Bjorn's chest before Gavin could stop him. Bjorn merely turned his attention from Gavin to the First Knight. His expression was unconcerned. Mathen froze in astonishment, merely looking at the sword in his hand as if it had betrayed him.

"Do you mind?" Bjorn asked after a moment.

In Hrothgar's name! Gavin thought. *He's just like Valerian. We are nothing more than ants to him!*

"Actually, ants are very important creatures," Bjorn said, answering Gavin's thoughts. Mathen withdrew his sword from Bjorn's chest, bloodlessly, and examined it closely.

"And I assure you," Bjorn continued, ignoring Mathen, "you, as a man, are much more important in my eyes than any mere insect."

"What did you mean, 'Not anymore'?" Gavin asked.

"I am no longer Bjorn," Bjorn replied. "Now, and for the past thousand years, I have been Bairn."

"Majesty, you must not listen to this man," Mathen said. "He is a demon!"

"No more so than you, First Knight," Bjorn said. "You were born one of us."

"You lie!"

"Your mother was born with the Gift," Bjorn said. "She defied our law by marrying outside of the Circle and yet remaining with her Circle."

"These are lies!"

"When your father discovered her secret, he could not bear to think that he had married a magess," Bjorn continued. "He convinced himself that a magess had taken the place of his wife with her Art, but the magi do not have such skills. He beat your mother to death with his bare hands in front of you."

"*Gods!*" Gavin said.

"She was not my mother!" Mathen shouted. "She was a filthy magess! She killed my mother!"

"Your father killed your mother," Bjorn said. "You already *know* this, but you have buried this memory because you had to. You've had to hide the truth from yourself to survive, just as you've hidden the memory of how your father would beat you whenever you cried for the loss of your mother."

"No-ooo!" Mathen screamed.

"You *will* remember!" Bjorn shouted, stepping toward Mathen. "We can no longer afford to let you kill us for the sake of your madness. You *will* remember!"

The First Knight of the Sacred Hunt collapsed to the ground screaming like a woman.

"Bjorn!" Gavin shouted. "You're torturing him! Just like Valerian tortured all of us."

"Oh, no, Gavin," Bjorn replied coldly. "This is *much* worse. Valerian tortured us with phantoms. Mathen is being forced to witness the truth which he has hidden from himself for decades. If he can endure this, however, he will become whole for the first time in his life."

Gavin looked back down to where Mathen writhed on the ground, battling with demons he had been unwilling to face his entire life. The scouts had withdrawn from the three of them in a circle. Gavin and Bjorn stood alone and watched Mathen. Finally the screams and wails subsided, replaced by wracking sobs.

"Mama," Mathen moaned. Bjorn knelt down and took Mathen in his arms as the First Knight cried like a child.

"Mama," Mathen sobbed. Bjorn looked up, toward the fortress, and a woman appeared before him. She knelt down where Bjorn cradled the sobbing priest.

"Take him," Bjorn said. "Put him in one of the guest rooms in the inner keep and watch over him."

"Yes, Lord," the woman said. She tenderly took Mathen from Bjorn, and then both were gone. Bjorn rose to his feet to face Gavin.

"You and I have much to discuss," Bjorn said. "Send your men back to the remainder of your forces and come with me."

"Do I have a choice in this?" Gavin asked.

"No," Bjorn replied.

"People will not accept this," Gavin said. "*I* will not accept this."

"You think people will refuse to accept that they do not have the right to murder their neighbors?" Bairn asked.

"Not when those 'neighbors' are mages!" Gavin said.

"Sadly, you are probably correct," Bairn said. "At least not until the consequences have been applied a few times."

"You seriously intend to enforce this edict?" Gavin asked.

"I do," Bairn replied. "Assault or murder of one of the magi without cause will result in punishment similar to the offense. Death for murder, removal of a hand for assault, removal of genitalia for rape, removal of property for theft."

"How do you intend to enforce such an edict?" Gavin asked.

"How do you intend to stop me?" Bairn asked in reply.

"So, the MageLords *have* returned," Gavin said bitterly.

"In a sense," Bairn said. "Fortunately, *this* MageLord has no interest in ruling your lands or people. My *only* demand is that my people be allowed to live their lives in peace. In return, I shall guarantee that none among them shall attain the Power that I have attained or otherwise interfere with your governance. Those who do shall answer to me."

"What do you need with me?" Gavin asked.

"I simply need you to turn around and go home," Bairn said. "If you do not, I will be forced to destroy your army. Do not force me to do that."

"When do you intend to make this pronouncement?" Gavin asked.

"On the morrow," Bairn said. "As daylight sweeps the world, my law will be made known to everyone."

The door opened into the sitting room, and Raoul stepped in.

"Raoul will show you out," Bairn said. "Remember, he is almost as powerful as I. Do not give him any difficulty."

"Yes, *Lord*," Gavin replied, spitting out the word.

"I think you will come to learn that I am *not* Valerian," Bairn said. "Come to me at any time. You are always welcome in my hall, King Gavin."

Gavin turned and left the room without a word. Raoul followed him out and closed the door. Bairn sighed. This would be a long process and, doubtless, many would die before his laws were accepted.

Baron William had risen from his bed just before dawn. He did not know why, but he had awoken with the feeling that someone had called out to him.

"I am Bairn," a voice said from his window. William rushed to the window and looked out. What he saw chilled his blood.

The figure of a man floated in the air high above his palace.

The figure was large enough to be easily visible, and William recognized the face—it was Bjorn.

"I am a MageLord," the voice said, "and I have Power over you."

Hrothgar preserve us! William thought. Gavin was marching against *this*? William wondered if he would ever see his king again.

"I have no desire to alarm you," Bjorn continued, "and I have no desire to harm you. However, I demand that you stop harming my people.

"From this day forward . . ."

Abdul ben Yosif watched the figure floating above the city with a mixture of elation and fear. Bairn *had* returned! After all the centuries, the day had finally arrived.

"From this day forward," Bairn was saying, "any attack against a mage or magess that is made without cause will be punished most severely. If the mage dies from the assault, those who committed the offense shall die as well. If the assault does not result in death, the offenders will suffer the loss of one hand. If both hands have already been taken, the offenders shall be put to death."

Gods above! Abdul thought. This would cause mass panic! He was amazed that it had not happened already. He looked around, but people only stared skyward as if mesmerized by what they were seeing.

"The rape of one of the magi shall be punished by the removal of the offender's genitals," Bairn continued. Herrold watched the figure that floated above the lodge. It was definitely Bjorn, but he had introduced himself as Bairn.

This explained much. It explained why Theodr had returned to tell them they had no need to fear Gavin's arrival and why he, and all of Bjorn's family, had left the lodge.

"Theft from the magi shall be punished by compensation made from the offender's possessions," Bairn said, "and imprisonment of the offender within his own mind for one year. These punishments shall be administered without mercy against any who violate these laws."

Herrold felt very thankful that his people lived separate from the ungifted. He could only imagine how these pronouncements would be received.

"The following laws shall be observed by all of the magi from this day forward," Bairn said. Herrold listened with renewed interest. What restrictions was Bairn going to place on all of *them*?

"No mage may hold power or authority over the ungifted," Bairn said. "Any mage who attempts to take such a position shall be removed by me. No mage may attempt to acquire the Power of the MageLords. Any mage who so attempts, whether the attempt is successful or not, shall be put to death."

Herrold relaxed. These restrictions were not severe. Some of them they had lived by for centuries.

Molin watched as the man he had once known as Bjorn spoke from above. What had driven Bjorn to this madness—claiming to be Bairn returned and presuming to dictate to the people of Star Hall?

"All mages shall wear a pin or amulet identifying themselves as being under my protection," Bjorn said. Molin stiffened at that pronouncement.

Now I know *he has gone mad!* Molin thought. Did Bjorn expect the magi to walk openly under the sun after they had hidden for so long? Did he not realize that hundreds would be killed? Did he truly think he could prevent that, no matter his Power?

"These items shall be distributed by the High Magus of each Circle," Bjorn continued.

Behind him appeared five people in black trousers and tunics with sword belts of silver or gold. Two were men, three women.

"These people, and any like them, are my knights," Bjorn said. "They speak with my voice and my authority. They wield my Power. They, and others like them, will enforce these laws among you. Obey these laws and you need have no fear of them. Violate these laws and you will answer to them and to me, no matter your station."

Temple Father Olaf trembled in fear at the apparitions that had appeared over his altar. The MageLords *here*, in the very House of Hrothgar! He had arrived to find the statue of Hrothgar cast to the floor in fragments and this man, Bairn, promising dire consequences to any who harmed a single mage.

"I have a special message for the Temple of Hrothgar," Bairn continued. "From this day forward your so-called 'Sacred Hunt' will cease. If a single mage is taken by the Hunt, I will raze the temple responsible for that action to the ground. I will grind the stones to powder, burn all else to ash and stake the bodies of your priests around the perimeter as a warning to any who would hunt us."

"I have your First Knight," Bairn continued. Mathen appeared beside Bairn. He looked different somehow. Humbled.

"He has something to say to you," Bairn said.

"I repent of my crimes against the magi and renounce my priesthood to Hrothgar," Mathen said. "I have learned that the magi mean us no harm and seek only to live in peace among us. In the name of Hrothgar I have committed atrocious acts of murder against women and children. I . . . am sorry."

Olaf's blood chilled at Mathen's statement. What had this monster done to him to make him speak thus?

"Mathen has committed serious crimes against the magi," Bairn said, "but he has learned that this was wrong. We hereby forgive him for his actions until now and place him under our protection. Any person who seeks vengeance against this man shall answer to me *personally*."

"The Hunt is *over*!" Bairn said. Then he, and all those with him, were gone.

Bairn sat back in the sending chair. Twenty-four hours of constantly sending the same projection, delivering his edicts in every tongue in the world, had exhausted him more than any pitched battle against another Lord.

But there could be no rest. Now the identifying pins and medallions had to be distributed to the High Magi of each Circle.

And then all hell would break loose.

Miranda stepped from her home with her heart in her throat. Today, by order of Bairn, her secret would be a secret no longer. The pin that rode on her left shoulder would label her as one of the magi to any who saw it.

She had scarcely walked a score of paces down the street before she was seen.

"A witch!" someone shouted.

Gods above! she thought. Now she was going to die.

"There's one o' them!" someone else shouted. People surrounded her.

"Blasted witch!" a man shouted in her face. "Ye think ye're filthy tricks will save ye?"

Someone grabbed her hair from behind. As she was pulled over backwards, she saw a knife raised in the air above her.

"Oh, gods!" she cried.

A slender, black-gloved hand grabbed the wrist of the hand that held the knife. Around Miranda, the mob that had encircled her was hurled back as if by a mighty wind.

"Did you think we were merely *jesting*?" a woman in the garb of Bairn's knights shouted to the crowd as they climbed to their feet. Many tried to flee, but they were stopped as if by a wall of air.

"By rights I should take a hand from all of you!" the woman continued. "Fortunately for you, I arrived before more than one of you had laid hands on this woman."

Miranda rose to her feet from the mud of the street. The woman had brilliant red hair and fiery green eyes. She held a man off the ground by his wrist as if he were nothing more than a scarecrow.

"Watch!" the woman commanded. She carried the man over to a stairway leading to the apothecary and laid his arm across the banister. With a single smooth motion, she drew her sword and severed the hand that had held the knife. Then she picked up the man by his tunic and hurled him into the crowd. She also picked up the severed hand and hurled it into the crowd on the other side. People recoiled from both. The hand lay in the street like an accusation.

"What were you going to *do*?" the woman demanded. "Put the magess to the fire? Perhaps you would like to know what that feels like?"

"No!" someone shouted. "Please! Have mercy!"

"*Burn!*" the woman said coldly. The crowd began to scream. As Miranda watched, the townspeople fell to the street, writhing in agony. There were no flames, and no burns appeared on them, yet they screamed like any who had suffered the fire.

"Please!" Miranda said, taking the woman's arm. "Spare them!" The screams stopped.

"This woman you would have killed has begged me to show

you mercy!'' the woman said. ''As she is innocent, here, I have decided to grant her request. You should thank her. 'Tis more than you deserve.''

''Go about your business,'' the woman told her softly. ''They will not trouble you again.''

Kaftan Jalim watched as the mage screamed. His chief interrogator was torturing the man in the throne room at his order. His people would see that he was not afraid of phantoms conjured by demons!

The bar across the doors to the throne room shattered, sending slivers of ironwood flying across the room as the doors burst open. Two men walked into the room. One was the man who had called himself Bairn, and the other was one of his warriors.

Jalim's soldiers rushed to stop them. As Jalim watched, they were hurled to either side of the throne room as if by a raging desert wind. Jalim turned to flee through the door behind the throne. It would not open.

''There is no escape, Jalim,'' a voice said behind him. Jalim turned to watch as the two men advanced toward the throne.

''You have no authority here!'' Jalim shouted. ''I rule these lands!''

''I have the *only* authority here!'' Bairn replied. ''I have the Power to do as I please, and neither you nor all of your kingdom has the Power to stop me.''

They walked up to where the mage hung from his chains. The manacles opened of themselves, and the man floated gently down to the floor as if his weight had left him.

Bairn knelt by the mage. With a pass of his hand, the man's wounds were healed. The mage's eyes fluttered open. Jalim felt as if his heart had risen into his throat.

''Lord . . . Bairn,'' the mage said. ''You have come for me.''

''I have,'' Bairn said softly. Then he rose to his feet and turned to face Jalim's interrogator.

''Take his hand,'' Bairn ordered.

''Yes, Lord,'' the warrior with him said. He dragged the interrogator to the worktable as though he were a mere child. His arm was laid on the worktable, and his hand was severed.

''Give me your sword,'' Bairn told the warrior. ''Then bring the kaftan here.'' Jalim backed away as his personal guard stepped in front of him. The black-clad warrior said nothing. He merely walked up the steps to the throne. When the guards stepped toward him, they were thrown aside as though by an invisible hand. The warrior grabbed Jalim by the tunic and lifted him from his feet with one hand. He carried Jalim to Bairn and threw him down at the MageLord's feet.

"I believe your orders were to torture this man to death," Bairn said. "And so you have pronounced your own fate. Raoul, place him on the table."

"Yes, Lord," Raoul said.

"Dog!" Jalim shouted. "You will *die* for this!"

"I think not," Bairn said. With a single stroke of the sword, he removed Jalim's head. Bairn lifted the head by its hair and showed it to those assembled in the throne room.

"Nothing can protect you from my laws," Bairn told them. "*Nothing!*"

He set the head back down on the table, and he and Raoul walked out of the throne room. No one tried to stop them.

Bairn had never been so glad to see his sitting room. Here a single day had passed. For him and his people, the ordeal of this first day had been much, much longer.

They had spent a day in the first village. Once that day had passed, Bairn had translocated them to the next village, town or city and had taken them back a day in the process. It had been the only way they could be everywhere they were needed. Soren's knowledge of time travel, forcibly extracted from his mind, had been useful. That, and the knowledge of elemental Power, were secrets Bairn planned to share with no one.

They had literally been to thousands of places. Bairn had lost count, but he believed that at least five years had passed from their perspective.

"That is what I call a long day!" he said, collapsing onto a chair. It had been worth it, however. None of the magi had died, and they had been forced to kill or maim only a few of the ungifted. For most, a brief moment of extreme pain had been enough to convince them not to defy the new edicts.

The most painful cases for Bairn had been those magi who had sought to abuse their new protection. He had no choice but to burn the Gift from their brains and banish them from the Circle.

"Do we have to do this *again* tomorrow?" Rowena asked,

falling onto the sofa across from him. Izabel took the chair next to Bairn. She said nothing.

"I expect not," Bairn said. "Almost everyone in the world has felt our Power at this point. Most of them will not be anxious for a repeat of today's lessons. Between the six of us, we should be able to deal with the few who are less receptive in a single day."

"Thank the Power," Izabel said. Helga came into the room, awakened by their conversation.

"Did the day go well, husband?" Helga asked, sitting on the arm of his chair. Bairn took her hand and smiled tiredly.

"Not as well as I would have liked," Bairn replied. "But much, much better than it could have."

Epilogue

AT THE CENTER of the City of Bairn stood the Palace of Bairn. Bright yellow banners waved in the sunlight. Just outside the palace was the Ambassador's Quarter. Here large estates provided housing for visiting kings, sultans and emperors. It was more a part of the palace than the city, although much traffic from the city passed through the gates of the Ambassador's Quarter.

Just outside the wall surrounding the Ambassador's Quarter was the city itself. Over twenty thousand called the City of Bairn home. Most were shop owners and artisans employed by Bairn or the noblemen who lived in the Ambassador's Quarter.

The city also had a permanent population of transients—pilgrims and those seeking the favor of Lord Bairn. Ten thousand could be housed in free quarters outside the southern gate of the Ambassador's Quarter in what had come to be called the Supplicant's Quarter.

Farmland surrounded the city for a day's march in all directions. Ian had heard that between two thousand and three thousand farms surrounded the City of Bairn. He now stood on the same hill from which he had first seen the palace, over twenty years ago.

The fortress of Bairn had only come under siege once, when the Temple of Hrothgar had raised forces from throughout the clans and attempted to unseat the "MageLord." The siege lasted for an entire season, but only because Bairn had completely ignored the attacking army. No attack had been able to damage the outer wall, no sapper could dig beneath it and no attack could be launched over the wall. Finally, with their morale broken, the invaders had simply gone home.

The Temple of Hrothgar had not lasted long after that. Bairn had taken no action against them. They had merely fallen out of favor as a new generation had come of age.

"It's *big*, father," his son, named Bjorn after an old friend, said to him.

"It has grown since I saw it last," Ian said to his son of fifteen summers. "This is where it all happened. This is where the Hunt was destroyed."

"What was it like, living during the Hunt?" Bjorn asked him.

Ian looked over to his son. He was approaching forty summers himself, but that question made him feel old beyond his years. Could an entire generation grow up with no real concept of the Hunt? With no understanding of the madness that had kept them in hiding for centuries?

"I hope you never know the answer to that question, son," Ian said. "Let's go."

They mounted their horses and rode down the hill toward the gates of the city.